By AMY LANE

I0691593

Behind the Curtain
Beneath the Stain
Bewitched by Bella's Brother
Bolt-hole
Christmas with Danny Fit
Clear Water
Do-over
Fish Out of Water
Food for Thought
Gambling Men: The Novel
Going Up!
Grand Adventures (Dreamspinner Anthology)
Hammer & Air
If I Must
Immortal
It's Not Shakespeare
Left on St. Truth-be-Well
The Locker Room
Mourning Heaven
Phonebook
Puppy, Car, and Snow
Racing for the Sun
Raising the Stakes
Shiny!
Shirt
Sidecar
A Solid Core of Alpha
Super Sock Man
Tales of the Curious Cookbook
Three Fates (Multiple Author Anthology)
Truth in the Dark
Turkey in the Snow
Under the Rushes
Wishing on a Blue Star (Dreamspinner Anthology)

Published by DREAMSPINNER PRESS
www.dreamspinnerpress.com

By AMY LANE (CONT.)

CANDY MAN
Candy Man • Bitter Taffy • Lollipop • Tart and Sweet

KEEPING PROMISE ROCK
Keeping Promise Rock • Making Promises
Living Promises • Forever Promised

JOHNNIES
Chase in Shadow • Dex in Blue • Ethan in Gold • Black John

GRANBY KNITTING
The Winter Courtship Rituals of Fur-Bearing Critters
How to Raise an Honest Rabbit • Knitter in His Natural Habitat
Blackbird Knitting in a Bunny's Lair

TALKER
Talker • Talker's Redemption • Talker's Graduation

WINTER BALL
Winter Ball • Summer Lessons

ANTHOLOGIES
The Granby Knitting Menagerie
The Talker Collection

Published by DREAMSPINNER PRESS
www.dreamspinnerpress.com

Readers love *Winter Ball*
by AMY LANE

"…it was really no surprise to me that I fell in love with *Winter Ball* – this is a unique and fun story that fits right in with all of Amy Lane's other stories."

—Gay Book Reviews

"Everything about this story is perfect—from the rec league to Skip's job, from the bumpy road to the amazing cast of characters. I love it."

—Joyfully Jay

"*Winter Ball* is romantic and sweet, and funny and touching. I loved these guys and their journey so much."

—The Novel Approach

The plays that matter don't happen on the field...

Winter Ball

"Simple, sweet story"
Publishers Weekly

AMY LANE

"This is a sweet, touching story with plenty of humor, sex that spans from tender to dirty, and a range of emotion that should satisfy anyone looking for a good character driven romance, especially friends-to-lovers fans."

—Sinfully Gay Romance Book Reviews

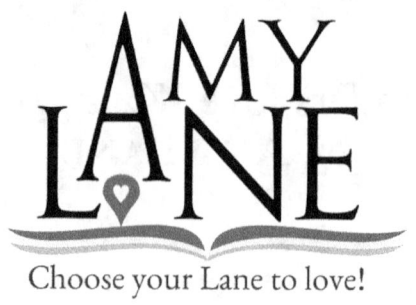

Choose your Lane to love!

More praise for AMY LANE

Tart and Sweet

"I enjoyed this book and this series... If you've been enjoying the series, then you'll definitely want to pick this one up."

—Joyfully Jay

"Amy Lane has done it yet again: Pure. F*cking. Magic"

—The Novel Approach

"...I honestly can't say that it's my favorite, if you go by my ratings, because I loved them all... but if you make me pick...well then, I think I might have to tell you this one is my favorite."

—My Fiction Nook

Fish Out of Water

"This is a great read for anyone who likes unraveling a mystery to make sure the right party pays, opposing backgrounds coming together to make each other better and decent people finding their happily ever after."

—Alpha Book Club

"...a good novel which seems to be the start of a series as there are threads left dangling. I would be happy to continue reading."

—Prism Book Alliance

Summer Lessons

AMY LANE

Published by
DREAMSPINNER PRESS

5032 Capital Circle SW, Suite 2, PMB# 279, Tallahassee, FL 32305-7886 USA
www.dreamspinnerpress.com

Summer Lessons
© 2016 Amy Lane.

Cover Art
© 2019 Tiferet Design
http://www.tiferetdesign.com/

ISBN: 978-1-63477-893-0
Digital ISBN: 978-1-63477-894-7
Library of Congress Control Number: 2016913749
Published November 2016
v. 1.1

Printed in the United States of America
∞
This paper meets the requirements of
ANSI/NISO Z39.48-1992 (Permanence of Paper).

Meet Mason Hayes

Twenty-seven years ago

"MOM! YOU shouldn't let him run around naked like that!"

"But Mason, it's beautiful outside. Seriously, how many days do we get like this on the peninsula?"

Mason was oblivious to the gorgeous March sunshine on his little brother's bare ass. "But *Mom*, his penis is showing!"

Janette Hayes had been in her early thirties when she started having children. Mason would always think of her as she was on this spring day, in her sundress, her bare, pale feet digging into the lushness of the lawn of their tiny Redwood City backyard. Her dark brown hair cascaded down her back with only a few strands of silver to mark the fact that her nine-year-old son had aged her worse than cigarettes and heroin—her own words, leveled at Mason for most of his life.

"I know his penis is showing," his mother said gently. "He's three—he doesn't care if his penis is showing. He can run around the lawn and pee in the corners."

"But *Mom*, he's gonna get the flowers pregnant!"

Later he would acknowledge that this look on his mother's face—mouth open and closing in shock, dark eyes wide as saucers—was something he saw a lot, but that day it sort of stuck in his mind. It was the first time he realized that he horrified people just by speaking.

"No!" she protested, gasping a little. "You can't get flowers pregnant, honey—"

"But we had the *puberty* video," Mason told her earnestly. "And the puberty video says that it's the boy part that gets people pregnant."

"Oh God, your father must have signed that. I do *not* remember that permission slip."

"You signed it with my math homework and my English homework and the history test I got an A on and the science test I got an A on and—" Mason remembered everything. Sometimes his brain was so busy remembering

1

things that he forgot that words, meaning, and people's reactions all had a sort of car wreck whenever he opened his mouth.

"I *get it*, Mason, I have only myself to blame! Now what you may not have gotten from the fourth-grade puberty video is that that thing—"

"A penis."

"That penis can only make a human *woman* pregnant if it is inserted into the vagina and allowed to discharge—"

"Touching it makes it feel good," Mason said. "But the video didn't say that—I figured that out for myself."

"That's awesome, Mason, but maybe you *keep* that to yourself for a while, okay?"

"But I don't understand! Why does it get big when you touch it, and how come boys can't be pregnant!"

"Because boys don't have a place in their bodies to make babies," his mother said, her voice indicating she was hanging on to her patience by a thread. "That's why they have to put the penis in the girl's—" She paused and took a breath. "—vagina."

"But I don't want to *touch* a girl's vagina!" Mason wailed. "I don't want any girls touching my penis! I only want *boys* touching my penis, but you just told me that boys don't have any place for my penis to go!"

"Oh." His mother blinked. "Okay. That's a whole different story."

"Is it a good story?" Mason asked urgently, trying not to cry. "Is it a story where the boy kisses the boy and gets his penis touched?"

"Sure," his mother said, dazed. "That can be a story."

"Then why wasn't it in the video?" Mason demanded, furiously upset. "And where does the penis go?"

At that moment his brother Dane let out an excited squeal. "Penis go *pee-pee*!" he shouted, and then he proceeded to water his mother's begonias.

"How did this happen?" his mother whispered. She looked like she had the night Dane had discovered chocolate syrup could be used to paint walls and the cat.

"He aimed and shot," Mason said helpfully. "Just like Dad showed us with the Cheerios in the toilet. And how come he can touch his pee-pee outside and I can't touch mine in my pants?"

"Because he's *three*, Mason. *Three*. And you were in *school*, and all pee-pee touching needs to be done in private."

"But what if another boy wants to touch my penis? How will I know?"

2

"Oh dear God."

"But Mom, God doesn't like it when we touch our penises. That gross girl in school said that in front of the entire class! Why would you bring him into it?"

"Mason, would you like some Kool-Aid?"

Mason smiled at his mother, distracted and happy about it. "Yeah. Do we have cherry?"

"I hope so. Watch Dane. Mom's going to go get some Kool-Aid for both of us." Mason would figure out later that Mom's Kool-Aid had a healthy dollop of vodka, but then, who could blame her at that point?

After Mom got up and toddled unsteadily into the kitchen, Dane tilted back his head and laughed uproariously. "Pee-pee!" he shrilled. "Going pee-pee!"

"Yeah," Mason said glumly, resting his chin on his hands. "You enjoy that now while you can, little brother. According to Mom, they have to get locked away in the dark when you get older, and the only time they can see the light is when they visit vaginas."

"Ginas!" Dane crowed. "Ginas ginas ginas...."

"Gross."

"Ginas gross," Dane repeated happily.

Later, when Dane came out too (in a slightly less harrowing and more coherent confession when he was thirteen), Janette would turn to an ecstatic Mason and say, "I blame you."

His father denied that there was alcohol involved, of course, but she'd had vodka and Kool-Aid that day too. Mason would start to wonder if the drink held some special significance. His mother certainly did drink a lot of it in the years to come.

Twenty-three years ago

"SORRY, MOM."

"Mason...."

"She was being stupid!"

"Your teacher?"

3

Mason looked around the bright, busy walls of the time-out room. "Yeah. We were supposed to write a story about what our family would look like in twenty years."

"That's nice," his mother said encouragingly.

"It was," he grumbled. It had been. "I drew pictures," he said, because this had felt like going above and beyond the call of duty for eighth grade.

"Can I see them?" His mother smiled prettily, and he pulled the offending pictures out of his binder, hoping for another few moments alone with his mother before the principal came in.

"Here."

"Oh, nice," his mom said, encouragement in her voice. "You in a tie, a nice young man with yellow hair and a suit, and two kids, and a dog! The dog is a nice touch, Mason. Your brother would approve. So what's wrong with this?"

"The teacher said I couldn't write my family that way," Mason said, getting indignant.

"Because there's two boys?" his mother asked, her voice hardening.

"Yeah." Mason felt the injustice keenly. "And I said you were okay with it, and the teacher said it wasn't possible for two boys to have a family, and I said, 'Just because the penis isn't going in a vagina, that doesn't mean that two boys can't have a family together.'"

Next to him he could feel the air in his mom's lungs whoosh out in a rush. "There's that word again," she said, sounding tired.

"But I used it right this time!" he complained. Because there had been other times, right after the puberty video, in which he'd been informed that the word "penis" was absolutely not appropriate to use. Like when a little girl tried to kiss him and he said, "I don't want girls touching my penis!" Or when a little boy asked him what he was going to be when he grew up and he said, "I'm going to be a businessman and have a husband, and another man is going to touch my penis!" These times were bad.

But this time… Mason was *sure* this time was right.

"Yeah, yeah," his mother said, tilting her head back and massaging her temples. "This time you're right and the teacher was wrong, and the next hour is going to be a *treat*!"

Oh, speaking of…. "Hey, isn't it snack day?" Mason said, brightening. His mom usually took them to a fast-food place for a soda or a cookie on Thursday.

"Yes, it is," his mother told him. "And if I get through today, I'm ordering *extra* cookies for Mommy!"

"How about Kool-Aid," Mason said helpfully. "We just made some yesterday."

"And I just bought a fresh bottle," his mother said under her breath. At that moment, the teacher came in and his mother stood up and rolled up her sleeves.

She drank three giant glasses of Kool-Aid and vodka that night.

And Mason got another eighth-grade teacher when he went back to school in the morning. This one was very, very careful to say it was okay for two men to be the daddies.

Twenty years ago

"Sorry, Mom."

"Mason...."

"He was kissing me and it just sort of slipped out."

"That word slips out a lot, Mason. What were you doing kissing in the middle of school?"

Mason looked up from the slick gold-brown surface of the table in the conference room and tried to gauge his mother's expression. She would have looked happier with a Kool-Aid in her hand. He went back to studying his fingers as he tried to erase *Fuck Hope* from the table with just his spit alone.

"Mason...," his mother warned.

"It was lunch," he said defiantly. "We were making out under the bleachers."

"That's nice," his mother said, her voice dry. "Do we even know this boy? Have we met his parents? Do we have their phone number? Or, hey, his *name*?"

Mason fidgeted. "Kyle," he muttered.

"That's a nice name. Are we ever going to meet him?"

Oh God. "No," he said, squeezing his eyes tight.

"Why not?"

Oh God. To his *mother*? "Because I asked to touch his penis and he punched me in the face."

His mother let out a breath. "Uhm, was there..." He could hear her thinking. "...*context* for this request?"

Mason sighed. "He had his hand down my pants?" And it had felt *good*. Really good. Mason couldn't lie—Kyle had been squeezing and stroking and… *damn*.

"Oh." His mother sighed. "That's not what he told Principal Curtis."

"Yeah. I think he was okay with feeling me up, but I said the magic word and he freaked."

His mother rested her forehead against her hand. "Mason?"

"Yeah?"

"How would you like to go to private school?"

"Do I have to hide the fact that I'm gay?"

Her sigh shook the world. "No, no—gay is fine. Just… maybe tell them you're celibate?"

"God, college can't come soon enough."

"You are telling me."

Seventeen years ago

TODD SLEZCYK was so damned hot.

Tall, but not taller than Mason, and rangy, with dark blond hair and eyes the color of a butane flame, he dressed casually in loose 501s and tight athletic T-shirts and often let his beard grow to an adorable stubble. He was a member of all of the civic organizations, including the newly formed GSA and the Tree Huggers' Club and Young Liberals Are Us.

Mason followed him willingly into all of those organizations, because Todd's reputation for putting out after a really stirring political meeting was legendary. Mason's friend Corbin actually told Mason that Todd's dick got bigger during the announcement of the winner of the presidential election, right up until he found out it was Bush, when he came prematurely and shriveled like a raisin.

Since Corbin started dating a guy from Stanford then—someone who didn't get all limp and sad when Bush was on TV—Mason took that as license to move in. He'd play old Clinton footage if he had to, but he was going to suck Todd Slezcyk's penis if he had to fail poli-sci to get his attention!

His move came in late spring, when he and Todd emerged from a meeting defending the need for the GSA to the dean of students. The dean had seemed like a nice enough guy—middle-aged and conservative, but once he met Todd and Mason and realized they were human and not the gay stereotype from every bad disco movie *ever*, he told them he'd accept their petition to be an official club during Rush Week for the fall semester.

Todd was *stoked*, jabbering all the way across the quad to the dorms, his body throwing off heat as he capered to the time of his driven political drums.

Mason nodded excitedly, throwing in his two cents when Todd would let him, but inside, his groin was buzzing and his cock was at half-mast and even his *nipples* tingled with excitement.

Oh glory be and hallelujah, Mason Hayes was getting laid!

He'd been waiting through two years of college for this!

"So," Todd said, bouncing on his toes like he yearned for a soapbox, "did you see how that worked? The political process at its best—we followed the protocol and whoop! There you go, social change!"

"Yeah, Todd, you were awesome!"

"I mean, it was incredible, right? And with that one act, we can give a place for gay and bi and questioning students to feel safe, and for their friends to ask questions and not be afraid of censure—we *did* that, Mason! Wasn't that a rush?"

It had bored him senseless. "Such a rush!" he agreed, wondering how often he was going to have to go to meetings like that in the course of his life. When he grew up and got a real job, he was *definitely* going to find ways to ditch out on meetings where one person talked and everyone else in the room tried not to nod off, because that was the *worst*.

But right now he'd just like Todd to stop bouncing on his toes because he was pretty sure that, like Mason, Todd was sporting a semi.

"So are you ready for next week?" Todd asked, his blue eyes sparkling in the light from one of the streetlamps.

"We have to wait until next week?"

"Well, *yeah*. That's when we elect officers for next year's student council—Mason, you've been helping me campaign all semester!"

This was true. Mason was actually a top-of-the-line banner painter—he could come up with a campaign slogan at the drop of a hat. He was, in fact, thinking of making a banner for his *bed* that read "Mason Hayes! Get him laid!" because nothing else seemed to be working.

"Oh," Mason said now in a small voice. "I remember. In fact, you know, maybe you wanted to come up to my room and talk about the campaign?" He gave a flirty smile—or what he thought of as a flirty smile— and maneuvered so Todd was back against the wall of Mason's dorm. They were kissing distance—*kissing distance*—away.

Todd looked away and blushed. "Mason, that's really sweet, but, you know... I get really...." He bobbed his head and thrust his hips playfully. "*Excited*, you know?"

Oh yes! This was *exactly* what Mason had been hoping for! "Well, *yeah*," Mason said, nodding, leaning, nodding. "That's... you know... maybe we can go up to my room and... get excited *together?*" *Please, Todd—please, let's get excited together. Let's touch each other's penises together, oh my God, let's lose my virginity together!*

The look on Todd's face was kind and tender.

And most definitely not yes.

"Oh, Mason—I'm sorry, man. But I'm bi-questioning, remember? I've experimented with men, and I have a woman waiting in my room to further the experiment." He smiled like Mason should be happy for him. "This could really further my career as an activist, you know?"

Mason gaped at him, trying to put this all together. "But...." He reached down and cupped Todd gently, massaging, feeling Todd respond to his touch. "But... but you want *me*, right?"

Todd's eyes rolled back in his head and he thrust forward, clutching Mason's shoulders. "Well *yeah*, Mason, but I've got someone back at my dorms, man, and...."

Mason kissed him. He'd become the make-out king in the past two years, but somehow he just never seemed to get past second base. That didn't mean he didn't know how to kiss, though, and he pillaged Todd's mouth with every bit of expertise he had.

Todd moaned and bucked against his hand, bringing his arms up and wrapping them around Mason's neck. Oh, oh yes. His taste, oh! And the feel of their chests together, yes! And his cock in Mason's hand... oh God... please....

"Mmm," Todd breathed. "You are making it so very hard to resist." He smiled coyly from under blond lashes.

Mason bit his lip, his stomach exploding into a nest of butterflies. "And isn't a pole in the hole worth a cock in the bush?"

Under his hand, the promising steel of young lust wilted into revulsion.

Which was exactly how Todd looked at him as he pulled away and wandered dispiritedly down the path to his own dorm.

Mason moaned and banged his head softly against the brick wall. "I'm never going to get laid."

When he got back into his dorm room, his cell phone tinkled in his pocket, so excruciatingly loud his roommate grumbled and fell out of bed. God, one day he'd figure out how to fix the settings. Face hot, he stumbled into the hallway and flipped open his phone.

"Hi, sweetheart—just wanted to see if you're driving home over spring break."

"Hi, Mom," he said, both mortified and relieved to talk to his mother. Yeah, she'd seen every embarrassing moment in his life in living color, but yeah—she'd always managed to make them better. "Uh, okay. Sure." Since he and Todd would obviously not be hooking up for the sex of a lifetime.

"So." She cleared her throat delicately. "Will you be bringing any, uh, friends home?"

"No, Mom. Still a virgin."

His mother's sigh of disappointment gusted through the earpiece. "That's too bad, sweetheart. Your father and I are rooting for you!"

He let out a helpless chuckle and pinched the bridge of his nose. "Good news is, at least I'm not using the word 'penis' anymore."

He recognized her vodka-and-Kool-Aid voice. "No?"

"Nope. I scared this one away talking about the president."

"Well, your father and I think he's a dick too, if that helps."

Mason couldn't help it. He laughed. "It helps. You help, Mom."

"Well, that's my pleasure, hon. We look forward to seeing you."

"Love you," he said, knowing his voice pulsed with homesickness and not caring.

"Love you too."

She hung up, and he leaned against his door, still chuckling. Well, yes, sex would have been nice, but you couldn't beat family.

And later that semester, when Mason *finally* lost his virginity to Todd Slezcyk, he thought that sex was woefully overrated. He still loved his family, though—and his mother, bless her soul, told him to keep trying. Eventually the sex thing would live up to all the condom commercials.

9

Seven years ago

MASON LOOKED at his watch and sighed. Gordon was late.

Gordon wasn't his first boyfriend, or even his second or third—but he *was* the first boyfriend Mason could see himself spending the rest of his life with.

And Mason was going to ask him to move in at dinner tonight.

He'd had reservations for a month—a lovely table in a restaurant by the bay. He'd recently bought a house in Walnut Creek and had been making the hour-long commute into the city every day. Gordon had been leaving his San Francisco apartment to come stay at Mason's house nearly every weekend for the past seven months, and while they seemed to agree on everything from politics to books to movies, those weekends were….

Well, boring.

Blowjobs on Friday night. Butt sex on Saturday—Mason always topped. Snuggles Sunday morning.

Mason wasn't complaining, per se, but he was hoping that if they actually *lived* together, they would discover, perhaps, the joys of Sixty-nine Monday, Blindfold Tuesday, and Mason-Gets-to-Bottom Every-Other-Thursday. He loved Gordon as a friend and liked him as a lover, and maybe if they took this up another notch, he could love him as both.

He was in the middle of a glass of champagne and visions of Sex-Toy Saturday when his phone rang.

"Gordon?" he said happily, hoping this meant Gordon was close by—maybe just caught in traffic, since his office was a scant two miles away from the restaurant.

"Mason? Uh, so, you're at the restaurant?"

"Yeah! Are you on your way? I can order."

"No… uh, Mason, I hate to do this on the phone."

Oh God. "Really? I've had reservations for a month, and you're going to do this on the phone?"

"How do you know what I'm going to do?" Gordon whined. "Dammit, Mason, that's pretty presumptuous of you!"

"Well, *tell* me what you're going to do!"

"I'm going to…." He could *hear* Gordon cringe. "Break up with you."

"I *knew* that's what you were going to do." Sex-Toy Saturday died a quiet death. "Why?" He didn't care why. He felt like asking was a courtesy, really—a sense of closure for Gordon that Mason didn't need.

"Mason... I care about you—I do. But... you know. We just have different needs. You... you like sex. I... I'm not so crazy about it."

And Mason heard the unspoken two words in that sentence. "With me. You're not crazy about sex *with me*."

"I didn't say that...."

"You didn't have to. Talk to you later, Gordon. If you want any of your stuff, you'll have to come get it yourself."

"Mace, don't—"

Mason hung up. Goddammit. Here he was at a place where they served some of the best steak and lobster in the city, the kind of place where the amuse-bouche alone went down the throat like butter, and the guy he'd hoped to share it with didn't want to share anything with him—not even spit.

Fuck.

He signaled the waiter, who looked at him apprehensively. "Is the other member of your party—"

"Not coming?" Mason said shortly. "Perfidious? Really boring in bed? Yes. Yes, he is."

The waiter, a young man a little younger than Mason, looked Mason up and down and then smiled prettily. "I'm not boring in bed," he said bluntly. "And I'll be happy to come."

Mason blinked, pleased. The waiter had dark brown hair, brown eyes with green flecks in them, and a square jaw with dimples in his chin. He had a smile that could get cooked spaghetti hard.

"Are you getting off soon?" Mason said hopefully.

"Well, my shift's over in fifteen minutes," the kid said. "Maybe I can get off later."

"What's your name?"

"Logan. Yours?"

"Mason. Logan?"

"Yeah?"

"How would you like to be part of a new tradition?"

"What would we call that?" Logan asked, standing so close to the table Mason could see the sizable package outlined in his slacks.

11

"Find-Someone-to-Fuck Friday."

Logan's throaty chuckle warmed Mason to his toes. "I am so there."

"Order for us both," Mason told him, enjoying this very much. "And then come join me."

The next morning Mason woke up in a hotel room covered in come next to a trashcan full of condoms. His wallet was missing. There was a note next to the bed.

Paid for the room, left your car keys. Took the cash and the credit cards. You were a sweet lay—but maybe next time buy a dildo. Less expensive and easier to clean.

Mason rolled over on his back and peeled the sheets off his despoiled body.

Yep. It had been a great ride, but maybe he should stick to Masturbation Monday for a while.

Eight months ago

"MACE, I'M sorry."

Mason looked up from the tumbler of Glenlivet he'd poured himself just before Dane walked in the door of his Walnut Creek home.

"Not your fault," Mason said, knocking back the whiskey with a shocking disregard for how much it cost. Well, Mason's job was sort of spectacular. He could afford the best. It had been one of his primary attractions for Ira.

And then Ira had started fucking Mason's boss.

Now the job and the money and the house were no longer attractive.

"How did you find out?" Dane asked, grabbing a tumbler for himself and sitting down kitty-corner at the rather long table. Mason and Ira had entertained a lot in the past four years. Mason wasn't so great at entertaining, really—he still managed to say the wrong damned thing at the wrong damned time. But Ira had been *spectacular* at it, ordering the right wines, knowing the right jokes, knowing how to tell them to the right people.

Mason had been so grateful, actually, because Ira had smoothed the way with Mason's boss. Mason's first social interaction with the man had been to tell him how much he enjoyed casual Fridays, because his first job out of college had been for a guy with a stick up his ass who made employees wear polo shirts to company softball games.

There *were* no casual Fridays at Bent-Co. Mason had been showing up in khakis and polo shirts on chutzpah alone.

Fuck.

But Ira had been able to make Roy Carruthers see the humor in the situation. And apparently Ira enjoyed doing that so much that he and Roy got together at least twice a week to laugh and laugh.

Or that's what Mason assumed they had been doing when he picked up his dry cleaning during his lunch hour one day and spotted the two of them coming out of a hotel lobby, laughing and razor-burned and chummy.

And then he'd looked at Ira's credit-card summary—he left his reports on the desk in the study, where they both sat and did bills and used the home console—and saw the twice-weekly expenditures. Oh, wasn't that nice. One day one of them got the drinks and the next time that guy got the room.

Wouldn't Roy's wife be surprised?

But Mason wasn't going to be the one to tell her. He had enough trouble cleaning his own house—and that's what he did. But first there was the argument, and the denial, and then there were the recriminations on Ira's part, about how Mason was some sort of savant who couldn't be around people and who didn't have a romantic bone in his body and who might have been great in the sack but whose pillow talk was awkward and disgusting.

Mason didn't know what to say about that. He liked to talk about sex. He liked to touch and taste and feel—for him, sex was all about the senses. There were no bright lights, no trips through the tunnel to see Jesus—there was just the glory of physical sensation. The rest of it—the building a life part—that was the part where his heart got all squooshy.

He had not, as of yet, connected the two.

He'd told his mother that when he'd called to tell her about the breakup, and he'd heard her sigh from Redwood City. "Oh Mason—honey, you have the best heart. And when you find someone—*the* someone—it's going to be someone who gets that about you."

"The only person who gets that about me is my mother," he'd said, trying to make things light.

"And your little brother, who thinks you walk on water."

"Sh—let's not tell him the truth, okay?"

"I think your little brother has it spot-on, Mason Hayes. If you're going to disillusion him, you're going to have to tell him yourself. He's on his way over."

And that's where they were now. Dane had hotfooted it over from their parents' house, where he was living as he finished stage one of school, to apparently drink really expensive Scotch.

"So he was cheating on you for how long?" Dane asked, sipping appreciatively. He'd changed his major three times as an undergrad, and the money his parents had saved for his education had run out. He was currently working two jobs to pay for his tuition—he told Mason once that he was starting to believe Miller really *was* beer.

"Two years." Mason took a gulp, because as Ira said, the finer things in life were wasted on him.

"What a douche nugget. You want I should take a hit out on him? I work with some really unsavory people at the restaurant—they know people."

Mason laughed, feeling the burn behind his eyes. "I'm sure they do," he said, loving his little brother so much in that moment that he forgave him completely for coming along as a baby and sucking all of the attention from Mason. "And no—it's okay. He doesn't make that much as a graphic artist—"

"He's not that good, Mace. He's not. I mean, I never told you this, but I used to bring your guys' holiday cards into school and have the real graphic artists make fun of them. They enjoyed that. They enjoyed that a lot."

And the laughter burbled up, unstoppable, much like Dane himself. Dane was just as odd a duck as Mason was, but Dane made that work for him. He wore his hair messy and his beard neat, and the fine lines developing in the corners of his big brown eyes were mostly from laughter and a little bit from confusion—Dane's love life was less conventional than Mason's in that he wore his condition of singleness like a beacon, right up until a sudden passion sucked him away from his family, his studies, his bills, and his common sense. After he almost got kicked out of school—and changed his major for the third time—his parents had given him a good talking-to and then pulled him toward a shrink.

With a few memorable glitches, Dane had taken to his new medication regimen like a champ, and the last four years of pre-veterinary school had been much less turbulent. But Dane was still not looking for a permanent lover, and Mason worried about him.

Until right now, when it appeared Dane had the right idea all along.

"So," Dane said, taking another drink. "I got accepted to Davis."

"For veterinary school?" The school was famous for that field. "That's awesome!" He smiled at his brother in relief—good news. He'd needed it.

"And I'm going to move out of Mom and Dad's house and be all on my own far away." Dane looked at him calmly and blinked his wide-set brown eyes at his big brother, and Mason looked at his little brother and understood.

"Are you worried?" he asked, wishing Dane all the happiness in the world but knowing that sometimes happiness was so much harder than it sounded. Bipolar disorder was never going away, and Dane put on a good game face, but balancing his meds had been a big fat pain in the ass. Having a combo now that even allowed him a sip of Scotch was a victory, and Mason would totally trade places with him if he could. Mason didn't need friends or lovers—God knew he managed to fuck up any combination of the two. But Dane deserved it all.

"Yes," Dane said, smiling briefly so Mason would know he was serious. "Yes, I'm worried. Mom and Dad are… you know. Mom and Dad."

"Awesome," Mason said quietly, because who could argue.

"Yeah. And Mom has this way of making me remember my meds without nagging, and Dad has this way of just grounding me when something has triggered me and I need to take that one pill for the really bad days, and…." He shook his head. "And is it stupid that I *like* not going off the deep end? That I *like* knowing that if I lose my shit, someone will be there to catch me?"

"No," Mason said. "Not at all."

Dane looked up at him briefly and swished his glass around. "So, can you leave all this behind and catch me?"

And that's how Mason decided to move to Sacramento with his little brother so Dane could go to school and Mason could get a new job and they'd both know that somebody was there to catch them.

But sometimes your little brother isn't the person who needs to catch you. And sometimes you need to be ready to catch somebody else.

So, Five Minutes Ago

"HE WAS cute," Dane said as he and Mason got into the car. They were parked in front of a modest house in a tiny Citrus Heights suburb, where Mason's friend Skip had thrown a lovely Christmas party for his friends on his rec league soccer team—and Mason and Dane.

"Skipper?" Mason asked wistfully, because yeah, Skip was cute. Six foot three, blond, blue-eyed, with this sort of open kindness in his face that forgave anything—even Mason's inappropriate come-on when Mason first called him for tech service.

Some things never changed, and Mason's foot-in-mouth disease was one of them.

"I've met Skipper," Dane said dryly as Mason started the car. "I thought he was cute then, but he was taken then. Still taken now."

Mason grunted, not wanting to talk about his crush. "And Richie is a good match for him," he admitted, feeling gracious.

"If anyone hurts Skip, Richie will kill them and stuff their body in a car trunk and put the car in a crusher," Dane said matter-of-factly. "The guy's like an arctic shrew—he looks cute and fuzzy, but if you put him and three other shrews in a bucket with the lid on, when you open the bucket the next day, there's going to be a fat Richie and a whole lot of blood."

Mason's eyes widened. "Did you take your meds today?" he asked, a little panicked because it was the holiday season and things had gotten hectic. They were driving down to Redwood City tomorrow to spend Christmas with their parents, and Dane had endured a grueling series of finals that had ended two weeks before.

"Yes, Mason, I took my meds!" Dane waved his hands. "You're missing the point."

"And what's the point?" Mason piloted the Lexus SUV through the small neighborhood. He'd had a sedan before they moved, but just like with the house in Walnut and Ira and his job at Bent-Co, Mason wasn't sorry to see the change. He was now vice president of product quality at Tesko Tech. He still didn't actually know what he did, and he was sadly still in a lot of meetings. He made enough to pay the mortgage on a decent-size house in

16

Fair Oaks, and his commute to work wasn't bad. Dane's commute to school was heinous—he left early three days a week and came home after eight—but Mason made sure he didn't have to work during his last few years of school.

Well, he'd made some money on the Walnut Creek house, and he had nobody to support. If you couldn't spoil the shit out of your little brother, what was your purpose in life?

"The point was, that Jefferson guy—"

"Terry Jefferson?" Because Mason and Jefferson had talked for quite a bit while Jefferson's mother sort of hunkered in the background, glaring at them.

"Is Jefferson's first name Terry? Because all the soccer guys are like… like last-names only. I swear I heard Skip call his own boyfriend Scoggins when he was talking about their last game."

Mason laughed. "Yeah, so what did you call Clay?"

"Clay's straight," Dane mumbled, but the car got suddenly heated and Mason started to doubt if that was true.

"As far as I know, so is Jefferson."

"Bisexual is a thing, you know," Dane said with dignity. "I've harbored embarrassing feelings towards women sometimes."

"Why would you be embarrassed about that?" Mason asked, laughing. Mason was pretty much a 5.8 on the Kinsey scale—but Dane could be a 3 or 4 easy.

"Because my type is usually, like, my fortyish severe female professors. It's weird."

Mason shook his head and tried to negotiate through the patchy fog between Citrus Heights and Fair Oaks. "Yes, yes, it is."

"Thanks, Mace, for helping me accept myself."

"Oh, I'm totally there," Mason laughed. "I totally accept that you're weird."

"Okay, so I'm weird. But that doesn't mean that Terry—"

"Jefferson."

"Okay, Jefferson, wasn't putting out… feelers."

"No, he wasn't!" Mason hung a left on Madison in fog so thick he couldn't see much on the other side of the intersection. Like everyone else driving at twelve o'clock on Christmas Eve, he was taking a lot on faith.

Dane started doing an impression of the young man who had brought Mason a napkin full of cookies as they'd stood around the fire pit in Skip's backyard.

"'Gee, Mason, you have some decent muscles for a guy who claims he only golfs. Are you sure you don't run too?' 'Well yes, Jefferson, I do run, but I feel like a lazy bum for not running marathons because that seems to be a thing here in Sacramento.' 'Well gee willickers, Mr. Hayes, you could always join Skip's soccer team if you're looking for more exercise. Skipper would be *happy* to have you, because then I could get laid and you and me could stop crushing over the tall oblivious blond guy!'"

At this point Mason was laughing so hard he was afraid he'd wreck the car. "Oh my God, Dane, you are so full of shit!"

"I am not," Dane replied mildly. "I can't believe you can't see it either."

Mason thought carefully back to those few hours of huddling around the fire pit, drinking hot chocolate and talking.

And Terry Jefferson, who looked like a kid—and hell, was even younger than Dane—with carefully streaked brown hair worn in one of those wedges that would go back into a tiny bun on the top of his head if he wanted to.

Tonight it had hung partially in his brown eyes, and he'd had a way of looking out from under it at Mason that made Mason forget about Skipper entirely for a moment.

It had also made him remember Logan the perfidious waiter and that one night of really awesome sex that had set him back about two grand.

It had been the best sex of Mason's life, honestly, but it had also been one of the best lessons.

Still….

Terry Jefferson had the flirty easiness of Logan the perfidious waiter, but he also had a shy way of biting his lip when Mason paid attention to him, and a narrow, rectangular harlequin's face, with a slender jaw and dark brown eyes over a pert, irreverent nose. He looked like he enjoyed the flirting, and he was good at it, but he didn't get much practice at it. In his head, Mason replayed his conversation outside under the stars that night, before the low fog had rolled in.

"So, would you consider playing soccer?" Jefferson had looked sideways at him through that wedge-cut hair, his hands buried in the kangaroo pocket of his Sac State sweatshirt. "Skipper always needs more people."

"Well, I'm sort of the old man of the group," Mason said, looking around. "I didn't realize how young Schipperke was when we first started talking." Yup—Dane was probably one of the oldest here, at not-quite-thirty, and besides Jefferson's mother, who hung back on one of the patio chairs, swaddled in blankets so thoroughly that Mason couldn't get a bead on her appearance, that left Mason as the oldest. "I'm afraid I'd hold you all back."

Jefferson laughed and pulled his wedge back, letting Mason see his warm brown eyes. "Naw, man—it's not like that. We just play to play, really—winning's, like, a perk. We enjoy it, but we like the friends better."

Mason smiled, feeling like a grade-schooler. "Really? I mean... I'm sort of a social nightmare, but I'd love to play a sport." He'd played soccer as a kid—until he'd told Tommy Perkins that the nylon soccer shorts made his penis get large if he forgot to wear his jock, and suddenly nobody invited him to their birthday parties anymore.

"A social nightmare?" Jefferson cocked his head almost coyly and moved closer to the fire pit, shivering. It was around forty degrees out in Skipper's backyard, and Jefferson was wearing cargo shorts, because he was apparently one of those men's men who didn't care about pneumonia. Mason took a side step to give him more room, and Jefferson... moved closer. Mason had to stop scooting because he was about to get really friendly with Dane's friend Carpenter, and Carpenter claimed he wasn't gay, so Mason didn't want to freak him out.

"Did you just hear me call him Schipperke?" Mason asked, half laughing but mostly despairing because he couldn't seem to stop. "First time I talked to him on the phone, I teased him because his name's Skipper Keith—"

Jefferson's laughter was low from his stomach, like he meant it. "That's fantastic! I can't believe he didn't tell us this!"

"Because every man wants to be known as a small fluffy dog," Skipper said dryly, overhearing their conversation and holding out a tray with more cookies. Mason took one on autopilot and thanked Skipper with a hint of embarrassment.

"Skipper Keith," Mason said with meaning. "I mean, if someone told you their name was Bison Friese, you'd take notice, right?"

"Is that a dog?" Skipper asked, looking puzzled.

"Oh my God, Skip!" Jefferson crowed. "Remember the little fluffy dog from *Shrek*?"

Mason's heart stalled. He hadn't been a kid when those movies came out, but Jefferson and Skip had.

"Yeah," Skipper said, rolling his eyes. "Loved those frickin' movies."

"I, uh, haven't seen them," Mason said abashedly.

Jefferson's grin caught him by surprise and socked him in the stomach. "We can watch them together sometime," he said.

At that moment, a voice quavery with peevishness but not age seemed to slice right through the happy banter that Mason had been so enjoying.

"Terrence! Are you going to get me some hot chocolate or do I have to go fetch it myself? And try not to put too much whipped cream on it. Makes me gassy."

Mason tried to catch Jefferson's eyes to smile and let him know that parents were universally embarrassing, but then he saw Jefferson's unguarded expression instead.

Terry Jefferson was mortified. And miserable. And suddenly Mason, who would have said he possessed no empathy, became acutely aware that a man who would bring his mother to a Christmas party very possibly lived with his mother day in, day out, and while this might be an okay thing for Mason and Dane, it was obviously not a picnic for Jefferson.

"Right on it, Mom," Jefferson said. His eyes slid to Mason's, and right when Mason was about to offer to join him, Carpenter asked Mason when they were going golfing again, and Jefferson was gone.

Until Dane called him up to Mason's memory, and suddenly Mason was seeing signals he hadn't noticed in that particular moment.

"He's too young for me," Mason said reflexively.

"I don't see that as a problem," Dane said, doing that thing with his lips that made them pop out from the cave of mustache and scruff.

"Really? Your brother dating a guy eleven years his junior. That doesn't squick you out?"

"You assume that you're actually eleven years more mature than this guy, and really? I don't think that's the case."

Mason boldly refrained from rolling his eyes, partly because he didn't want to wreck the car in the fog. Oi! The fog got worse and the streets got narrower near the river, and Sailor Bar was practically in Mason's backyard.

"I don't even know if this guy is gay," Mason grumbled, because yeah. He'd made that mistake too.

"Jefferson might not either," Dane said with a smugness Mason had never felt. "There's that whole bisexual thing too—he might be bi and not know it yet. Think about that—you could be his older-man awakening. Doesn't that do something for you?"

"Give me indigestion? Jesus, Dane, you are *not* reassuring me about thi—"

"I think Carpenter's bi," Dane said out of the blue.

Mason's breath caught in his chest. "He said very clearly he's not gay." Mason remembered that moment, because he'd seen the corners of Dane's eyes droop in obvious disappointment. Well, Mason's own eyes had been drooping that day, because he'd actually gotten to *meet* the Schipperke of his dreams, and it turned out he was everything Mason had envisioned. Tall, handsome, smart, kind... and taken. Don't forget taken.

"Yes, he did," Dane said, sounding complacent. "But he did not say he wasn't bi."

"Uh, Dane—" Oh God. Please don't let Mason's little brother get his heart broken by a big bear of a guy who wouldn't hurt a flea but who couldn't be expected to change his sexual orientation on the basis of Dane's hopes.

"I'm not crazy," Dane said mutinously. "Or I am, when I'm off my meds, but imagining a straight guy is gay has never been one of my problems. Now please, Carpenter and I are going to take months and months. I rely on you for entertainment. Entertain me and tell me you're going to get his number from Skipper and call this guy."

"No," Mason said shortly, pulling into his driveway finally. The house on Eastwood Street wasn't flashy, but it had a lovely arched patio and carport, two stories, and four bedrooms. That was one for Mason, one for Dane on the other side of the house, and two guest rooms that shared a bathroom in the middle. Unlike when they'd been growing up in their parents' tiny home on the peninsula, they didn't have to share a room, and they never had to pretend not to hear the other one masturbate for the rest of their lives.

Oh. And there was an enormous swimming pool in the back, with a fenced-in deck and an attached hot tub. This was not a thing Mason had asked the realtor for, but that was only because he didn't realize he'd be house-shopping in August and that August in Sacramento tried to kill people with fire and suffocation.

Once he knew that, he was grateful for the real estate agent trying to up her commission, because the pool had been in use through October.

All in all, he liked his new digs—and his new job, even if he wasn't sure what he did. *Mostly* he signed papers and made suggestions, and then he asked people to carry that out for him, okay?

He'd gotten two promotions in four months. He was apparently *really* good at his job.

Which was not going to save him from his brother's dogged determination.

"No why?" Dane asked as they pulled into the carport.

"No, I'm not going to call him, because tomorrow is Christmas, we're driving down to Redwood City, and I'm sure Jefferson has plans. And we'll be back the day after tomorrow, and I'm spending the rest of the week on home improvement."

Dane flicked him a glance. "What kind of home improvement?"

"I don't know—it's *your* Christmas present. You tell me what we're going to paint your walls and how we're going to tile your bathroom, and all the rest will follow."

Dane blinked at him. "I take it this is under the tree?"

"In card form, sure." God, Mason was so bad at Christmas. What he really needed was a giant gift card that said "I Tried" on it, so his family could understand that this was just one more social skill he'd never mastered.

Dane pinched the bridge of his nose and squeezed his eyes shut, and for a moment Mason really hated himself because he'd totally disappointed his little brother. But when Dane opened his eyes, they were red-rimmed, and his smile was the same sweet one he'd had as a baby, when he and the cat had made peace and all of his internal combustion functions had recently been executed.

"That's a really nice present," Dane said, like Mason had somehow achieved world peace. "That's thoughtful—including the week you're taking off to help with the work." He swung out of the car, and Mason saw him wipe under his eyes and thought that Dane really needed some sleep and some rest and some time to recoup after the stressful semester.

Dane went into the kitchen through the carport, and Mason followed him, putting the bread loaf and cookies that he'd gotten from Skip and Richie that night on the table. Breakfast in the morning. Dane paused at the refrigerator and pulled out the milk carton to pour himself some chocolate milk to wash down his meds. When he was done, he leaned back against the counter in the dimly lit kitchen and regarded Mason soberly.

"What?" Mason said after a moment.

"Why won't you ask him out? He's friends with Skip—the worst that can happen is he can say he's wild about breasts and vagina, and you know you can start again."

Mason fidgeted, not wanting to state the obvious but needing his brother to understand.

"Da-ane…." And that sounded like a second-grader whining. Well done!

"Ma-son!"

Mason glared at him. "Has it ever occurred to you that maybe I'm just never going to find the right guy? That there is something deficient in me, something that fucks things up at the last minute, something that says the wrong thing or does the wrong thing or—"

"No," Dane said and kicked back a healthy swallow of chocolate milk. "No, it has not occurred to me."

"But Dane…."

"I know—you told me. All lose, all the time. I think it's bullshit."

"Then you haven't been living with my penis."

"Thank God or that would be gross."

Mason groaned and tilted his head back, remembering the way he could almost see the stars in Skip's backyard.

"Have you noticed," he said randomly, "how different it is here than it is in the Bay Area?"

"If by different you mean repressed Bible-belt mentality with none of the dedication to the arts we're used to seeing in the city? Yes."

Mason laughed—sort of. "I… I keep thinking that I'd like to do something with my life—"

"You're a very well-off man."

"Yes. But… I don't know. I just keep expecting the world to be all… bright and promising like it was when we were kids. Like, I found out what sex was, and that it involved my penis, and I was expecting there to be days when my entire body felt like fireworks and I could see God."

"Damn," Dane said with a whistle.

"Have you ever had those days?"

"Only when I was on an upswing. Have you?"

Mason laughed unhappily. "Once. He took my cash and credit cards and left my car keys."

Dane grimaced, the expression clear even in the semidarkness. "Oh Mace."

"I just… I don't want another relationship—not if it's not going to be awesome, you know?"

He'd put so much of himself into saying that. He thought Dane would understand.

"You'll never know if it's going to be a prince until you kiss him," Dane said practically.

Mason sighed. "I'm going to bed."

"Me too. I'll make breakfast in the morning. And give you your gift then."

"Is my gift a sausage burrito?"

"No, smartass, it's not. Now go to bed. I want you to drive tomorrow so I don't get homicidal."

Whatever.

DANE'S PRESENT turned out to be a gorgeous framed print of Vincent Van Gogh's *Starry Night*. Done a lot? Well, yes, but Mason didn't care. Having it in his living room made him really happy.

They left at noon, hoping to pull into Redwood City around three, and just about the time Dane nodded off—thank God because he was often a nervous passenger—Mason's phone rang.

Mason put it on speaker and hoped Dane could continue to sleep through anything like he had when he'd been a baby.

"Hey, uh, Mason? This you?"

"Yes…."

"I hope it's okay I'm calling. I got your number from Skip. This is, uh, Jefferson? Terry Jefferson?"

"Yeah," Mason said, hating his brother for the absurd little adrenaline spike that hit him right in the chest. "Last night, Skipper's house. I was there."

"Of course you were. Anyway, after you left last night, I asked Skip if you could play soccer, and he said sure, he would have asked you sooner but he thought you only played golf. As. If."

"I play golf," Mason said, a little affronted.

"Do you *like* golf?" Jefferson asked suspiciously.

"If I'm playing with friends," Mason said, Hazel Avenue turning to Highway 50 as he spoke. "Why am I defending golf?"

"Because usually only rich douche bags play golf," Jefferson said, disgust lacing his voice.

"Well, I'm a rich douche bag. Sue me. Why are you calling again?" And here was the interchange. Mason hated this section of freeway because it was usually muddling—but lucky him, the road was almost empty today.

"To ask you to play soccer with us peasants."

Mason snorted softly. "Can I wear my white cleats and expect you to clean them?"

He heard Jefferson's reluctant snort on the other end. "You can expect all sorts of things. Mostly expect to have a beer after practice and pizza after the games and dirt rubbed into your face during play. We only win sometimes."

"Sounds compelling and life-changing—I'm in."

"Are you *looking* for compelling and life-changing?" Jefferson asked, and even though he was still being playful, Mason couldn't help remember what he'd been trying to say to Dane the night before.

"A man can always hope," he said a little wistfully.

"Yeah." The sigh on the other end of the line hurt something in Mason's chest, but he couldn't say why. "I've given up hope. I'll take soccer instead."

"Would you take golf, or are you too scared of rich douche bags?" The words were out before Mason could stop them.

"Fine. I'll play your silly rich person's game, since you're going to clean your own cleats and all."

Mason was about to fist pump before he realized he didn't know if this was a date or not. Or if Jefferson was really gay. Or if he'd be interested in Mason if he was.

"So when's good for you?" *Caution, Mason, caution—let's try not to say anything about sucking on his neck and fondling his penis before we know the important things.*

"No time is actually *good* for me," Jefferson muttered, "but since we have three weeks before the next soccer season picks up and my mom's used to me being gone on Saturdays, can we fit it in there?"

Mason had to think about it. Tee times usually had to be reserved a couple of weeks in advance at almost any course in the area, but…. "How early can you be there?" he asked hopefully. "Because if we can do a six-thirty tee time, we can squeeze that in."

Jefferson's low-throated chuckle was one of the dirtiest, most sexually arousing things Mason had ever heard.

"Squeezing things in? I can do that."

"Gurgh." So help him, it was the only thing he could say. That one sound, and he was suddenly sporting a chubby in his family gathering slacks, and his only hope was that he didn't go for full-blown wood or he'd renew the lease on his circumcision.

"So, the Saturday after New Year's? Like, a week and a half from now?"

"Yeah," Mason managed. "I'll call you if they're full up."

"I can do full up too," Jefferson said, and how did that sound suggestive? Mason hadn't been laid in nearly ten months—that was the only answer for how "full up" could sound like an orgy porno.

"I, uh, don't know how to take that?" Apparently Mason took it like sex on tap, but that was probably his own hormonal imbalance at this point.

"Reserve the day, even if you can't reserve the course," Jefferson said cryptically. In the background, Mason heard his mother's voice shouting, "Terrence, are you going to be on the phone all day? It's Christmas. Do you even care? Weren't we going to church in half an hour?"

"I'll be there," Jefferson said, his voice firm. "You just text me with where."

"Will do," Mason said, and then, because he could hear some of the desperation in Jefferson's voice, "I promise."

"See you then." And then he hung up.

"Dane!" Mason hissed, grabbing his phone from the island console and thrusting it at his brother.

"What?" Dane snarled, because losing sleep had never been his favorite thing.

"I need you to do something for me—"

"Now?"

"Shut up and reserve a tee time for me at Timber Creek."

"You woke me out of a sound sleep for a *golf game*? I'll never make you breakfast burritos again!"

Mason fumbled with one hand and *made* Dane take the phone. "What you just slept through was Jefferson calling me up and scheduling a golf game. And inviting me onto the soccer team. And… and laughing. Laughing like… like chocolate-coated hormone sin. And *I really need to play that fucking golf game!*"

He was hyperventilating, oh yes he was, but his groin still ached a little from that laugh. And his heart was still beating with the adrenaline high of being called up and… oh hell. At the very least it was a play date with a friend, and since Ira had gotten all of those with the split, Mason was going to take that at face value and run gleefully onto the golf course.

"Oh. I *slept* through that? Talk about unfair." Dane straightened up and started messing with Mason's phone. "Of course, you need to make that reservation *right now*. But you know what the price is gonna be?"

"You need to stop somewhere?"

"I'm feeling like a highly caffeinated milkshake. Next Starbucks you see."

Awesome. He was going to be side-seat granny driving all the way to San Mateo. But that was okay, because Mason had a *play date* with a guy who could get him hard with just a *laugh*.

Even if Jefferson was straight, it was the most exciting thing to happen to Mason since Skipper didn't sue him for suggesting gay porn as a perfectly appropriate office activity.

"HOW ARE you doing, son? Have you met anybody?" Mason's father, Roger, was *the* most dad-looking dad Mason had ever met. He looked like Ferris Buehler's father, or the dad in *American Pie*. Not that those two dads looked alike, but Roger Hayes gave off that same "dorky dad doing his best" vibe. He was tall, with silvered brown hair, a thin, handsome face, and a kind smile. Mason's mother had sat next to Mason at the principal's meetings and the teacher's meetings and the meetings with baffled parents—and Mason's dad had listened to the breakdown and then taken Mason and Dane out to eat and asked them what *else* they'd seen that day.

It had been the "what else they'd seen" that Mason had lived for.

If Dad could focus on the other 95 percent of the day besides the part that Mason had fucked up, then Mason could believe there was more to his life than just his fuckups.

It was that simple.

It's what had gotten Mason through 95 percent of his life, actually.

So Dad's gentle probing into Mason's love life wasn't a bad thing, really—Mason just didn't know how to answer.

"Have I met anybody? Well, I had a terrible crush on a guy from work," he admitted. "But he's sort of taken."

"That's not promising," Roger said. "Not gonna lie."

Mason's smile stretched his cheeks. His dad could say things like that—"not gonna lie"—in spite of being born and raised on the peninsula in a conservative neighborhood. He could blend in anywhere, unlike Mason, who had needed to channel Fred MacMurray just so he could talk to Skip on the phone without going "Nurk!"

"Well, the good news is that he's a friend now, and his boyfriend isn't going to stage a hit, and his best friend is now Dane's best friend too."

"Wow—he may not be happiness, but he sounds like a carrier."

Dad. "He is." Mason let out a breath, and some of his carefully nurtured optimism about Jefferson faded, and some of his worry about Dane surfaced. "But, you know, Dane's getting his hopes up about the friend, and I...." God. Dane had been such a gleeful baby. And when his moods were balanced, he was a pretty gleeful adult. But Mason had been there through some of his dark times—had carried him kicking and screaming to the doctor's once after a bad breakup, when he'd holed up inside his dorm and stopped eating.

Mason would do anything to make sure his brother didn't get his heart broken.

"You worry," Roger said, making himself comfortable in the recliner next to the couch where Mason was sitting. They were pretending to watch *Jurassic Park* on television, because it was a better alternative than football, which nobody in Mason's family followed. Dane and Janette were in the kitchen, doing the actual cooking. Mason and Roger *liked* food—they were fans, in fact—but they were not actual participants in the food-making sport. If it hadn't been for Dane, Mason would have survived on chicken sandwiches for the past five months.

"You don't?" Mason said, his voice throbbing with anxiety for his little brother.

"No, I do." Roger laced his fingers around his knees and stretched. "I just... I'm getting a bit old, Mason. There comes a time when you have to have faith in your children, even if they've got problems."

"You're not old," Mason said automatically, but he could do math too—if he was thirty-six, that made his dad not in his sixties anymore.

"Okay, I'm not old." Roger smiled at him gently. "But I *do* have faith in you."

"It's just easier to do that when I keep my mouth shut," Mason said glumly.

Roger's smile turned wicked. "Why would you want to do that when your words always give us the most delightful surprises?"

Mason's eyes burned. "Thanks, Dad."

"Has Samuel L. Jackson been eaten by the fucking velociraptor yet?"

"Nope—but the gamekeeper who looks like the velociraptor has."

"Spielberg did that in *Jaws* too—it's a handy trick."

Mason nodded and smiled at his dad, but he really couldn't talk right now. He was too busy getting excited that some guy who thought he was a rich douche bag wanted to play golf.

Break for Balls

DANE'S CHOICES for painting his room and tiling his bathroom were bold and simple—sky blue and white. Mason couldn't complain, because the colors brightened the house but they didn't clash with the neutral carpeting in the hallway, and when Dane accessorized with dark purple bedding and curtains, the extra color gave the whole thing a pop.

They stood back the Friday after Christmas and looked it over, both of them sweaty and filthy and really, really glad that they could turn the water back on after the incident with the water main when they were replacing the toilet.

"We did good," Dane said in awe.

"You did good," Mason praised. "I was a credit card and a strong back."

"No, seriously—you looked up how to use all the stuff. That one wrench looks like something you see in cartoons only—I don't know how you thought it was a real tool."

Mason laughed, secretly pleased. The truth was, he'd been studying how to redecorate Dane's rooms for a month. "Ira hired someone to do the house in Walnut Creek," he confessed. "I just… I wanted to, you know—"

"Prove you didn't need that two-timing fucknugget to make your house a home?" Dane supplied.

Mason wrapped his arm around Dane's sweaty, paint-spattered shoulders and hauled him into a hug. "Just my baby brother, whom I love," he said sweetly.

"Yeah, yeah—I'm cleaning up. We already made that deal. Now go shower. Don't you have a golf game tomorrow?"

"Next week!" Mason called as he trotted off to shower. But speaking of…. He grabbed his phone and texted Jefferson as he waited for the shower to get hot.

Ready for golf next week?

I'm ready for golf TOMORROW and I've never even played.

Oh hell. *Shit—I could try to find a driving range to visit to work on your swing.*

30

How about I teach you soccer?

Mason stared at the text. Oh. Okay. Well, if whatever they were doing didn't work out tomorrow, he still had a tee time next week. Why not?

He refused to get excited about it. Any of it.

But he couldn't shake Jefferson's eyes peeping shyly out at him through his hair either.

MASON SHOWED up at Tempo Park bright and early Saturday morning, cleats in hand, wearing shin guards, soccer socks, and knee sweats.

And a hooded sweatshirt over his long-sleeved shirt and gloves, because it was nine in the morning in the rat-tail end of December, dammit!

Jefferson arrived as Mason was on his second trip around the field. His green Toyota coupe belched a big cloud of black smoke before it puttered to a stop.

When he got out, he was wearing soccer shorts and a T-shirt, and Mason felt a surge of annoyance. It was obvious the guy was just aching to get out of the house and away from an overbearing mother, but she couldn't be bothered to nag him about wearing a sweatshirt?

"Aren't you freezing?" Mason called out as he jogged up the hill toward the parking lot.

"Like a brass monkey with no nuts," Jefferson retorted, throwing his ball over Mason's head and into the center of the field. "Can we do another couple of laps?"

It would figure that he was way faster than Mason without even trying. Mason finally just told him to run on his own while Mason kept at his steady jog-trot that got him around his neighborhood in the morning.

When Jefferson veered off from the outside of the soccer field to the center, with the ball, Mason headed that way, unsurprised when Jefferson used his toe to pop the ball up to his knee, and his knee to pop it up so he could bounce it solidly off his head. It arched over to Mason.

Who caught it wetly in his arms.

"Mason, you're killing me," Jefferson said, but he was laughing as he said it. He'd pulled his wedge back into a brief ponytail, the shorn sides of his hair still thick enough that Mason couldn't see any scalp through the stubble. Mason suddenly wanted to touch his scalp, feel the strands of hair through his fingers, but Jefferson's voice called him back. "Now set it down and use the inside of your foot to pass it to me."

Mason did, feeling like the world's tallest, gawkiest, most awkward human.

"Oh my God. *Killing* me." Jefferson passed it back, making an obvious turn to his foot so Mason could see him using the inside of it to pass. "Now don't be a toe-poker. You have more area on the inside of your foot, so more control. Now send it back!"

Again, and again—it was like a game of catch with your dad, except with your feet and a big vinyl ball, and they moved around the field as they kicked. And except Mason's dad had never actually played catch because of that whole coordination thing.

Jefferson kept up an insane patter of trash-talk-slash-encouragement the whole time.

"Yeah, see that? You toe-poked it. You see where it went? Southern Angola, that's where it went. Now watch me run for it, 'cause you like that, you crazy bastard, yes you do. Okay, see what I did? I *passed* it. Did you see where it went? It went *straight to you*. Notice that? Notice that it went straight to you? Wasn't that nice of me? Now can you frickin' *pass* it this time? Oh, that's nice—you stuck to the continental United States that time, now can you *use the side of your frickin' foot* for sweet Christ's sake!" And so on.

Mason didn't participate in any of the patter—he was too busy running for the ball and listening, bemused, as Jefferson bossed him around as no man had bossed him around before, in or out of bed.

Finally Jefferson got irritated and booted the ball the hell off the field. Mason gave him a weak wave and went trotting after it, dribbling it back slowly and with great concentration, sticking his tongue out of the side of his mouth like a little kid.

He got up to where Jefferson was ready and very carefully popped the ball over, using the inside of his foot, breathing a sigh of relief.

"Woo-hoo!" Jefferson bounced straight up, pumping both fists, and then he ran full barrel to Mason, arms out, so Mason had no choice but to catch him in a massive sports-guy hug.

Mason managed to lift him up and whirl him around. The feeling of his tight, muscular body so solid against Mason's thighs did the same thing Jefferson's laugh did.

Mason whirled to a stop and set Jefferson down, feeling giddy and a little dorky and embarrassingly aroused.

"Water break!" Jefferson crowed. Then he grabbed Mason's hand and hauled him up the hill to the small concrete bathroom with the drinking fountain.

He *grabbed Mason's hand.*

That was pretty much Mason's only warning.

He found himself dragged into a freezing bathroom made of cinder blocks with a concrete floor. It must have been cleaned the night before, because it didn't smell bad, but it was damp and wet and colder than the frosty soccer field, which at least sat in the sun.

As Mason looked around, surprised to find himself in such a place, Jefferson put two icy hands on his cheeks and the world stopped.

Mason looked immediately into an intense set of brown eyes with crinkles in the corners, while he responded to a laughing, mischievous smile.

Oh. Oh yes. It wasn't imagination and he wasn't being an awkward perv—this guy liked him, and he liked the time they spent together, and—

And his mouth was hot, wet, and heavenly as he pulled Mason down into a heart-stopping, ravishing kiss.

Mason had been waiting his entire life to be kissed like this. He wrapped his arms around Jefferson's shoulders and pulled him closer, creating a warm cocoon in the shiver of the bathroom. Jefferson's tongue grew more aggressive, as did his hands, sliding under Mason's sweatshirt and T-shirt, shaping the muscles in his stomach, the density of his chest, and—

"Oh! Damn!"

The almost painfully engorged points of his nipples.

Jefferson laughed as Mason gasped, and pinched them again. Mason bucked up against him, mostly hard and filling fast, and Jefferson shoved a knowing hand down his sweats and grasped his cock without shame or apology.

"Oh my God." Because… *hand on his penis.* It was all he'd wanted since he'd first seen the puberty video, and suddenly this nice man was doing the thing he'd always craved.

"*Nungh*…." And doing it well.

Jefferson squeezed and stroked and took Mason's mouth again while Mason's central processor completely shorted out. He didn't think about the cold, or the fact that he didn't know this man well, or that they were in a semipublic place. All that got through was *Hand. On my penis!*

And then Jefferson wrenched away from him and sank to a squat, pulling Mason's sweats and Under Armour with him.

Mason's vision went a little gray around the edges as Jefferson squatted there and grinned up. His hand kept up that stroke with the twist at the end and the thumb digging into his pee slit, and the other hand danced around Mason's balls.

"Admit it," Jefferson said wickedly. "You expected this."

"Wanted," Mason admitted, naked and unable to play coy. "Didn't exp—*eep!*"

He wasn't proud. Jefferson's mouth, hot and treacherous, engulfed him, swallowed him to the *root*, and then sucked back, keeping a delirious pressure on the crown. Mason had watched videos and *practiced* blow jobs like this, but nobody he'd been with had ever been as grateful as Mason was now.

"Oh God," he moaned, wishing he was comfortable enough to even lean back against the wall. They were in a *public bathroom*—and that thought, of his cock out in the air, of Jefferson squatting before him and servicing him for no reason at all, made his ass clench, his taint tingle, and his balls swell.

Jefferson pulled back and fisted his cock some more, stroking hard and fast and relentless. For a moment Mason could hear nothing above his own heartbeat and rasping breaths, and then the cold air hit his wet cockhead as Jefferson pulled back and said, "Spread your legs. I want to play with your hole."

Oh fuck comfortable. Mason spread his legs and leaned against the sink, his body open and exposed to the cold, and his cock deliciously chilling with every pant of Jefferson's hot breath. Then his cockhead was swallowed into the heat again and two fingers, slick with spit but not polite, shoved up into his asshole.

He saw stars and dumped come down Jefferson's throat.

His hips were still thrusting when he heard the sound of flesh against flesh. He looked down and saw Jefferson's hand blurring on his own exposed cock, and then the vibration of Jefferson's moan around his crown sent him into one more spasm of climax.

And Jefferson's come hit his ankles, shins, and shoes.

"Oh God," he whispered, massaging Jefferson's scalp through his hair. Sometime between kiss-me-now and fuck-my-mouth, Mason had pulled the rubber band out of Jefferson's hair, and the wedge was back, falling in front of his brown eyes as he smiled up at Mason almost shyly.

Mason touched his face tenderly, not sure what to say, and that's when they heard the car pull into the parking lot.

Jefferson grimaced and stood up, pulling Mason's sweats with him and covering him up in one swoop. He was about to bend down for his own shorts when Mason squatted. "Let me," he said, bemused. "I mean… the least I could do."

He gave Jefferson's cock a little kiss and stood, pulling the soccer shorts and Under Armour up with him. He cupped Jefferson's cheek and, mindful of what sounded to be an entire soccer team unloading from the car they'd heard pull in, he gave a sweet, gracious kiss.

"Not that I shouldn't have told you earlier, but I'm HIV negative," he said when it was over.

Jefferson rolled his eyes like it was no big deal. "I use rubbers when I fuck," he said bluntly. "Me too."

"But how would you know that—"

He shrugged. Oh my God, did nobody teach this kid what serious was? "The likelihood of me getting HIV from a blow job is less than 1 percent," he recited. Then he rolled his eyes. "And man, your *cock* was just…." He shook his head. "Mm… what is that thing? Seven inches? Eight? It's *enormous*."

Mason was torn between feeling a little bit used and objectified and thinking he might have found his soul mate. "Mostly what it's been is underappreciated," he said with feeling. Then, because Jefferson was shivering, he reached out and pulled him against his chest almost gruffly. "Let's get out of here," he growled. "I'll take you to pancakes or something."

For a moment—a sweet moment—Jefferson collapsed into Mason's arms and shuddered, and Mason thought, *Oh wow. This is it. Love at first blow job. I thought that was just a fairy tale, like Cinderfella.*

Then Jefferson pulled back—reluctantly, it seemed, but with purpose. "Sounds awesome," he said with a sigh. "But I don't get much unsupervised time a week." He smiled crookedly. "So, soccer and a bathroom break." He winked and then turned and led the way out of the bathroom.

35

Mason followed him, uncomfortably aware that he had spunk on his sweats and his shoes and his skin, and that his cock had been put away wet.

And that he was just as confused about Terry Jefferson as he had been before they went into the bathroom.

Jefferson made no effort to talk, intimately or otherwise, heading first for the field, where a group of teenagers were passing his ball. He didn't ask for it back, but instead chased down the kid who had it, stole the ball back after a spirited, furious battle, and then kicked it to Mason with amazing control.

"Catch it!" he called, and Mason did, because apparently that was his *only* soccer skill. The kids put up a fuss, but Jefferson turned toward them with a shrug while he was running backward away from the field. "It's my ball!"

He was soundly booed for that, and he turned toward Mason, still jogging as he offered a salute behind his back.

Mason looked down to the field and saw that another kid was dribbling a ball up from the tree line and figured that they weren't going to die without Jefferson's ball. Relieved, he started walking toward the battered little Toyota.

"I'll take that!" Jefferson reached for the ball.

Mason turned away from him, guarding the thing with intent. "Wait a minute—you'll get it back when I know when we can see each other again!"

Jefferson's guffaw echoed down into the park. "Mason, don't we have golf next week?"

"Yes, but—"

Jefferson popped the ball through Mason's arms. Mason flailed for it, but the end result was predictable—Jefferson grabbed the ball and threw it inside the Toyota.

"I'll see you then," he said.

For a moment Mason was going to put his foot down, and then it hit him. Jefferson's mouth was open and laughing—but his eyes.

His eyes were begging. Pinched at the corners, limpid, almost wet—he was *begging* Mason not to make a big deal out of this.

"Can we see each other longer?" he asked with a sigh.

Jefferson popped him on the ass like any other athlete would pop a teammate.

"Course—but we may not want to hit the whole game on the course, if you know what I mean." He winked and slid into the car, cranking the motor with the confident turn of the key.

The car rattled off, leaving Mason staring at its trail of exhaust, fighting the absurd impulse to hold out his hand and whisper, "Call me," to the air pollution Jefferson left in his wake.

WHEN HE got back home, he passed Dane, keenly involved in an online game of *Destiny* with Carpenter over the PS4. All Mason knew about the game was that sometimes he could hear Nathan Fillion's voice, and that was pretty sexy, but other than that, there was an awful lot of bloodshed for a Saturday afternoon.

For a moment he expected Dane to put his game on hold and make some sort of clairvoyant pronouncement along the lines of "You smell like come!" but he didn't. He saved that for when Mason got out of the shower, put on clean sweats, grabbed a book, and cuddled up in his corner of the couch.

"Good game?" Dane asked, his eyes on the screen ahead of him.

"Not bad—more like a clinic. He taught me the basics." On the soccer field. Apparently he was like blow job pro in the bathroom—Mason had learned just from the pressure of his tongue and palate alone.

"Good. Gonna see him again?"

Mason was so tempted, right then, to spill out, "Yes, and I'm probably going to get blown again, but that doesn't stop me from being confused as fuck!"

Instead he shrugged. "Well, we're going golfing next week still."

"Promising!" Dane turned and graced him with a smile before going back to his game.

Mason made plans to pack a sweatshirt for Jefferson, and wet wipes, rubbers, and lubricant for whatever else might come... er, pop... er... show up.

He wasn't going to turn down more sex, no matter *how* confused he might be about it.

LILLIAN BRADFORD, Mason's secretary, was a crisp, efficient woman in her fifties. She left her hair color at iron gray but always made sure it was perfectly coiffed in pinned curls, and she wore pressed, navy-blue suits to work every day. Mason had actually paid attention to the cut and length of the jackets and skirts to see if she wore *different* suits in the same color or just the same suit. Turned out she owned four different suits in the same color, but that didn't stop the impression that the woman was unsusceptible to the vicissitudes that shook the earthly masses.

She'd been the one to tell him that Schipperke (as he still thought of Skip) was "a tall gentleman, fair hair, and a strength to the jaw. Would I say he's handsome? Very. And fit. And…." She had looked up and to the right then, as though accessing a hidden file in her brain, her no-bullshit blue eyes steady as steel. She returned those eyes to Mason's face and continued speaking as though she hadn't paused. "Vulnerable," she said. "Mr. Keith is vulnerable, and a bit naïve."

Mason had already gathered that by how easy it had been to fluster poor Skipper. "He's young," he'd said wistfully.

"More than that, sir." Lillian had compressed her lips tightly. "That boy, sir, is in desperate need of some mothering, and all he seems to know is men. I would suggest you keep that in mind if you're seeking a… a connection with him."

Mason *had* kept it in mind. He'd kept it in mind that she apparently thought he was a merciless cradle robber and that he should probably lay off his IT phone tech fascination entirely. When he'd come into the office after he and Dane had run into Skipper and Carpenter on the golf course, he'd told her—somewhat dispiritedly—that Skipper was well and truly in love with Richie.

"That is too bad, sir. I would very much like to see you happily matched."

"Have we been watching *Pride and Prejudice* again, Mrs. Bradford?"

"*Sense and Sensibility*, sir. It's my husband's favorite. Something about when the eldest Miss Dashwood bursts into tears just melts his crotchety old heart."

"As it should," he'd replied. She'd turned to leave, the military precision of her heel pivot showing twelve years in the Air Force before she'd married, opted out, and stayed home to raise two sons. "Mrs. Bradford?"

"Yes, sir?"

"Thank you. For, you know, helping me meddle in my own love life."

"Of course, sir. And sir?"

"Mrs. Bradford?"

"Do keep trying."

That had been after Thanksgiving. Now, after New Year's, when pretty much the entire office was coming in after pretending they were working from home, she stood in front of his desk, crisp and efficient as always, at the beginning of the day.

"Good morning, Mrs. Bradford. I trust your holidays went well?"

"Not so much, really, sir. My boys both brought their wives, neither one of which is interested in procreating and both of whom have decided… ideas about things."

"Ideas?" He rarely heard her actively disapprove of anybody.

"Well, Michael's wife is an environmental activist, and she was appalled to see that we'd gotten a Christmas tree from a lot. She seemed to feel that the tree had been tortured and murdered to be brought to our house, and that if we were truly good people, we would have bought a fake tree years ago."

Mason's eyes got big. He could not imagine… not even… oh God. Who would contradict Lillian Bradford in her own house?

"And the other wife? Chad's wife?"

"Well, Chad's wife is also an environmental activist, and she seemed to feel that a fake tree is pandering to the evil plastics industry, and that to buy one would be giving our capital to a heartless polluter that poisons children in developing nations and who feeds the unwilling spoonfuls of arsenic, lead, and cadmium in an effort to destroy all of the fertile soil on the planet."

Now Mason's mouth was hanging open. "Uhm…."

"I was, of course, in quite the quandary. I even"—her brows drew together, and she lowered her voice as though confessing a shameful secret—"grew a bit emotional."

He could see that. She and her husband had been celebrating Christmas for the sweet sake of pagan rituals!

"I'm so sorry," he said, almost afraid of what happened next.

"Oh, don't be." She nodded decisively. "My husband came home in the middle of the debate and said—and I quote him here, sir, as his language was quite salty. He spent his military time as a Marine, you know—but he said, 'It's a fucking Christmas tree, and you will be fucking grateful for the things we have, or your mother and I are cashing in your goddamned Christmas presents for tickets to a cruise we never had the money to take. Now you assholes get the fuck out of my living room for a couple of hours and let me and your mother look at the lights.'"

Mason wanted to cheer. "Your husband is something special, isn't he?" His throat was all thick and everything. "That reminds me of how my mother used to stand by me through school."

Mrs. Lillian Bradford's face relaxed, became matronly and soft. "Your mother must be a very special woman."

He nodded. "As are you, Mrs. Bradford. I do hope your family calmed down."

She held out her hand and tilted it—a little yes, a little no. "The women and I reached détente, and the boys apparently went in to buy us a cruise. I'm going to call it a win."

"Fair enough."

"And yourself, sir?"

Mason grimaced. He was hoping to get out of this without having to make a full disclosure, but he was pretty sure Mrs. Bradford had just admitted to actual tears of frustration, and it was his turn to put out.

"Well, I met a nice young man at Schipperke's Christmas party."

Mrs. Bradford's face practically lit up. He wondered if, since both her sons were occupied with strong women who clashed… erm… strongly with their mother, maybe Mrs. Bradford enjoyed hearing about his romantic attempts because *men* she could deal with.

"You did? And what was his name, sir?"

"Jefferson. Uh, Terry Jefferson. We, uh, met to play soccer."

The lines on her handsome face grew a little deeper. "Is that all, sir?"

Oh dear. He was *not* telling Mrs. Bradford that he'd gotten a blow job in an awful concrete bathroom at a public park.

"Well, there was… there was a hope?" Okay, he could say that. "A hope for more. But…." He let out a sigh, wondering how to phrase this. "Mrs. Bradford, you have two sons."

"Yes, sir."

"They're married."

"Yes, sir."

"How old are they?"

"Michael is twenty-seven and Chad is twenty-five. Why do you ask?"

"Because he's young—twenty-five—but his mother… she's sort of all over him. Where's he going, who's he seeing, why isn't he home to make her happy. I think… I think rec league soccer is his only out. I mean… is that normal?"

She frowned. "Where's his father?"

Mason shook his head. "I have no idea."

"Well...." She pursed her lips. "Some people...." And now she scowled. "No. I shall be blunt. My daughters-in-law are very strong-willed and very vocal—and as difficult as that is sometimes, I am relieved. It means my sons are strong men and can handle a woman's strength."

Mason nodded sagely. "With you as their mother, I have no doubt."

"Thank you, sir. But not all women use their strength. Some women assume that to be weak is to be 'good.'" She quirked her eyebrows in lieu of quotation marks. "You understand what I mean? 'Good'?"

Mason had to laugh. "Mrs. Bradford, I think you have the wrong person to ask that. I lived in the principal's office. I had to change schools after the first time I made out with a boy. There was nothing about me that was 'good'—except my mother, who insisted that my heart was better than anything that came out of my mouth."

And that stern face softened again. "I think you know exactly what I'm saying, then, sir. Some people use weakness as a way to exert their will. It's one of the reasons I joined the military—I was not that woman. Some women didn't have a choice—some women were beaten for showing strength, some ridiculed. Those women often... they use manipulation to get what they want. Perhaps this young man's mother does not want to be alone."

Mason sort of gaped at her, because it really could be as simple as that. "But... when does he get his own life?"

"That could be a very serious problem," she said soberly. "Are you sure you wish to continue this association?"

"Yes," Mason said, nodding slowly. "Yes, I think I do." He smiled briefly, and then they launched into the series of—ugh!—meetings that made up the rest of their day, but he spent all of his spare attention questioning what made him say that.

He thought at first that he was remembering the blow job when he said it. But that wasn't what he was remembering at all.

He was remembering that unspoken plea in Jefferson's eyes to just... just say yes. Just let the blow job happen. Just commit to another date just like this one.

To just, please, don't leave him alone.

Schwing!

SURE ENOUGH, Jefferson showed up to the golf course at the asscrack of dawn wearing cargo shorts and a long-sleeved T-shirt. Mason had been waiting for him in the car, and he pulled out a thick hooded sweatshirt that said *Stanford* on the front and threw it at him as he approached.

"There's a dress code?" Jefferson asked, sounding a little hurt. His car had barely made it into the parking lot—Mason wouldn't have asked him someplace that made him dress up.

"No, but you make me cold looking at you. There's gloves in the pocket, and a stocking cap too."

Jefferson started putting on clothes while Mason reached into the car and pulled out two large lattes and a small pastry bag. "Here," he said when Jefferson looked warmer. "Hold that while I get the clubs out of the trunk."

"I don't have my own clubs...." And it was like this was the first time he'd thought about it.

"Don't worry—you're only an inch or two shorter than Carpenter. It's nice to have your own fitted clubs, and you can rent them if you don't, but he's got a really nice set. Standard loft, standard flex—they should be fine for a beginner."

Jefferson looked at the clubs curiously as Mason set the bags down behind the car to slam the trunk. "They don't look like golf clubs on TV."

Mason laughed a little. "That's because the new shit is technological as hell. It's actually scary. I had to do research—I'm talking, like, *weeks* of research to order my last set. I felt stupid, right? Because I just wanted to *play*."

"Then why all the research?" Jefferson handed Mason his coffee so they could each grab their clubs and trolley them in. Mason took the coffee and noticed that Jefferson had downed his and was starting on the pastry bag with limited ceremony. Hungry. He was hungry and didn't remember a damned sweatshirt or gloves when it was thirty degrees outside.

Mason wondered if the level of worry in his stomach was worth the possibility of sex, but he didn't have an answer for that, so he answered Jefferson's question instead.

"'Cause they're sort of spendy," he said, avoiding the issue. Fact was, his set of clubs cost more than Jefferson's car was worth. *Carpenter's* clubs cost the down payment, at least, on Mason's own car.

Jefferson had only been a little wrong when he'd said golf was a sport for rich douche bags. Mostly about the douche bags—or at least that's what Mason was hoping.

He really tried not to be a douche bag.

"Well, they look like some sort of weapon from *Star Trek*. I mean, if they're spendy too, these things should be able to take a dump for you, you think?"

"I don't know," Mason said mildly, "I sort of prefer to take my own dumps. Gives me time to think."

Jefferson laughed. "Yeah, I read in the bathroom. Freaks Mom out—she thinks I'm wanking off."

"No," Mason said, as completely serious as Jefferson appeared to be. "You don't wank off in the bathroom—that's uncomfortable. Definitely in the bedroom. Soft mattress, nice lighting—"

"Right?" Jefferson's excited nod was sincere as only a twentysomething talking about sex could be. "It's like, hey, if this is the romance I'm getting, it had better be good!"

"Or at least comfortable!"

"I'm saying." Jefferson gave a sunny smile, and they walked into the club in perfect synchronization.

And then Mason realized that they'd been talking about *masturbation*, and his next conversation—the one with the girl registering golfers for their tee times—was not nearly so smooth.

"Uh, yeah. Just two guys and their clubs… uh, swinging their sticks… uh whacking… erm, beating balls around the bush, I mean into the holes, the ones with the sticks in them, I mean…." Meltdown. Complete and total verbal meltdown. Mason closed his eyes and rested his forehead against the cool varnished wood of the counter, linking his fingers behind his neck.

"I have a reservation for Mason Hayes and Terry Jefferson, please?" he tried in a weak voice.

"Yes, Mr. Hayes," she said, sounding amused. Well, she was Jefferson's age—that age group seemed to be perpetually amused by dorks who couldn't speak. Or maybe Mason was projecting. "Your tee time is in five minutes. Here's the key to the cart. You two had better hurry!"

"Yes, thank you," Mason croaked, and then took the keys and the registration packet, shouldered his clubs, and slouched out of the lobby toward the carts.

Jefferson followed, barely containing his glee.

"*ZohmyGod*!" he chortled as they emerged into the chill of the fog. "I mean, you warned me—you *warned* me you had moments like that—but until I saw it in action… damn."

Mason shook his head, glad that at least his penis was hiding in mortification, because for a minute there it had been peeping out in hopeful curiosity. "That's not as bad as it gets," he confessed, face burning. He handed his key to the valet, who trotted down to the end of the line of golf carts, gesturing for the two of them to follow him.

"Oooh… tell me." Jefferson's eyes were big and honey-brown, and they fastened on Mason's face like he was *Game of Thrones* and *Destiny* and the all-stars basketball tournament all rolled into one.

Mason laughed even though he didn't feel like it and slid into the cart as the valet exited. "Maybe we should concentrate on your golf game," he said mildly. "I'm dying to see you play."

Jefferson snorted indelicately. "I'm surprised as shit you actually brought clubs for me—I swear, I thought this was a euphemism for sex."

Ouch. "Was soccer?" he asked curiously, because that blow job hadn't felt planned.

"Nope. Soccer was to see if you'd be interested in sex—"

"Or interesting enough to have sex *with*," Mason said dryly.

Jefferson was silent for a moment, and Mason turned his eyes away from the course long enough to see him frowning. "Why would you think I wouldn't want to blow you?"

"Because I am incredibly conventional," Mason said.

"Except for when you start talking to random strangers about your balls." Jefferson smirked.

"Not really a point in my favor." Mason had stopped praying to be swallowed by the earth around the time he had to change schools for asking to see a guy's penis—but as a way to cope, it hadn't been bad. It beat the hell out of trying to find something to say to a guy he hoped liked him for more than his penis.

Jefferson's buddy pat on his thigh was not reassuring. "No, no—it's cute. You look all corporate guy, but you're just not that smooth. I'm not a fan of smooth, really. Not always sincere, you know?"

Mason frowned a little and negotiated the cart along the path. "Never thought of it that way." Ira, Gordon—smoother than turkey shit. Todd—another silver-tongued snake-fucker. All he'd ever put together about them was that they had a quality he did not.

He'd assumed he'd been the one lacking.

"You should," Jefferson said grandly. "It's always a lot easier if you assume the world is wrong and you're right. If you assume the other way around, we may as well pray for the earth to swallow us up because we're not doing jackshit right!"

Mason slid a sideways glance at him, wondering when he started reading Mason's secret prayers from high school.

Then he saw it—that slight vulnerability to Jefferson's lower lip, a glint in his eyes.

He's talking about himself.

"You're right," he said, completely serious. "World's wrong, we're right—I don't know why I've never seen it before."

"Yes!" Jefferson crowed, pumping his fist. "Bring on the clubs and the ball!"

Fierce words—oh yes they were.

They came to a halt and got out of the cart; then Mason set up the ball and chose his driver, explaining all the way. "See, this one's my driver. I'm picking a three-iron because this hole isn't very deep, and iron gives me control. If it was a longer distance, I'd pick wood, because wood hits farther. Kay?"

Jefferson grunted, busy turning a full circle at the tee. "There's no woods," he said. "I mean, there are a few trees, but I was sort of hoping there'd be deep woods somewhere."

Mason looked around Diamond Oaks and grimaced. "There's some willow trees over there," he said. "Uh, you have a thing for trees?"

Jefferson rolled his eyes. "Yeah, Mason. I really want to blow a tree."

His words hit Mason in midswing. Mason scratched, glaring helplessly at Jefferson as he recovered the ball.

"Sorry," he said, sounding reasonably contrite.

"Just… just let me hit a couple of rounds," Mason found himself pleading. "Let me teach you how to swing the club—"

"Heh heh!"

"—at the very least!" he begged. "Then we can go out to pancakes after nine holes. My treat."

Jefferson squinted and cocked his head. "Like a date?"

"You can blow me in the car at the pancake place," Mason offered, feeling like he was imposing. But it was okay, because Jefferson perked up at the mention of the sleazy sex behind a restaurant in broad daylight.

"Sure," Jefferson said cautiously. "But… the sex has to be meaningless."

A little part of Mason's heart shriveled, but he was used to that. "Okay. Fine. Maybe I can give this time."

"You'd want to?"

Mason sighed and set up to swing. "If you just let me beat the crap out of the ball with the stick, I'd *love* to." He pulled back and paused to see if Jefferson had anything to add.

Beat… beat… beat… and swi—

"Do you really like giving?"

And scratch.

Mason sighed and turned around, checking to see if next party was coming their way. So far, so good—apparently only diehards went golfing when it was still dark and cold as fuck.

"I'm *gay*, Jefferson. You name a thing about a penis, and I'm pretty sure I'm a fan. Now can I hit the damned ball?"

"Gay?" That narrow harlequin face compressed, one eyebrow going up and the other dipping down, skewing the shape of him, making him look like a polygon instead of a rectangle.

"Aren't *you* gay? Or at least bi?"

"Well… I like blowing guys," Jefferson said hopefully. "And getting blown by them. And butt sex is great. But I can't be gay or my mother would kill me."

So. Much. Wrong. With. That.

Mason's brain blew a fuse—he turned back, fucked his form, and whacked the holy shit out of the little ball.

TWO HOLES later, the sun was rising and the chill dew was soaking in through their shoes, socks, and the cuffs of Mason's jeans. Jefferson was dancing at every hole while Mason tried to instruct him in golf, and Mason had to concede.

This wasn't working.

He stood behind Jefferson, hands on his thighs, as he corrected his stance, his back, his arms, his grip, and his swing.

On the one hand, it was great being so close to him—and on the other, it was torture being so close to him.

And on the third hand, they now had a backup of two other parties who needed to play through.

"Okay," Mason said, letting a lot of breath out on his exhale. "Are we good? Knock that little fucker up and over, and then the rest of it is short game."

"Yeah, fine," Jefferson said, but Mason saw his eyes had glazed over. He was done.

"I'm going to move back and let you go for it, okay?"

"God, yeah, faggot—move back and give the guy some room!"

They both jerked their heads around to see the foursome waiting for them to get their shit together—all blandly handsome guys in their fifties with capped teeth.

Mason wanted to smack them—except he knew he was going to be a nonbigoted version of them in about twenty years, and he hoped someone would have some patience with him.

"I'm sorry," he said with forced cheer. "My friend is new. Once we finish this hole, you guys can play through."

"You're *apologizing* to him?" Jefferson asked, furious.

"We're holding up the line," Mason said. "Don't worry—it's all my fault. I talk too much."

"He called you a—"

"Jefferson, just swing and we'll get out of his way, okay?"

Jefferson scowled at him, then scowled at the guy with the capped teeth and the plaid pants, and then grabbed Mason's face and planted a big, bruising kiss on him.

Mason stood, stunned for a minute, and about the time his brain said, *This doesn't happen often, open mouth, extend tongue,* Jefferson pulled back and gave him an apologetic little peck on the lips. Then he turned to the ball and, with decent form, whacked it as hard as he could. They grabbed their clubs under the gimlet eye of the jackass with the Brylcreem and took off, Mason flooring their golf cart to maximum revs.

"Wow," Mason said, wondering when his heartbeat was going to slow down.

"It wasn't your fault, it was mine," Jefferson said.

"You're new—he should be more patient—"

"I didn't realize we were holding up the line. I was being an asshole, thinking you were talking down to me when you were just teaching me. It makes me check out."

Mason had seen him doing that. "I'm sorry. Golf isn't really your—"

"You tried so hard at soccer. Give me another chance?"

And for once he wasn't looking into the distance or to the side. He was looking hungrily at Mason's face, like for approval. Mason—who had pretty much written off pancakes *and* the blow job at this point—felt himself warm again.

"Of course," he said, smiling tentatively. "If you want to learn—"

"I want to try again," Jefferson said seriously. "Please?"

"Of course." Why not? They were there.

They got down to the hole and Jefferson took Mason's advice and putted effectively. They finished the hole about five over par—which, on the one hand, stunk on ice, but on the other? It showed a learning curve, and Mason was all for that.

They hurried to the next tee, doing their best to get ahead of the foursome that appeared to have it out for them.

It went better until, three holes later, Mason stood behind Jefferson, adjusting his form and correcting his swing, and Jefferson suddenly fidgeted upright.

"Uh, Mace?"

"Yeah?"

"Don't take this the wrong way, but… you're sort of getting a stiffie, and I'm trying to concentrate."

The wash of heat made Mason's sweatshirt stick at the collar. "Yeah. Course. Go ahead."

Jefferson got back into position and then paused and looked over his shoulder. "Uh, it wasn't unpleasant," he said with a helpful smile.

Mason flushed again and concentrated hard as Jefferson made another vastly improved swing.

IN THE end they finished nine holes just a breath away from the party behind them, and between thirty and three hundred strokes over par.

Mason had given up keeping score on the second hole. He let Jefferson drive them back after the ninth hole while he completely made up numbers so he could submit their scorecards to the club.

"Why's it so important that people know what my score was anyway?" Jefferson asked as Mason decided that five over par at every hole did *not* look suspicious.

"Well, there's leagues, and people looking to play with a partner and stuff. And mostly just tradition, so you can look up another golfer's handicap and—"

"Oh," Jefferson said, suddenly completely okay with fake scorecards. "So like seeding."

"Like what?"

"Like a seeding tournament, where all the teams in the league get together and then you know which teams will be matched."

"Yes—yes, exactly."

"But we were awful."

"Well, I'm not writing that we're prodigies!" Mason laughed. "Besides, if you ever want to play again, I'm setting us up so we're even."

"So… like, you'd play again?"

Mason smiled a little, thinking about how amenable Jefferson'd been after the run-in with the jerk who used the f-word. "Yeah. Once you decided to learn, it went really well." And *bam*, his flush was back. "And… you know. Coaching you from, uhm, behind was pleasant."

Jefferson cast him a grin that was all teeth and then steered the cart into the parking queue. "Excellent! Pancakes first or pancakes later?"

Oh God. Public sex. "Pancakes first," Mason said grimly. This way he could at least be sure that Jefferson ate.

IHOP was not exactly haute cuisine, but there was literally no way to screw up strawberry pancakes. Jefferson made his chocolate banana, and they spent their meal talking about other foods that should be dessert but that got served as entrees. Mason was pretty sure honey-walnut shrimp was the number-one entry, but Jefferson said he couldn't see eating seafood for dessert—there was something fundamentally wrong with that—and went with Ritz crackers and Dr Pepper.

"You eat that for lunch?" Mason was appalled. "Like, don't you leaven it with soup or anything like that?"

"Well *now* I do," Jefferson laughed. "But when I was a kid, there wasn't always soup. Sometimes there was just crackers and soda. I mean, food stamps, you know? They only go so far."

Mason blinked at him. "No," he said. "I didn't know that."

He saw the wash of heat up Jefferson's cheeks. It left a faint red crescent at the razor edge of each cheekbone. "You've probably had cash all your life," he mumbled. "Sorry—embarrassing story." He tried to mask his mortification in a cup of coffee.

Mason's brain shorted out again and he blurted, "I got kicked out of school for asking to see my boyfriend's penis."

Jefferson spit out his coffee. "You did *what*?"

"We were necking under the bleachers, he was feeling me up, and I thought I'd be a gentleman. He decked me."

Jefferson stopped mopping up coffee from the front of his borrowed sweatshirt. "What an asshole." He frowned, the expression looking about as fierce as a Chihuahua licking your hand. "Why did he do that?"

Mason sighed, remembering the half-strangled apology the kid had gotten out when Mason and his mother had left the principal's office that day. "He didn't want to admit he was gay. It was one thing to make out with me, but if I asked about it and he did it, that meant something entirely different."

Jefferson slow blinked and set down his wad of napkins. "I don't… my mom would fucking kill me," he said, looking back up at Mason with that plea in his eyes.

"Fine," Mason agreed rashly. "But… can we go somewhere besides the car? My house is in Fair Oaks. It's about ten minutes away from Skip's. I swear, nobody will be there."

Jefferson pulled out his phone and checked the time. "We've got about two hours," he said softly. "Let me go clean up."

As soon as he was gone from the table, Mason signaled for the waitress to give him the check, and whipped out his phone.

Are you home? he texted Dane.

Just woke up. Why?

Because you need to leave.
FOREVER?
NO—for two hours.
Why?
Because he's skittish.
So you want to get laid.

Well duh. *And I don't want to scare him off.* Mason took a deep breath. *He's not out to his mother.*

I'm not his mother, Dane texted stubbornly. *I'm two bedrooms down from you—pretend I'm not here.*

Mason sighed. *Okay—you pretend you're not here either.*

Fine.

"SO YOUR house is going to be empty?" Jefferson asked as they walked out to their cars.

"Sure," Mason lied, and Jefferson looked at him sideways. Mason blushed. Again. God, adulthood was *not* what it said in the brochures. "My brother is asleep in his room. He's still recovering from finals."

Jefferson stopped dead, worrying at his lower lip, and Mason turned toward him, wrapping his arms around Jefferson's shoulders protectively, the way he'd wanted to do since they'd met up that morning.

"Don't worry," he murmured in Jefferson's ear. "Dane won't say anything. He just wants to sleep in."

Jefferson leaned against his chest, rubbing his cheek on Mason's shirt. "It… I mean, I *am* sort of revved up from the game."

"It'll be like having sex in a dorm room," Mason promised. "Everyone would just as soon pretend it didn't happen."

Jefferson shrugged, still not meeting his eyes. "Tech school," he said indifferently. "It's where I met Skipper. I monitor the machines in a string of quickie marts. I'm sort of their tech guy." He smiled briefly. "Not a dorm room, Mason."

He shot a look from under his streaked hair, the kind of look that made Mason's heart sore and a little achy, and Mason caught his chin in front of an IHOP in Carmichael and kissed him.

Jefferson tried to make the kiss greedy, to take everything, like they were going to go at it in the middle of the day behind an IHOP.

Mason pulled back and kept it sweet, ending with a kiss against Jefferson's temple.

"So, like that?" Jefferson asked, his voice a little broken.

"Yeah," Mason said. "Like that. C'mon. I'll drive you and bring you back to your car."

Jefferson shook his head. "Okay. I guess if you were going to steal away with my body, you'd at least make sure Skipper had another player for the team."

Mason grinned and kissed him briefly on the lips before backing up and trying not to get the shit beat out of them in a not-exactly-gay-friendly little suburb.

"Anything but pissing Skipper off," he said gravely.

Jefferson nodded like it was completely reasonable, and they got into Mason's car.

Jefferson talked nonstop as Mason drove—mostly about the things he saw as they passed.

"Dude, did you see that? That squirrel was like… suicidal! What makes them do that? They run in, they run out, they run in—"

"No peripheral vision," Mason said. "They can't see to the side, so suddenly they're like, 'Oh! Car!'"

"I did not know that! Why do cats get stuck in trees?" He was looking at Mason like he held the secrets of the universe, and Mason was suddenly afraid his well of useless facts was as shallow as a saucer of milk.

"Because their claws curve to help them climb up!" he said triumphantly.

"Oh wow! Again, I did not know that! So, why does hummus taste so good?"

"Tahini oil and lemon juice?"

"Excellent!"

"Are you going to make your own now?" Mason asked, trying to maybe pin him down on a subject.

"How would you do that?"

"Cooked chickpeas, tahini oil, lemon juice, garlic if you like it—"

"Really? So, like, I could buy that shit?"

"Yeah, although specialty stores have—"

"Okay. So I can make hummus. Like in a blender. That's awesome. 'Cause it tastes great on the bread Skip makes, but I don't like to ask Skipper to make it, right? But if I go, 'Hey, Skipper, I'll make the hummus if you make the bread,' then I've got something to bring to the table, right?"

"Right," Mason said, bemused. "Why don't you get Skipper's bread recipe, and then you could make your own?"

"Because bread is Skipper's *thing*, you understand?"

They were at a stoplight when he said this, and Mason turned to look at him. "Thing?"

"It's green, Mace."

He turned back to the road and stepped on the gas. "Green? I mean thing?"

"Yeah. Like, Skipper likes to take care of us, but he doesn't have many mom tricks. So, like, he keeps extra sweatshirts in his car, and power bars and Gatorade during games, and for holidays he gives out bread. But it's like all he's got. So, you know, I just bought chips and whatever, and it was good. I didn't have anything to give him for the bread, and I couldn't take away his thing, right?"

It made a twisted sort of sense—sort of. "But... but my ex used to spend hours swapping recipes and looking stuff up on the Internet and trying new stuff out. Why couldn't you do that?"

Silence.

Mason turned right down Fair Oaks Boulevard and made his way toward Eastwood Street.

Silence.

Unnerving silence.

"What?" Mason said at last, glancing at him.

"I just... I mean, you know. Never thought of that."

Mason shrugged. "I, uh—I mean, I guess we both saw our parents do it."

"Why?"

"Why what?"

"Why were they exchanging recipes?"

Jesus Christ, were you raised by wolves?

Mason took a deep breath and tried not to alienate the guy who'd just sat through the world's worst golf lesson in order to suck Mason's cock.

"Because it's a social thing," Mason said. "You know—like sharing sports tips, but, uhm, food."

"Oh." Jefferson gazed off into space. "Oh wow." And then he turned what was probably a blinding smile on Mason. "Oh *wow*. Do you think Skipper collects recipes?"

"If he doesn't, he might like to. Some of the other guys might collect them. I mean, everybody eats, right?"

"Yes!" Jefferson punctuated this sentiment with a pound against the dashboard and then sank back into his seat. "But not everybody cooks. I shop and cook, and I'm really bored, and my mom doesn't know anything but hot dogs and spaghetti. I keep trying to bring stuff home, but like, Chipotle is way too advanced and cutting-edge for Mom, you know?"

"Uhm, yeah. So, uh, what's your mom's… uh, what does she do for a living?" Okay, that sounded neutral, right? And not at all like "How did your mother completely destroy all functionality in her baby boy?"

"Nothing," Jefferson said, unperturbed. "She was really young when she had me, and my dad split, no alimony, and so she did the welfare thing. And then I got a job and I could support her."

Mason was in his neighborhood going 10 miles an hour, which was a good thing or he might have wrecked the car. He tried really hard to imagine Janette Payton Hayes sitting static, doing nothing until her sons supported *her*. The image didn't compute.

"She… I mean, it's not ideal, but she didn't get a job?" His mom had degrees in marketing and finance. She'd made enough money to semiretire in her thirties so she could have children.

And it was just occurring to Mason that sometimes you had to know such a thing was possible before you did it yourself.

"Why would she get a job?" Jefferson asked, sounding blank. "She was raising me."

For a moment Mason's future was poised on a knife-edge: absolutely lose his shit about how wolves would have done a better job at raising Jefferson than his mother apparently had and lose any chance of having sex for maybe the next year, or….

Or be quiet and see where this went. Be quiet and bring him sweatshirts when he forgot. Be quiet and stock his car with granola bars for game days and start looking up recipes and cooking websites and maybe giving him some advice about always having rice and noodles on hand, and a can of mushroom soup for when things went wrong.

Be quiet and accept Jefferson for who he was and the limitations in his life, and maybe, week by week, show him how to reach for more.

Oh, Mason had never been good at being quiet. For better or worse, he'd ventured into life with an open mouth, full speed ahead.

"My mother had a job," Mason said, shrugging like a capable, independent mother wasn't the thing that had kept his life—and Dane's— from hurtling into chaos. "I just can't imagine her asking me to support her. You must be very strong."

"Really?" Jefferson sounded entranced. "You think I'm strong?"

Mason swallowed. "You have no idea."

And they were home. He pulled into his driveway feeling an absurd affection for the new home, for the great oak trees that hovered over the fenced poolyard and could be seen from the street, and for the unfenced property behind the pool that featured a creek that fed into the river.

It was beautiful here. He'd been happy about the archways and the shapes of the doors and the swimming pool, but now, with Jefferson right next to him, looking for things to wonder at, he was so very glad he had something with which to inspire wonder.

"This is pretty awesome," Jefferson said, voice breathy.

"You like?" Mason felt his chest swell. "Uh, I mean, rich douche bags live here."

Jefferson's laugh rippled along Mason's spine; it was a child's laugh, unabashedly delighted. "That's okay—I know one of those guys. He's not bad."

The compliment did more than ripple Mason's spine—it penetrated through to his chest and his stomach.

"Well, let's see if he's got any tricks up his sleeve," Mason said smugly, and he led the way.

Dane had been downstairs to make coffee and toast a bagel—as evidenced by the mess on the counter—but he was blessedly absent as Mason pulled Jefferson through the house and up the stairs.

"Nice!" Jefferson said, his voice subdued. He tugged on Mason's hand so he could look around at the hardwood floors and the stenciling up near the ceiling in the hallway. "Did you do the painting?"

"Well, yeah. We redecorated Dane's room, and we added the stencils because, you know—sort of boring off-white without it."

"I thought it was ecru," Jefferson said smugly, and Mason grinned at him and pulled him forward into a kiss.

Slow.

This kiss was a little slower. Mason had time to explore his mouth, to nuzzle his cheek, to cup his jaw and go deeper.

Jefferson sighed, relaxing completely against him. Mason slid his hands along that compact, muscular waistline and palmed the smooth skin at his back before shoving up his shirt to touch it *all*. Jefferson's gasp in his mouth told him he wasn't used to being touched all over, and Jefferson's hands down the back of his slacks told him he wasn't patient about new discoveries.

"Shh...." He kept kissing but walked them, one step at a time, to his partially open door. He backed into the room, Jefferson returning kiss for kiss, and as soon as they'd cleared the door, he groaned and shoved his hands under Jefferson's thighs, hoisting him up so he could wrap strong legs around Mason's hips.

"Condoms?" Jefferson panted.

"We're not even undressed!"

"But... but *now*!"

Mason turned around and lowered Jefferson slowly to the coverlet, then secured his wrists over his head with one hand.

"But *wait*," he said firmly, and then took his hand away and glared meaningfully.

Jefferson grinned and clasped his hands, a solemn promise to keep them where they were supposed to be.

"This is not kinky," Mason growled.

"Suuure it's not." Oh, his eyes were squirrel-bright, mischievous as a pixie's, and Mason wondered—not for the first time—who had the upper hand here.

He peeled Jefferson's sweatshirt off, and Jefferson parted his hands and helped him, and then Mason dealt with the T-shirt as well.

The man underneath was pale, with brown hair starting on the chest. He was muscular, but not defined like a gym rat. No, all of this muscle came from a guy who ran around the soccer field or the track or his own damned head until he was ready to drop from exhaustion.

His ribs showed under his skin, and Mason wondered if he'd take a bagel for sustenance on the way home.

Suddenly Jefferson broke character, holding his hands in front of his chest.

"Not a model." He blushed.

Mason pulled his hands away and firmly placed them over his head again.

"Quiet," he instructed. "I'm looking. You're...." His voice failed. He wanted to say *beautiful*—would Jefferson accept beautiful? "You're awesome," he said, his eyes burning.

He couldn't remember ever having to be so careful with a lover in his bed.

"You think so?" That smile—God. For all his precociousness, he was incredibly... innocent, right here. "I mean, not scrawny or—"

"Perfect," Mason muttered, lowering his head so he could taste that chattering mouth. Mm... he did so love total surrender.

He kissed, and more, and more, until Jefferson flailed his hands a little. Mason pulled back and put them firmly where they belonged.

"But I want to touch you!" he whined.

"Oh, yeah. Hold on. Right there." Mason stepped back and shucked his shirts—sweat, polo, and tank—and then undid his belt and toed off his shoes and socks before letting his slacks fall down with the thump of his belt and phone and wallet.

Then he went to work on Jefferson's shorts.

"I don't get to look?" Jefferson complained. "You spent, like, forever scoping me out!"

"You complain a lot," Mason judged. "I think maybe you should just hang out and experience." The cargo shorts had no belt, and the only things in them to thump were the phone and the wallet. Mason stopped for a moment to admire the laundered white of Jefferson's boxers against the pale peach of his skin, and to cup his calves and circle his ankles, appreciating the slick, coarse hair under his palms.

Jefferson groaned and pointed his toes. "That's nice," he hissed. "Mm... I like that!"

Mason smiled, even though Jefferson's eyes were closed and he couldn't see it. He kept rubbing, calves, shins, and then upper thighs.

Jefferson blinked at him, startled and, judging by the way he arched his back, extremely turned on.

"That's... uhm—" Mason kissed the inside of his knee. "Oh! Wow, so you wanna—" Mason dragged his tongue up to the hem of his boxers. "Yeah, damn, you might wanna—" And coyly poked his tongue in the leg hole. "Take those off!" Jefferson hissed, arching his back.

"You're bossy," Mason murmured against the crease of his thigh. The swell of flesh under Jefferson's boxers was taking definite, pleasing shape against the fabric, and Mason nuzzled it before sucking at the little dark spot of pre.

"You're *slow!*" Jefferson gasped, and then Mason engulfed his cockhead through the cloth, and he braced his feet against the mattress and arched into Mason's mouth. Mason chuckled with his mouth full, and Jefferson moved his hands up and down so much, Mason grabbed them and moved up so he could pin them meaningfully to the bed.

"Jefferson," he said softly into a bare ear. "*Terry.*"

"What?" *Terry's* body had relaxed under his, and Mason tried to radiate warmth and protectiveness, since he'd never mastered raw animal sex appeal.

"We have time." Gently, he licked the shell of Terry's ear, then caught the lobe between his teeth and nipped. "Your turn to receive."

He kissed down Terry's jaw and stopped to nibble, enjoying Terry's moan very much. When Terry started to fidget, he moved on to a pebbling pink nipple. He explored the flat of it with his tongue and then nibbled daintily with his teeth and then, as Terry started to thrash around, he pulled it hard into his mouth.

Terry jerked, knotting his hands in Mason's hair, hissing. "I'm going to come from that alone!"

Mason gave another suck and let it pop out of his mouth. "That can *happen*? *Really*? Let me try the other one!"

He pushed over a little and started to play, enjoying the salt of Terry's skin and the peculiar pink taste of that specialized bit of it while Terry tried to protest over his head.

"But… no—if I come now, we'll miss the—oh God, Mason, aren't you gonna touch my… oh… oh… *cock*!"

Mason felt that fine, compact body tremble beneath him, and he shoved his hand under the waistband of Terry's shorts and squeezed. The hot, silky spill over his fist rewarded him, and he grinned, moving down to strip off Terry's boxers while he was still quivering. Tenderly he wiped the come off Terry's cock and then off his own hand, placing a little kiss on the head when he was done.

"Good?" he asked, pleased.

"Yeah, but you never—"

Mason engulfed his cock in one big, sweeping swallow and cleaned it off in a long pull back, shuddering in ecstasy when Terry began to knead rough fingers in his hair.

He repeated the motion slowly, with pressure on the shaft and teasing on the head, and Terry let out a long, breaking groan from the pit of his balls and then, blessing of blessings, surrendered again.

His legs flopped open, splaying indecently, and his rough kneading turned gentle, accepting. The taut, quivering muscles in his stomach stopped shaking, and his cock began to harden again.

Mason wrapped his fingers around it, impressed by the girth, and then pulled back and teased the bell delicately with his tongue. Terry let out breath and murmured, "Oh, God, Mason—what you're doing to me…."

Yes. "What would you *like* me to do to you?" Mason rested his weight on his elbow and turned excited eyes up to meet Terry's. "Anything… uhm…." He wet his finger in his mouth and then slid it slowly, firmly, down between Terry's brown-furred testicles, behind them, into his crease.

Terry lifted his legs and spread his thighs, using his hands to spread his cheeks apart, as wanton and as needy as anything Mason had seen, including in porn.

"*That*," he demanded. "Can we do *that*?"

Mason laughed softly and took advantage of his position by licking across one buttcheek straight to the dead center of the target.

"Maaaasoooon…."

He just kept licking.

Terry lost his mind, writhing, moaning, begging, but Mason wanted him that way. Wanted to show him what time and a bed could do.

Wanted him to see what a date could be.

"I'm gonna," Terry panted. "I'm gonna… again… please, Mace—please!"

His voice, throaty and broken, hit Mason in the groin, and he bucked against the comforter. *Oh God!* He hadn't realized he was that close.

He pushed up and wiped his face on his shoulder, then tried to roll to the side to reach into his end table.

"Where are you going?" Terry wrapped his legs around Mason's chest, and Mason half laughed.

"Condoms?" he asked. "Lube? C'mon, Terry—they're right there!"

"Aw… *dammit*!" Terry dropped his legs and Mason scooted quickly, grabbing the supplies from his drawer before sliding his briefs down his legs and kicking them off. Then he sat up on his knees in front of Terry, appreciating the view while he dealt with the condom and drizzled lube.

"Wait," Terry said softly, reaching out a hand.

"What?" Mason leaned down, covering Terry's body with his own, supporting his weight on his elbows.

"I didn't get a chance to…." He stroked Mason's chest, his shoulders, dropping a sweet kiss on a straining bicep.

Mason stared into his eyes, warm and brown and bright, and had a hard time swallowing. "Next time," he whispered, taking his mouth.

He pulled away reluctantly, aware that time was passing, and he needed… just needed. Carefully he positioned himself just as Terry said, "Next time?" with all the hope in the world in his voice.

"Yeah," Mason gave a sigh of comfort, like he was coming home. "Next time." And then he thrust carefully inside.

Terry palmed his skin, squeezing and rubbing, finally cupping his neck and holding on while Mason thrust and pulled, rocking in and out in that exquisite dance of flesh and release.

"Good," Terry panted, squeezing his eyes shut and gasping. "You're good… so…."

"Good?" Mason grinned playfully and lowered himself for a kiss.

Terry returned it with interest, and Mason had to pull away or he'd stop the whole momentum of fucking for the sake of a drugging, wet-mouthed lip-lock that seemed to have everything and nothing to do with the dynamics of cock and ass.

Mason surged forward, growling with frustration, wanting *everything*, and Terry grunted at the impact.

"Again," he whispered.

Mason slammed into him again.

"Yes, more!"

And again.

And again, and again, and harder, until Mason's skin ran slick with sweat and Terry's face sheened with his own moisture, but it wasn't quite… was almost, almost….

"Come," Mason pleaded. "Grab yourself, Terry. Grab yourself and—"

"*Coming!*" Terry reached between them and grabbed himself, the frantic beating of his fist hitting Mason's abs, but Mason didn't care.

Because Terry's ass was squeezing tighter, a giant band of rubber muscle gripping Mason unmercifully.

"Yes!" Terry cried, and the ripples of orgasm in his body jerked Mason hard, harder, hard enough to—

"Yes!" he rasped, convulsing in climax, forced, finally, to close his eyes against the dark-eyed harlequin beauty of the man in his bed. He collapsed, chest heaving for air, and buried his nose in Terry's shoulder.

Fabric softener, sweat, some sort of oil for his hair… and warm animal, sex pheromones, and unfettered joy.

Terry wrapped his arms around Mason's shoulders and murmured quietly into his ears.

"That was amazing. I can't even… didn't you get bored?"

Mason pulled back far enough to let it be seen that he was rolling his eyes. "What in the hell—"

"But you spent all that time…." Mason felt Terry's skin heat up as he flushed. "You know… that time…."

"Making love to you," Mason said, thinking that as vocabulary lessons went, this one wasn't bad.

"Oh…." Terry's mouth went slack, his lower lip as vulnerable as anything Mason had ever seen.

"We were making love," Mason insisted. "Is there anything wrong with that?"

"I just didn't know that's what that was," Terry said, eyes big. "That's… that's awesome."

Mason wished he could bury his face in Terry's shoulder forever. "It is," he said tenderly, dropping a kiss on his sweaty forehead. "Would you like to do it again?"

"Yeah!" Enthusiasm unbound, and Mason smiled weakly.

"Good," he said quietly, lowering his head for another kiss. Terry gave it to him, but Mason could feel his cock softening in the chill. He pulled back from the kiss and glanced at his clock, heart sinking. "Are you sure you can't stay another…."

Terry glanced too, and his unhappiness was palpable. "No," he said, looking away. "I'm sorry."

Mason kissed him one more time. "Next week," he said. "After the soccer game."

And that smile, the one that said Mason would never know the gift he'd just given—*that* smile practically blinded him. "I'd like that."

Mason closed his eyes against the separation and then rolled away. He disposed of the condom and stared blindly around for his clothes. "Me too," he said, voice thick in his throat. A weekend thing? Was that what this was? What they'd just done had felt much bigger.

"Hey," Terry said, putting his hand on Mason's back. "I… I mean, maybe I can get away other nights too."

Mason swallowed and nodded, not meeting his eyes.

Terry's hand fell away, and he found his boxers and yanked them up with unnecessary force. "I knew it," Terry muttered. "You're going to get all pissy and possessive—"

"No," Mason said quietly, standing up and finding his own underwear to put on. "I'm not. I… I like spending time with you, that's all. It doesn't all have to be sports and sex."

"Oh." Terry paused in the act of pulling his shirts on. One of those was the sweatshirt Mason had provided for him, and Mason wasn't going to say a word about Terry having something of Mason's on his body. "What do you—"

"We could see a movie," Mason suggested hopefully. "Or you could come over and watch one. Or play… well, I don't play them, but my brother plays video games, or…."

Oh Lord, this was embarrassing. This was like being in grade school and looking for a playmate after the debacle of the puberty video.

Terry hadn't put on his shorts yet, but that didn't stop him from moving into Mason's space and wrapping strong arms around his waist. "My mom is… needy," he said at last. "She wants me home all the time I'm not working. And I keep trying things—got her enrolled in classes or job placement or stuff—but…." He let out a half laugh. "She's so mean, Mason. Nobody wants to talk to her. But I'm all she's got. I… I don't know how to—"

Mason captured his chin and kissed him as sweetly as he knew how. "Just think of me when you can," he said, his heart twisting in his chest. "Just… if you can come over, don't worry about time for sex. It can be time for television. If you're near Tesko and it's lunchtime, text me—we can eat together. I'm just…."

Terry's lips twitched. "Think bigger," he said, then laughed a little at the dirty pun. "You want me to think bigger than a meet-and-fuck."

"Yeah." Mason's heart untwisted—not completely, but enough to beat.

"I can't promise you movie dates or anything like that."

And then it stopped.

He must have made a sound then—of hurt, or disappointment, of something—because Terry took his cheeks in both hands and looked up to meet Mason's eyes through his wedge of streaked brown hair. "Wait," he said softly. "I'll tell you what I *can* promise, if it'll help."

And oh! Mason hadn't counted on how much this interlude would mean to him, because it was like spring had arrived in the bleak, foggy January.

"What?" he asked, knowing he sounded young and needy, and too damned hurt to be embarrassed about it.

"I promise I won't do this with anyone but you. So, you know, next time, remember the lube, forget the condoms. That is if…." Now Terry bit his lip.

Oh.

"Yeah, I want that. As long as we're doing this, we're only doing this with each other."

Whatever *this* was—but it would have to do.

Cookies and Curry

THEY MADE their way downstairs in a subdued sort of quiet, only to be stopped by voices—and the smell of baking.

Terry's eyes got big and Mason grimaced, shrugging. They knew both those people.

"I'll sneak out the front," Terry hissed.

Mason rolled his eyes. "Do you think Dane hasn't told him?"

That brought Terry up short, and he didn't actually make any sound, but Mason had been able to lip-read "fuck" since the fourth grade.

"Mason!" Clay Carpenter called excitedly. "Jefferson! Is that you guys? Come in here—we're baking cookies."

"C'mon," Mason said philosophically. "They smell pretty good."

Carpenter's broad, semibearded face peeked around the corner. "You guys—chocolate chip! What are you, inhuman?"

They walked into a disaster of flour and cookie dough and chocolate chips. Dane was on his hands and knees wiping off the sides of the cabinets, and as they entered, he looked up guiltily like a little kid.

"You weren't supposed to see it until it was clean." He grimaced.

"Isn't Carpenter supposed to be helping?" Mason asked, and Carpenter grinned.

"I'm on for dishes, but Dane knew where the cleaning supplies were."

"Why baking?" Terry asked, bouncing on his toes. "I mean… Subway has really good cookies."

Carpenter's palpable disgust made them both laugh. "For one, the smell is half the pleasure. For two, this is a step on the Make Carpenter Less Fat plan. I've been an *awesome* dieter for the last week, and my carrot on a stick was homemade cookies. Dane promised me. So here we are, making cookies. And when I'm done doing dishes, we're going to sit down with some milk and gorge like ten-year-olds. I've earned this."

"You're not fat," Dane said staunchly, pushing himself up on the counter. "This is Make Carpenter Healthy, not Make Carpenter Less Fat."

Mason took in Carpenter's husky form and had to concede that he'd slimmed down since Thanksgiving. Then he looked anxiously at his brother to see if his hope had spilled over into infatuation yet.

Mason couldn't tell, but Dane looked happy, and Mason wouldn't shit on that. "Well, I'll just take my cookies and run, then," he said, amused. There were two-dozen misshapen but warm and gooey cookies cooling on racks on the counter, and the stove timer said more were baking. He pulled out some paper towels and, hissing at the heat, loaded them up with cookies. "I'll be back in half an hour," he said, bumping Terry's arm with his own and holding out the cache of purloined cookies.

Terry took them without a word, big-eyed and a little shell-shocked.

"Hey, Jefferson," Carpenter said as they were leaving. "You going to practice Thursday?"

Terry nodded, suddenly a little more comfortable. "Yeah, why?"

"'Cause we need you. Jimenez is on a business trip, and Singh and his family are in Hawaii. Without you, we're fucked."

"Mason's playing too," Terry said, and Mason met Carpenter's surprised gaze.

"You play?"

Mason grimaced. "I stand around looking awkward and occasionally kick the ball." Honesty—nothing beat it.

"He's a toe-poker," Terry said matter-of-factly. "But then, put him on defense and all he's gotta do is look scary."

Mason smiled with all his teeth and Carpenter cracked up.

"Yeah. You're terrifying. But we still need you, so practice."

"We're gonna get creamed," Jefferson said, but he didn't sound like he was put out about it. "But who cares—we'll be playing!" He bumped Mason this time, and they made it out the door.

THE COOKIES were gooey and delicious, and Terry made yummy porn sounds as he forked lumps of warm cookie into his mouth with two fingers.

"You sure you don't want the las' one?" he asked through a mostly full mouth.

"Nope. I'm old—I'll get fat." Which was partly the truth, but most of it was that he hadn't made that bagel he'd planned on, and Terry obviously needed cozening.

"You're not old," Terry said, taking another bite of cookie and closing his eyes in bliss. "You're hot."

Mason guffawed. "Uh...."

"No, seriously—you're... groomed."

"I'm old," he said. "That thing you're doing with your hair? I'd look like a jackass. I'm still listening to Offspring and the Killers, and you're listening to Imagine Dragons and Grouplove. I'm old."

"Imagine Dragons is passé," Terry said ruthlessly. "But that's okay. They're still pretty hot too."

"D'oh!"

Terry's throaty laughter followed, and conversely, Mason didn't feel so old anymore.

But he did feel awkward and sad as they pulled up next to Terry's car. "So, uh... Thursday?" he said brightly.

"Yeah. Practice!"

"Do you want to get dinner or something, you know, afterwards?"

Terry blinked. "You want to?"

"Not *sex*, Terry. *Dinner*."

"Oh. Okay—yeah. After the beer in the parking lot, we can go to Denny's or something."

Awesome. "Sounds like a plan," Mason said. "Look forward to it!" And some of his desperation must have broken through his voice.

"It's a plan," Terry said softly, pausing with one hand on the door handle.

"Then have a good week." Mason tried a smile. Failed.

Terry turned away from the door and kissed him softly. "Was the best... making love, I guess, ever," he said, brown eyes intent and sober on Mason's. "I'll... I'll text you over the week."

"Deal," Mason breathed. He'd never been anyone's best ever. "See you Thursday."

Terry grinned and bounced out of the car. Mason waited until the piece of junk started up before pulling away.

The sun was peeking out of the fog, and Mason thought that a nap would feel good about now. He really felt like pulling the covers over his head and not coming out.

CARPENTER AND Dane almost had the kitchen cleaned by the time he got back, and he passed up the nap for a corner of the couch while the two of them went after electronic enemies with bloodthirsty glee.

"Mason—Mace!" Carpenter urged, poking his shoulder. "You're up. Don't you want to play?"

Mason shook his head and leaned his chin on his hand. "Naw—you guys are entertaining enough. I'll watch."

To his embarrassment, Dane put the game on pause. "What's up?"

Mason glared at Dane and tried not to flick his eyes at Carpenter like a sitcom hero.

"Give it up, Mason," Carpenter said gruffly. "I was here long enough to make cookies, and you guys weren't quiet."

"Aces," Mason snarled under his breath. "He'll be thrilled." But Mason couldn't be too mad—Dane had been doing something with a friend, something safe and happy, and Terry hadn't been too upset in the end.

Carpenter shrugged. "He's got nothing to worry about. Skip and Richie came out to the club after Thanksgiving. It was all good, people were chill—"

"Obviously not too chill, because Skip had a bruised cheek," he pointed out, remembering standing in his office and watching Richie drop Skip off that morning. He hadn't asked—hadn't been close enough to Skip as a friend to ask—but he was putting it together now.

"Yeah, well, that guy was an asshole without the homophobia—and Skip hit first."

"Seriously?" Dane interjected, and Carpenter nodded, grinning.

"Skip's got a bit of a temper. Like, Richie's asshole stepbrothers pissed Skip off in a wrecking yard once, and Skipper threw a sledgehammer through a car window. He was all modest too, like it wasn't nothing, but Richie was like, straight through the windshield."

Mason had to laugh a little. "Okay. So I get it. The team's fine with the gay. But I don't think *Terry* is."

"Jefferson?" Carpenter asked—*Clay* Carpenter, and Mason had a moment of fury for bullshit male codes that said the soccer team all used their last names because that was manly.

"Yes. His name is Terry Jefferson. And I don't know if he's had a normal relationship in his entire life, and everything I say and do makes him look at me like, 'Here is the rich douche bag in his natural habitat. Watch as he looks fruitlessly for dinner after sex. Look, rich douche bag, look! You are playing with a different breed of asshole now, and there is no dinner to be found!'"

He had to stop because Carpenter and Dane were hanging on each other helplessly, laughing until they cried.

"It wasn't that funny," he said with dignity after they'd stopped.

"Oh my God, it really was," Dane panted, catching his breath. He stayed there, leaning on Carpenter, and Carpenter didn't seem to notice.

"Jesus, that was awesome," Carpenter confirmed. Then he sobered and looked at Mason perceptively. "But not so easy to live through."

"No," Mason said shortly.

Carpenter grimaced. "I don't know him that well, honestly. You know who you should ask, don't you?"

Of course. "Skip."

Carpenter shrugged. "He's the captain of their little ship, as far as that goes."

Mason scrubbed his hands through his hair. He hadn't put any product in it, and it was sort of a curly riot at the moment. He liked it like that sometimes. "I don't understand him either," he confessed, feeling pathetic.

Carpenter sighed. "You know, Dane talks about your folks all the time. My folks are just like 'em. Still a couple. Got their shit together in a paper cup. It makes you feel invincible, right?"

Mason thought about all those times he'd sat in the principal's office and known that his mother and father would love him regardless. "Yeah."

"When you don't got that feeling, like you can screw up and it'll be okay, you stay a kid a lot longer, at least in your head. Because you don't know how to do anything else. Nobody showed you how."

"Great. Because I didn't feel old and creepy enough."

Carpenter shot him a white grin through his scruff. "Anybody can see you're a big kid pretending to adult, Mason. But you at least know how to pretend. Anyway, talk to Skip. They've known each other as long as Skip's known Richie—he might have some info."

Mason nodded, feeling a little better. But he still didn't play the next round, because he was too busy watching his brother and Carpenter destroy the enemy like old and blooded brothers.

Or like two guys working hard at not falling in love.

MONDAY HE called Skipper through the tech line.

"Tesko Tech Business Services, this is Skipper Keith!" God, he sounded happy. Happy, perky, and sweet. He had from the first time Mason had called his department and gotten him. And Mason, coming off of Ira and worried about Dane, had asked him to come up to his office and watch porn.

The thought of it still made his cheeks burn.

He expected himself to just blurt out things like that—but to have that unfortunate victim of his social ineptitude turn into a friend? Embarrassing.

"Hello, Schipperke," he said now, making himself sound jovial and smooth. He always tried to channel his father when he did this. Or Fred MacMurray. "How are we doing this morning?"

"Well, apparently we're having lunch with a VP in the east wing, because he got his brother to take our friend out for lunch, and we don't want to eat alone."

Mason laughed. "I thought I was being smoother than that." Dane had been happy to do it. And so had Carpenter.

"You could have just come eat with us," Skipper said reprovingly. "Me and Carpenter don't bite."

"Yeah, but I wanted to quiz you shamelessly about your friend, and that's easier to do when you don't feel like you're being a rat fink. So, my office? I promise I'll have something delivered. Anything you want."

"Thai food?" Skipper asked hopefully. "I keep trying to get Richie to try it, but he says nobody he's known has eaten it and lived. I'm hoping if *I* eat it and live, then maybe we don't have to eat pizza all the time."

"What's wrong with pizza?" Mason asked, although he'd hit the age where the onions gave him gas.

"Ponyboy keeps getting into it."

"Ponyboy?"

"The puppy. He can reach the counter, you know."

Mason had known they were *getting* a puppy. He hadn't realized it had happened already. "What kind of puppy?"

"We have no idea, but they told us it was eight weeks old, and it's already the size of a pony."

"And it likes pizza."

"The only things it likes better than pizza are garbage and cat shit."

Mason laughed, genuinely delighted. Skip and Richie had apparently seized each other's hand and decided to trot boldly into the future, even if the future was filled with unknown quantities such as Thai food. And dogs.

"Well, I look forward to you telling me all about it," he said, happier now even if Skip didn't know a damned thing about Terry.

"See you at lunchtime."

He rang off and looked up to see Mrs. Bradford waiting in his doorway.

"Did you have a good weekend, Mrs. Bradford?"

"Can't complain, sir. The mister and I drove up to the snow."

Mason blinked. "Did you go skiing?"

She gave a shudder. "Good Lord, no. We sat inside the bed and breakfast, drinking hot chocolate and looking out the window, going, 'Oh, look. Snow.' It was thrilling."

"I imagine so," he laughed. A part of him wondered if maybe the two of them hadn't found other "thrilling" things to do while looking at the snow, but the thought of Mrs. Bradford and sex would knock him off his game for maybe the rest of his life.

And he wasn't doing great as it was.

"How was your weekend, sir?"

Mason sighed. "I played golf," he said, unable to shake the confusion in his voice. "But that was Saturday. Sunday, my brother and I tried to redecorate one of the guest bedrooms."

"Tried?"

Mason shrugged. "Well, we succeeded, but I went with green and cream, thinking it would be handsome?"

"As it should have been."

"I picked the wrong…." He shuddered. "Green."

"How bad could a green be, sir?"

He closed his eyes and shuddered again. "Like an olive barfed on a rotten lime."

She let out a bark of laughter and her eyes crinkled at the corners. "That *is* an epic failure, sir. Do you have plans to fix it?"

"Yeah—next weekend, I think."

"That would probably be a mercy. Are you ready for your first meeting?"

Mason nodded. "Yes, ma'am—but is there any way you could order some takeout Thai food delivered?"

She barely raised an eyebrow. "Of course, sir. Anything in particular?"

"How about two helpings of mild green curry and one of pumpkin curry. You really can't go wrong."

"But that's what you said about green and cream," she told him in all seriousness.

Mason found a real smile coming up from his toes, when he could have sworn he'd be stuck with that sort of achy, anxious expression he'd been wearing since he woke up.

"Point taken. Make sure it's a really *good* Thai place, or Skipper and his boyfriend may be feeding their dog pizza for the next twenty years."

She laughed again and then sobered. "Mason, does any of this banter have anything to do with the young man you saw last week?"

Mason felt his face heat. "It's sort of a way not to think about him," he confessed, feeling raw. "He was my golfing buddy on Saturday."

Mrs. Bradford nodded as though things were beginning to fall into place now. "Was this a good thing or a bad thing?"

Mason closed his eyes again, and this time, instead of putrid green, he saw the wonder in Terry's eyes as he peeped at Mason through his hair.

"It was an amazing thing," he said, but no amount of remembering the amazing could shake the trouble from his voice.

"Understood, sir," she said.

"I wish I did," he told her and then nodded in dismissal before he could spend any more of his morning worrying about Terrence Jefferson.

SKIPPER TOOK to Thai food like a pro, dumping the curry over the rice with unabashed curiosity. He took the first bite and whimpered, pleasure written all over his square-jawed Captain America face.

"This is good," he moaned. Then he opened his eyes like he'd discovered a bone or something. "Is it bad for you?"

Mason smiled. "No, sir—chicken, vegetables, and coconut milk. There are way worse things."

"Mm." He took another bite and savored. A few more bites, appreciating every one, and finally, when he was at the slowing down part of the meal, he focused on Mason.

"You look like shit," he said bluntly. "What's wrong?"

"Nothing!" Mason protested. Then he sighed. "Well, we tried to decorate the guest room, and it smells like paint and it looks hideous."

"That's it?"

Mason avoided his blue-eyed gaze. "That's a thing," he temporized. "It's a true thing."

"But is it the only thing?"

Mason let out a breath. "So. Uh, your friend Terry—"

"Jefferson?"

"His first name is Terry!"

"I know what his first name is—we went to Disneyland, for heaven's sakes!"

Mason squinted at him. "Is that a team-building thing?"

Skipper squinted back. "I had to see his driver's license. We did not suddenly grow close and bond because it was four guys in a hotel room. But still, yes, I do know his first name is Terry. I know his dad left when he was still a baby, and I know his mom's a piece of fuckin' work."

Oh good. An opening. "Mm… could you maybe, you know, define that a little more specifically for me?"

Skipper chewed his rice thoroughly and regarded him with suspicion. "I need to know why you're asking."

Mason took a bite of his own curry—he'd gone with half green and half pumpkin and was wishing he'd gone with all pumpkin, because it was delicious. He swallowed and wondered how much to trust this sweet young man who had, thankfully, not tried to have him hung out to dry for sexual harassment.

Well, when he thought about it that way….

"I'm… well, we're sort of involved?" Oh yeah. That was mature.

"Sort of?" Skipper frowned at him.

"See, that's my problem too."

Skipper's frown was not unfriendly—it was more… contemplative. "Well, I didn't know he was gay, but Richie had a feeling, so I'm not really surprised."

"So, he's not… out?" Mason had figured this out for himself.

Skipper shook his head. "See, that's…." He flailed with his fork, flinging rice indiscriminately. "It's that whole…." He flailed again. "See, Richie and I were doing it for weeks before we even said the g-word."

"Goal?" Mason was actually busy ducking rice—it was the only thing he could come up with.

"*Gay*, Mason. I mean, thing about guys like me and Richie? Sixty years ago and we wouldn't be working in an office. We'd be working in a factory or a mill or someplace. World changes and we end up in IT—but we're not suits. We're not you. There's this whole… thing—you know and we don't."

Mason closed his eyes and tried to think like someone he *hadn't* grown up with. "Schipperke—"

"Like *that*," Skip said triumphantly. "Like what that damned dog is called! Like how to wear a suit—"

"My dad taught me—"

"See!" Skipper bounced in his seat—and he wasn't a small, bouncy man.

"Skip, I'm still not—"

"Money, Mason. But not just money, because I met some of Carpenter's rich people, and they were douche bags."

"I'm really starting to hate that stereotype," Mason muttered.

"But see, you're the good kind of stereotype. You send your secretary down with TheraFlu. You agree to be on my soccer team even though we're just a bunch of hosers who like to get dirty. You're a nice guy. But…." Skipper closed his eyes and shook his head like he was coming to a reckoning. "My mother drank herself to death in our apartment, Mason. While I was in school. I had to get a job at a burger joint so I could eat, and all I ate was burgers, and I was a mess! Now I'm not saying everybody don't—doesn't—have their baggage. For all I know, your pain is way worse than mine—"

"No," Mason said numbly, thinking there wasn't enough Thai food in the world. "Not even."

"Well that's good to hear, because mine is bad enough. But guys like Jefferson, like Richie and me, that's the hand we're dealt, and we don't have a safety net to help us get our shit together in a paper bag. So whatever Terry is dealing with, he's not used to help. He's not used to *words* that'll help. All he's used to is what he's got, and he might not even have a picture in his mind of anything better than that."

Mason's turn to flail. "Movies—television, books—"

"Well, yeah. But I watch shit blow up on my TV and that never happens in real life. For all I know, those TV people in happy families are just that—TV people."

Mason found he had to still his breathing, and suddenly words— hateful words spoken by the people Ira used to invite to their dinner parties—hit him full-on. Things like *background* and *education*, uttered in tentative tones, like these things were lacking in whomever they were talking about. For the first time in his life, Mason realized what wealth and privilege really were.

And that there was a barrier between the people who had them and the people who didn't.

The barrier wasn't money itself, like most people thought. It was *resources*—it was the belief that the world out there could help you instead of just kick you in the teeth.

This was the thing that he had and Skipper and Richie and Terry did not.

It was the thing Carpenter had been trying to tell him.

It was a thing he didn't know how to fix.

"But…," he said, sounding plaintive like a spoiled child. "I… I care about him. Do I not get to care about him because I'm a rich douche bag?"

Skipper laughed a little and finally set his fork down, like he couldn't eat anymore even though he was about halfway done. "No. I don't think that's how it works. But it means you need to help him see bigger than what he's got. It's like…." Skipper sighed and looked at Mason unhappily. "I really hate talking about myself. I hope you know that."

Mason grimaced. "I couldn't miss it if I was blindfolded," he said honestly.

"Well, good. Because this is me being a friend, and now you know. But Richie and I, when we were first getting together, he didn't want to leave his dad. Not because he couldn't afford to live away or because he was afraid of being on his own, but because his dad, he was the only family Richie had. And he's a bigoted asshole, so if Richie left him for me…." Skipper stood up and started wrapping up the food on the table.

"It was permanent," Mason said, understanding.

Skip looked at him square on, a wealth of understanding loading down his broad shoulders. "It *is* permanent. And it's scary. So Jefferson—*Terry*— if his situation with his mom is awful, well, he thinks that's just his life. You may want to keep going like you are until he can see there's more to life than just what he's got now."

"Patience," Mason said, feeling stupid because it was obvious. "You're talking patience."

Skip nodded. "And… like, use your words. He won't. You need to give him words to use."

Mason nodded, thinking about chocolate chip cookies and promises to be monogamous because condoms were a pain in the ass. "Better words," he said softly.

"Yeah. Macho male bullshit is only romantic if one of you translates," Skipper said pragmatically. Then he shrugged and smiled shyly. "That sounds really fucking wise of me, I know, but truth is, I've got a whole three months of relationship under my belt. Let's see if Richie and I haven't screwed things up in a year, and I'll tell you how much of this works."

Mason laughed. "Sit down, Skipper—you've wrapped up lunch, but we've still got half an hour to go. I brought some cookies from home. Do you want some?"

Skip bit his lip. "I'll have to run an extra block, but sure!"

They dug into the cookies Mason had brought in a baggie. Mason watched his friend looking just as blissed out as Terry did and had a useless wish that everyone he knew had had a Janette Hayes to make them cookies when they were kids.

Or a someone. Anyone at all.

THURSDAY NIGHT was stormy and blustery—no practice. Mason texted Terry just to be sure, but he was expecting the *Can't get away. Sorry, no dinner!* that he got back.

Miss you, he texted truthfully. *I missed you all week.* Mason had tried—he'd sent cute little pictures from the Internet, pictures of his brother asleep with shaving cream in his hand (because Mason and Dane really *were* twelve), and pictures of him awake with shaving cream in his hair.

He'd gotten back the occasional LOL, but nothing beyond that, and Mason was wondering if he wasn't getting brushed off, which, after all of that research, sort of hurt.

A lot.

I want to come have dinner, he got back. *Mom doesn't like the rain. It freaks her out.*

Wow. That was more truth and emotional availability than Mason had assumed he'd get in a month! He'd take it!

Dane hates the rain too, he confessed, looking at his brother on the other side of the couch. Dane was flipping through the channels dispiritedly, and Mason reminded himself to ask Dane about his medication. *It triggers his depressive episodes sometimes.*

Your brother gets depressed?

And oh crap. Mason had forgotten that Terry didn't know everything—or anything, really—about his life. Well, Skipper said it was up to him to provide a road map. *He has bipolar disorder. If he doesn't take his meds he goes up up up and then comes crashing down. It's scary.*

Beat, beat beat, and Mason felt the absolute terror of wondering if he'd jumped without a safety net and landed on a cliff.

He always seems so together. I had no idea.

He IS together, Mason texted, girding himself for a brief educational text interlude on mental health. *His brain chemistry just betrays him.*

"Who are you texting?" Dane asked, and Mason jerked, sending the phone up in the air before catching it.

"Ta-da!" he said, and Dane clapped. Mason inclined his head modestly and answered the question. "Terry. We were going to do something tonight, but no soccer."

"Oh!" Dane replied, sounding very innocent of any knowledge that he was being gossiped about. "Getting-to-know-you texting. It probably should have happened three weeks ago." He nodded sagely. "Oh well, better late than never. I'm settling on shotgunning *Vinyl* and eating popcorn. Are you game?"

Mason shuddered. "Ugh. I'd rather kiss Bobby Cannavale—"

"I wouldn't mind that, actually."

Mason glared at him. "It's like you're not even my brother. I'm going upstairs to talk like a human being."

"Fine—but don't knock Bobby until you've crushed on him."

"Dane, just no."

Mason took his phone upstairs to his room. By the time he got there, Terry had left a string of texts that he had a hard time deciphering.

So he hit Call, because fuck it, texting was a young man's game.

"What're you asking?" He threw himself back on his bed and kicked off his slippers.

Terry sounded disgruntled. "I'm just… you know. How does your brother seem so normal?"

Mason grunted and tried to recall his conversation with Skip. "Have you ever pulled an all-nighter?" he asked. One of Dane's triggers was a stressful week of finals.

"Yeah, when I was in tech school. I'd get off work and go to school and stay up all night to do my homework—"

"Exactly. How long did you go without meaningful sleep?"

Laugh. "About two days."

Mason couldn't laugh. "Dane went about three weeks. He started ripping out walls in his dorm, painting them." Mason closed his eyes, remembering his mother calling him up, panicked, and how he'd had to clock Dane in the jaw, stun him, to get him in the car to take to the psych ward. How the place was awful, even with health insurance, and how Mason and his parents had taken shifts so Mason's sweet baby brother wouldn't be alone in that place, and the painful reconstruction of Dane's life after that. This had been before Ira, and Mason had been so desperate afterward for calm, for "normal." Thinking about it now, he realized he'd equated *boring* with *normal*.

"What's the crash like afterwards?" Terry asked perceptively.

Mason's throat swelled. Suicide watch. Dane lying unwashed in bed like a dying fish. Hearing the words "I want to die" coming from his baby brother.

"Bad," he whispered hoarsely. "It's… for full-blown bipolar, it's bad. So there's medication and talking and more medication and more talking. He has to keep a journal every day. He has to talk to a doctor every week. And the thing is, when everything is level, he's Dane. And…." Mason smiled. "You've met him. It's worth it. It's worth it to find normal, you know?"

"What's normal?" Terry asked, sounding raw.

Mason let out a sigh and wriggled under the covers. He was wearing sweats—he might as well settle in for a convo. "I like to think it's something that doesn't hurt." He remembered Ira. "But that doesn't bore the shit out of you either."

"Doesn't hurt?"

Mason thought about it. Thought about all the times he'd opened his mouth and fucked up a relationship—and how badly he wanted someone to see past the dumb things he said and look at the things he actually did. "Yeah. Something that makes you feel good when it's working. That doesn't make you afraid it's going to get yanked away because you say or do the wrong thing once or even twice. It's a relationship with a do-over clause."

"Huh," Terry said.

Mason resisted throwing the phone across the room. "That's all you've got?"

"I just… I know you're thinking you want to hear what I've got in mind for a relationship, but, uh, I've never *had* one, really. I mean, queer guys don't get a relationship, do they?"

"Well they do *now*," Mason said, trying not to cross his eyes or sound like a condescending shit. "Thirty years ago, not so much. Nobody expected us to have a family. I mean my *mother* expected me to, and that's what mattered, but I get it." And suddenly he remembered his gay history, riots at Stonewall, AIDS activism—all of it. "For a while, close encounters in bathrooms were all we got. But not anymore."

"Not according to *my* mom," Terry said glumly. Then he let out a sigh—and it turned out to be one of the best sounds ever. "She's… I mean, I want to say she's, like, mentally ill, but I don't think that's right. Dane can't help himself. Or, I mean, he *can* help himself, and, you know, that's what he does. But she… it's like her heart died when I was a kid. And the only thing that makes her happy is now it's my turn to take care of *her*."

"But that's not fair," Mason said, so relieved—so damned relieved—to actually say it out loud.

"But she didn't have to have me, you know," Terry told him matter-of-factly. "She could have gotten an abortion. I'm lucky to be alive."

Mason's heart stopped. Literally. In the silence that it left behind, he could hear the big whoosh of its last beat roaring through his ears.

"Your mother told you that?" he asked, not sure where the breath had come from.

"Yeah. Whenever I was bad."

"That's a horrible thing to say," Mason rasped. "That was her choice—she had no right to inflict it on you."

"But, you know. I'm the reason her life was so hard."

"Terry?" Mason said, hoping he wasn't moaning. He hurt. His *entire body* hurt.

"Yeah?"

"You're awesome. You're… there is so much more to you than what your mother tells you. You just need to get out of the house more to see it." Augh! Terry should have been having quickies with a counselor or a psychologist or someone who knew the words—*anyone* who knew the words. Every second they were on the phone, Mason felt like he walked a tightrope between what he should say and what he wanted to blurt out. What he wanted to blurt out was "Get the hell out of there, move into your own apartment, leave her to rot, then come date me!" Which would have suited all of Mason's needs perfectly, but Mason was starting to figure out that he'd had a lot of his needs met already, and this wasn't about him *at all*.

"Huh."

"I hate that word."

Terry laughed. "Sorry—I just don't have any others. That was… that was a really nice compliment. You know we're going to have to play together without actually practicing as a team, right?"

A total non sequitur, but Mason was so damned glad to move away from the hard stuff. "Well, like you said, let me sub for the defenders. I can't do too much harm there, right?"

"Mason, we're gonna get creamed—I told you that. But you can't feel bad about it. See, when I first started playing, I was afraid Skipper was gonna yell at me for fucking up so badly, because we couldn't win for *shit*, right? But Skipper was like, 'Dude, we're out here getting exercise, we have a beer after practice, we get to play like little kids—what's to worry about?' So I'm telling you, yeah, we'll lose. But it's not… wait!" He sounded excited. "It's *exactly* like golf. It's like, 'Who cares what *actually* happened in the game, as long as the scorecards say we can play together again!'"

Mason found himself smiling. God, when he was a kid, he'd imagined it would all be that simple. "That's excellent," he said, feeling optimistic in spite of the rain hammering at the roof. "We'll be like the Bad News Bears."

"I've seen that movie!" And again he sounded excited. "Although the older one was like… whoa. They let kids *smoke* in that movie, and you're like damn, shit was messed up a long time ago."

Mason had to laugh. "Yeah—remember, I was *born* a long time ago."

"What's the thing about the age, anyway?" Impatience tinged his voice. "I said you were hot."

"I guess… I just thought my life would be settled by now, you know?" Oh God—Mason's early midlife crisis was going to bore him, and that would be it.

"Well, maybe you're lucky. Maybe if it had settled the way you'd planned earlier, that would have sucked, but if it settles the way it is *now*, there will be no suck, and you'll have a better life."

The wind gusted and the rain poured—and Mason relaxed, happy. "I can't argue with you," he said, his voice an awed whisper. At that moment the lights flickered and went off entirely. Oh hell. "Terry, I'm going to go check on Dane, okay?"

"Did your lights go out?"

"Yeah," Mason soothed, getting out of bed. "Do you get nervous when that happens?"

"Sounds like a total pussy thing when I say it, doesn't it?"

"No. Actually, Dane doesn't like it either." He padded to his doorway and the lightning flashed, and he screamed and fell back into his room.

Dane screamed and started to laugh, anxiety turning it into a cackle. "Mason?"

"Jesus, Dane, you scared me to death!"

"Well, you *know* I'm a big baby in the dark!"

"Yeah, well, so is Terry. C'mon. Crawl in. If I put the phone on the charger before I go to sleep, it should wake us up in the morning."

Dane docilely followed him back into the bedroom. "I turned everything off, so it's not going to all blast on in fifteen minutes."

And Terry said, "So you're just going to let him crawl into bed with you?"

"Since we were kids, yeah. Mom let him do it until he was sixteen years old."

"Which was pretty funny when Dad got up to pee and wasn't expecting me," Dane chuckled.

"You are so warped," Mason muttered, crawling into his bed, glad it was a king-size, because puppy piles weren't his thing.

"So," Terry said, his voice growing thin with his own fear and something else Mason couldn't define, "you'd... you wouldn't laugh at me for crawling into bed with you."

Mason's heart gave a vicious twist in his chest. "No. I come from a family of big scared babies—you'd be part of the crowd."

Terry and Dane laughed at the same time, and Mason rolled over to one side, knowing Dane would roll over to his other. "Sounds... cozy," Terry said. "Real... cozy."

"Well, it will be, until he starts ripping burrito farts under the covers."

"Yup," Dane said, sounding drowsy already. "Saving them for you."

"Just lay there and pretend to sleep," Mason muttered. "I'm trying to be romantic."

"That's what he said," Dane giggled, and Mason rolled his eyes in the dark.

"Mason," Terry said in his ear, claiming his complete attention. "Don't hang up yet, okay?"

He was scared. Mason could hear it—same as Dane had been.

"No," he said softly. "I won't. I promise. What do you want to talk about?"

"Tell me about college," he said decidedly. "I want to hear what I missed."

So Mason launched into the story of Todd Slezcyk and the lost virginity and listened as Terry laughed, more and more quietly each time. He must have fallen asleep finally, the phone next to his ear, because when Mason hit End Call, he could hear a faint snoring on the end of the line.

He hung up and put the phone on the charger, aware that the electricity had come back on sometime in the last half hour, but all his lights were turned off, so he was still good.

"Todd Slezcyk was an ass," Dane mumbled into the dark, startling him awake.

"Well I know that *now*," Mason laughed, so happy the story had done something to ease Terry's anxiety that he didn't care if Dane heard or not.

"You should have known that then. Who picks politics over sex, Mason? I mean, seriously."

Mason chuckled tiredly. "Todd did."

"Well, I'm glad you and Terry are a thing now. He has more sense."

Mason hmmed because he didn't want to wake Dane up when they both had to be up early in the morning. The truth was, he wanted so badly to talk to someone about Terry, to see if he'd done the right thing, if he was saying the right things, if he was even hoping for the right things, but he'd pretty much exhausted his circle of friends this past week, and he figured he was going to have to deal with it on his own.

His last comforting thought was that for the first time, talking to someone until they fell asleep seemed like a talent and not a hideous social faux pas.

The Dangers of Toe-Poking

TERRY HAD been right and the rain let up the next day. Saturday dawned bright and sunshiny and frosty as hell, the grass coated with ice, even at eleven, when they were all meeting.

The other team wasn't there yet, so Skipper made them run drills, the first one being to take turns taking goal kicks at Carpenter, who was apparently their pro tem goalie.

"Serious, Skipper," Carpenter panted. "It's like you want us to lose!"

"That's not true," Skip said, motioning Mason forward to kick the ball. "But we don't have another goalie, and Mason can sub the defenders. I think it'll work better if Richie subs all the midfielders and strikers."

Well, of course. Richie had enough gas for a jackrabbit army. He could probably sub the other team too.

Dane, the rat, waved from the sidelines, absolutely determined to be their cheerleader and not to play at all. Dane had taken dance lessons through school—he hadn't been great, but he claimed it as his athletic skill, and Mason let him. Now he ran on the treadmill and followed yoga tapes in his off times, which was fine, but Mason was going to tell Mom on him if this game went as south as Mason expected when Dane could have helped. Suck it up, buttercup—if Mason had to make an ass of himself on the soccer field, he wasn't letting Dane escape.

Mason ran determinedly forward and toe-poked the ball at Carpenter, who caught it neatly and threw it back to the line, where Owens took his turn to dribble it toward the goal.

"Mason, dammit!" Terry called from his place in line. "Do you remember nothing?"

"Yeah, yeah, I get it—the inside of my foot. I get it."

"No, because if you got it, you'd do it!"

Mason scowled at him. "Don't be mean," he said shortly. "I feel enough like an idiot as it is." He trotted to the end of the line and jogged in place to keep warm.

Terry was a few bodies in front of him, and as Mason watched, his expression turned inward.

"Yeah—sorry 'bout that," he said, turning around and catching Mason's eye. "Channeling Mom for a minute—scares the shit out of me when she just pops out of my mouth like that, you know?"

Mason nodded. "Bet it's like coughing up a gopher," he said in total seriousness.

The three guys between him and Terry disintegrated, and Terry snickered. Skip looked up from where he was directing everybody and shook his head.

"What in the hell did you say?" he asked Mason helplessly.

"Gopher!" Cooper howled in front of him. "Oh my God!"

Mason shook his head and Terry winked, and then it was Terry's turn. He used the side of his foot, and it was like he drew a lovely hyperbolic line from his foot, around Carpenter, and into the net—and the ball followed that curve.

Mason could only stare stupidly, impressed as hell, as Terry turned around and trotted back to the end of the line and Carpenter picked himself off the ground to dust off his knees.

A HALF an hour later, Carpenter wasn't the only one with grass stains on his knees and ass. As Terry had predicted, they were getting creamed at five goals to one, and Mason and Richie were as exhausted as the rest of the team from cycling on and off the field to give other people a break.

There was no banter in this kind of play, just a solid, balls-out determination to keep running until you dropped and to give each play your best until you folded. But Mason's feet were like lead, and he was developing a sore spot in his hip from all the sudden reversals on the grass field, and he had to *actively* work at turning his foot sideways to kick the damned ball like he was supposed to.

And sometimes he forgot.

Like toward the end, when the ball came rolling toward the goal in an obvious save and Mason ran to boot it across the field. He didn't lift his foot entirely off the ground as he shifted forward to kick it, and his toe poked into a hummock of grass on the uneven field, bent back, and Mason's momentum sent him sprawling as his ankle turned underneath him.

For a minute he lay facedown in the mud, waiting for the pain in his ankle to hit and hoping the earth would swallow him.

Then the pain in his ankle hit, and there was no room for hope.

"*Time!*" Skipper shouted, and Mason became aware of the muddle of feet still jostling for the ball near his head. "I said *time-out*, assholes!" Skipper yelled, as winded as the rest of them. "If you kill my fuckin' boss I'm gonna fuckin' destroy you, now move, goddammit, move!"

"You mean he's really hurt?"

Mason pushed himself up on one arm and tried not to whimper. Up, up, over to his ass, and oh mama, yeah, that sucked.

"Yes," he gasped. "Yes, really hurt."

Terry suddenly crouched by his side. "You're a mess," he said grimly. "Did you mean to land face-first in a mud puddle?"

"Yes, of course, I've been planning it all day." He closed his eyes and tried to pretend he wasn't thinking about throwing up. Terry squeezed the back of his neck, and Mason took a deep breath, and then another, and the pain receded a little. Skipper crouched at his feet, probing his ankle with gentle fingers.

"It's swelling like a motherfucker," Skip said grimly. "Dane, you want to drive the car down here and—"

"I'll get him," Terry said, popping up from Mason's side. "Here, I'll go get my car—I'll be right back!"

He disappeared like a magic pixie, and Dane gazed at Mason's ankle in horror. "He's going to take you to the hospital in his Toyota?"

"God," Richie said, watching him grab his keys and phone from the pile by the side of the field before sprinting up the hill, "that thing's smaller than my car. Skip, Mason can't ride in that thing, can he?"

Skip looked at Mason with wide blue eyes. "Uh, boss? Uh, are you sure you don't want to, you know, go with Dane?"

Mason took a few deep breaths and tried to find a balance between extreme pain grimace and blissed-out smile. "Did you see that?" he said. "He's getting his car!"

"Oh God," Skipper moaned, smacking his face.

"I don't even believe this," Richie muttered, running a hand through his wild red hair. "Skip, your boss is an idiot—*you* don't even like riding in your Toyota, and it's *your car*."

"Richie, go get me the ice packs in my gym bag, okay?"

"Yeah—good idea, Skip!" Richie ran off, that boundless energy almost an assault on Mason's senses. The other team had pretty much gathered to themselves at this point, and Mason wondered if they were laughing at the big clumsy guy who face-planted and now needed the entire world to administer to his boo-boo.

"This it, Skip!" Richie called, waving the bag in the air.

Skipper smiled benevolently at him like he'd done something amazing. "Yeah, Richie—that's it. Bring it back, 'kay?"

"That's so revolting," Cooper muttered, shaking his head at Richie, and Mason would have taken offense, but Skipper grinned.

"His energy, or the fact that *he* actually knows how to help a guy?"

"His energy," Cooper replied, laconic. Cooper was sort of a big country boy who had played defense for the same reason Mason subbed it—he just didn't move that fast. Skip laughed, and Mason realized that he was new to this little group, and unless he could come back and play, he'd be just a footnote in its history.

At that moment they all heard the loud rattle and backfire of an engine that hadn't been serviced in years, and Terry came putting down the field.

Richie got back with the gym bags—Mason's too, which he handed to Dane—and Skip pulled out an ace bandage and an ice pack, making busy while Terry wended his way around the squishier parts of the field. He came to a stop at the boundary line for their particular pitch.

Mason breathed shallowly through his nose for a moment while Skipper, with absurdly gentle movements, wrapped the ice pack to his ankle, taking his shoe off and putting it in Mason's bag when he was done.

"We own a Lexus," Dane said, coming out of what appeared to be a trance as he'd fixated on Skipper wrapping Mason's ankle. "Mason, he's just going to take you away in that thing when we came in a Lexus SUV. What in the hell?"

"Here, Skipper, help me up. I need to get some of the mud off so it doesn't wreck his upholstery."

"Yeah," Carpenter said, getting on Mason's other side and offering a solid shoulder. "That's the problem with Jefferson's car. Too much mud on the upholstery."

Richie smirked and smacked Carpenter playfully on the arm and then fussed around Mason with a towel he'd grabbed from the sidelines. "You're really okay," he said, rubbing the rough cloth over Mason's forehead and cheeks. "It's mostly on your face and stomach—you won't leave no assprints, so don't worry none, okay?"

Mason nodded gratefully and then held on tight to Skip and Carpenter as they helped him hop toward the side of the field where Terry was headed.

"But…," Dane muttered unhappily, "Mason—we *have* a *Lexus*!"

"Let it go, Dane," Carpenter told him gently. "It's not the fucking car."

"I am totally missing something," Owens muttered.

"Or missing *out* on something." Galvan smirked back. Mason glanced at them in time to see them locking surprised glances, and then Carpenter accidentally bumped his ankle and his vision went too black to see.

By the time the team had escorted him, en masse, to the car, he was pretty sure he was going to cry in a totally unmanly way, but he managed to control himself as they slid him in, and Dane thrust his gym bag on his lap. Terry had scooted the seat way back and thrown all of the trash behind the seat, so if Mason could ignore the smell of feet and the fact that his ankle was at a rather cramped angle for something that seemed to be growing exponentially, the ride wouldn't be that bad.

"Call Sutter Urgent Care," Dane told him, sorting through Mason's gym bag until he found his phone. "Here. Call them and tell them you're coming. They'll have a wheelchair out for you and someone to help you in it."

"I can help him," Terry said, nodding. "I'll make sure he's okay."

Dane's eyes got big, and he obviously tried not to sweep the car's interior with his gaze. "He'll want a wheelchair when he gets there," he said diplomatically and then he glared at Mason like it was Mason's fault Dane was a snob and loved the Lexus.

"Wait!" Skipper held out his hand, and out of nowhere Riche smacked another ice pack into it. He crouched at Mason's feet and wrapped it around from the other angle, which also served to prop Mason's foot up more comfortably.

Mason's gratitude made his eyes water. "Thanks, Schipperke," he rasped, and was rewarded with a hard squeeze on his shoulder.

"Give us updates. Jefferson, you let us know if you need to go and he needs a ride home, okay?"

"We *have* a *Lexus*," Dane repeated, like nobody had heard him the first time, and then Carpenter shut the door and Terry put the car into gear.

The uneven field jostled the car unmercifully, and for the first five minutes, Mason concentrated on keeping his ankle still so he didn't throw up. Eventually the car hit solid pavement and Mason opened his eyes. "Left," he murmured. "You know where Sutter is?" The closest hospitals were in Roseville, not far from each other.

"Yeah. Skipper's got Kaiser."

Still, it took Mason a minute to process what those two things had to do with each other. "Money," he grunted. "Sorry." All of Tesko employees got to choose, but Kaiser was cheaper. And, of course, if Skipper had been born in Kaiser—possibly on welfare, if his childhood had been as bleak as he'd said—he would have kept his number for life. Sutter was pricier, but the reputation for service was better. Great. He even had bourgeoisie health insurance.

"No, don't be—I wasn't trying to be shitty. I'm glad it's the good kind—you could be waiting at Kaiser for a while."

That reminded him! He grabbed the phone and called urgent care, reporting his ETA as fifteen minutes. When he hung up, he leaned his head back and sighed.

"This is so embarrassing. You know it's probably a minor sprain—you totally would have hopped up and scored a goal or something." Mason tried not to picture himself going right over and flat on his face. "God—way to make an impression!"

Terry's schoolboy giggle didn't exactly surprise him. "Yeah, it was pretty epic. We'll be giving you shit for that for years. Like, every time you come down the field, someone'll yell 'Timber!'—it'll be great!"

For years? Oh hell. "Yeah, if I wanted to relive fifth grade again."

"No, no—see, when you get to be a grown-up, it's good to do that. When you're a kid, you don't know how to own that shit, but now? You just make a whistling sound like a tree falling, and you'll be in!"

Mason chuckled in spite of himself. "I never thought I'd be using my fifth-grade social skills to make friends as an adult."

"Why are you?" Terry asked.

The question caught him by surprise, but he didn't have to think about it long. "Right before Dane and I moved to Sacramento, I had, like, a major breakup."

"Bummer. Did you cheat?"

Mason let out a harsh bark of laughter. "Of course not. No, he did. With my boss. It was weird. I mean, *I* was the one who was sort of fucked over—or fucked under, I guess. But they ended up with all the friends in the split." Mason shrugged, trying to remember the last time he'd really missed Ira. "It's just as well. He thought I was an idiot, and he liked to talk down to me. I... I hate it when I think I'm a rich douche bag who might be just like him."

"No," Terry said, merging onto the freeway with the practiced ease of someone who knew this stretch of road well. "No, you're great. You're nice and you treat me like a human. Don't worry—once we start calling you Timber and you laugh with us, you'll be in!"

"That's comforting," Mason said, thinking it was true. "Maybe you can come golfing with me, Carpenter, Dane, and we can think of a good nickname for *you*."

Terry laughed. "Squirrel!"

"Where?" Mason didn't want to look—a squirrel on the freeway was just too tragic.

"No, *me*, dumbass. I'm the squirrel. That could be my nickname."

"Only if you get to climb the tree every now and then," Mason said, liking the dirty pun.

Terry did too, because he laughed. "Lots of times. This squirrel wants to climb that tree up his ass *lots* of times."

"Just—" Mason winced as the car hit a bump. "—not tonight."

"Yeah."

They were quiet until the hospital. A nurse was waiting outside with a wheelchair, and Mason got taken away to fill out paperwork. Terry met him upstairs at X-Ray, where the wait was supposed to be a good hour, and Mason smiled at him gamely from his semidoze against the back wall.

"You found a parking space?"

"Ugh. Yeah. Took forever."

Oh. Oh no. He was on such a short leash. "You, uh, could always leave if you have to, and call Dane or Skip."

Terry scowled. "Is that what you want? Would you rather have your brother or Skip here with you?"

"No." Mason closed his eyes and thought wistfully about warm cookies and milk and comfort things. "No, I'd rather have you."

The hand on his shoulder was a surprise—but a nice one. "That's why I volunteered," Terry said. "Even if your brother was probably right. Your car would have been more comfortable."

Mason smiled but kept his eyes closed. They'd given him some pain meds, and the world was so lovely and floaty that he didn't want to see self-recrimination or try to deal with the convoluted squirrel path of Terry's brain.

"It's enough that you're here." Until Terry grabbed his hand, he didn't realize he'd said that out loud.

"That's nice," Terry murmured. "One of the nicest things ever, and you're hurt too. I'll stay as long as you need me."

Longer than a doctor's visit, Terry. I'll need you for a nice long time.

About fifteen minutes into the wait, Terry's pocket buzzed, and he pulled out his phone. Mason had already texted Skip and Dane the pertinent info, so this could only be the big bad she-wolf herself.

"Yeah, Mom. I told you, I'm staying with my friend. Because he's hurt and he needs me, that's why. No, you might want to take the bus, then. I can't take you to Carol's. I can't. No, I told you that two hours ago—if she offered to give you a ride, you should have taken her up on it. No. I showed you how to use the bus last month. The stop's a block and a half away. You should go. Because I'm not coming home tonight, probably. Because he's still in X-Ray, that's why. Because he's my friend and he needs me, Mom. I'm sorry if that bothers you, but it's true. I gotta go. No, don't call back. I'll block your calls if you don't behave. Bye."

With a grunt, Terry shoved the phone back in his pocket and then took in Mason's wide-eyed gaze. "Sorry. Didn't mean to get so loud."

"You did that?" Mason asked, his heart pounding with what could only be wonder. "For me?"

Terry smiled fondly, not a squirrel or a flippant kid or a flight risk—not for this moment. "Yeah, Mason. I'm…." He looked away. "You deserve a nice guy."

"I do, right?" Mason smiled back at him. "I've got one."

At that point the nurse called his name, and he was taken in for X-rays that hurt him possibly more than the original injury. He got to go sit in the doctor's office after that, and Terry sat with him as he was shown how to wrap the foot and told to ice it every day, because it was a sprain but it was a *bad* sprain, and he probably wouldn't be able to play soccer for another month.

"Or golf?" Mason asked plaintively.

"Or golf," the doctor confirmed. "The good news is you can probably walk short distances—like from your car to the office—in about two weeks. Can you live with that?"

Mason regarded the doctor—a genial man about his own age—with deep suspicion. "What if I said no?"

He was rewarded with a laugh. "I don't know what to tell you, Mr. Hayes. Sometimes hurts just take time to heal. But don't worry—when it's gone, it should be gone forever, so you'll be okay."

Mason nodded and tried not to pout, but he apparently fooled nobody.

"Don't be a baby," Terry told him after he'd been loaded in the car in front of the hospital. "Do what the doctor says—go home, levitate it, ice it—"

"Levitate it?" Mason had an odd vision of his legs just rising up for no reason.

"Isn't that the word he used? And do I go left or right here?"

"Left. And I think he said elevate, but I can't be sure. I thought I was the one on all the pain medication. Where did that come from?"

"Hunger," Terry said sourly, steering with muscle like the wheel was stiff. "It's almost four in the afternoon!"

Mason groaned. "That explains it. Okay—food on the way home. Your choice, I pay."

"Deal!"

And then Mason remembered that conversation at X-Ray. "So, uh, do I get you all night? For real?"

His eyes were closed against the sun through the windshield, but he heard the definite joy in the answer.

"Yeah! Yeah—I mean, she's already mad at me. It'd be stupid not to just do that. I'll stay over." His sigh gusted through the little car. "I just wish you were up to more... you know...."

"Acrobatics?" Mason supplied. "Well, don't worry. We can do plenty with me on my back, trust me." He was tired and woozy from the pain meds, but if that's what it took to get Terry to stay the night, he'd do it.

Terry made a funny little sound—half laugh, half surprise.

"Not necessary," he said after a moment. "Tell you what—I'll take you home, get some takeout—"

"Wait!" Mason checked his phone as it buzzed. "We can get something light on the way, but nothing huge. Dane's making lasagna." Aw, that was nice. "It's my favorite—we just need a snack to get us through until six."

"Oh." Terry sounded disappointed. "I can't do anything for you, really. I'm sorry."

Mason blinked and tried to come out of his wooziness. "You can get me home. You can sit next to me on the couch and help me up to bed. Don't worry, Terry—just being there counts."

They were at a light, so Terry glanced at him. "You say that like everybody thinks that," he said quietly. "Life isn't always as easy as just being there."

Mason grunted. "God, no. Trust me. I've been there my entire life— I've just never been the right person in that spot."

Terry made a wounded noise. "That's bad," he said unhappily. "If you're not the right person, how am I even going to come close?"

And in spite of the crappy day, Mason's heart twisted. "Come to my house, eat my brother's lasagna, and sit next to me on the couch," he said simply. "I swear to God, that's all I need."

Terry reached over and gently touched Mason's thigh. "That much I can do," he said.

Mason was so happy, his eyes burned. Or maybe his painkillers were wearing off—he was really too tired to tell.

THEY STOPPED for a soda and a snack, and then Mason got to sit in the recliner as master of the DVR while Dane recruited Terry to help in the kitchen. He pretended to watch a rerun of *How I Met Your Mother* when he was, in fact, listening to Dane try to tease some conversation out of Mason's squirrely houseguest.

"So, you service PIN machines?" Dane asked after he'd put Terry to work ripping up lettuce for the salad.

"Yeah. It's… well, boring. There's not much to it, usually. You check if the network is up, you check if the machine is getting power, make sure the sensors aren't gummed up. Biggest problem is that people are stupid."

Dane chuckled. "Define stupid."

"Like, 'Help me, Mr. Jefferson, sir, my machine don't work because it's ten years old and nobody can read the numbers and it only has room for a four-digit PIN and most people have a longer one than that. And no, I don't want to buy a new system, you must be working for the company, how many commissions do you get, boy, and gee, can you blow me while we're bitching at you 'cause you look pretty cute in them jeans!'"

Mason grimaced from his throne, and he heard Dane making sympathetic noises in the kitchen.

"Yeah, you're right. People are stupid. I work the emergency clinic two days a week now as part of my internship. We get these cats so infested with fleas they're sick with it, and people yelling at us for putting pesticides on their animals and how it's going to make them sicker. It's like, 'Well, you could have given your cat some flea treatment a month ago, but you didn't, did you, so stop yelling at us now!'"

"Ugh," Terry muttered. "Yeah, that's irritating. I mean, most of the time when a doctor tells you something, it's pretty important. I don't know why people suddenly think they know better when it's an animal."

Dane grunted. "'Cause sometimes the doctor is an outdated idiot. Don't trust all the people in the white coats, Jefferson—but don't blow off someone who's making sense either."

Terry's pained grunt came in loud and clear. "God, I hate it when people tell me that. I'm not that smart—sometimes I just need someone to tell me what to do!"

Mason's eyes flew open, and he remembered with feverish clarity their time in bed, and how much he'd hungered to have someone direct him, tell him it would be okay, just trust.

"Don't we all!" Dane laughed. "And it's a good thing you're dating my brother, then—he's a bossy asshole on the best of days."

It was on the tip of Mason's tongue to holler "I am *not*!" from the living room when he heard Terry stammer.

"Dating? We're not… wait—we're just playing sports together and… I mean, dating, don't you have to go on…. What's it called what we're doing, anyway?"

Oh dear.

"Dating, Jefferson. You have chosen dates and times to meet and engage in both platonic and nonplatonic activities. That's dating."

Terry's skeptical grunt echoed through the living room. "Why in the hell would your brother want to date me when he can fuck me for free?"

The sound of breaking glassware followed, and for a panicked moment Mason thought his brother had dropped the lasagna. He jerked upright, moved his swollen ankle injudiciously, and let out a sound like Snoopy getting hit in the balls.

"Alggghhh…."

"Just a glass!" Dane hollered. "Don't panic, we still have food!"

"Good to know," Mason gasped. "Could you maybe send Terry here with a glass of milk and my pain meds?" It was obviously time for another dose.

Terry came in, milk in hand, and put a Vicodin in his palm. Mason had recovered himself by then and curled his fingers around Terry's, then looked up into that wide-eyed harlequin face. He still had smudges on his cheeks from the game, although his hands were clean down to the fingernails.

"It's called dating when you want to spend time with someone," he said, holding fast when Terry tried to pull away.

"Oh God," Terry mumbled. "I didn't know you could—"

"I'm dating you because I want to spend time with you. Honestly, if we hadn't had sex yet, I would have been finding ways to be near you. So, you know, maybe remember that if someone asks." He let Terry pull away, popped the pill in his mouth, and washed it down with an angry swirl of milk.

"Never had anyone ask before," Terry said, looking miserable. "Except girls who wanted to go out."

"You ever…?" Not that he couldn't be bi, but Mason was curious.

Terry shook his head. "Not once. I mean, I don't get that much time to myself, you know? Had to be something I absolutely wanted."

Oh. Yeah, that was nice to hear. "Well, you absolutely want me. And backatcha."

He nodded, some strands from the knot of hair at his crown falling forward. Then he bent down and kissed Mason's cheek. "Your brother's real nice," he said softly. "But I think I'm getting in his way."

"You need to help him anyway," Mason told him soberly. "Helping the family in the kitchen is sort of a test."

Terry looked surprised. "Of what?"

"Whether you're willing to be part of the family," Mason told him reasonably. Ira had tried to help Janette in the kitchen all the time. She'd repeatedly turned him down because he got bossy and elitist about the food, but at least he had tried.

But the look on Terry's face was skeptical. "And that gets me…?"

"Free lasagna and cookies?"

Ah—there was the look of something clicking. "Okay, I get it now. I'll go finish up and bring you a plate."

He left and Mason went back to pretending to watch the rerun. But all Dane and Terry's conversation was based on getting dinner set up and plates full, so Mason didn't learn anything else interesting by eavesdropping, and he really *was* starving by the time food was served.

He managed to clean his plate before he fell asleep, and both Dane and Terry helped him up the stairs.

"You both may want to shower," Dane told him as they set him on the bed. "I'll go get Terry some sweats since he's more my size."

He left, and Terry darted an apologetic glance at Mason. "I sleep naked," he whispered.

"You may want underwear so your balls don't get twisted," Mason replied back, because that was why *he* always slept in boxers. Terry nodded like this was new and important information, and maybe it was the pain meds, but Mason finally realized that he'd met someone who saw life in the same terms Mason always had: how best to care for and feed that strange animal that had been born between his legs.

"You're so clever," Terry said in admiration.

Dane showed up right then with clothes, which Terry said thank you for before disappearing into the bathroom.

"You going to be able to bathe yourself?" Dane asked, concerned.

"I'll get his help if I need it," Mason replied mildly.

Dane sucked air through his teeth and pulled thoughtfully at the scruff on his chin. "Uh, Mace, he means well and he's better than pretty much any of the losers you've dated, but… uh, helping not his strong suit."

Mason grimaced. The lettuce had been torn up into really big chunks. His jersey still smelled like ranch dressing because it hadn't been easy to eat.

"We'll work on it together," he said with dignity.

"Well, here's a plastic bag. Let me rubber band it to your ankle so you can work on it together and not have the damned bandage get wet."

"D'oh!" Yeah, Mason should have thought of that.

"You're really stoned, Mace. Just don't sign anything permanent tonight, right?"

"Deed to the house is secure," Mason said soberly, and Dane rolled his eyes and patted his head.

"No more soccer for you!"

"Not true," Mason said. "We have to go. We have to cheer on the team!"

"Oh God."

"But you *like* Carpenter!" Mason was stoned, but he was also confused.

"I do. But he gets beat the hell up at those games and it's hard to watch."

Mason frowned. "Yeah, but if you give a shit, you deal with that. Why else would Terry drive me to the doctor's office and stay for lasagna?"

Dane cocked his head and wrinkled his nose. "You know it sucks how often you're right. I'm going to bed now—don't pass out before Terry gets here to help you shower. You smell like ass."

That thought alone kept him awake.

Terry came in a few minutes later, a towel wrapped around his waist. "I was going to get dressed, but then I remembered you'd need help, so guess what? We're showering naked."

Mason thought hard at his penis, but it mostly yawned and rolled over sleepily. "Goddammit," he muttered.

"Doesn't do what you wanted it to?" Terry asked sympathetically, putting his shoulder under Mason's arm. "Yeah—mine was getting all frisky when I got naked in your bathroom, and then I reminded it that you were hurt and, you know, nothing. I'm stunned. First time that thing's been quiet since I was eleven years old."

"What happened when you were eleven?" Mason asked, hopping carefully into the bathroom.

"Mikey Ingalls showed me what happened after he made his hard. It was *very* interesting, believe you me."

Mason chuckled, and he would have launched into the story of the puberty video and his social justice outrage at nine, but he needed to concentrate to undress and get under the spray.

Terry helped, undressing him in that impersonal way that people have when they're focused on something. It wasn't until Mason got under the spray that Terry's hand slid across his stomach, and then the rest of Terry climbed into the shower and plastered himself along Mason's back.

And Mason relaxed like he'd forgotten how to breathe for a week and only just now remembered.

"This is good," he said, the comfort making his chest ache. "Thank you."

"I needed it too," Terry mumbled. "You're not supposed to get hurt, Mason. Not with me."

"Anything can hurt you," Mason said, wondering if they were talking the ankle or his heart. "All you can do is take worthwhile risks." Ah, there was his business school coming out. It was nice to know it was good for *something*.

"My stupid soccer team isn't worth—"

"Friends," Mason said shortly, thinking about how everybody had gathered around him. Skipper, Carpenter, Richie, the other guys—they'd all been concerned. It was dumb animal camaraderie, and he couldn't remember ever having the rest of his herd giving that much of a shit. "You. Worth it."

"Well, if you're not healed by the end of this season, there's always another one," Terry said practically. He straightened then and grabbed the washcloth, soaping Mason's back and then his chest with brief, practical motions while Mason used both his hands to keep himself balanced in the tub.

"You ticklish?" Terry asked at one point.

"Only a little—"

"I'll go fast."

It was his only warning that the cloth was going to get personal, violate his underarms, his ribs, and then, oh God—"Eek!"

"I've got to wash your balls, Mason. They're sweaty."

"Yeah, but—oh my God!"

"Heh heh heh."

"That wasn't my balls—eeee!"

"You're cracking me up. Now let the water hit you and I'll get your legs. You really are still wearing a mud puddle."

"The water isn't going to hit any of those places you just washed," Mason said with dignity. His cock, balls, and asshole were sparkly clean, thank you very much.

"Yeah, but I might want to rinse them off with my tongue, so maybe try to make sure I'm not gagging on soap, okay?"

And just like that, Mason's penis was back online.

EVENTUALLY TERRY rinsed him off, helped him out of the tub, dried him off, and got him into boxers and a T-shirt. Terry put on a clean pair of Dane's boxers and left the T-shirt on the dresser with the sweats, and then gave Mason a hand into bed.

He set Mason up on his side, his ankle propped up with a pillow, and told him to just stay there and turn off the light. Mason was in the process of reaching above him when Terry disappeared under the covers, pulling Mason's boxers down just far enough, and his mouth…. Mm. His mouth was doing one of Mason's favorite mouth things down there with Mason's cock.

Mason couldn't move or he'd risk jostling his ankle, and he was too tired and too stoned to do more than lie there and let Terry minister to him while he moaned quietly, tugging gently on the clean strands of Terry's hair under the covers. It didn't take him long to issue a sleepy climax down Terry's throat.

Terry popped up out of the blankets then and kissed him softly, and Mason closed his eyes, falling into the kiss, and the one after that, and the one after that. When Terry pulled away, Mason was barely awake enough to grumble.

"I didn't get to do anything for—"

"I ain't never slept next to anyone all night," Terry whispered. "This is as good as sex!"

Mason groaned and pulled him tight, settling his head on Mason's shoulder. "Better," he whispered, falling asleep. "It's even better."

Balls Off the Table

TERRY GOT up once in the middle of the night to use the bathroom, and then came back and settled in Mason's arms. Mason woke up in the morning with a vicious need to pee, and Terry woke up and helped him groggily. By the time they both got back to bed, they were awake enough to talk.

"God," Terry mumbled. "I want to just stay here next to you all day."

Mason wouldn't have minded that. Terry was powerfully built but not thick—sort of like a snake or a jackrabbit, where every ounce of weight was put into muscle. And he fit against Mason's chest, and his ribs, like a puzzle piece cut just for him.

"I wish you could," Mason said back. "Can you?"

"Well, what did you have planned?" Terry regarded him with sleepy eyes.

"Dane and I were going to try to repaint the guest bedroom. It's heinously ugly because we fucked up green last week, and we want another try."

Terry grunted. "I got no idea how you could fuck up green. That's probably a rich people's thing."

"No, I think it's a that-color's-uglier-than-dog-puke thing. What was your day going to be?"

"Nungh." Terry burrowed closer into his chest.

"That's not a good answer."

"It's stupid. I just… I mean, you and Dane were painting last week, and you showed me pictures, and I realized that you could change your house, and I got this stupid wild hair—"

Mason was waking up a little now and suddenly terribly interested in what he'd had planned. "What sort of wild hair?"

"God, Mason, it's so embarrassing. My mom got her house from her parents and hasn't done squat with it. The place has this, like, shitty yard out back, and it's all overgrown weeds and shit, and junk and snakes probably and mosquito puddles and…. God, it's a fucking jungle."

"You were going to clean it out?" Mason asked, intrigued. He'd never cleared out a jungle before. "I can help."

"You can not, moron—you sprained your ankle. You could watch me, and that's embarrassing."

"I could direct," Mason said grandly, suddenly liking this idea very much. "And I'm not your only option for help, you know. Maybe call Skipper and Richie, offer them some beer, call the other guys on the team."

"Today?"

Oh yeah—a bit much to do at the last minute.

"Next week," Mason yawned. "Today, let's go back to sleep for an hour. When we wake up, maybe we can get Dane to go out for doughnuts."

"I'll glaze *your* doughnut," Terry chuckled wickedly.

And then he fell asleep.

DANE WOKE them up an hour later with doughnuts and a big glass of milk to share. Mason struggled to sit, and Terry sacrificed all his pillows to prop Mason up.

"So," Dane said when they were all settled, "what are we doing today?"

"I gotta go home soon," Terry said apologetically before biting into a chocolate glazed. He chewed and swallowed blissfully. "Well, maybe in an hour."

"While you're here, we should plan cleaning out your mom's backyard," Mason said, suddenly excited about having another home improvement project.

"Is this before or after we fix the guest room?" Dane asked skeptically, and Mason shrugged.

"It's only green?"

"No, it's not only green. It's the green that makes ogre barf look beautiful and pure, you asshole. Are you telling me we have to live with that for another two weeks?"

Mason tried to do that begging-with-his-eyes thing that Terry was so adept at, but Dane was the baby brother and as such was apparently immune.

Terry finished off his doughnut and looked up to see the eyeball standoff still underway. "Uh, so, how long will it take to repaint this disaster?" he asked cautiously.

Dane smiled at him with pointy teeth. "Well, if you set up while I'm at Lowe's getting a better color, probably two hours."

"That is way underestimating," Mason warned. "It took us all last Sunday."

"Yeah, but the tarps are still down because we saw it dry and tried not to hurl," Dane retorted. "I swear, if Terry can fix the tape up while I go get any other fucking color but that one, it won't take that long at all."

"Fine," Mason said, in prime negotiations mode. "You do that—*but* you have to plan the work party for Terry's yard next week. We need six people besides me—"

"You're sitting on a folding chair and supervising!" Terry protested.

Mason grunted. "Well, okay. So you two—"

"Carpenter," Dane supplied.

"Carpenter," Mason conceded. "And Skip and Richie and—"

"Anyone else I can get Carpenter to ask," Dane finished. "Deal. What will we need?"

Both of them turned toward Terry, who was in the middle of his second doughnut.

"Are you naked?" Dane asked into the sudden silence.

Terry looked down at his bare torso, and Mason watched as a flush traveled up his stomach, outward from his pectorals, and liberally splashed his neck and ears. "I've got boxers on," he mumbled, taking another bite of doughnut. In the pause afterward, his nipples pebbled, and Mason choked back a smirk—and on the temptation to scope out his crotch to see if anything else perked up.

"Work party," Mason rasped. God, they'd slept together all night, and he'd been so stoned he hadn't been able to *fuck*. The unfairness of that seemed overwhelming right now. "We need to plan the work party."

"Yeah," Dane said, looking pointedly at the desk in Mason's room—so, pointedly *away* from Mason's sort-of boyfriend. "What will we need?"

"Uh, work gloves?" Terry forgot his sudden embarrassment. "Work gloves, jeans, boots—God knows what's back there. We need something to cut back the weeds and shit—"

"Pruning shears and a Weedwacker," Mason supplied.

"Yeah—we don't got none of that. And I don't know where we're going to put all the shit—"

"Rent a dumpster," Dane said, ticking it off on his fingers.

"Sustenance," Mason said seriously. "Dane and I can bring a big thermos of coffee and doughnuts—"

"And pizza and beer for later," Dane agreed.

"Wait!" Terry burst out, suddenly panicky. "Guys, we can't all go tramping into my mom's house. She'll shit her pants!"

Mason shrugged. "We'll set up outside—"

"But it's cold!"

"That's what the coffee is for." Mason didn't see the problem. "And if it gets too cold, we'll let people go out on errands in the heated cars. Honestly, Terry, as long as guys can get into the bathroom to take a leak, I think it'll be okay."

Terry frowned at him, eyebrows working like a small dog's. "You know, if everyone shows up to do something nice for us, fuck her if she can't deal, right?"

Well, that was a little harsh, but if that's what it took to launch Terry into home and possibly life improvement? "Sure." Mason nodded. "And you know, if you want to maybe try to get her to go to a friend's house or something, we could be done before she even knew we were there."

Terry's eyes widened until they were practically an animated forest creature's eyes. "That would be the best thing ever," he breathed. "Let's do *that*."

Mason and Dane nodded enthusiastically. "Deal!" Dane said. "So, we all have jobs to do there, and you and me have jobs to do today. Mason, I'm going to put the doughnuts downstairs while you dress, and then *you're* going to go lay on the guest room bed and *I'm* going to get out the tape and the brushes for Terry. Are we all planned out?"

Terry grabbed his third doughnut. "Five more minutes," he said before washing his bite down with milk. "Ab banks bor be bobuth."

Dane looked into the woefully depleted box, which he'd probably hoped would last him at least until the next day, when he had to leave at six in the morning so he could get to Davis and park by eight. "Anytime," he said philosophically. He stood up, grabbed the box and their milk glass, and left to go get the folding chair and tape, leaving Terry to get Mason dressed and ready.

MASON WAS in the middle of explaining to Terry how to tape the border between paint colors—and how to anchor the tarps to make sure the carpet and the bed didn't get spattered—when Terry's phone rang in his pocket.

Mason was sort of depressed that Terry had been able to use Mason's cord to charge it when he saw the look on Terry's face when he answered.

"Yeah, Mom. No, won't be gone all day. Be home in a couple of hours. Helping my friend with his house—painting his guest bedroom, actually." Terry listened for a moment and grunted like she'd reached out and smacked him. "Because they're nice and they made dinner for me. No, I don't feel taken advantage of. Not *here* at any rate. No—I'll come home when we're done. Because. Because they're helping me do something next week. No, it's not expensive, and if it is, I'll pay. Because. Because. Because it needs to be done. Because I said so, Mom, and I'm paying rent. Yeah, that does too give me the right to talk to you like that—I'm trying to get friends to help us fix our house. Please, Mom, don't be awful about it. Well that's fine. You go where you gotta go when it's happening. No, I'm totally serious. We don't need you there to supervise. We've got Mason. Yeah, he'll still be hurt—that's why he's supervising. You know what? I'm done. I'll be home around one. Bye."

He shoved the phone in his pocket and met Mason's look of sympathy with something so naked and pitiful that Mason held out his arms.

To his surprise, Terry rushed into them. "You must think I'm dumb," he mumbled against Mason's chest.

"No!" Mason held him tight, not even arguing that the chair was probably going to collapse under their weight. "I think she's awful, but that's not your fault."

Terry held him tighter. "It's so embarrassing," he said, the admission obviously costing him. "I hate that she gets to do that. She calls me up and I've got to go running."

"You didn't this weekend," Mason pointed out, wanting so much for that to become the norm.

Terry looked up from his chest and smiled. Tears spiked his lashes into a star, and his face was blotchy from rubbing up against Mason's chest. "That's right," he said proudly. "I didn't."

"Nope. And you made plans for next weekend."

Terry shrugged. "Yeah, but I've made breaks for it before," he warned. "She bitched about Disneyland for a year."

Mason hated to suggest it, but oh! He felt good in Mason's arms. "Moving out?"

"Yeah." The word came out as a sigh. An agreement. A prayer. "I wanna. I keep thinking, you know. You put this idea in my head. We get the house fixed up so it's not embarrassing. Make it so someone else would want to live there with her. Or she could sell it. And then I can get an apartment or something." He closed his eyes for a second, smiling. "Go to soccer, stay out with you. Go out to beers with my friends after work. Not having to worry. Or explain myself to her."

He looked up at Mason, his eyes big and trusting. "I could spend an entire day in bed with you."

Mason's groin started to tingle, and he groaned. "Really? You mention that *now*?"

Terry laughed a little and stepped back, wiping his eyes on his shoulder.

"Yeah—this weekend sucked without sex. You think your ankle'll be up to it next weekend?"

"As long as we stay on the bed, I think it's okay."

Terry backed away and turned toward the wall he'd been taping. "Sex on a bed is pretty sweet," he agreed. "First time I got it up the butt, I was in a car, and lube was not to be found. Telling you, having shit handy—and a *bathroom*—that's living right there."

Mason could either be appalled or he could laugh. He laughed, because Terry was going to clean out his mother's backyard next weekend, and he was going to work to be free.

And he wanted to keep having sex in a bed.

"DID WE have ourselves some adventures, sir?"

Mrs. Bradford, as always, looked impeccable—even as she raked Mason over with her eyes, taking in the bandage and the crutches and the scuff on the cheek that he'd gotten when he'd toppled into the mud puddle.

"We played soccer with Schipperke's team," Mason replied, taking her clipboard from her to see what he needed to sign. "Results were… mixed."

"I don't have the MBA, sir," she said, voice like toast. "You'll have to explain to me the difference between 'mixed' and 'disastrous.'"

Mason pursed his lips. "Well, disastrous would have been if I'd sprained my ankle and he'd left me to rot. Mixed is when I sprain my ankle and he rides to my rescue in his dying vehicle, and then stays the night and helps my brother paint the guest room in the morning."

"Hm," she considered. "Given what I know of your love life, Mr. Hayes, why is this not a triumph along the lines of the stage play *Hamilton*?"

Mason gave her a side-eyed glare that bothered her not at all. "Because. He's still attached to his mother. And when he becomes *unattached* to his mother, he's going to need to figure out why he's so attached to *me*. I don't want to be his father figure, Mrs. Bradford. For one thing, that's icky. For another, it's…." He thought about the terrifying, exciting freefall of sex and desire he felt with Terry, and his face fell. "Heartbreaking," he finished weakly.

"Ah," Mrs. Bradford said softly. "So I don't believe any platitudes about loving something and setting it free would help here?"

Mason sighed. "Well, since it's not love and he's not free yet, they might be a bit premature."

"I shall file them handily away, sir."

"How very forward-thinking of you, Mrs. Bradford. So tell me, on a scale of one to ten, one being comatose and ten being a day in the park with a Frisbee, how awful are my appointments today?"

"I would rate your day a solid 1.5, Mr. Hayes. But given that you are not likely to be throwing a Frisbee for the next week—"

"Month," Mason corrected.

"Good Lord—from *soccer*? Well, fine. Given that playing in the park on a sunny day is not an option in any sense of the word, how about I bring you some coffee and you can feel productive and proud of your work ethic."

Not. Promising.

"Sounds awesome! Bring on the day!"

"Yessir."

"But, uh, Mrs. Bradford?"

"Yessir?"

"Could we maybe invite Schipperke and his friend Carpenter in for lunch so I don't get tempted to gnaw on my wrist?"

"I'll order Thai food."

"Thanks, Mrs. Bradford. Carry on."

"So," Skipper said, dumping his rice on his plate like Mason had showed him last time, "we're doing a work party at Jefferson's on Sunday? Well, beats the hell out of ripping out my kitchen linoleum and painting the whole damned thing. Richie's over the moon."

"Right?" Carpenter took some pad thai and then started adding red curry. "Working on someone else's place is always so much better than working on your own. 'Cause when you're done, you're like, 'Oh, hey! I helped do this!' and then you go home! But when you work on your own place, you're like, 'Oh, look—I have sixty zillion other things to do to make it all work like I want it to!' So, yeah. Other people's houses are the best."

Mason had never thought about that. "Well, I'm just glad he helped Dane paint over ogre-barf green this weekend."

Carpenter looked up. "What color did you decide on? He showed me that shit last week—I gotta tell you, I've never seen green look so bad!"

"We went with navy," Mason told him. "It's hard to fuck that up, and hey, it's a guest room and guests can't afford to be picky and say, 'You know, navy is as boring as hell and I don't want to live here anymore.'"

"True that," Skipper said.

"Yeah, but you and Richie still need to get to the kitchen," Carpenter said. "It looks like the seventies changed a diaper in there."

Mason almost snorted curried rice up his nose, and then, given the color, was just as glad he hadn't.

"Which is why we eat in the living room," Skip said. "And that reminds me." He looked up at Mason. "Tell your little brother that we're doing pizza and video games this Friday, my house. You're welcome too, but Dane's a genius at it."

"You guys play over the… the whatsit? The PS4?" Mason felt old.

"Yeah, Mace, the PS4," Carpenter said seriously. "You know, maybe you want to bring Jefferson."

For a moment Mason thought about it—hanging out at Skip's, watching Terry be young and excited about video games someplace he was a little more comfy in than Mason's house. Then—

"If Terry can get away from his mother Friday night, I'd just as soon stay at my place and get laid," he said frankly, and then wished for a bunker to hide in, or an emergency call, or the president of Tesko to run in saying, "Mason Hayes, help us, you're the only executive who can!" because that was exactly the sort of thing that didn't get him invited to dinner parties. Ever.

He winced and looked at his two lunch companions.

Who kept eating their lunch.

"Dude, sounds totally legit to me," Carpenter said, nodding sagely.

"Can't blame you a bit," Skipper agreed. "Carpenter didn't even see me on the weekends when Richie and I were dating."

"Yeah I did. You roped me into your weird soccer cult, remember?" Carpenter didn't look put out much as he munched steadily through his brown rice and pad thai.

Skip smiled. "Yeah, but you like it. I'm just saying—getting laid sort of trumps hanging out and playing video games, and if it doesn't, I think you're doing shit wrong." He nodded soberly, and Mason took another bite of lunch.

All things considered, he was starting to wonder if he'd been hanging out with the wrong people his entire life. Either way, he was sort of glad he'd discovered the right people now.

MASON KEPT on a good face, but fact was, his ankle was killing him by the end of Monday. It hadn't let up by Thursday, so Dane made him stay home during practice. They were both surprised when they heard Terry's car in the driveway.

Terry knocked on the door, carrying a tray of coffees with cookies to go with them.

"Not homemade," he apologized as Dane let him in and gestured him to the front room.

"But very appreciated," Mason told him. Coffee was going to keep him up until the small hours of the morning and make his Friday a living hell, but Mason didn't give a shit. They'd been texting desultorily that week, and Mason was getting disheartened.

God, he was starting to live for Terry's pretty brown eyes and unpredictable smile, but he wasn't sure—not really—whether Terry liked him just as much.

Coffee and cookies at eight o'clock at night just might mean he did.

"You got sad," Terry said bluntly, sitting down next to him on the couch and handing him his coffee and cookie. "In text. You got sad. Needed to make sure you were okay."

"I'll be in my room," Dane announced, grabbing his own coffee and cookies. "I need to study. And watch old Tom Hanks/Meg Ryan movies. It's a moral imperative." He swanned out, and Terry settled back into the couch and sort of muscled himself under Mason's arm.

Mason took the hint and leaned back, arm around his shoulders, savoring his heat.

"I miss you during the week," he confessed, balancing his cookie. Terry took it from him, opened the cellophane wrapper, and fed him a bite. With a wash of coffee to swallow it down, it was perfect.

"I'm starting to miss you too," Terry said moodily, feeding him another bite of cookie. "I don't remember missing someone before. It chafes like jeans when it's too hot."

"Not comfortable," Mason agreed when he washed down that bite too.

"I cover stores in your area tomorrow for service," he said abruptly. "How 'bout I bring you lunch tomorrow at one. Good?"

Mason couldn't have stopped his smile if he'd tried. "It'll get me through the day," he said.

"It's only sandwiches. I'll text you when I'm in line, okay?"

Mason clutched him a little tighter, relieved when he didn't wriggle to get away. For some reason Mason had been expecting a squirrel. He was surprised when he got a man instead.

"Mason?"

"Yeah?"

"Don't I get a kiss for bringing you dessert?"

Mason smiled into his harlequin face and some of the fear in his heart reknit itself into hope. Leaning carefully, he put his coffee down while Terry put the rest of the cookie down on the table in front of them. "God, yes."

Sweet. His mouth tasted like coffee and cookies, and as Mason kissed him harder, longer, languorously, the two of them melting into the couch and mindful of Mason's ankle, Mason was continuously recognizing the difference. Not a squirrel. Not a child. A man. Terry's hands on his chest knew what they were doing, and his kisses—slow and drugging—made Mason sob for breath.

Terry shoved his hands under Mason's shirt and rubbed him, simply feeding his skin hunger, until Mason ground up against him in frustration—and accidentally tweaked his ankle and let out an unmanly yelp.

"Oh!" Terry sat up. "Oh no!"

"We have to stop?" Mason whined, only partly because his ankle hurt.

"Yes, dammit. A bed—you said a bed would work, and this isn't." Terry scowled at him, and his pocket buzzed, and he sighed. "I have to go anyway." He leaned forward and kissed Mason on the forehead. "I just needed to see you. It was good seeing you. Not enough, but good." He pulled back and Mason read his eyes again: begging for it to be enough.

"Can you stay the night Saturday?" Mason pleaded.

Terry grinned shyly. "Yeah. Yeah, I think I can, if I can leave early Sunday to get my mom to her friend's before you all come over."

Mason's stomach uncoiled a tiny bit more. "We can do that," he promised.

Terry took his mouth then, hard and brief, a man's kiss, before tearing off for the door.

Mason was left staring at the door long after he'd let himself out, harboring an almost forlorn hope that someday, Terry would unleash that same tiger who'd just kissed him stupid, and Mason would finally get to bottom.

"ARE YOU sure he's coming, sir?" Mrs. Bradford asked.

Mason looked at his phone and nodded, trying not to yawn. Dane had apparently found the YouTube channel of his dreams this past week, because he'd woken Mason up every night giggling at his computer.

Okay, time to make a decision. His phone said *There by 1:00.* It was 1:05, and Mrs. Bradford was about to go out to lunch herself. She knew Mason ate at his desk sometimes, and since he hadn't brought anything, she was offering to bring him back something just in case.

He was just about to tell her to get him a sandwich that he could take home if he didn't eat it when he got a text from Skipper.

Jefferson's downstairs—security thinks he's lost.

Oh shit.

I'm omw—tell him I'm coming.

WAIT! He's embarrassed. Just tell security to lead him up here.

Oh hell. Mason picked up the in-house extension and talked to the security guy downstairs. Mike sounded dubious, but he agreed to escort the guy with the takeout up to the fifth floor of the building and to Mason's office.

"He's on his way," Mason said happily, and Mrs. Bradford raised her eyebrows.

"Mike's not a very good security guard," she said bluntly. "He is, in fact, the reason people make fun of them."

True on both counts. Out of shape, lazy, and clearly happier playing with his phone than actually making sure everyone who got through the front doors of Tesko belonged there, Mike Buford was not an exemplary employee by any stretch of the imagination.

"And your point is?" Mason asked hesitantly. He knew where this was going.

"Why wouldn't he let your friend in the door?"

A knock sounded, and Mason stood up and hopped one-footed to the door, gesturing Terry inside. He was wearing cargo shorts and a tank top (it was forty-two degrees outside) with a baseball hat on backward, and tennis shoes.

He grimaced apologetically at Mason and then looked around the office. "Oh geez," he said, taking in the wood paneling and the cream-colored carpets. Mason's furniture was standard Tesko issue—pine with sort of a salmon-and-green color for the cushions—but Mason had gotten to order from the catalog, and he'd chosen the most comfortable chairs he could. The desks were a nice warm camel color, and the varnish was the deep expensive kind that resisted cracking.

Mason liked his office, but he didn't think much about it.

Apparently Terry couldn't think of anything else.

"Thanks, Mike," Mason said quietly, waving off Mike's attempt to explain why he'd detained a friend of one of the VPs. "Terry, this is Mrs. Bradford. She should actually be making all the big money, because without her, I couldn't do my job. Mrs. Bradford, Terry Jefferson."

Terry turned around from his contemplation of a seascape—one that Mason had actually chosen—and smiled at Mrs. Bradford tentatively.

"Uh, nice to meet you?" Oh hells. He was really nervous—and so uncertain.

"It's a pleasure to meet you," she said, inclining her head regally. "Mr. Hayes, since you seem to be eating, I'll take myself out to my own lunch hour."

"Thanks, Mrs. Bradford enjoy."

"Mr. Bradford is meeting me," she said, and for Lillian Bradford, her expression was almost girlish.

She left and closed the door, and Terry looked around disconsolately. "This is really nice," he muttered. "They almost didn't let me in through the door."

Mason grimaced at him. "You're cold," he said at last, and used his hand to balance on the chair in front of his desk while he hopped closer.

Terry bridged the gap, and Mason rubbed Terry's arms with his palms. "Why don't you ever wear a sweater?"

Terry smiled hesitantly at him. "I just never remember," he said after a moment. "I remember yours most often, but it needed to be washed, and I forgot to get it out of the dryer."

Mason wrapped his arms around Terry's shoulders and pulled him against Mason's chest. "I'll keep you warm," he said, and then he remembered his gym bag in the far corner of the room. He'd had to have Skip go get it out of his locker in the company gym that morning because he didn't want to just leave it there over another weekend. "Or better yet— here, help me balance; I left the damned crutch back at the table." He held out his hand, but Terry rolled his eyes.

"You sit and eat, I'll fetch and carry." He helped Mason into the closest chair—*not* the one behind the desk—and then went to grab the bag.

"Just unzip it—there's a sweatshirt in the top," he said, setting up the sandwiches, chips, and sodas on napkins. "These look good. Where are they from again?"

"Mr. Pickles." Terry came back wearing Mason's green track jacket zipped up to his neck. It was too big and did nothing to change the criminal waif vibe that had so freaked out Mike Buford, but at least he was warm. "Are you happy now?" he asked, leaning over Mason's shoulder to switch the sandwiches. "I got you the teriyaki chicken, and I've got the pastrami with cream cheese."

Mason closed his eyes and shuddered. That sounded heavenly. "Probably a good idea," he conceded. "I'm going to be fat at the end of the month."

Terry dragged another chair so they were sitting knee to knee. He unwrapped his sandwich while studying Mason's face curiously. "That wouldn't be so bad," he said after a moment. "Your chin won't disappear. I'd still do ya." He grinned then and took a bite of his sandwich.

Mason bit his lip, a little shy because from Terry that was damned near poetry. "Well good," he said after a moment of feeling dumb. "Because my ankle will be up to some *really* rocking sex by the time the month is done."

Terry's eyes went to half-mast—in slow motion. It was like watching a squirrel turn into a napping panther. "I *really* want to get you into a bed again," he said, voice all breath.

Mason swallowed. *I will not give him a blow job in my office. I like this job and I want to keep it.* "Yeah. Uh, so tomorrow night? After the game and beer and pizza?"

"Yeah?" The jungle cat went away, and Terry looked around the office furtively. "I, uh… doesn't take a genius to figure you have better choices than beer and pizza."

Heat crept up Mason's face. "The furniture is really ugly."

Terry bounced. "But comfy!" he said, but his acknowledgment that this wasn't his usual lunch digs was still there.

Mason turned and took a bite of his sandwich. "This is pretty good," he said. "I've never heard of this place."

"It's local." Terry unwrapped his own sandwich uncertainly, but Mason didn't know what to tell him. It was just an office. Nothing about it was as awesome as having someone who would bring him lunch for no other reason than awkward conversation.

"I don't know any of the good local places," he admitted. "In the Bay Area, I knew all the cool places to eat. I… I knew where to bring a date to impress him, and I used to read all these magazines for new places to try."

Terry looked more disheartened with every word. "I… I like my basic places. Mr. Pickles. I get a number fifteen every time."

Mason nodded. "Yeah. See, me and Dane—we've been getting used to it here. And… we like it. I mean, once in a while, I wouldn't mind going down to San Francisco to do something fun, but… most of the time, living your life, if I'm having fun doing the basic stuff, then that's all I really want."

The rigid set of Terry's shoulders relaxed, and he picked up his sandwich and took a bite. "I could probably use some horizon expanding," he admitted when he'd swallowed. "I mean… my whole life has been in this town."

"I've never been with someone who liked to travel," Mason said. "Ira's idea of a good time was a cruise."

"That's traveling!" Terry laughed.

"That's traveling snail style," Mason muttered. "You're taking the whole world with you. I sort of want to backpack through Europe one day. I mean, I speak some French—"

"I speak Spanish pretty good," Terry said brightly.

Mason looked at him adoringly. "That's amazing. I only speak a little bit of French from school. I was never very good at it."

"Well, I took it in high school, but I work with a lot of guys who speak it. It's probably not, you know, Spain Spanish, but I can get us to the bathrooms, right?"

"Totally necessary," Mason agreed, taking a chip. "That's what I know too. So we're set. Trip to Europe, a definite possibility." His mouth went dry as he suddenly thought of a more attainable goal. "After you come home with me on Saturday and spend the night."

Terry turned his head sideways from his sandwich. "Would you really take me to Europe? I'm not…." His gaze swiveled around the office again. "Uh, European."

Mason reached out with a napkin and got a dollop of cream cheese from the corner of Terry's mouth. Terry caught hold of his hand and met his eyes.

"I think we could be European together," Mason said through a dry throat.

"I'm not rich, Mason," Terry said after a charged moment. "I thought it was just money, but the more we do this, the more I'm getting it. It's the good health insurance and an office that looks too good to let me in it and a secretary who looks like she'd peck my eyes out if I moved wrong. I… you were nice. You were funny. You were a big, goofy moron on the soccer field and I just…." He dropped Mason's hand. "I wanted you. I didn't know what I was doing."

"I did," Mason told him, his heart crumbling. "I knew what you were doing. You think I'm funny. Nobody thinks I'm funny, Terry. I've got a long, disappointing history of guys who begged me to shut up before they had to admit they knew me. You think I'm nice. I… I know a lot of guys who wouldn't even put that on their list of things to care about. I wanted you too. I mean…." Oh, how embarrassing, to talk about talking about sex. "I want to talk about sex all the time. I want to *have* sex—with you!—all the time. And… nobody—I mean *nobody*—I've ever met actually made that a priority. You gave me a blow job when I was recovering from a doctor's visit. It was exactly what I needed. Not one guy has ever given me exactly what I needed without stealing my wallet when he was done."

Terry's eyes widened. "True story?"

"Sadly yes. But you're missing the point."

"The point is if I can't get away from my mother to make love in a bed, I'm not much of a catch," Terry said practically. "So yeah. I'll stay the night. I'll leave early to clear her out, and then you and the soccer team can come and help me with my stupid bullshit house thing."

Mason's heart stopped crumbling and started beating again. "That is the best plan I've ever heard."

Terry took a swig of his soda. "I can see why you needed to move here," he said after a minute. "Those people where you lived, they were probably all right folks. But they weren't yours."

"No," Mason said, blinking rapidly. "You're my people."

"Yup. Wanna bite? I promise I won't kick you outta bed for being fat." He held out his sandwich, and Mason took a salty dreamy bite of heaven.

"Mm...."

"Here. Let's trade halves. I got you my second-favorite one, so that'll work."

They did, and when their gourmet lunch was once again situated on white butcher paper, Mason grinned at him. "Best lunch ever," he said, meaning it.

Terry glanced at him shyly and looked away. "Yeah. I should bring you lunch more often. Fridays good?"

"Fridays great."

Oh God. Fridays great. He had a standing lunch date. For a brief shining sandwich, Mason was as happy as he'd been as a kid, when all of sex loomed ahead of him and the grown-up world held untold promise of glory.

Sexy Saturday

"DANE, YOU need to get up," Mason said patiently.

"Ma-son!" Dane huddled deeper into the blankets.

"Dane, man, we're going to miss the game. It starts at ten."

"Go without me," Dane whined, pulling the covers over his head. "Nobody will miss me."

Mason scowled. Uh-oh. "Carpenter will miss you," he said, hating himself for using Carpenter when he might be rancid bait.

"Carpenter can't be there," Dane mumbled. "His sister is in town, and he has to go spend the day with her kids."

Ah. "Well, Skip and Richie are your friends too." Which should concern Mason—Dane didn't seem to be making friends at Davis. His first two quarters had produced good grades, but it felt like Dane was making a sojourn of penance every time he left the house.

Dane turned his head fractionally on the pillow. "They're probably not talking to me," he confessed, eyes closed against something he was imagining from the video game gathering the night before. Mason had spent the night on his bed, watching old movies while reading porn. He didn't know how the movies ended, but the evening had ended just fine.

"What did you say?" Mason asked, curious. So far he'd discovered his new peer group was pretty hard to offend.

Dane groaned and covered his face with his hands. "I told Skip that when he went back to school and got his real degree, he'd know how much bullshit there was in the school system."

Mason winced. Tacky, yes, but not irreparable. Mason had said way worse things. "What did Skip say?"

"That he was afraid of the cost, not the bullshit," Dane muttered, hands still over his eyes. "God, was I a dick?"

Mason thought about it. "No. Not a dick. He's not going to hate you for one thing."

"Yes, he will."

"No, he won't."

"Yes, he will! He's Carpenter's best buddy, and now I've pissed him off and Carpenter will never speak to me again!"

Mason remembered these discussions from when Dane was in high school—the impossible pile of mental crap that Dane had obsessed over and cycled around in his head and cried over when it never seemed to stop. For years Mason and his family wrote this off as just Dane, hypersensitive Dane, spazzing out about stupid shit until he couldn't think.

It hadn't been until that trip to the psych ward, Dane lying in a fetal curl, sobbing about how he'd ruined his life by refusing a movie invitation, that it had hit Mason—and their parents: this was how Dane's brain worked.

The blessing was Dane—happy, joyous, brilliant, enthusiastic *Dane*.

The drawback was Dane obsessing over the smallest perceived imperfection until he lost his ability to function.

Not on Mason's watch.

"He will too speak to you again," Mason said brusquely. "And you know what? It's only eight o'clock. You should call him up and have him bring his niece and nephew to watch him play—"

"He didn't want them to see him hauling his fat ass around the field!" Dane said, eyes open now—and bright and red-rimmed.

Augh!

"He'll be there," Mason promised rashly. "He'll fucking be there. Now get your ass out of bed and shower. I'm going next and you know I'll take all the hot water when I do."

Fucking ankle. It made a trip across the hall feel like a trek through the goddamned Sahara, without a friendly camel.

"Really?" Dane asked hesitantly, sitting up.

"Dane," Mason vowed, lowering his voice and trying not to yell. "I will get Carpenter to the field if you do two things for me."

"Shower and make coffee?" Dane asked hopefully, looking away.

"Shower and tell me if you've been remembering your meds."

Dane's grimace told Mason plenty.

"Why not?" Mason asked, keeping his voice even.

"'Cause I don't want to be a fucking freak who can't function without them!" Dane shouted.

"You're not a fucking freak, you're my baby brother!" Mason shouted back, feeling his eyes burn. Dammit, he'd *seen* it happening. Dane being moody, Dane being manic, Dane giggling to himself until the wee hours of the night over something on YouTube.

This was the other side.

"Dane, I'm going to call Carpenter right now. If you're not out of bed by the time I get back, I'm throwing you over my shoulder and chucking you in the goddamned shower!"

"You can't do that!" Dane said, sitting up in bed but keeping the covers over his ears. He looked like a nun. "You've got a sprained ankle! You can hardly walk!"

"Well it won't be a picnic for either of us!" Mason snarled, but inside, he was relieved. If Dane was worried about him, it meant Mason might be able to get him out of bed—and get him to take his meds. The next couple of days were going to be rough, though. The whole thing was about keeping the levels of medication in Dane's bloodstream even. Dane *knew* that, but school had been taking most of his attention, and sometimes, dammit, someone forgot.

Or got proud and didn't want to accept help anymore. Even from the medicine that sustained his reality.

"Fine," Dane snapped back, throwing the covers back. He was fully clothed from the night before, which was *not* a good sign.

"Fine!" Mason yelled, scrubbing his face with his hand. "I'll be back in ten minutes to check on you, and Carpenter will be on his way to the game!"

"He will not, because he hates me," Dane groused, but there didn't seem to be any passion behind it, so Mason one-crutched his way to his bedroom for his phone.

He sat down for a blessed second while he hit the number and was not surprised when Carpenter sounded as out of it as Dane had.

"Mason?" he grumbled. "Why?"

"Look, can your niece and nephew come and watch you play soccer?" Mason asked abruptly. "Please? Dane forgot his fucking meds and you're my carrot on the stick."

"What?" But he sounded awake now. "Why would he—"

"You'll have to ask him. But he needs to get up and take his meds and try not to overdose on the self-loathing today. And he needs to see you because he loves you." Oh shit.

"Loves me how?" Carpenter asked, but not like he was suspicious or the earth moved or he was afraid.

"Does it matter?" Mason asked, suddenly defeated. "Does it matter how he loves you? No. What matters is that you're the one person in the world he will get out of bed for today."

Of course Mason saw the flaw in this logic. Dane needed to get out of bed for himself—that was the ultimate in goals. But that wasn't going to happen until he got his levels back.

"No, it doesn't matter," Carpenter said, not sounding muzzy. "Course I'll be there if he needs it. That's what you do."

Oh God. He didn't say "that's what friends do," but he didn't say "that's what you do when you love someone" either. Goddammit, Carpenter, specificity was more than gravity!

"Okay," Mason replied, giving up. "Good. And while we're on what you do for someone, you need to not bitch about fat, okay?"

"What?"

Mason hit his forehead with the heel of his hand. "Don't say things about how ugly you are running around fat. It depresses him, Carpenter. You're the best friend he's had since grade school. I don't know why—you two were love at first sight, I was there. But when you bitch about your weight, it fucking weighs him down. So bring your niece and nephew, and I'll watch them from the gimpy corner, and you go run your heart out."

"Wow," Carpenter said wonderingly. "It's like hearing my mom, but I don't resent you nearly as much."

"I'll take that as a compliment," Mason said with a grunt. "See you on the field."

He pushed himself up from the bed and decided to let his hot water depletion wake them both up. The less he had to hop, the better.

THEY GOT to the field an hour later, showered, dressed warmly, caffeinated, fed, and, thank the gods, drugged. Mason had taken his pain pill, Dane had taken his medication, and they were able to greet the team with high fives and smiles when they came to the sidelines after warming up. Terry grinned shyly at Mason as they all huddled in a circle, and Mason winked back.

Terry was wearing Mason's hooded sweatshirt today, his hands hidden in the overlong sleeves. The stocking cap from their day golfing was tucked snugly around his ears, and Mason's heart gave a poignant throb. Mason could take care of Terry. He seemed to have fucked up with Dane, but Terry, at least, was warm and happy with the world today.

The guys shed their sweatshirts, and Terry came over to hand his to Mason. "You're sitting down, right?" he asked, glancing over to where Dane was setting up two camp chairs next to two tow-headed children on tiny Disney pop-up stools. Carpenter had run over there after the break and was apparently introducing everybody.

"Yeah." Mason nodded. "Kids. I'm not great at them, but they're Dane's favorite people."

Terry grinned at him, and Mason pulled a grin out of his toes to give back.

Terry's face fell. "What's wrong?" he asked, puzzled, voice dropping.

Oh. Oh no. Mason wasn't prepared for that. "This morning was… rough," he said quietly. "Dane forgot his meds for a couple of days. The next week is going to be a bumpy ride."

Terry nodded thoughtfully. "Can I still… do you still want me to come over?" he asked, his eyes shadowed.

Mason's jaw was tight and so was his throat. "Oh God, yes," he said, wanting to hold somebody so badly. "Dane and Carpenter are going to spend the whole day with the kids. I think Dane might even be going over to meet Carpenter's parents. We have the place to ourselves."

Terry cackled, running backward to join his team. "You could put a rock band in the living room and still have your place to ourselves." He turned around and trotted forward then, leaving Mason to make his slow way to the chairs.

When he arrived and sat down, Dane covered him up with a bright orange fleece blanket emblazoned with *Giants*, which they used when they caught a game at AT&T Park. Tucked into the cup holder was a venti caramel latte, which, along with gloves, helped keep Mason's hands warm.

"Do you have everything?" Dane asked soberly. "Are you as snug as a sultan in a swing?"

Mason shook his head. "I'm great," he said. "I'll have to pee in a few minutes—then we're in trouble—but other than that, well done!"

"Good to know," Dane said. He looked at the little girl on the other side of him. "What do you say, Holly-bell? Will you have to go to the bathroom in a minute?"

Holly-bell regarded Mason with unfriendly brown eyes. "No. Not with him."

Mason arched an eyebrow at Dane, who shrugged. "Well, we can go as a group," he said diplomatically. "Jason, do you have to pee?"

"How come she's Holly-bell and I'm just Jason?" he asked, way too surly for one so young.

"Would you like to be Jason-llama?" Dane asked, his rather wonderful mind pulling that from thin air.

"What's a llama?" Jason asked—damned suspicious for a seven- or eight-year-old. He actually had a no-bullshit line that arched between his eyes, something Mason would normally associate with a fifty-year-old marketing director who had been through the cola wars.

"It's a pack animal originally from South America," Mason told him at the same time his sister said, "It's that thing Kuzco was in *The Emperor's New Groove*, dummy. We just saw that last week."

"That was an awesome movie," Dane said, keeping the peace like he always did. "Do you want to be Jason-llama?"

"I don't want llama-face!" Jason protested. "Make it something else!"

"Jay-bird," Mason muttered under his breath. With this kid's attitude, he would be behind bars soon enough.

"I like that!" Jason said chirpily. "She can be Holly-bell and I can be Jay-bird and—"

"Look! Uncle Clay just saved a ball!" Holly-bell chimed in. "Go, Uncle Clay, go!"

They all turned and cheered, and Clay cannoned the ball back into play. Thank God—the kids actually knew soccer, and watched and cheered, and Mason could concentrate on Terry.

From a strictly observational view, he was both an amazing player and an exasperating one.

He was amazing because he was squirrel-quick and an amazing ball handler. As soon as he saw an opening, he could steal the ball from the opposition's best forward and be driving down the center line toward the goal.

He was an exasperating player because he was frequently out of position, and he didn't know where any of his teammates were. If he got stopped at the goal line, he had no idea where to pass the ball. Skipper would be yelling at him—"Jefferson, dammit, you got three goddamned forwards, use us!"—and he'd be playing footwork games with the opposition's defense.

Mason was surprised Skipper didn't just chuck the ball at the back of his head.

But he didn't. Nobody did. Instead, they called out to him, frequently, and pulled him back into the game they were playing and not the one he'd locked himself into at the goal line. They didn't often score a goal that way—and twice they had an offsides penalty—but nobody seemed put out.

But the third time Terry did it, right before the half, Mason let out a big sigh.

"Gonna say anything?" Dane asked quietly.

Mason thought about it. "He needs to see how it should work," he said after a moment. "He needs a picture in his head. I wonder if there's any pro soccer on this afternoon."

"There's always pro soccer somewhere," Dane muttered, hitting his phone. After a few moments wreaking whatever magic he knew, he grunted. "Good. Done. We're set up to tape a game happening in Brazil in ten minutes. As soon as you're home, look it up on the DVR. You can use it as foreplay."

"*Dane!*" Mason hissed, glancing at their young and grumpy companions.

Who were both busy jumping up and down because Richie had just scored a goal.

Mason clapped and yelled "Yay Richie!" while the whistle blew and all the guys went to get a water. Terry and Carpenter came wandering down to their corner of the field, both of them carrying water and extra energy bars for their audience, and Mason smiled weakly.

"Energy bars," Dane muttered. "Ugh. I'll be pooping for days."

"Mom says those are bad for you," Holly-bell said wisely. "She tells Uncle Clay they make him fat."

Dane jerked around toward the little girl with the beginnings of a snarl issuing from his throat, and Mason tapped him on the shoulder to calm him down.

Holly-bell giggled. "That was funny, Dane. Do it again!"

Mason grabbed his wrist. "Dane?" he warned, and Dane took a deep breath and let it out.

"Your Uncle Clay isn't fat," Dane said sweetly after a moment. "And if he thinks energy bars help, well then, let him eat them."

"Good job!" Mason said to their approaching heroes. "You got any gas for the next half?"

Terry looked over his shoulder, embarrassed. "Skipper says I would if I thought more than ran," he apologized. "I have trouble seeing the field."

He handed Mason a water and a breakfast bar, and Mason caught his hand. "I think I have a way to help," he said brightly. "After the game when you come over, okay?"

Terry cast Dane and Carpenter a furtive look, but they were busy explaining how granola bars were not fattening as long as you didn't get the kind with chocolate and marshmallows and how they would hold the kids over until they went for lunch.

He looked back at Mason. "All day?" he said, a little bit of wonder in his voice.

"Dane will get home sometime in the evening," Mason warned, but Terry shook his head.

"All day," he repeated, nodding. "It'll be great."

And then—oh God—he kissed Mason's cheek like it was the most natural thing in the world before he and Carpenter ran back into the fray.

"Stop that," Dane ordered.

"Stop what?" Mason watched as Terry launched himself at the ball fearlessly, and then, per usual, ignored his teammates to drive it to a standstill.

"You are *rubbing your cheek like a teenaged girl*!" Dane snapped.

Mason dropped his hand and picked up his coffee, which was down to the dregs. He still felt the tingle on his cheek.

OF COURSE, after the game—which they lost, two goals to four—there was the usual postgame wrap-up around Skip's car. Mason balanced on his crutches and talked about the plays and how good Carpenter was as keeper and how Richie had scored two goals.

Terry said playfully, "What about me, Mace—you got any praise for me?"

"He don't got shit," Richie said irritably. "You don't see the field, dammit. You gotta pass it from midfield!"

Terry looked abashed, and Mason shrugged. "He's a little right," he admitted, "but you're an awesome ball handler."

"Heh heh heh," Terry laughed like a twelve-year-old, and the whole team groaned.

Mason's face flamed—which wasn't bad, really, because he'd been starting to think he'd never feel his toes or his cheeks again.

"Not quite how I meant it," he mumbled.

"Yeah, no." Thomas, their hipster schoolteacher, stole Mason's stocking cap and smacked him in the head with it. "You walked right into that one."

"Limped," Mason said with dignity, snagging the hat back. "I *limped* into that one. But that's okay, because we're going to go watch a pro game on TV—I'm pretty sure if he just saw a game, that would help. There's this sort of…." Mason made vague gestures with his hands. "This *puzzle piece* thing that happens when you guys do it right. I think you'll see it on screen."

"Ooh," Skip said, eyes wide. "That's a good idea. In fact, we should take in a Republic game in the spring."

"What's the Republic, and why would we be watching a game?" Dane asked suspiciously.

"Wait, I know this one!" Oh, for once Mason had inside info. "They're the local soccer team, third division, I think. Tesko helped sponsor their new field. In fact, if we want to get a ticket bundle, I think I can get us a discount."

And like that, Mason had the entire team's attention.

Before they broke up for the afternoon, Skip agreed to get everybody's money, and Mason agreed to ask HR for dates and times, as well as details on how many tickets they'd need to get the discount. Mason and Dane had gone to Giants games and 49ers games all their lives. He'd never seen people get so excited about third-division soccer—but then, he'd never been this excited about a Giants game either.

But the group broke up—cold and ready for some hot chocolate—and Dane went off with Carpenter to apparently spend the day with those two *charming* little assholes who had whined for their Nintendos during the entire second half. Mason anxiously watched him get into Carpenter's Ford SUV.

Dane looked in his element, spouting nonsense and teasing the kids with almost every word.

He looked *content*, and Mason caught his eye and nodded fiercely. Dane patted his pocket—where his night dose of meds sat—and Mason nodded again, this time in acceptance.

Dane was an adult, and this was the best he could do.

"So," Terry said as he slowly walked Mason to the Lexus. "You want I should stop for food on my way?"

Mm—food would be good. Just sitting in the cold and watching had given Mason a massive appetite. "Yeah—and I'll make us some hot chocolate. It'll be ready by the time you get there."

Terry nodded, looking pensive. "Will you tell me what's wrong then?" he asked plaintively.

Mason blew out a breath. "It's nothing you can fix," he said honestly. "Like I said, this morning just... just sucked."

Those squirrel-bright eyes grew sharp and canny. "How bad? I mean, I like your brother, but how bad does it get without them?"

Mason shuddered. "He's a real butt-hurt asshole," he muttered. "I've got no other words. But... but you know. *Dane.*"

"Yeah. So worth it to see the good guy in him, right?"

"Yeah." He opened his car door as the keyless entry beeped welcome. "And he's going to have a good day."

Hopefully, so was Mason.

TERRY RAN in with sandwiches and a duffel bag before the water and milk had even started to heat. He excused himself to shower while Mason finished up and microwaved some soup. They ate lunch and drank hot chocolate while watching the game Dane had taped, and while they didn't know either of the teams (Terry wasn't sure if he'd even heard of the *country*), they chose their good guys and their bad guys and watched the play.

Terry seemed to be in awe.

"Okay, I see it now. I mean, I *see it*. Skipper is always telling me to play my position, and I never got what that meant. Did you see what happened there? He was in the perfect place, and he passed it, and the forward took it in! Oh my God—it's like... I can't even *tell* you how much this makes clear. And wow—lookit these guys with the ball. I mean, you said I was good, but these guys—they're so damned fast. This is amazing—oh look! He's got it! He's going in! Go, go, go, go, run, you little bastard, run—*goal! Goal! Goal!*"

Terry leapt off the couch, hands overhead, shouting and jumping, and Mason leaned back against the couch and laughed.

Play resumed and Terry collapsed next to him, laughing as well and holding his stomach. "Man, that's fun. None of my work guys watch sports—I didn't realize how awesome it was just to do that!"

Mason bit his lip, feeling like a sham. "I'm not really a sports guy," he confessed. "I've gone to live games because that's, like, an event. You eat garlic fries, and you cheer with the team and try to catch T-shirts. But I didn't get how much fun it was." Terry's eyes were resting on his face, his mouth parted softly. His cheeks were flushed and his hair fell softly down one cheek, almost dry from the shower. "Until now," Mason whispered.

"You get it now?" Terry asked, eyes crinkling.

"Yeah."

Terry moved forward a little. "How's your ankle?"

"Better?"

Laugh. "That's a lie," he acknowledged.

Mason would have shrugged if he wasn't half lying down. "It's better than Thursday," he said truthfully.

Terry's smile crinkled with mischief at the corners. "Is it good enough to prop up on a pillow while I ride you like a show pony?"

Mason laughed, feeling giddy. "I can't be a stallion?" he asked a little plaintively, pulling Terry across the couch while he lay down flat.

Terry placed a little kiss on the corner of his mouth. "Stallions are assholes," he muttered before tracing the seam of Mason's lips with his tongue. "I finally got a guy who wants to show me that slow is a thing."

"Oh," Mason murmured, running his lips down Terry's jaw. "Now the pressure is on. I've got to be a blue-ribbon winner."

Terry shifted, placing his weight more fully across Mason's chest while he went for Mason's earlobe. "You're not allowed to prance anymore."

Mason moaned—Terry's groin was pressed against his, and that hot breath in his ear, with the playful little nip, that was making the whole area swell in delicious discomfort.

"If I'm not prancing, how you gonna ride me?" Mason panted. He reached for Terry's backside and kneaded. Tiny, muscular ass—but he didn't mind.

Terry chuckled, strained and dirty, and moved sideways so he could reach down Mason's body, cup his erection, and squeeze. "I'll ride the… the whatyacallum—"

"The saddle pommel. Oh!" Because Terry had undone his belt and his fly and was thrusting his hand into Mason's underwear. "Cock. Just ride my cock...."

Terry's laugh tickled the skin of Mason's throat. "You tortured me last time," he hummed, running his teeth along Mason's collarbone.

"Two weeks, Terry!"

"Yeah, but I want it to be good." He started tugging at Mason's shirt and sweatshirt, and Mason helped him out, seizing the hems and wiggling so he could throw them over his head. While he did that, Terry pulled off his own shirts and shimmied out of his sweats and boxers, then stood to kick them off with his shoes.

Mason reached out from the couch to run his fingertips along the length of Terry's erection. He purred at the softness of the skin and the way the shaft bobbed happily at his touch.

Terry caught his hand just as he was skating his thumb across the edge.

"I can't stroke?" Mason complained. "Stroke? Taste? Touch?"

"Let me get your pants off," Terry ordered. "Geez, you're bossy. I mean, I know you got the big office and all, but I'm giving you sex. Take orders for a minute."

"Yessir," Mason snapped out playfully.

Terry's knees appeared to wobble, and he wrapped his own fist around his cock and stroked, very slowly. A bit of precome spurted out, and he caught it on his thumb and then thrust his thumb into Mason's mouth.

Mason sucked hard, scraping the soft flesh with his teeth and meeting Terry's eyes.

"You want me to order you around some?" Terry mumbled, like he'd never even thought of such a thing. "Be not like a toy, like... like...."

"Like you're my partner," Mason gasped. "Unless, you know, you just want me to beat off in front of you, 'cause...." He slid his hand under his pants again and made a pass of his own, keening when he came to the end.

Terry flicked his wrist as it disappeared. "Stop that," he ordered. "I'm going to get you naked, and then we're gonna see something."

Mason reluctantly let go of himself and started pushing down his jeans and underwear. Terry helped him out the rest of the way, pausing when he got to Mason's sock-covered feet.

The one with the bandage on it swelled under the cuff of the pants, and he tugged at the edge with exquisite care. When the pants came free, Terry looked up at Mason and grinned like he'd accomplished something.

Mason grinned back. God—look at what he'd done, just to not cause pain.

Then Terry moved his outside foot so it rested on the floor and began his real path of seduction. He started by kissing along the inside of Mason's knee, dragging his tongue up along his thigh. Mason gasped, caught between ticklishness and arousal. Terry upped the pressure, pushing with his lips and suckling hard, tight mouthfuls of flesh.

Arousal won, and Mason melted, spreading his legs as wide as they could go, exposed and open to the air and to Terry's bold touch.

He licked the crease of Mason's thigh and then danced around Mason's scrotum, taking one testicle gingerly into his mouth.

"Oooh…." Mason massaged Terry's scalp under his hair, lost in being tended to, being made love to like sex was an awesome thing.

"Here," Terry said practically. "Lift your ass… and… yeah." He shoved a pillow under Mason's pelvis and placed his palm on each cheek, spreading.

Fucking *awesome*.

First he traced the predictable path from the back of Mason's balls to Mason's crease and along his hole. A *rim job*. Mason had given them a lot but hadn't gotten many, and Terry's finger petting, pushing gently as Terry licked and spat, lubing him up, almost made him come.

"Ohmigod ohmigod ohmigod," Mason chanted as that finger thrust in, the burn of the nerve endings setting *all* the tender parts on fire.

Terry pulled back enough to stroke Mason's cock and say, "*You* like that!"

"Yesssss…." Oh, Mason wanted more. He did. He wanted to be fucked, reamed, taken—but nobody had wanted to do that for him.

"I've never topped before," Terry said, pushing up on his elbows to pull the crown of Mason's cock into his mouth. He sucked hard once and then let Mason pop out, wet and dripping precome in the faint chill of the air.

"Nungh…." He couldn't even make the words.

"And I *really* want to sit on this," Terry said, squeezing his cock from the bottom to the bell.

"Nungh…."

"And I brought lube." Terry reached to the tangle of clothes and pulled a small bottle out of the pocket of his sweats. "See?" He punctuated that with a lick across Mason's cockhead, digging his tongue into the slit as he went.

"Ohh…." Mason's whole body was shaking and on fire. He didn't care. Something—*something*—had to give.

"So I'm pretty sure I can—nungh!—sit on your cock without hurting you," Terry panted, and Mason opened his eyes in time to watch him reach back, fingers coated in lube, and start to prep himself.

"Can I watch you do that?" he begged.

Terry smiled wickedly, but he didn't do what Mason asked. "Do what?" He grunted, humping backward, probably fucking his own fingers, damn him. "Watch me stretch my asshole out?"

"Yeah."

"Does that turn you on?"

"Yeah!"

"Well, tough," Terry moaned, his hand moving quickly. "I'm going to get up and sit on your cock and fuck myself on it, and all you can do is thrust up when I tell ya!"

"Oh God," Mason moaned, loving Terry taking charge, loving his dirty talk, loving that he was at this man's mercy. "Yes. I'll fuck you on command, you little shit. Just sit on me, dammit, *please*!"

Terry laughed and scooted up until he was straddling Mason's hips. He sat, catching Mason's cock in the cleft of his bottom, and rocked back and forth, taunting them both.

Mason arched his head back and thrust up, knowing he was being teased and enjoying it. Terry's entrance, slick and open, caught the ridge under Mason's bell, and again, and again, until Mason groaned.

"I'm gonna come," he threatened. "Gonna make you a big mess, and you're gonna be left high—*ahh*…."

Terry rose on his knees and positioned Mason's cock at his entrance, the lube and the stretching giving them purchase. Terry slid down slowly, his face slack with concentration.

Down… down… so tight, warm and satiny—oh, to be inside somebody, it was almost sacred.

Not almost.

It was glory.

Terry came to a trembling halt flush against Mason's body, and for a moment they regarded each other soberly. Terry's hair, clean and soft, fell over one eye, and his lips were parted as he breathed in quick pants. Mason ran his palms up Terry's thighs, his soft-skinned stomach, his tender ribs, and Terry gasped, falling forward and rocking in small, controlled movements.

"You feel so *good*," Terry moaned, rocking faster. Mason cupped his shoulders, his neck. For a moment he held his bright-eyed harlequin face between both hands. Terry started to hump frantically then, losing his rhythm, and Mason seized his hips and took over.

"Stay right there," he gritted, using his good foot for leverage and his core for strength. With Terry suspended above him, he started to rocket his hips up and back, not low enough to fall out and not high enough to really smack into Terry's ass.

Terry lowered himself just enough and sobbed, "Mason, harder."

Oh yeah. Harder.

He pumped his hips with everything he had, and Terry's cock flopped on his stomach, leaving a wet smack mark with every thrust. Terry was leaning slightly forward, hands on Mason's ribs as he steadied himself. Mason thought that if his stomach muscles held out, they could do this all day, but he only did so many crunches in the morning, so they'd better wrap it up.

"Terry," he gasped, not slowing. "Can you jerk off for me? I want to see it, baby. Just stroke it. Come on my stomach, okay?"

Terry nodded, dreamlike, but he sat up a little and took charge of his own body again. He wrapped his fist around his girthy cock and squeezed hard enough to turn the head purple. Then he stroked slowly up.

Watching the slow progress of that stroke while Mason was rabbit-fucking him from the bottom was one of the most excruciatingly awesome moments in Mason's sex life.

"Don't slow down," Terry begged, going back for another stroke.

"Killing me!" Mason breathed, but what a way to go.

Stroke by slow goddamned stroke—and Mason's stomach muscles burned and his ankle ached, and God, he just wanted to feel that clench around his cock. Terry's cock was swollen, weeping precome, and it was murder to see it so close and not to taste it.

But Terry kept begging for Mason to keep fucking, and Mason wouldn't stop unless his heart exploded.

Then Mason shifted his angle just… right… *there*. Damn! His cock hit the spot, *the* spot, the magical prostate spot, and Terry's throaty, gutsy scream reverberated around the first floor of the house. He convulsed, asshole tightening around the base of Mason's cock as come spurted, hard and hot, across Mason's stomach, chest, and chin.

Mason closed his eyes at the last minute—you only made that mistake a couple of times before you just gave it up—but the image of Terry's face, wanton, unguarded, lost in orgasm, seared across his eyelids as he exploded into climax.

Ahh—*augh!* He could not seem to stop coming, even as Terry collapsed across his chest, limp and mewling for breath.

Finally—*finally*—Mason stopped rutting inside that slim, fine body, and Terry gave an exhausted whoop and let Mason fall out.

Come leaked out of Terry's ass and began to trickle down Mason's balls, and Mason made a mental note to clean the throw pillow under his hips before anyone else sat on the couch. It was the only thought he had for a few.

"Thought I was gonna have jizz spurting out my eyeballs," Terry panted into the silence.

"That was impressive," Mason admitted. "You know we're arc-welded together with spunk, right? When you sit up, all my chest hair'll rip out."

Terry laughed helplessly. "Well, I'll have to stay here awhile."

"Fine with me—you're the one who's going to get cold."

"Damn."

They breathed together, their bodies remembering what to do after the cosmic reboot of orgasm, and then Terry nuzzled his ear. "That's another first," he whispered.

"Riding a guy like a show pony?" Mason asked, smiling.

Terry shook his head, unexpectedly serious. "Getting to boss someone around," he said, regarding Mason with his squirrel-bright brown eyes. "You… you let me have power, you know? I didn't know I could be that guy. It's great."

"I enjoyed it too," Mason said weakly, and Terry pushed up for the kiss.

Mason wrapped his arms around that narrow back and took him in, kissing back, allowing Terry to take the lead while protecting him from the chill.

When they were done, both breathless again, Terry pulled back and grinned. "I'm going to need another shower."

"Me too. And I need to clean the couch."

Terry winced. "Yeah—don't want someone sitting on that cushion. Awkward. How 'bout you limp upstairs, and I'll clean up this shit here. I'll join you in the shower and we can watch some more soccer in your room."

"You make good plans," Mason said sincerely. "I couldn't get much past 'I just had sex and it was awesome.'"

Terry tilted his head back and laughed, and then kissed Mason thoroughly one more time for good measure. "It *was* awesome, right?" he asked, suddenly worried.

Mason nodded with all the enthusiasm in his soul. "Definitely. Why?"

Terry shook his head and looked down, studying Mason's ear with great intensity.

"What?" Mason prompted, jiggling them both.

"I just… I've never done that either. Had sex that got better. Usually I get hot for someone, and we do it, and… then that's it. And if we try again, it's awkward and suddenly I want more from it. But you? Every time has been more. Every time we're together, it's different. And you look at me…." Terry shook his head and then buried his face against Mason's neck.

Mason wrapped his arms even tighter. "Like how?" he asked, kissing the edge of Terry's ear. He had holes along the rim like he'd worn studs at one time, but not now.

"Like I matter," Terry said, turning his head sideways so they could look into each other's eyes. "You look at me like I matter. Like my opinion, and the things I say, and whether the sex is good for me—like it all matters."

Mason's eyes burned with the truth of that. "You do," he admitted, raw and open and naked in his living room. "It does."

Terry nodded and blinked rapidly, then rolled off Mason and turned to help him sit up. "Here, let me put your boxers on," he said. He slid them up, gentle and mindful of Mason's wrapped ankle, and then heaved Mason to his feet and gave him his crutches. He managed all of that without making eye contact, and Mason sighed in exasperation.

"Terry?"

Terry shook his head and looked away.

"Baby, look at me."

Reluctantly he turned back toward Mason, eyes limpid in the falling light of late afternoon.

"It was important to me too," Mason told him, knowing it was foolish to say this so soon, after so little between them. But dammit, he already knew there wasn't much he wouldn't do to spend an afternoon this way. Even if it involved soccer on television and throw pillows that needed washing.

Terry nodded, wiping his palm under his eyes, one at a time. "I'm not sure I can trust that yet," he apologized. "But the way it makes my heart feel—that's new too."

Mason pulled him against his chest for a moment and then wobbled. Terry helped him get his balance—and apparently achieved his own in the process.

"Go," he said, voice firm. "It'll take you forever. I'll be there before you even get in the shower, probably."

Mason nodded. "Bring up snacks and water and stuff," he said, starting toward the stairs. "We'll build a fort and watch TV and pretend we're six."

"I never did that when I was six," Terry said, and Mason half turned toward him.

"Dane and I did that whenever it rained. Mom would give us Kool-Aid, and lace her own with vodka, and we'd have a good time."

Terry laughed then, hard, and Mason turned around and left him to it.

THEY SPENT most of the day in bed, taking turns with the remote and catching each other up on their favorite movies. They'd pause and talk and then start again, Mason sitting up on the bed and Terry lying with his head on Mason's stomach so Mason could play with his hair.

They were in the middle of *Office Space* when Terry started talking, blindly, without reference to what was happening on television or even their last topic.

"See, I think the thing is, my mom, she just never had anybody tell her there was a world like this. Like she could take a class and get a better life. I mean, this movie, all these guys took college and they got a better job—and it made them not appreciate it, I think, because they're *really* unhappy. But she doesn't know any of it. As far as she's concerned, all of the nice jobs, the nice clothes, the good things—those are for other people. She gave up on those when I was born."

"You're not the reason she's unhappy," Mason said, his heart aching a little.

Terry turned his head and smiled up into Mason's eyes. "I know that," he said. "Now. I mean, even just a couple of times, I think I made you really happy. And you're like, part of this whole other life. I don't know the password or the secret handshake to get me into the whole other life—all I know how to be is nice to you."

"That's my favorite secret handshake," Mason said, pulling Terry's hair back from his forehead. Gah! His face was so young, so pretty and vulnerable—Mason felt unworthy, oafish and gawky, just looking at him.

Thank God Terry's earthy laugh came next. The laugh that made Mason's cock *and* heart swell, both at the same time. "You're sort of easy, you know that?" he asked. "As long as someone grabs your dick, you're happy."

"And yet so few takers before you came along."

"And I don't get that." Terry scrambled up so he could rest his head on Mason's shoulder. "I mean, why wouldn't people like a nice guy like you?"

Mason shrugged, careful not to dislodge him. "There's not really a premium on niceness," he said, hating to whine. "People like the aggressive corporate type or the guy who likes to talk a lot. I just…." He grimaced. "I guess I only care about being nice to people who are nice to me back. I'm horrible at kissing ass at work—seriously. The reason Mrs. Bradford and I get along so well is that she looks at my schedule and tells me who's an asshole and who I should bother to talk to. Then I work with those people and we get stuff done. It's not that hard, really."

"Yeah, it just took an MBA," Terry said dryly. "I don't even know how you went to school for so long."

Mason thought of Todd Slezcyk and snorted. "I was trying to get laid. It's how most of us made it through school, you knew that, right?"

Terry gave a long, slow blink. "That had never occurred to me," he said. "You mean people spend as much time thinking about sex as I do?"

Snort. "God, no. Just me, I think. Because I've been looking my whole life to find someone who thinks an afternoon in bed is as awesome as a hike to a farmer's market to find organic brussels sprouts or something."

"Please tell me you're kidding." The horror on Terry's face would have been comical if Mason hadn't spent too many weekends like that with Ira to count.

"My last ex had a thing for organic produce and cooking stuff—I mean, I get new recipes and all, but God! Shopping! Why?"

Terry chuckled. "I don't really have exes. There's guys I've fucked and you."

Mason looked at him. Just looked at him until he squirmed as he sat.

"You're better," he clarified.

"So glad to hear that." Mason kissed the top of his head and then asked the thing that had been pressing on his chest forever. "Can you leave her? Can you move out? Do you want to be a grown-up bad enough to do that?"

Terry took a deep breath, and then another, and then a third. Every time he let out a breath, he collapsed a little more, becoming part of the landscape of Mason's chest. "Yeah," he said after the last breath. "I'm going to start cleaning up her house. When she gets to a place where she can take care of herself, I'll get myself an apartment or something." Terry looked up at him hopefully. "And then we can have lots more days like this one."

Mason smiled widely. That sounded like a plan.

But it must not have been wide enough.

"Is your brother going to be okay not at home?" Terry asked tentatively. "Because most of you is here with me, but some of you is...."

"Worried," Mason supplied. "And I'm sorry." He grimaced. "This might be a good time to tell you that the worry never goes away. Dane will be dealing with this for his entire life, and I'm going to be worrying for him that long. Even if he finds someone, you know?"

"Yeah, but if he finds someone, then you got a cocaptain, right? Someone you can work with who's *not* Mom and Dad?"

Mason remembered the helpless anger from that morning and the incessant anxiety that came from trying to monitor his brother's anxiety levels.

"Yeah," he admitted. "A team approach would be nice. It's just so private. You know, *my* boyfriend and then Dane's, when he gets one. It would just be okay to not feel alone."

"Not alone," Terry whispered. "I can't promise much, but for right now, not alone."

They were quiet then, and Mason reached for the remote to turn the movie back on when Terry stopped him by putting an ear to his chest.

"I can hear your heart," he said, a smile in his voice.

"It's beating special just for you," Mason said, not sure if he should be proud of that line or cringe.

"It's warm, just for me," Terry said.

"Course."

He hit Play on the movie and Terry stayed there, listening to the warm beat of his heart.

At around six they went downstairs and warmed up some soup for dinner, and then they went back upstairs, where a lazy hand job turned into an intense sixty-nine that left them both breathless. Terry went and got a washcloth and wiped Mason down, his motions efficient and gentle.

And that turned into a kiss.

Which turned into Mason propping one knee on the bed while he stood up and fucked Terry into the mattress from behind.

Terry's noisy hollers as he came made Mason *very* glad Dane wasn't there. Something about how uninhibited he was, how eager he was to enjoy what they were doing, made the sex…

Amazing.

And exhausting. Mason was sort of glad when they finished off that last time. He thought he might be starting to chafe. When Terry collapsed limply on the bed, giggling, Mason figured he'd had his limit too.

"You okay?" Mason asked, nuzzling his ear.

"I had no idea," Terry whispered, turning to look at him.

"No idea what?"

"That you could literally fuck yourself out. I've never felt like I could have enough."

Mason tried not to look disappointed. "Well, I mean, *today* we're sort of done," he conceded.

"Yeah, I know. But tomorrow, we could do this again!"

Mason rolled his eyes. "If we weren't cleaning your backyard."

Terry hid his face. "Augh!"

They got dressed again and watched more movies, entertaining each other in a thousand somnolent ways.

Dane got in around nine, and Mason went downstairs to greet him. He looked tired but calm and maybe, possibly, happy.

"Good day?" Mason asked, hopping toward the fridge for the chocolate milk.

"Good company," Dane said quietly. "Carpenter's good company, you know that."

Mason did. He figured he and Skip and Carpenter would be having a lot more lunches together. "Were the kids okay?"

Dane's smile lit up the kitchen. "Yeah. They were awesome. Apparently Carpenter's sister and her husband are leaving for a stint with Doctors Without Borders in June. Carpenter and his parents are on for babysitting—that'll be fun."

"Just in time for summer vacation." Mason gave quiet, fervent thanks for his day job.

"Swimming, the zoo, trips to San Francisco." Dane's teeth flashed in the midst of what was growing into a full beard. "Mom will be thrilled."

Mason nodded, wondering if he should broach the one little glitch in the plan.

"I kissed him tonight," Dane said quietly, his joy suffusing the air like balm.

"Yeah?" Mason squeaked.

"He responded. It was only a couple of seconds, but there was tongue." Dane poured his own glass of chocolate milk and leaned against the counter, throwing back a couple of meds.

Mason's heart started to beat again. "Next move?" He had never actually seduced a supposedly straight boy. He had no idea.

"Wait," Dane said. "Hope."

And there went Mason's heart to his feet. His face must have shown it.

"I said hope," Dane told him. "Not fantasize. Although that too. Don't worry, Mace. I keep telling you, I know the deal."

Mason closed his eyes and came clean. "I always worry," he said. "Always. This morning was rough."

"I'm sorry," Dane said.

Mason opened his eyes to see Dane studying his chocolate milk. "I know. Just… I'm going to nag you. Like be paranoid for a week or so. You understand?"

Dane met his gaze and nodded. "Yeah. I get it." He looked away and changed the subject. "So, Terry?"

Mason didn't try to fight the smile that crept up. "I'm going to bring him a snack." Chocolate milk and cookies.

"Mace."

Mason reached for the glasses and poured Terry a cup, and then turned around to get the cookies behind his head.

"I'll carry those up for you," Dane muttered. "Why didn't you send him down?"

"Because he cleaned up after lunch and dinner and I'm tired of feeling like an invalid." And he really was gaining weight. Water aerobics at the work gym helped, but it didn't do the same as a good run through the neighborhood.

"So are we really spending our Sunday cleaning out his backyard?"

"He says there's blackberry bushes. I'm going to need you to go buy those Teflon gloves Dad uses for roses and two kinds of garden shears. I already texted Skipper about everybody wearing jeans and long shirts and waffle stompers and—"

Dane held up a hand. "Oh my God, calm down, Mason. You got the job! You're the top dog organizer of the entire world, Mr. MBA. I'm just asking—what's your endgame here?"

And Mason was proud, because they had one. "Help him clean up his mom's house. Help him move out and be his own person."

Dane regarded him steadily.

"Hope he comes back," he conceded with a sigh.

"See?" Dane said, smugly superior. "Hope. It's a fucking thing."

Brambles and Brush

TERRY LEFT early the next day, after a lingering kiss and an admonition for Mason to stay in bed for another hour. Mason had managed a half an hour before he pulled Dane out of bed and got them both ready so they could go to the hardware store and buy several sets of gloves, some clippers, and the super-strong garbage bags that wouldn't puncture if you tried to shove a spear through the sides.

When they arrived at the tiny ramshackle house in Carmichael, Mason's first thought was that Terry hadn't been exaggerating when he'd talked about his mother's backyard. There was a rotting wooden fence keeping the garden entropy from taking over the driveway, but the brambles and weeds were literally too thick to see through.

Mason seriously wondered about going back to Lowe's and asking if they sold machetes.

Carpenter arrived, and he and Dane set Mason up with fleece blankets and a folding chair and those wonderful little hand-warmer things. Skip and Richie showed up about the same time Terry got back from taking his mom wherever he'd taken her. Terry had tried to explain where she was going, but he outlined a series of stops, from her friend's house to church to the mall to somewhere else, to a place where someone would be who would drop her off at six. Mason didn't follow it. Mostly he was glad she was gone.

Terry waved at everybody and then ran inside the house and came back wearing jeans—for once—and a long-sleeved denim shirt. He'd also tied his hair up in a bun, and as he came out of the house, he was sliding Mason's stocking cap over it and pulling the warm blue wool over his ears.

He greeted Skip and Richie while Carpenter and Dane were still fussing with a way to prop Mason's foot up so it didn't hurt. When they were done, he walked over to Mason's chair and copped a squat, grabbing one of the little chemical hand-warmer packets out of the box.

"So you break open the little pellets inside and they keep you warm?" he asked curiously.

Mason nodded and squeezed the ones inside his gloves. "Yup. Love them."

Terry grinned, opened up a packet, and shoved it up under Mason's shirt.

"Wha—"

He fiddled with Mason's clothes for a moment, intense and searingly personal, and then settled the packet between Mason's T-shirt and his sweatshirt, right over Mason's heart.

"Gotta keep it warm," he said, peering into Mason's eyes with a twinkle in his own. "So it can keep on warming me up."

Mason's flush made up for the frigid gray fog that blanketed them all and the lack of even hope for the sun. "Just warm for you," he promised.

Terry kissed his cheek again, then stood up and asked Skipper what they should do first.

Although Dane gave Mason crap about being a weenie and letting his friends do all the work, the truth was, the next couple of hours were hard to watch.

They started out one cut at a time, cutting the blackberry bushes and weeds that grew over the fence, and then worked their way through the next foot, and then the next one, and then the next one.

Richie and Terry kept up a blue streak of cursing as they filled up trash bags with brush, brambles, trash, old boards, newspapers, rusty garden implements, pots, birdcages, and the wooden leftovers of what might have been a chicken coop.

The gloves helped, but everybody—Carpenter, Dane, Terry, Skip, Richie—ended up with big scratches over their faces, and Mason turned out to have a job after all: first aid. He swabbed a lot of hydrogen peroxide and Neosporin that day, and then taped gauze over the offended areas.

After two hours they had worked their way about halfway through the yard, and besides being both sweaty *and* freezing, scratched, bleeding, and disheartened, they were also hungry—and running out of room.

The trash bags covered most of the driveway.

They paused for a moment and had a discussion about what to do next—nobody had a car big enough to haul—when a big pickup truck with extra rails built on for gardening implements pulled in front of the house and Cooper hopped out with Menendez by his side, because you never could have enough soccer buddies to help.

They made an unlikely pair—Menendez, small with curly dark hair and movements like a spring-loaded toy; and Cooper, tall, with broad shoulders and long limbs, as well as a wealth of thick reddish-brown hair he'd pulled back from his face into a ponytail. Mason had enjoyed playing soccer with both men, and he could tell from the suddenly alert, active cant to Terry's shoulders that seeing them was a welcome surprise.

"Wow!" he said, bouncing. "Where'd this come from?"

"It's my dad's," Cooper said. "He's got like five of them in his business, but this one's got the weakest rack on it. We use it for hauling. Tony knows where the dump is—he's got a buddy who works there."

"Who's Tony?" Richie asked blankly.

"*I'm* Tony, asshole!" Menendez spoke up. "Jesus, you don't even look at a player roster?"

"I just thought you were Menendez," Richie said, not apologetic at the least.

Terry shrugged. "I gotta admit, I woulda been hard-pressed to remember your actual first name. I mean, do you even know mine?"

Menendez gaped at them—and then flushed. "Gerry?" he hazarded.

Cooper busted up. "And I'm Wyatt! Pleased to meetya, everybody—it only took six years. Now do you want us to haul some trash?"

"A-fuckin'-men," Terry sighed. "I'll call you anything you want, just help us get this shit out of my driveway before dark!"

It took them four more hours—and three trips to the dump outside of Roseville—to clear out Terry's backyard. In the end, it also took two Weedwackers to get the chin-high weeds down to knee level, and Terry used his old push mower to reduce that to stubble. Skipper jury-rigged a couple of cage lights from his and Cooper's cars so that he and Richie could rake the last batch of cigarette butts, condoms, and bubble-gum wrappers from the stubble that remained. Everybody was filthy and exhausted, everybody had war wounds, and everyone had a war story about some horrible thing they'd discovered in the course of the day.

For Skip it was a cat skeleton. For Richie it was a pile of chicken bones. Carpenter had stepped in rabbit remains and screamed like an actress in a horror film.

Someone's dog had been crapping steadily in the back corner, where the fence had broken down years ago. Dane had stepped in *that* pile, and had been scraping the crap out of his waffle-stomper for an hour.

About the only thing that *wasn't* wrong was hunger, and that was because Mason had ordered half-a-dozen extra-large pizzas from the nearest Round Table a little after noon, and people had been noshing steadily on that. He'd also run to Starbucks for a giant traveler of coffee, and that too had been appreciated.

But now they were done. All but the last bag had been hauled, and they stood, loose-limbed and happy with their day's work, underneath the cage lights and told their horror stories like warriors after the battle.

"Oh my God!" Cooper was whooping. "That fucking gravel pile on the other side of the house—did you even *see* that shit?" he asked Carpenter.

Carpenter had a few bruises and punctures on his thigh that indicated he had *not* seen the pile of fish gravel before he got there with one of the Weedwackers.

"Oh hell," Dane swore, coming out of the dusty, cramped house. They'd all gone in at one time or another to use the bathroom or wash their hands. The last of the pizza now sat in a box on the battered Formica table. "Dammit, Clay—here, come back inside and I'll put some Neosporin on that shit."

"I'm fine." Carpenter waved him off. "Promise. It's only a flesh wound."

"That could get infected," Mason said, a subtle warning in his voice. Dane would obsess, and whatever was between them, this was one of those sitches where it was easier to give in.

Carpenter blinked. "Fine, fine—geez, you two. Mason sprains his ankle and we're all tragedy bound." But he went.

"They think *you're* bad," Terry said staunchly, "you should have *seen* Richie and Carpenter freaking out when Skipper was sick in November."

Mason started to laugh. "You mean when he answered the phone 'Tesko's teeth, how can I burp you?'"

There was general laughter.

"That's not what I said!" Skipper protested.

"How would you know?" Mason teased. "I've never *heard* anyone so stoned on cold medicine!"

Richie shook his head. "You guys should have heard him when he got home. He kept telling me he was going to join the gay soccer league with the cat."

There was more generalized laughter, and at that moment, a car pulled into the driveway.

Terry moaned. "Guys—this is gonna be… well, awful, okay? Ignore everything she says. I'm hella grateful. You need me for *anything* and I'm your guy. Rodents in the plumbing, monsters in the closets, I'm totally there."

And with that rather cryptic promise, he trotted to the incoming car to help his mother.

"Who are these people, Terrence?" his mother snapped as soon as the door opened. "What have you been doing all day?"

The false and desperate brightness of Terry's voice made them all cringe. "My friends and I cleaned up, Mom. Look—we've got a backyard now. Took all day."

"Why would you want to do that? It's just gonna get crapped up again. Waste of time."

From across the driveway, they all saw Terry's agonized look toward them as they watched the exchange.

"I want to make the place good so you don't have no trouble with it," he said. "You know, so I can go get an apartment and you'll be okay."

"You can't live by yourself," she snapped. "You're a kid. Jesus, you're covered in dirt. And you brought a bunch of people I don't know here? What were you thinking?"

"I was thinking I'm fixing the bathroom next weekend," Terry said, his voice bleak. "The toilet's leaking, and Mason almost fell through the floor."

He had, in fact, rolled his bad ankle again. He'd been trying to move without crutches, at least to the bathroom and back, but he'd needed Terry's help to get to his chair.

"Who the hell is Mason?"

"He's my…." Terry's voice faltered. "He's my friend, Mom. He's my uh—you know. *Friend.*"

Mason grimaced, and Skipper squeezed his shoulder. Well, as coming out went, it could have been worse.

"I'll just see about that," the woman promised. She stuck her head back inside the car and said something to the driver—it must not have been too friendly, because the car peeled back almost before she could shut the door. "Bitch," Terry's mom said succinctly. "Like I wanted to sit next to her retarded dog anyway."

"Mom, that's the only person left who will talk to you."

"Shut up. Who's this *friend* of yours?"

Terry's mother came forward into the circle thrown off from the cage lights. She wasn't bundled as she had been at Skipper's place, and her hard-dyed blond hair was pulled back from her face in a tight ponytail.

She was wearing a plain blue sweatshirt and ill-fitting blue jeans with a cut Mason remembered moms wearing when he was in the third grade. Her face was the same shape as Terry's, and her eyes were brown behind the squint, but her mouth was tight and pulled in at the corners, and her nose wrinkled with distaste.

Poor Terry. Mason wasn't sure what had twisted her, but the process seemed to have been irrevocable and highly painful for anyone in the vicinity.

"Mom, this is, well, my soccer team, really. That's Skip and his boyfriend, Richie—"

"You brought fags to my house?"

It was like water crashed over them all and congealed on their skin in an icy rime.

"Mom, that's fuckin' rude," Terry said after a shocked moment. "They're my *friends*, dammit—"

"Why are you hanging out with them? Do you want me to think *you're* a—"

"Yes," Terry snarled, grabbing her arm. "Yes, that's fine. You think what you want."

"*Terrence—*"

"Whatever. I just asked these nice people to come to *your house* and clean up so when I leave I'm not leaving you in a shithole. Now unless you want me to leave *tonight*, you need to tell them you're sorry."

For a moment they locked gazes and stood, furious and shaking, in the center of the frigid, foggy driveway. Finally she turned her sour gaze to the group of men who had labored for her home.

"Sorry," she snapped, then looked back at Terry. "Let go."

"Now tell them thank you," he growled.

"I am not—"

He shook her. Not hard, just enough to emphasize that he was there.

"Thank you all for doing something I didn't ask you to do," she said nastily.

"We were glad to do it for our friend, ma'am," Skip said. "We'll come back and help him any time."

Terry squeezed the bridge of his nose and then looked at Skip and nodded. "Thanks, Skip," he said gratefully. "I don't know how to pay you back."

Richie's almost inappropriate laughter seemed to break the spell of horror that had settled upon them. "You said it yourself, Jefferson—monsters in the damned trees. You owe us Halloween cleanup for the next five years."

Skip slapped his arm—"Richie!"—but Terry's face lit up with joy and relief.

"You hold me to that," he said softly. Then he turned back to his mother. "Now, let's get you inside before you can scare them away. Mason bought pizza. There's leftovers for dinner."

"Wait, Mason? Isn't that your—" She took time to sneer. "—*friend*?"

"Yeah, Mom, but forget about—"

Mason, leaning heavily on Skipper and Richie, had pushed himself up to balance precariously without his crutches.

"Ms. Jefferson?" he said politely. "I'm Mason Hayes. It's, uh, a, uh, experience to meet you."

He would have thought he'd totally blown it, but Terry was standing next to his mother, nodding and holding a thumbs-up. "Experience?" she asked, arching her eyebrows. "Not even going to try 'nice'?"

"You gotta earn nice," Cooper—Wyatt—said from his spot in the circle. "Mason fed us today—if he doesn't think you're nice, we're all behind that."

There was some general noise about how food was good, and they were all about food, and Mason got some pats on the back.

"You all are easy," he said, just softly enough to elicit several smirks and a few snorts. Oops. Accidental dirty joke during a tense moment—he had a new thing to add to his FML list of stupid things to say while adulting.

"Whatever," Terry's mom said, crossing her arms.

"I might try a little harder if I knew your name," Mason lied.

"Julie Jefferson. What do you care?"

"I just want to know the people important to Terry," he said in complete sincerity. "Terry talks about you all the time."

She snorted. "Bitches about me is more like it."

"That may be true," Mason said, "but maybe if you said nice things to him, he'd say nice things about you."

"God. This is my life? A bunch of idiots in my driveway and some fag telling me how to raise my son?"

"I just really would like you not to hurt my boyfriend," Mason said, allowing some of his own temper to show. "He's perfectly functional until you open your mouth."

Julie gaped a couple of times, and Mason turned back toward his chair. "Guys, wanna help me fold this up again? I'm thinking it's time to pack it up."

By the time they got the chair in the back of the SUV and rounded up the cage lights, Dane and Carpenter had come out of the house, followed by Terry, who was apologizing profusely, sounding young and destroyed.

"Guys, I'm sorry. That thing she said, that was horrible, and I just hate that you all came over and—"

"Stop," Mason said, his heart hurting too hard to even put words to it. "Terry, c'mere." He swung around in the passenger seat so he was facing outward from the car door, his feet braced on the runner. Terry moved between his knees without question.

"I'm sorry," Terry said, near tears. "It's so stupid. It was… I mean, it was horrible, but it was a good day. You all came over and helped and I was…." He took a shuddery breath, and Mason met Skip's eyes over his back.

That quickly, the guys all disappeared to their cars. Skip's last words were "Meet at Starbucks—hot chocolate on me!"

The cars all pulled out, and Dane leaned on the driver's side of the car, giving Mason and Terry some privacy.

By the time everyone had disappeared, Terry was crying softly against Mason's chest.

"Sh…." Mason kissed his hair. He understood. For a day, Terry had been independent, capable, and accepted. Mason had wanted to be like that his entire life. For a moment, Terry had held the keys to the adulthood castle, and then the one person who should have built up that castle for him had ripped the keys from his hand and stomped the castle to splinters.

"I'm so pathetic," Terry choked. "I am so grateful for you guys—"

"Then concentrate on that," Mason said. "You have friends. They showed up. They helped. They'll do it again."

"But my mom—"

"Can jump off a fucking cliff," Mason snarled, hating her more in that moment than he'd ever hated another human being. "We won't talk about her. We don't think less of you. Just let us know—you can sleep in our guest room or on Skip and Richie's couch. We'll come—someone will come every weekend—to help you get the house to where you feel you can leave." Mason fought against every instinct he had to throw Terry into the car and rescue him like he was a princess in a tower. Or to sink a few grand into improving a home that would eventually end up in the possession of someone he hoped to never speak to again. "You tell us, okay?"

Terry nodded and looked up finally, embarrassment and humiliation etched clearly on his features. "You'd be willing to come back?"

"We'll pretend she's a mosquito," Mason said grimly. "A mosquito we can't squash, but sort of a blood-sucking annoyance who spreads bad karma like a disease."

Terry laughed shortly and then offered another one of those ridiculously pleasing kisses on the cheek. "I want to spend another day in bed," he said frankly.

"Well, maybe if my ankle gets better, we can spend part of the day in bed and part of the day doing something more interesting." A movie in a theater, even.

Terry smiled wistfully. "I'd like to play golf again," he said, surprising Mason very much. "You're a good teacher."

"Then we will." Oh, a rash promise, but Mason would have made a thousand of them. "Summer mornings—I'll reserve a tee time for every Sunday, before it starts to get hot. Just for you."

Terry looked around the concrete-colored air of dismal January. "You're planning awfully far ahead."

Oh. Mason shrank back into the car a little. "I'm not getting bored," he said, hoping he could keep it light.

Terry's smile lit up the darkness like a magic moon. "Me neither—and everything bores me. So summer it is." This time his kiss hit Mason's lips and lingered. He pulled away, saying, "Thanks, Mason. You're... I gotta...." He held his hand uncomfortably to his chest. "I gotta figure out the right word."

He turned and trotted back into the house, and Dane sank thankfully into the driver's seat and closed the door with a thud. "So, are we meeting at Starbucks for chocolate?" he asked hopefully. Well, he and Carpenter had flirted like always, but this time their flirting had been... more intense, Mason thought. Maybe hope was the order of the day.

"Of course." Mason swung into the car, did up his belt, and shut the door. Behind his eyes he saw Terry rubbing his chest and searching for the right word.

Mason knew that word. He'd used it before mostly for a lot of assholes who thought they knew what it meant.

He was starting to learn that you didn't really know what it meant unless you felt the broken glass of worry that went with it.

Everybody Hurts

BY MID-MARCH, Mason was ready to play again—but Dane had stopped taking his medication twice, and soccer should have been the last thing on his mind.

"Dane, so help me, I will *call Mom*!"

Dane looked up from the driveway, where he was sitting, knees drawn up to his chin, rocking back and forth. His hair had grown over his collar, and his scruff had turned into actual beard. He didn't look hip at this moment, he looked homeless—and the fact that he was wearing Carpenter's supersized college sweatshirt didn't do him any favors. Mason had been getting breakfast together and telling him to hurry up and take his meds when Dane had sprinted past him and out to the carport.

Mason tackled him right when he got to the SUV, and Dane had crumpled, trying hard not to weep against his knees. Mason had given him a moment to calm down, and had gone inside for his medication and some milk and some goddamned food. Dane had lost twenty pounds since January, and he didn't have that much to lose to begin with.

Goddammit. Dane needed Mom, or Dad, or fucking Carpenter, even as a friend. Mason was not doing this right, he just fucking wasn't.

"You always want to call Mom—what's the fucking matter, Mason—not man enough to deal with the crazy person by yourself?"

"*You're not crazy*! You're just undermedicated! And if you don't get up and eat this sandwich and take your meds and get into the goddamned car, we're not *going* to the soccer game, we're *going* to the fucking psych ward!"

Dane's mouth dropped slowly open, and Mason hated himself more in that moment than he had in his entire life. "You wouldn't," he whispered, hurt as a baby. "Mason—that place—"

Mason sank to a squat and shoved the pill in his fist into Dane's open mouth and then thrust the chocolate milk at him. Dane swallowed, staring at him resentfully, and Mason put the sandwich in his other hand.

"I'm going inside for my bag," he growled. "If you are not in the car and ready to go by the time I get back, I'm dragging you in by your Jesus hair and taking you to the fucking hospital."

Dane's eyes washed over with tears. "I don't want to go there," he all but whimpered.

Mason couldn't watch his baby brother cry. His eyes burned, and he wiped them with the back of his hand. "Please don't make me take you. Please? God. Please, just work with me here. The game. Carpenter. The things you love. They're there, inside you. I know they are. Just… just take a deep breath and remember they'll come back. I know you're sad now—I know it. But those things aren't gone forever—they're just hidden, Dane. Please, man. You gotta keep looking."

They were forehead to forehead, and Mason couldn't ever remember feeling as desperate about anything as he had at this moment. *C'mon, baby brother—c'mon. I know it's hard. I know that the world feels like broken glass right now. I know going outside and dealing with people is scaling an obsidian cliff. But don't give up. God, Dane, don't fucking give up.*

"He never kissed me back," Dane said brokenly. "I thought…"

Mason's heart seized. "But Dane—even if he *does* love you, how are you going to see it when you're like this? You can't see *me,* and you've known me all your life."

Dane closed his eyes and leaned his chin against his knees, and lost the battle with sobs. Mason gave up on being on time and turned around and sat with him, their backs against the car, his arm draped around Dane's shoulders.

Dane eventually leaned his head against Mason, and the sobs died down. "Go get your bag," he said softly. "I'll make us better sandwiches. God, Mason—salami for breakfast?"

"If you don't cook, you don't bitch," Mason said, his voice clogged. But he pushed himself up and then gave Dane a hand. Dane went in for a short, fierce hug, and then they went back to their morning like it never happened.

BUT YOU can't just erase a moment like that from your heart.

"Jesus, Mason," Terry said with respect. "I've never seen a soccer ball go that far. What the hell's gotten into you?"

Mason smiled tightly. "Bad morning," he said, and by now Terry knew him well enough to know what that meant.

"Sorry," he said, and to his credit he managed not to look at Dane, who was wrapped in blankets and glaring balefully at the field.

Mason shrugged, but he was pretty sure he fooled nobody—a supposition that was backed up by Carpenter as they stood waiting for Skip to score on the other side of the field.

"He looks like hell," Carpenter muttered. "So do you. Is there anything you can do to help him?"

Mason laughed bitterly. "I force fed him his meds this morning. You got any other ideas?"

Carpenter grunted and play came their way. Mason charged the offense, kicking the ball right out from under his foot and straight to Richie, who was half a field away. Play shifted to the other side of the field and Menendez whooped at Mason and high-fived him.

"I don't know what's got you pissed off, man, but use that shit!"

Mason eyed the soccer ball grimly, even as Skip took Richie's pass and ran it to the goal. "I totally intend to."

The half came, and Carpenter and Mason stood together, gulping water. "I was going to take him to my folks," Carpenter said quietly. "My mom loves him. I don't know if he can turn that shit away."

Mason nodded. "Good plan." He'd never met Carpenter's family, but Mason and Dane were such mama's boys, he couldn't see Dane not responding to mothering from an actual mom. "He's got meds for tonight and tomorrow, but he needs to do homework in the afternoon. He's falling behind."

Carpenter grunted. "God. Another year after this—that's what you said?"

Mason closed his eyes, and Terry came up next to him, patting the small of his back in a gentle way that had nothing to do with guys on the field. "Yeah. If we can just get him through till May, maybe we can lighten the load and make it two."

"I'll see what I can do," Carpenter said, and Skip called them back to play.

Mason looked down at Terry, grabbing his hand before they turned away from the bench. "Thanks," he said softly.

Terry shrugged. "I'll see if I can do better tonight."

A wave of lust—pure, unadulterated, without tenderness or sentiment—assailed him, and for a moment, he could have taken Terry right there, in public, snarling and biting, like an animal.

Oh God.

Mason shied away from the image.

"I might be a bastard tonight," he apologized, wondering if he could find words to tell Terry that he didn't want his boyfriend—or whatever they were—to see him this way.

Terry winked. "I'm a bastard all the time. Bring it!"

"C'mon you guys! Get your ass out here!" Skip called, and that was the end of the half.

MASON WAS busy talking to Dane and making sure he'd be okay to go with Carpenter when Terry waved and said he'd meet at Mason's house with sandwiches. Well shit—Mason was going to have to remember how to be a person, how not to wear his fear and his frustration on his sleeve.

God. Please let him keep it together—as settled into routine as he and Terry had become, Mason was positive he was one harsh word, one accidental blurt away from scaring him off forever.

He got to the house to find Terry waiting on the doorstep, sandwich bag in hand.

"I'm going to shower first," he said with a quick peck on Terry's cheek. "I still have game-stink on me."

Terry scowled, putting the sandwiches on the counter. "You still got game *mad* on you. I don't know who you think you're kidding."

"About what?" Mason let him in and followed him to the kitchen, pulling out the potato-leek soup he'd made the night before, just for their Saturday together. "Here—let me set this up to warm."

"No—we'll eat it later." Terry took the soup out of his hands and put it back in the refrigerator, surprising him.

"Why later?" Mason mumbled, and then Terry turned toward him and kissed him, hard, almost angry, shoving him back against the counter and shoving his hands up Mason's shirt to pinch his nipples.

"Mm?" Mason tried to pull back. Enthusiastic—yes. But never angry, never harsh.

"Shut up and use me," Terry snarled. "You gotta do it to someone, you might as well do it to me."

"Not to you," Mason said, trying to take a stand. His hand shook, but he managed to caress the skin of Terry's cheeks with his fingertips. *I love you.* "Never to you."

Terry's face contorted into a battle sneer. "That's why I'm best for the job." And then he climbed Mason like a tree, wrapping his legs solidly around Mason's hips and capturing Mason's mouth again.

God, Mason wanted. He cupped his hands under Terry's thighs and walked him to the stairs. Part of him was surprised his weak ankle didn't roll, but his cock—which felt like most of his functioning brain—was screaming *I WANT!* And Mason couldn't say no.

Terry wriggled out of his arms at the bottom of the stairs and hauled ass up, shouting, "Hurry, Mason, or I'll finish myself."

Mason was halfway up when the image hit him, Terry, lying in his bed, one hand on his cock, the other fiddling behind him, stretching himself, making him ready. Mason's vision went red, possessiveness sweeping through him.

Mine!

All of the juggling with words, the not trying to scare anybody, not trying to hurt anybody, trying to understand. Suddenly Mason just *wanted*—wanted to possess his lover like a cave man, wanted to take him, to *own him*—wanted no words or ideas between them, no other people.

He hurtled up the stairs like a meteor, arriving just in time to see Terry shimmy out of his jersey and shuck his shorts.

Mason didn't remember taking off his own clothes, but by the time he got to the bed, Terry was bent over the mattress, lubed fingers prepping himself, dilated, slick, and open.

Mason drove himself inside like a bullet, Terry's cry of pleasure/pain one of the sexiest things Mason had heard in his life.

It was the last thing he remembered hearing for a while, as he surged into his lover like a freight train, roaring and swearing, screaming "Mine!" whenever he could find breath.

Terry lay beneath him, panting, moaning "Yes, yes, yes—c'mon, Mason, give it to me!" and Mason gave and gave and fucking gave.

His climax seemed incidental in all of that fury, but when it rushed his spine and exploded outward, everything stopped—all the noise in the room, all the noise in his head, all the grief in his heart—and for that one moment, he lost himself in the beauty of orgasm, pouring his frustration into his lover's body.

He collapsed forward then rolled sideways, trying to catch his breath. Terry was still mashed into the bed, his fist moving feverishly underneath him. Just when Mason realized that he hadn't finished—was, in fact, chasing his own orgasm and maybe Mason should help—Terry let out a little "Oh!" and shuddered, his come hitting the bedspread beneath him.

And Mason realized what he'd done.

"Oh God," he whispered as Terry smiled tiredly through his fall of hair. "Terry, I'm so sorry."

"Don't be," Terry said simply, shrugging. He wriggled up so he and Mason were facing each other. "It's okay. I know how to take it like that."

Oh hell. Mason had used him, like all of the other guys Terry had known.

"I'm so sorry," he said again, his voice cracking. "I didn't mean—I never would have—" Except he had, hadn't he?

The smell of sex and sweat filled the room, and Mason came a breath away from rushing to the bathroom to throw up.

Terry's fingertips on Mason's cheekbones stopped him.

"Of course not," he said, equable and calm, like Mason hadn't just fucked him savagely, like a thing. "You're the only one who ever treated me like a person," he said. "But that's 'cause you're decent. When you're decent, you don't want anyone to see you hurt like that." A sweet, sad smile flitted across his face. "You trusted me, right?"

Mason nodded, out of words. "Yeah," he said, his voice fractured. He took a deep breath, and his chin wobbled. He tried to push himself up so he could go to the bathroom and pull himself together.

"Right?" Terry said softly. "You trust me?"

"Yeah," he said again, his voice broken completely. Oh God, he wasn't going to make it to the bathroom. Terry wriggled up on the bedspread, so Mason was even with his chest, and palmed Mason's head forward.

"Trust me," Terry urged. "C'mon, Mason. Trust me."

The first sob broke, the total helplessness, the pain of watching his brother in pain, the stupid unfairness of Mason's beautiful baby brother and the mental illness that sank its claws into him when Dane needed his sanity the most.

A flurry of sobs, a waterfall of broken, gasping tears, and Terry held him through them all, not saying much, just held him, kissing his temple, telling Mason without words that it was going to be okay.

Mason never remembered getting up and showering after that, or eating lunch either. They spent a couple of hours sweeping off the back porch and getting it ready for spring so they could sit out on the patio and eat, and then they went back inside and watched movies. Mason didn't say much, and Terry filled in the silence with chatter.

When they crawled into bed that night, Terry didn't move on him, didn't try to arouse him, just lay quietly in his arms for a minute.

"How you doing?" he asked into the darkness.

Mason closed his eyes and did an internal assessment.

"The only thing holding me together right now is you," he said honestly.

Terry hmphed. "That's probably bullshit," he declared. Then he kissed Mason just hard enough for tongues to get involved. He pulled back and said, "But it was a nice thing to say. Thanks, Mace." He touched Mason's cheek. "I hope you feel better in the morning."

Mason did—and he knew the truth.

It hadn't been bullshit at all, and it made him a little achy inside. Terry had the strength to hold Mason together when he needed it. Now he just needed to find the strength to do the same thing for himself.

The Short Months

DANE IMPROVED. Not overnight, but slowly and steadily, with a lot of help from Carpenter. Terry helped Mason when he could—but that fragile sense of togetherness was just not in a place to get stronger.

By the middle of April, they had established a rhythm. It wasn't a *great* rhythm, but there was just enough music and sex in it to keep Mason from begging for more.

Practice on Thursday, if they didn't have a game that day, where they agreed on the lunch that Terry brought him the next day. On those days Terry started wearing jeans without holes and one of two polo shirts, as well as tennis shoes and Mason's sweater. Mike didn't stop him at the gate anymore, and Mrs. Bradford simply assumed that Mason's lunch would be walking in the door sometime between twelve thirty and one thirty, the bearer sporting a bemused smile that never went away.

There was always a game on Saturday unless they were between seasons. Mason couldn't figure out what an actual soccer season was in this league—it seemed to be about six weeks, with a week in between, but he couldn't be sure. His ankle held, though, and that was good. As much as he enjoyed watching Terry play, it was a lot more fun to be involved—even if he was still a big gawky old guy who let more goals through than he kicked back into play.

Terry came home with him Saturday night. That was nonnegotiable. Terry turned off his phone as soon as he came to the game and didn't turn it on again until he and Mason left the next day to work on the house while Julie was at church or with friends or torturing small animals and the occasional child. (Mason couldn't be sure about that last one, but he was pretty sure all bad things came from Terry's mother, and not complaining about that during their weekends together was becoming more and more difficult.)

By mid-April, the floors of Terry's house were sound and laid with hardwood; the bathrooms were recaulked, resealed, retiled, and repainted; the siding was repainted; the roof was retarred; and the driveway cement repaired. Every room in the house had a new coat of paint and had endured a hearty scrubbing of all the dirt in all the corners; some even had new curtains.

Whether or not they'd all been able to make it to help with the weekend makeover, Carpenter and Skipper ate lunch in Mason's office every Monday, where they rehashed their weekends and talked about what else needed to be done before Terry could make his bid for freedom.

It was at one of these luncheons that Carpenter stated the obvious.

"So, like, our last chore is going to be to move Terry out of his mom's house. Does he have an apartment picked yet?"

Mason put down his fork. They were eating hamburgers from Chili's today, Skipper's treat, and Mason's had been dripping in wing sauce. He'd needed a fork and a knife if he wasn't going to completely destroy the shirt he was wearing.

"Uh, no," he said, feeling stupid. He'd known this was coming. *Known* this was coming. But the last thing they needed to do was fix and seal the eaves, and that was their job this Sunday.

It was time to set Terry free.

"Don't look so depressed!" Carpenter said, although *he* looked depressed enough for the both of them. Dane's mood swings were finally getting better—but it was a rough road. Carpenter had been taking him to his therapy and psychiatry appointments every week. Mason wasn't sure what their relationship was at this point, but given that Dane had no filter about his personal life and he had no *words* about what he and Carpenter were, Mason would put actual money down on Dane not knowing either.

But Carpenter had lost at least fifty pounds over the past six months, and Mason bet that thirty of them were stress and worry over a guy he *wasn't* dating.

Sort of like Mason's worry was over a guy he wasn't dating either.

"I... I don't know what's going to happen after he gets an apartment," Mason confessed, feeling foolish. Having these people as friends the past four months had become one of the biggest blessings. The foolishness came from his *own* hang-ups, about being older, about having more experience, about having an education.

The fact was, Skip and Carpenter couldn't have given a shit about Mason's supposed privileges—they treated him like a human. When Mason sounded like a peevish child or a sex-happy high school student, they just nodded like that was all okay.

No judgments here.

Mason was a fan.

"What do you mean, what will happen?" Skip asked, squinting. He'd gotten a veggie burger for himself, and Mason thought he'd ask for the same next time. He was still trying hard to lose the fifteen pounds he'd gained when he'd hurt himself.

"Why's he going to want to hang out with me anymore?" Mason asked, trying to leech the self-pity out of the words. "I mean, I'm great now when he's looking for two nights a week, but he's going to realize he can go out for a beer after work, and that he doesn't have to be home any time he doesn't want to." He gestured with his fork. "Maybe he wants a cat. We'll have to work to accommodate the cat. But it's going to take over his life. He won't have time to call me because of the cat, and then he'll forget to call me, and right now we've got a rhythm."

"You've got a rhythm with a cat?" Carpenter asked, obviously not keeping up.

"No!" Mason stabbed viciously at his burger and broke off a tine of the plastic. "I've got a rhythm with *Terry*. I think it's the only reason he remembers to come over. It's Friday, so we do lunch. It's Thursday, so we do practice. It's Saturday, so we do each other. I mean I don't blame him—living with that woman has fucked him over. All he can think of is the next thing that will get him out of the house and get *her* off his back. She's such a vicious noise in his head that he doesn't have time for his own thoughts."

"Oh my God, you're right," Carpenter said, entranced. "I've been trying to figure him out since November, but I think you've got it!"

"I'm totally impressed," Skipper said, equally wide-eyed. "I just thought he was a fuckin' squirrel."

"He is, and that's why," Mason said, his stomach roiling. "I'm over it—I like his squirrelly-ness—but it's gonna fuck me in the end."

"But Mason—"

He couldn't listen to Carpenter right now. His worry was too busy gushing out of his brain. "So right now the only reason that squirrel comes back to me is because I'm in the right spot in the maze. He's got the maze set up, he's got treats set up so he can get through it—I'm his weekend treat. Friday, Saturday, and Sunday. I'm what he lives for."

"That's fair," Skipper conceded. "So then what's the prob—"

Oh! Couldn't they see? Mason waved his maimed fork around some more. "What's going to happen when that's all gone, right? No maze, no rhythm, no reason to call Mason, Mason and Terry are no longer a thing!"

He gestured so hard his fork flew out of his fingers. Carpenter ducked, and it hit the wall behind him. Mason grabbed a napkin and soaked it in water from his bottle before getting up to wipe off the splat.

"So I have to help him do that," he said into the rather stunned silence.

"But... why?" Skipper asked, voice pulsing a little like Mason's heart.

The napkin started disintegrating, and Mason gave it up, throwing the pieces into the trash can by the door and hoping the custodian wouldn't hate him for the mess.

"Because," he said, staring blindly at the napkin muck against the ecru paint. "Because I want him happy and free. It's no good if I say, 'Oh, here you are, happy and free, but here's that minicage you built when you were miserable. Let's stay here.'"

He sighed and stalked back to his seat.

Carpenter handed him a new set of plasticware, and Mason broke it out in the sudden silence and tried to start again.

"He'll come back when the dust settles," Skipper said sincerely. "You'll still be the best part of his life."

"But you're right," Carpenter added.

Mason looked up and met his eyes and recognized the sympathy of one soul to another. It was the same look they exchanged when Carpenter was talking a moody, bitchy, *hurtful* Dane into the car, one insult and carrot on the stick at a time.

"I'm right?" He hated being right.

"He's got to figure out what life is like when nobody expects anything from him. It's... I mean, you want a grown-up. Grown-up relationships are choices. You can't choose your parents—but you can choose your friends and...." Underneath Carpenter's scruffy beard, Mason might have seen a flush. "Lovers," he said hastily, like the word was sacred. "Boyfriends. Significant others. Whatever."

"Is it really a choice?" Mason asked, looking at him with meaning. "Because I used to think so. I'd meet a guy, date a guy, take the relationship in increments. But this didn't feel like I chose it. It felt like... like I'd been *waiting* for this one person to wander into my life and make me feel good. And once he showed up, there was no choice at all."

Carpenter leveled a tortured look at him, and Mason returned it. Yeah, Mason didn't know the answer to Carpenter and Dane either—but he knew love when he saw it. Whatever it was they were doing, Carpenter needed to own up to that.

"I hear that," Skipper said unexpectedly. "But that's good."

Mason and Carpenter both stared at him. Skip smiled sunnily back.

"Why good?" Carpenter asked, like he was dying for the answer.

The look Skip sent him was so compassionate, Mason thought he must have more inside information about Carpenter and Dane than Mason did.

"Because you know what you have to do," Skip said, shrugging. "You don't have a choice. Whatever your person needs, you have to be there. 'Cause he's—yes, *he*, Clay, you're fooling fuckin' *nobody*—the one person who makes you happy. If you can do the thing, whatever the thing is, to return the favor, that's your *job*, right?"

So simple.

All those long talks Mason had had with Todd about the nature of love and politics, all those long talks with Ira about how to make a modern relationship work, and Skip had pretty much nailed it.

This person made Mason happy. Mason needed to return the favor.

"That's really wise," Mason said, feeling hollow and sad.

"Fuckin' brilliant," Clay snapped, but his voice was breaking, so he wasn't really mad.

Skip looked at him. Just looked at him. "Clay, what's so hard to admit? Your parents are liberal. I'm your best work friend and I'm gay, and you never gave a shit. Dane is your best friend in the world, and you're so damned in love with him it almost stops my heart. Why would it be so hard to just kiss him? Just fucking kiss him and see if the stubble bothers you?"

Carpenter scowled. "I *have* kissed him, and it was awesome. Do you think it bothers me that I'm attracted? That's not it at all!"

"Then what in the hell is it?" Skipper demanded, while Mason tried to file every word of this conversation to feed to Dane like dinner. A thing that would nourish his soul.

"You wouldn't get it," Carpenter muttered, throwing the last of his burger into the to-go box and starting clean up. "Look at the two of you. You'd never get—"

"So help me, Carpenter, if you are talking about the weight, I am going to kick you in the fucking balls." Skip stood up, furious. "I don't want to hear another goddamned word about your goddamned weight and why you don't deserve jack because you're a fat asshole who can't get his life together. You deserve fucking *everything*. You think I don't understand? You think I wasn't a fat kid with pimples? I leaned up, and so have you—and even if you hadn't, do you think I'd love you any less? Hell no. You're a fucking good person. *I* was a fucking good person. *Jesus*, Clay—you're breaking my fucking heart. Just give it a chance!"

Silence crashed the emotional tsunami, and for a moment Mason could only stare at Skipper, stunned all over again about the fineness of the man.

But he'd seen this in Terry, in his painful attempts to protect his friends and his lover from his mother's vitriol, too, in his tentative steps toward freedom. In that moment Mason realized why he'd fallen in love with Terry, and why it was irrevocable.

And then he realized that he'd fallen in love.

"I can't," Carpenter said, naked tears in his voice.

"Why not?" Mason asked, heart torn for him.

"Because I think the only thing holding him together right now is our friendship. You have to be strong inside to have a lover, and…." Carpenter met Mason's gaze almost tearfully. "He's not ready yet. I'd do it all, Mason. I'd come out, tell my parents, go to Pride Week in rainbow body paint and a thong—but he's still broken inside. I need to wait until he can deal."

Mason had to snap his mouth shut. "That is not what I expected you to say at all."

Skip nodded. "Yeah, gotta tell you, I am gobsmacked. You could have told me!"

Carpenter just shook his head, then stood up and started throwing trash away. "It was…." He smiled softly. "Private. Inside me. But then Dane started crashing and…."

"And all your love hurt," Mason said, with feeling.

"You know what it's like too." Carpenter shrugged. "It is—"

"If you say 'It is what it is' I'll vomit," Skip muttered. "'Cause what it is sucks. It's not 'what it is'—it's 'a situation ripe for improvement.'"

Carpenter let out the first cackle of laughter, but Mason was not far behind.

"Oh my God," Mason chuckled. "You need to be in management."

Skipper's skin was fair, and the two red crescents on his cheeks showed up brightly. "I was thinking about teaching," he said apologetically.

"I used to think an office building meant I'm a grown-up, but I'm really sort of over this one."

Oh. Oh wow. "You'll be amazing," Mason said. "When would you do that?"

Skip shrugged. "A couple of years. Apply for school, save money, that sort of thing."

Good. Mason knew that a change in job didn't mean a loss of a friend, but he was glad everything wasn't going to change immediately. He'd just gotten used to having friends at work who didn't terrify him with their judgment.

With a sigh, he started to help Carpenter with cleanup. "So, long-term," he said, with a sort of resigned determination.

"Yeah," Skip said, looking carefully at the two of them. "Long-term. As in, don't give up. As in, if it's important, it'll happen."

"Jesus, Skip, you sound all wise and shit," Carpenter chided, but he didn't sound like he was about to cry, and the moment lightened.

"Yeah, well, Richie and I knew each other for six years before we figured out what love was. I don't know what you two are bitching about. If it's worth anything, it's worth a little bit of a wait."

Mason reminded himself of those words when he went to help Terry with the last bit of work.

Terry's mom was there—had been there for the past month of Sundays—reading magazines, watching television, and generally sitting and glaring while her son and his friends fixed her house from a ramshackle hovel into something she could be proud of.

It had only been in the past couple of weeks that Mason had realized that Terry wasn't doing it for her.

He was doing it for himself, so that when he left, he could leave her with a good conscience, in a place where she couldn't blame him for her life when he walked out. His whole life, she had told him that he owed her—he owed her for his life, for his clothes, for his food.

She'd inherited the house—he'd never owed her for that. Fixing it was his payback for all that other shit.

His indentured servitude was over.

Mason was so proud he could burst.

"So," he said as they were putting the boards and the sealant away in the garage, "have you scoped out apartments yet?"

Terry shrugged. "One's pretty much the same as the others," he said, not sounding excited. "They're all shaped like shoeboxes. They're all small."

Mason blinked at him. For the past month he'd been talking about nothing but getting an apartment. This was how he felt now?

"Well, yeah," he said. "But some of them are closer to my house than others."

Terry straightened up from his crouch at the paint cabinet and turned, a faint smile on his face. "That's important?" he tested. "You know, that I'm close?"

Mason smiled even though his heart felt about at his knees. "It's probably the apartment's most important feature," he said honestly. "That you can stop by and say hi and…."

A grin split Terry's face. "I can run home and get clean clothes on my way to work in the morning?"

And a little part of Mason breathed easy for the first time in months. "Yes," he said, trying to hold on to his dignity. "That's really important."

Terry laughed and, in one of those movements that made Mason think of squirrels, leaped into Mason's arms right there in the garage. Mason barely stood firm as he wrapped his legs around Mason's waist and started to plunder his mouth. Oh! God, his kisses—so bold, so *exciting*. They had only gotten better from that first grope in the bathroom. They had only become as essential as breathing, like water in the desert, those kisses in Mason's soul.

Mason braced him up under his thighs and kept kissing, so glad his ankle had finally healed so he could do things like this, hold him, be strong and larger than life. Fiercely he cupped Terry's ass through his shorts and kneaded.

Terry pulled away for a moment and rested his forehead against Mason's.

"I'll look for an apartment tomorrow after work," he breathed. "You know what I wanna do now?"

"Come back to my place and have more sex?" Yeah, the day before had been Sexy Saturday—but it had also been Cookout in Skipper's Yard Saturday and Be Horribly Defeated by a Bunch of Twenty-Year-Old Art Students on the Soccer Field Saturday.

Now that their last job was done, Mason really wanted Sweet Sexy Sunday to follow Saturday.

Just this once.

"God yes," Terry murmured. "I'm gonna go get my clothes for work tomorrow and tell Mom."

Julie hadn't said much about Terry's bid for independence—but then, Terry hadn't given her much of a chance to.

They went inside, where she was sitting in the small, recently refloored living room, watching television with dead eyes.

"Mom, we're done with the eaves and I'm taking off," Terry said, acting for all the world like he did this all the time.

"It's Sunday!" she protested, looking up from the TV. "Who's gonna make dinner?"

"Well, Mom, since there's all those nice soups in the fridge and some salads in a bag, I figured you could do it. Dinner's been made!" He sent Mason an exasperated look before trotting up the recently repaired stairs to his eight-by-eight bedroom. Mason had been in it a couple of times while they'd been repairing the house, and each time he looked in vain for something, somewhere, some indication of who Terry was becoming. Mostly he saw a green-and-blue comforter and pictures of soccer teams on the walls. And those were recent.

But then, there wasn't room for much more than the bed and a dresser with his computer on it. Maybe, like a lot of tech guys Mason knew, all of Terry's personality was in the little box on his drawer.

Or maybe he wasn't the kind of guy who posted pictures and looked up porn.

Mason was very much looking forward to finding out.

"I don't know where he thinks he's going," Julie Jefferson grumbled. "He's got work tomorrow."

"He can leave for work from my house," Mason said neutrally. "I don't mind."

"Oh, I'm sure you don't. You just love having him over there so you can make him all fucking gay. You think you're a big man, right? With the fancy clothes and the car. You're a fuckin' *pervert*, and you've made my son one too. Fucking pansy-assed pervert. I can hardly *wait* until all this shit with the house is done—he won't have any excuse to hang out with you no more."

Ouch. Well, it was no more than Mason feared—but it hurt, and he was goaded into cruelty with his response.

"Whether he hangs with me or not is between us. But he's certainly not going to be hanging *here*—not after he finds an apartment."

"He's going to *what?*" she shrieked, and Mason winced. Well, apparently Terry had saved this little tidbit for later, not that Mason blamed him.

"Uh—"

"Hey, Mom—taking off. See you tomorrow night. Late. Got stuff to do after work."

Mason and Julie both turned toward his voice as he pattered down the stairs, a duffel bag with the logo of his tech company slung over his shoulder.

"You're moving out?" she demanded as he approached the landing. "And you didn't tell me?"

Mason glared at him too. "You didn't tell her?"

"I told you months ago," he snapped.

"That wasn't real!" she yelled.

"Oh!" Mason stopped glaring. "I'm sorry. I should have known better. Yeah, c'mon, Terry. Let's let her calm down."

"You think you're so high-and-mighty," she snarled at Mason. "Talking about me like I'm not right here!"

"Well, you don't talk to us like we're human," Mason said back. "I'm just returning the favor."

Terry came to where he was standing and bobbed his head toward the door. Back in January this exchange would have destroyed him, rendered him helpless, negated all of the strength and personal growth he'd worked so hard to achieve. But now he managed to ignore her, to hold himself together, and to function in the face of her vitriol.

Mason turned and followed Terry out, her ranting echoing at their backs.

Terry's composure didn't slip until Mason went for his car and Terry went for his. Terry paused and looked at Mason beseechingly.

"Look, I know this is a lot to ask," he started, and Mason's heart melted.

Four months ago he had barely accepted a ride from IHOP.

"Sure I'll take you to my place and drop you off," he said. "I can't think of anything else I'd rather do."

Terry climbed into the SUV then, and Mason gladly pulled away. Terry kept his eyes on the house, though, like he was searching for an answer in the freshly painted siding and the newly sealed eaves.

MASON STARTED up the barbecue while Terry was in the shower, and Dane came out to help. Marinated chicken and vegetables—Mason was determined to get that weight off, and Dane... well, he wasn't eating much these days.

"I hate that you're obsessing about fifteen pounds," Dane sulked, setting the plates out on the patio table. They'd bought basic furniture—the table was the same glass-topped, white-painted one every family in America had. But something about eating outside for the Battle of Mason's Bulging Stomach while the weather wasn't apocalyptic and the bugs hadn't yet regrouped made the day feel special. The oak trees that dominated the uneven terrain beyond the porch and the pool fence cast a soothing shade—a *lying* shade, Dane had called it last August, because it hadn't seemed to cool down a blessed thing—but the shadows were pretty.

Mason wanted to enjoy the shade and the idea that the home improvement projects in Carmichael were done, and he and Dane could start working on the porch on their house in Fair Oaks. He wanted to think about having Terry in his arms that night, and he *didn't* want to think about how it might be the last time for a while, or the second to last, or even the third to last—it didn't matter, because the word "last" was in there, and it hurt.

What he didn't want to do was spar with his brother.

"It's harder to play soccer with the weight on," Mason said evenly. "It's not all about vanity, okay?"

"Yeah, I know," Dane said savagely. "It's about health. I've heard it often enough from Carpenter. I think it's bullshit."

Ugh. Upon careful consideration, Mason had decided that Carpenter's disclosure at lunch that Monday was privileged information and that Carpenter was going to have to tell Dane himself.

But that didn't mean Mason couldn't say something about *this*.

"Carpenter's not trying to lose weight—or to attract you. At this point I think everyone pretty much knows you're his for the taking. He *does* want to be healthy. And I think that includes being healthy inside, where the bad eating was coming from."

Dane grunted. "I don't want to talk about that."

"Yeah, I know. Privileged info," Mason snapped. "I'm a fan."

"What are you so upset about?" Moodily, Dane picked up a twig that had fallen to the table from the big oak tree nearest the house and hurled it off the porch. "You don't have to be in love with the asshole."

"Who is amazingly worried about you. Please tell me you've taken your meds—"

"All weekend." Dane held up his hands. "Don't get your nuts in a twist."

"Tell me you've kept your fluids up and your blood sugar too." Because forgetting to eat and drink hadn't helped the past four months.

"Pure like an angel," Dane said, but his usual sarcasm was missing too. "Grilled cheese and an apple for lunch, sixty-four ounces of water, chocolate milk as a snack."

For a moment they regarded each other soberly. The wounds from March and April were still raw.

"Good," Mason said, mollified. He had to remind himself not to take his impending grief out on his brother. "Sorry. I'm just…." He smiled greenly at Dane. "I don't know what's going to happen next."

Dane shrugged, deliberately not taking the bait. "You're going to grill chicken on the barbecue. It's been marinating all day—it'll taste great."

"Right. And as soon as Terry's out, I'll jump in the shower. That's what's happening next."

And that suddenly, he knew how Terry had been thinking for the past four months. One thing to the next—the good things got you through the incipient fear of being rejected by someone you loved. He'd had practice with Dane, but this? This was the real thing.

THEY STAYED out, sipping iced tea and eating bites of melon from a bowl. They talked about silly things: what kind of frogs were chirping from the stream that ran in the ravine beyond, how hot it was going to be that summer, how stupid you had to be to run your library card through the credit card machine at a gas station. They laughed an inappropriate amount for people who had consumed no alcohol.

When the mosquitoes got too bad, they went inside, Terry pulling at Mason's hand until they vanished up the stairs, leaving Dane, knees drawn up to his chest, moodily flipping through channels.

When they got upstairs, Terry surprised him, though. Instead of devouring Mason, stripping him naked, and blowing him from the get-go, Terry started with a simple kiss on Mason's cheek.

Mason smiled in the shadows of the bedroom, as always ridiculously pleased by that gesture.

Terry traced the curve of Mason's lips. "Why you always smile like that?" he asked, close enough that Mason could feel every puff of breath.

"Because it's not about sex," Mason said back, running his lips gently along Terry's temple. "You don't kiss someone like that unless you care."

Terry pulled back, peering at Mason's face carefully in the dim light. "That's true," he said, sounding surprised. "Is that the only way you know I care?"

Mason couldn't make himself laugh like he should. "There's others," he said. "Practice on Thursday, lunch on Friday, sex on Saturday—"

Terry's fingers on his lips stopped the recitation. "You don't think that's… that's *all* you are to me, right?" he asked anxiously. "You… you *know* you're more to me than a thing to do on a certain day, *right*?"

His eyes were unreadable in the darkness, but Mason took a risk and hoped there was sincerity there. "I want to be everything," he whispered, just so Terry knew where they could go. "You have a lot on your plate. You don't have to go there until you're ready."

Terry gasped and traced delicate, tender lines on Mason's face with his fingertips. "Why?" he asked, confused. "Why would you want to be so important to me?"

The word ached in Mason's throat. "I'll let you know why if it happens," he said. He claimed Terry's mouth then, that sweet, wide, impudent mouth, and slipped his tongue between Terry's lips.

Their dance was gentle, giving and taking, Mason baiting Terry until Terry gave back in assertiveness, intensity.

When Terry took over the kiss, cupping Mason's neck, body hard against Mason's and imposing in his space, his taste, his passion, his assertion—it was the lovemaking of someone who *meant* it.

Mason allowed himself to be swept into the fantasy, to be overpowered and led. Terry kissed him backward, pulling down the covers and pushing him to the bed, then kissing along his neck until he got to the collar of his T-shirt.

He paused for a moment, sprawled across Mason while he played with Mason's sensitive nipples through the thin microfiber.

"You know, right?" he asked, sounding plaintive and lost.

"Know what?" Mason asked back.

"That… that you're important. The way I feel about you—that's… that's not how I've felt about *anybody*. I mean, you've had relationships and boyfriends and—"

"And nobody like you," Mason said simply. He couldn't think, now, about other times he'd said *I love you* to someone. They made him want to hide his head in shame, because he couldn't have possibly meant it, not then. He figured that maybe the reasons all those other times failed was because never, not once in all those years, had he felt like *this*.

Like he'd die if Terry didn't feel the same.

"Why?" Terry sat up and helped Mason out of his T-shirt, and then they both kicked off their shorts and flip-flops. "Why? What's so different about me?"

"You don't obsess about which wine goes with which meat," Mason said, rolling over so his naked body covered Terry's. He kissed to Terry's ear and bit softly, then continued. "You learned golf when you thought you'd hate it." And down that smooth-shaven throat to a vulnerable collarbone. He nipped a couple of times. "You didn't ask questions when my brother lost his shit." No. He hadn't. He'd just let Mason fuck him blind. "You are kind when you don't need to be, and funny because you like to laugh, and you don't humor me in bed, you just take what you want and give back."

He finished on a rush, the unabashed sentimentality making him want to hide his face, but the only place to hide was on the taut plane of Terry's stomach, and only the skin was soft.

Terry massaged his fingers through Mason's hair in reassurance. "You… you could have anybody," he said hesitantly.

Mason laved his belly button and then lapped delicately at the sensitive underside of his cock, tasting soap and salt and Terry. He gave the bell a quick suck and then pulled away, regarding Terry seriously up the length of his star-pale body.

"I don't want anybody," Mason said, knowing he sounded plaintive but unable to change it. "I want *you*. When you want me back like that, let me know."

He turned his head and sucked again, this time slow and hard, swirling his tongue at the end. "I want you," he whispered, taking that sweet length into his mouth again, pulling until the head was lodged in his throat. He pulled back and wrapped his fist around it, squeezing the same way he sucked, the way Terry liked it, while he tortured the slit with his tongue. "You."

Terry grunted, pleading, and pulled his knees up, spreading his thighs, exposing himself to Mason's lovemaking, trusting—as no one ever had—that Mason could do things right.

Mason wanted to do *all* the things right.

He shoved at Terry's thighs and nuzzled, pulling one testicle at a time into his mouth while Terry battered his fists against the mattress. Mason spread his cheeks after that, and licked, finding him clean and sensitive.

He sort of loved rimming Terry—he got vocal and encouraging as nobody ever had before. "Yeah, there. Love that. Like, stretch it. With your fingers—ooooh—that's right. God, keep going. I'm lovin' that—yes! Stretch, that's right, wider! More! Hit that—*augh, yes!*—spot!"

Mason would die to follow his orders.

Finally Terry clenched his fingers in Mason's hair, and his body started to shake uncontrollably. "*Now, Mason—please, now!*"

They kept the lube under the pillow. Mason could slick up so quick, Terry didn't even have to know he'd gone missing.

This time Terry rolled to his side, pulling one knee up in blatant exposure and begging. "Hard, Mason. Hard. Just you inside me—just, just hold me and fuck me and make it hard!"

Yes! Terry's clench around Mason's erection was all that heaven could hope for. Mason started pumping slow at first, but Terry couldn't deal with hard and slow.

"Faster—oh, dammit Mace, *faster*. Take me over, take all of me, fuck me till I *scream!*"

He begged that all the time, but Mason had yet to make him scream.

He didn't want to make him scream now.

So he paused in midstroke and did the unthinkable. Firmly lodged inside his lover's body, he ran his hand playfully, warmly, down Terry's flanks, his thighs, his stomach.

He took Terry's cock in his hand and squeezed from base to tip while Terry began to rock his hips frantically back and forth, needing Mason's length and girth bad enough to cry.

"Maaason!"

"You want me?" Mason taunted.

"Oh yes!"

"Anyone else?"

"No! Dammit, Mason, only you! Only you! You're all I want! Mine!"

"You sure? Sure no one else will do? Sure you don't want someone younger?"

"Mason!"

Mason's next few thrusts were unusually forceful. "What? Is that a no?"

"Only fuckin' you, dammit, now *fuck me*!"

Mason rolled so Terry was facedown on the bed, then thrust his hips as hard and as fast as he could. Oh yes—full possession. *Mine, dammit, mine!*

The slaps of their flesh filled the room. With a guttural moan and a scream, Terry convulsed without his own hand on his cock, orgasming fiercely and catching Mason in a vise so tight he almost couldn't come.

Almost.

His climax rolled through him, slow and vicious, pulling shaking, shrieking pleasure from the pit of Mason's balls. *He* screamed, muffling the sound in the sweaty skin of Terry's neck, which he bit at the peak of his come.

Terry moaned, shivering around the invasion of Mason's body, an aftershock rocking him, and then another. Mason gave one last used and exhausted spurt before sliding to the side and pulling him into an all-inclusive, spent, and needing hug.

They were a lot of things in bed—voracious, passionate, *loud*.

But they had never been like *that*.

Mason wished he had words to explain, to tell Terry what he was afraid of, but doing that would be like begging him to stay. Which was the one thing Mason couldn't do.

Instead he just held on tight, kissing the back of Terry's neck, his shoulders, his ears, trying to show without words all of the reasons Terry had to come back to him.

"Mason?" Terry asked, sounding sleepy and sated and maybe a little giggly from all the kissing.

"Yeah?"

"If I asked nice, would you come apartment hunting with me?"

"You could ask mean and I'd still do it."

Terry's chuckle calmed him, settled him somehow. "I'll ask nice 'cause that way gets me blow jobs."

Mason's turn to chuckle. "Just being you gets you blow jobs."

He rolled in Mason's arms, nestling against Mason's shoulders. "I only want them from you," he said quietly. "I'll let you know if that changes."

Mason closed his eyes, grateful. It wasn't much—but Terry was nothing if not honest.

It was everything.

"MRS. BRADFORD?" Mason asked Monday morning.

"Yes, Mr. Hayes?"

"Do you ever think of wearing something, I don't know, spring themed?"

"You mean not so blessedly hot?"

"Yes, Mrs. Bradford. That's exactly what I mean."

Mrs. Bradford cocked her head thoughtfully. "You wear a suit to work every day, Mr. Hayes. The other executives come in frequently in slacks and polos. Why is that?"

Mason grimaced—and then recounted the unfortunate story of the casual Fridays that weren't.

Mrs. Bradford raised her eyebrows. "Sounds like your boss was a real prick, if you don't mind my saying."

"Well, that's what my ex-boyfriend thought, Mrs. Bradford—which is why Ira spent two years sitting on him."

"D'oh!"

The sound was *so* at odds with her appearance. "So I'll make you a deal," he said when he was done laughing.

"What would that be, sir?"

"If you wear something besides heat-sucking navy, I will wear slacks and polos, and we might survive the summer."

A sweet smile softened her stern features. "I would like that very much, sir. Is there anything else?"

"Uh, yes, but it's not exactly work related."

She blinked slowly. "You're too gay to hit on me, Mr. Hayes—my curiosity is piqued."

"My friend, the one who comes on Friday—"

"Mr. Jefferson?" She inclined her head slightly, and Mason knew he fooled no one.

"Yeah. Terry. He, uh, is moving out of the house with his mother and is looking for an apartment. I was sort of hoping for something in Fair Oaks, but he doesn't... his job isn't... uh—"

"He doesn't make an executive's salary?" she supplied delicately.

"No."

"Do you know what salary he *does* make?" Her posture indicated no judgment whatsoever.

"I know what he does for a living," Mason said. "Does that help?"

"It does indeed. You give me a description and maybe a company, and I can come up with some apartments in his price range."

Mason smiled at her with nothing but the most profound gratitude. "Mrs. Bradford, is there some sort of reward I can put you up for?"

"Flowers on Secretaries' Day are nice," she said with a smile.

"Isn't that Administrative Assistants'—"

"I just want some flowers, sir. My husband doesn't do flowers. Is it so much to ask?"

Oh.

"You shall have flowers every week, Mrs. Bradford."

She looked at him limpidly. "You, sir, are the best boss in the world."

And with that, she turned on her heel and set about her day.

By the time they met again at lunch, she had a list of apartments in Terry's price range. And Mason had a standing order at the local florist's shop—one moderately priced bouquet delivered to Mrs. Bradford's desk every Monday.

She was more than worth it.

"WHY AM I taking Thursday off again?" Terry asked Thursday morning when Mason let him into the kitchen.

"Because we're a week from the end of the month. If we find an apartment today, we can pack this Sunday and move after the soccer game the Saturday after." Mason had done his homework.

"That's smart," Terry said, coming up behind Mason as he poured two coffees in aluminum mugs. He wrapped his arms around Mason's waist and rubbed his cheek against his back between his shoulder blades. Mason took a moment to close his eyes and savor.

"I had help," he conceded. "I asked Skip and Carpenter."

"Mm...." Without ceremony, Terry pulled his cargo shorts down and bent low enough to kiss a line up Mason's spine.

"Nungh!" Very carefully, Mason put the carafe in the coffeemaker and the mug in his hand down on the counter. "Wha—"

"Is Dane here?" Terry asked.

"No, thank God," Mason breathed. Terry's hands were busy kneading his ass and parting his cheeks.

"Good. Bend over." Terry put Mason's hands on the counter and nudged at his ankles until Mason kicked off his loafers and his shorts so he could spread his feet.

Mason had never felt so exposed, and for a moment, he wanted to hide. But Terry was tracing his tongue on an evil path, and Mason wanted him to find ground zero more than he wanted to save his own dignity.

Ahhh.... Oh yeah. Terry was good at this, and when he slid his hand between Mason's legs to fondle his balls and stroke his cock, his tongue felt even better. And even though this was impromptu and over *another* sink, Mason's body shook with yearning.

Oh man. *C'mon, Terry—you've got me wet and slack and bent over the counter and....*

The sensation of Terry's head nudging between his knees pulled him out of the moment. He looked down and Terry was looking up at him, Mason's cock at his mouth.

He winked and opened his mouth, and Mason almost sobbed.

And then he saw the bottle of olive oil peeking out from the cupboard where they kept the coffee.

Mason reached up and grabbed it, hands shaking. Oh God—hard and quick and dirty. Terry wasn't holding back on that blow job.

A few drops—that's all he needed—and then he reached back and... *ah*....

He moaned, body pulled tight like a piano wire between the two sensations.

Terry jerked back, mouth leaving Mason's prick, and Mason almost cried.

"What're you doin'?" he asked, voice full of wonder.

"You want in, go for it!" Mason whined, two fingers inside, thrusting, stretching. The angle was awkward, but he didn't care. *God*, it had been a while since he'd done this!

"You want *me* to…." Terry's voice throbbed with arousal, and Mason forced himself to stop with the fingerfucking so he could gaze at him fondly. "*Please?*"

Terry's mouth made a round little O, and he reached between Mason's thighs and grasped his wrist. "Stop," he ordered.

Mason glared. "You had better—"

Terry pulled his cock in for one more good suck, and Mason strained against that implacable hold on his wrist.

There was no yielding, and he whined, dropping his head to the counter.

Then that peculiar pressure between his legs again before Terry stood behind him. He pulled gently on Mason's wrist, and the emptiness that followed had him trembling with need. He held fast, fumbling for a paper towel while Terry fumbled for his own shorts.

Mason heard them hit the floor just as Terry's soft-skinned cock prodded his entrance.

"Nnnnn… please?" Mason whined.

Terry's cockhead pushed, and Mason broke into a cold, prickly sweat in anticipation. "I'm afraid I'll hurt you," Terry breathed.

Augh! "Only if you stop."

Ah… ah… ah… *oooh*….

Slowly he sank into Mason's body, farther and farther, until his pubic hair ground up against the tender skin of Mason's asscheeks.

For a moment they breathed while Mason tried desperately not to let his hands slide on the counter.

"Wow," Terry whispered. "Mace—you should see this! My *cock* is all the way in your *ass*. That's amazing! That's—"

"*Fuck me!*"

"Oh yeah." He pulled back. "Right." *Smack.* He thrust his hips hard, and Mason almost wept with relief. "Good?" he asked, stopping again. "I mean, that's what I'm supposed to do, ri—"

"*Terry!* Dammit!"

"Oh, sorry!" And thrust, oh thank God, and thrust again, and he wasn't stopping this time, and pull back, throw himself forward, ouch, that was a little hard—

"Gentler," Mason breathed, praying that wouldn't make him stop. It didn't. Just a little softer, a little slower, and—"Perfect. Keep doing that. Just that. Do that some more. *Oh my God keep doing that!*"

And yes! It was exactly right! It was exactly what Mason had been craving through three different relationships and one perfidious waiter!

Terry didn't stop, didn't waver—just kept that perfect, sweet-spot-hitting rhythm that had Mason burying his face in his arms and howling.

And then: "Mace, I'm gonna—are you gonna? 'Cause I'm gonna—" Oh hell. Mason moved his hand to his cock just as Terry groaned, "Come!" against his back.

Terry convulsed, his cock pulsing in Mason's ass, and Mason stroked frantically at himself, chasing that bright-dark light of orgasm. *Yes, yes, yes, yes, c'mon, please, oh my God so good so stretched so full and hot and wet, running down my thigh and—*

"Yes!" Oh yes. Climax took over his body, his ass clenched, his cock spurted, the sky exploded, the heavens wept, and oh my holy God, Mason Hayes had finally gotten topped by the man of his dreams.

Who was currently collapsed over his back, cock leaking down Mason's backside, sweating body sticking to Mason's skin.

Mason straightened up, groaning a little as his back released. He sighed and stretched and turned to pull Terry into a hot, sweaty, sexed-out hug.

"That was unexpected," he said into the sex-scented sunshine.

"You're telling me!" Terry panted. "God, that was awesome. I was so scared—I didn't want to hurt you, but… but it feels good when you do it to *me*, and I thought… I just wanted to… you know. *Give* to you."

Mason smiled, wishing they could just go nap now. "I want to give you the world," he confessed. Some of the ebullience faded, and his shoulders slumped. "But first, an apartment."

"Can we shower first?" Terry asked hopefully.

Mason laughed and kissed his sweaty hair. He'd worn it down today, and it hung lank over his eyes. April—already hot.

"Yeah," he said. "But first I need to wipe down the cabinets."

Terry looked down at the dripping wood paneling. "Ugh. Dude. Yeah."

So no nap. No second sex in the shower. And the olive oil stained Mason's boxers and shorts, just from pulling them on for the walk upstairs. He had to throw them away.

Sex—as messy as real life.

But as Mason stood in the shower and soaped Terry's hair, scrupulously stomping on his libido so they could go out and do what they'd planned, he remembered Terry trying so hard not to hurt him.

The only way to not get hurt was to keep going.

Getting an apartment was the next step in the "keep going" part.

Maybe they really were going somewhere.

"YOU LIKE it?" Mason asked, pleased. It was their fourth try, and the last apartment on the short list Mrs. Bradford had produced. The first three had been small and decrepit—one had a stairwell that had jumped out and bitten Mason as he'd walked up, and they'd had to stop to bandage up his ankle. ("Always the fuckin' ankle," Terry had said sourly.)

This one was small, but the carpet was new (or newly stretched), and there were ceiling fans in every room. The windows were strategically placed for flow through, so even though it was a top-floor apartment, it could still get rid of the heat, and the kitchen opened into the living room, so even though the whole thing was about the size of Mason's master suite, it didn't feel as cramped as the other three.

It was respectable. A kid's first apartment after moving out.

Mason really hated it. With all his soul. He had to keep reminding himself that Terry's key to seeing the world as a bigger place was paying rent on this much smaller place, but damn, was it hard.

"So my bed should go under the window," Terry muttered, and then he grinned. "You could fuck me in *my* bed for a change."

That suddenly, Mason didn't hate it anymore.

"Yup," he said. The place was hot, and they were both sweating, but Mason still moved behind him and kissed his neck. "And we can run around the place naked."

Terry laughed at that. "Which'll take about two minutes." He turned in Mason's arms then and frowned. "You won't mind? Coming here sometimes?"

Mason nuzzled his temple. "As long as I'm welcome."

"I… I mean, it's not as great as Skip's place, but Carpenter's giving me an extra TV and I'm getting Owens's old couch. We can watch movies."

He sounded so hopeful. "Sure." Mason had a good thought then. "So—what do you want for a moving-in gift? If Carpenter's giving you a TV and you have a bed and a couch, what can *I* give you?"

Terry smiled shyly, obviously pleased. "A… well, only if you have an old one or it's not too expensive. But I don't have a coffeemaker yet—or a microwave." He paused. "Or dishes, or cups. Or shower mats or towels. Or a dresser or…." His grin was wide and happy. "You know, I was all scared about this. I must have thought maybe six times about asking if I could sleep in your guest room or something. But I'm getting all excited. My mother's cups and glasses and stuff—that shit was *ugly.*"

Mason had to nod. There was no denying that Terry's mother hadn't given a crap about decorating.

"But I get to pick my own. That's gonna be *awesome*!"

"I can't wait," Mason said, his throat a little tight. "I'm so happy for you!"

It was hard to say—but he said it with a whole heart. Loving someone was easy, apparently. Letting him go was like swimming naked in eel wire.

MASON WENT for both the microwave *and* the coffeemaker. He presented them on Sunday, when he, Skipper, Richie, Carpenter, Dane, Cooper, Menendez, and some guy named Rudy from Terry's job helped him move.

Skipper rented a U-Haul, and Mason, Skip, and Richie helped get the stuff out of the house into the truck. They ignored Terry's mom, and she returned the favor, huddling on the couch and glaring at the men as they trooped up and down with Terry's furniture.

"You owe me for that!" she called as they left with each piece. And each time, Terry would remind her that he'd paid up her next four house payments.

Mason's stomach clenched at that.

It was one of the reasons Terry hadn't moved out on his own before. He'd been saving the money.

Mason couldn't think of someone who deserved it less then Terry's mother did.

But by midmorning they were set, and they caravanned from Carmichael to Fair Oaks, which all told took about fifteen minutes.

Of course to Terry, it was like jumping from the earth to the moon. He and Mason were the last ones to leave, Mason's car jammed with Terry's scant wardrobe. As Mason got into his car, Terry ran over and kissed him full on the mouth, and pulled back, smiling.

"What was that for?" Mason asked wonderingly.

"For being here and being awesome and not telling my mother to piss up a rope."

Mason laughed evilly. "That's only because I didn't think of it."

Those kisses on the cheek were still not getting old. "You're awesome," Terry said meaningfully. "Rudy thinks I'm lucky as shit."

"Rudy?" He was tall—taller than Mason or Skipper, even—and thin, with a shock of black hair, pale skin, and green eyes. Mason had grudgingly admitted to Skipper that he was damned beautiful, but there was no guarantee he even played for the boys' team.

"Yeah. He's a nice guy. He and I started talking a couple of weeks ago, which is why he offered to come help. He knew I was excited about it."

"He seems nice," Mason lied. He seemed like a pasty, scrawny boyfriend stealer, but Mason wasn't going to say that. For one thing, it would be embarrassing if it wasn't true, but for another?

Mason had made a show for Julie, but fact was, they weren't officially boyfriends.

Or a commitment.

Or anything with a name.

And Mason couldn't put one on him until Terry did it himself.

"He is. He found out that my soccer captain was gay and wanted to know if the guys were okay with it." Terry blushed. "I told him *I* was gay, and he said he was too. It's like… you know. A friend."

Of course. Mason knew how that went. In college he'd hung out with all the gay friends. At his last job, it had been his female coworker, Janice, and a couple of his managers.

Here, it was Dane and Skip and Carpenter.

You looked for people—not just sex people, but kind people. Terry had found his own.

"Well, I'm glad he found you. Maybe he can play on the team."

Terry smiled at him like he'd invented friendship. "That would be awesome! 'Cause, you know, now that you're good on defense, we need more subs. It would be great if we had more than one or two, you know?"

Mason thought he could play an entire game without a break if it meant Mr. Scrawny Pasty Green Eyes wasn't there, but then, Mason didn't get a say, did he?

"I think that's an awesome idea. Why don't you ask Skip?"

Terry grinned and hopped in his car, and they took off for the jump to the moon.

By that evening they had everything unpacked and in its place—including the new coffeemaker, microwave, and sheets Mason bought for Terry's bed. The sheets weren't fancy—a basic stripe—but they came with a comforter, and Terry got so excited Mason wondered if he'd ever had sheets not from the secondhand store before.

And then he felt bad.

This was Terry's day—his bid for independence. Even if Mason lost his boyfriend… friend… Saturday lover… these gifts needed to come from a whole and untainted heart.

Mason felt bad enough to try to make friends with Rudy.

It didn't go well.

"So, uh, Rudy. You know Terry—"

"Jefferson? You're the only one who calls him Terry." Rudy blinked at Mason with those dark-fringed green eyes, and Mason tried again.

"Well, yeah. But he's, uh, sort of special to me. Anyway, you guys know each other from work?"

"Yeah. I work at one of the service stations he comes to." Rudy regarded him with sober alertness, like he was just waiting for the next question.

"Working your way through college?"

"No."

Oh c'mon, kid, give me something to work with.

"Tech school?"

"No."

"Your master's degree on ancient religions?"

Rudy looked at him suspiciously. "Are you making fun of me?"

Oh hell. "No—I'm just trying to make friends. Terry—"

"Jefferson."

"*I* call him Terry. He's special to me, and you're his friend. I'd like to get to know you, that's all."

"I'm twenty-two, and you're too old for me."

"Rudy, would you like some popcorn? I'd like some popcorn. I think Dane brought some popcorn. Let's make everybody popcorn."

Mason made his way from the corner of the living room, where Rudy had just finished setting up the television and DVR, to the kitchen, where Terry and Dane were debating the best place to put the glasses.

Terry barely looked at him. "So you think the plastic thirty-two-ounce cups will fit here?" he pondered.

"How's it going, Mace?" Dane said, looking at Mason carefully.

"Peachy. I'm going to make popcorn." Mason tried not to give a death's-head grin as he said it.

"Why popcorn?"

"Because popcorn was the first word to come out of my mouth a minute ago and I'm grateful it wasn't *penis*."

Terry looked up then just as Dane guffawed. "Penis?"

"Yeah," Mason said grimly, looking out into the living room, where Rudy was apparently having a grand ol' time with Richie and Cooper. "It's another word for dick."

HE MADE popcorn, people snacked, and everybody—including Rudy—eventually left, and Mason sank to the couch with Terry in his arms. Once the people were gone, the air-conditioning kicked on, and it made the apartment suddenly sweet and cozy instead of stifling.

"Nice of everyone to come out," Terry mumbled, falling asleep on Mason's chest. "What'ya think I should do to say thank you?"

Mason thought of Terry's tight finances. "Thank-you cards are nice," he said thoughtfully. "Old-fashioned, but nice. And if you tell people 'Thanks, and let me return the favor,' then they'll call on you for help. It's a nice cycle."

"Mm… you know how to be a grown-up in the best ways," Terry mumbled. "I'll buy some cards on…." He sat up, putting his elbow in Mason's stomach.

That quickly he was standing in the middle of his apartment, turning a full circle.

"That's so weird," he said in wonder. "*This* is my home. And I can get here as late as I want on Monday. And leave whenever I want to. I don't have to ask *anyone's* permission to go to your house and stay the night. *Nobody* has to know where I am. *Nobody* cares."

"I do," Mason couldn't help but say. "But only so I don't worry."

Terry turned toward him. "Worry about what?"

"Worry about you getting home safe. Having enough to eat. Wearing clothes that aren't too hot or too cold or too full of holes." Mason's voice caught. "Being scared during thunderstorms."

The aching realization on Terry's face was hard to watch. "Being alone," he said softly. "Dealing with his brother without anyone to make sure he's okay. Thinking he's a big dork when he's really just...." Terry bit his lip. "Kind," he said at last. "The kindest person I've ever met."

Mason smiled crookedly. "You're easy to be nice to."

Terry threw himself into Mason's arms. "I'm not so good with days," he confessed, voice almost lost in Mason's T-shirt. "I... I might not return your texts. I... there's new people and...."

Mason kissed his temple. "It's okay," he said. "If I'm not important enough for you to come back to, that is not your fault. But... but I'll tell you. If I need us to be more than I need us, to be."

Terry nodded unhappily, and Mason saw his lips moving as he tried to work out exactly what Mason just said. It was the best he could do. Mason couldn't say it again, couldn't rephrase it more simply.

His chest ached so fiercely he couldn't hardly breathe.

THEY SLEPT that night on Terry's queen-size pedestal bed. No box springs. None. Mason woke up at five thirty in the morning and creaked out of bed, trying not to groan about his back. *Thirty-six, old man. Oh fuck. Thirty-seven.* His birthday had been in early March, when Dane had been at his worst. Mason had put a bright shine on things for his parents during their phone call and taken Terry out with the gift card they'd sent him.

And tried really hard to forget it meant he was dating a guy twelve years his junior.

But this morning, looking around the still-bare walls of Terry's first apartment, he felt his age settle into his bones. He looked down at where

Terry lay sleeping. He'd rolled over and hugged Mason's pillow, smiling a little, and Mason tried to memorize every line of that smile.

For a little while, I made him happy. Even if that changes and he isn't happy anymore, I need to remember this. It makes me a better person.

He slid into his clothes and kissed Terry on the cheek.

"Mason?" Those big brown eyes—they sort of slugged Mason in the gut.

"Gotta go get ready for work," he said, smiling. "You set your phone last night—you should be good."

Terry grunted. "See you Thursday?"

Oh yeah. Practice. "Or earlier—call me whenever."

A tiny smile quirked at the corner of his lips. "Text me. I like it when you send me shit."

Mason grunted and kissed his lips this time. "Then tell me thank you—I'm afraid I'm sending them to my brother half the time."

Terry frowned. "Some of that shit's really dirty!"

"You can see why I'd be worried."

Laughter, low and sleepy, tickled up Mason's spine.

This could work. This *would* work.

Another kiss, and he left.

HE GOT home and Dane and Carpenter were sitting at the kitchen table, drinking coffee. They were looking at each other warily, and both of them had red-rimmed eyes, but they were sitting intimately close, and whatever wordless communication was happening, Mason thought it was better done alone.

He slid past them, and Carpenter's voice stopped him as he was walking up the stairs. "You driving to work, Mace?"

"Yeah. Want a ride?"

"Sure. I'm coming back here tonight."

Dane jerked sharply like this took him by surprise, but Carpenter looked determined.

Okay. Fine. They asked no questions about him and Terry; he asked no questions about them. Fair.

Sort of.

"So," Mason asked as he negotiated the tiny thoroughfare of Sunset. "Sleepover?"

"I don't want to talk about it."

"You want me to be somewhere else?"

"If it gets as loud as you and Jefferson, I'll kill myself."

Mason almost swerved into a tree. "I beg your pardon?"

"Do you have any idea how thick your walls are, Mason? And still, I swear to God, I thought you were killing him Saturday night."

"You were there?" As far as Mason could remember, they'd gone out on a day trip that Saturday. "Dane said you didn't get back until one!"

"It was to spare your feelings. Good Lord, man—I've seen nature shows on bonobos that made less noise."

Mason's flush had pretty much suffused his entire body. "I'm sorry," he mumbled. "I had no idea—"

Carpenter let out a giant sigh. "No. I'm sorry. You're not that loud."

"Then why—"

"Because." Sigh. "Because. I'm nervous. And he's trying not to let me know how important this is. And we're both... I mean, the whole reason this started is because we liked each other, right?"

"Change is hard," Mason said, a little less mortified. And a whole lot more sympathetic. "Just... don't do anything out of character, okay?"

Carpenter grunted sourly. "Like have a relationship that doesn't end in tears, recrimination, and assertions that my fat ass is the end-all and be-all of the problem?"

"You're not fat," Mason muttered. Sixty pounds. He must have lost sixty pounds in the past seven months.

"Well, it's good to hear you say that. I'm freaking out, Mason—could you take me to Starbucks for a dessert drink and a cookie? I promise not to tell Skip if you don't."

"Deal," Mason said. He was sort of depressed as it was. "Do you want to get lunch today? You can borrow my car."

Carpenter's twelve-year-old-doing-wrong laugh was a balm to his soul. "So, perks to banging the boss's brother include access to the boss's car. I should have slept over months ago."

APPARENTLY DIETER'S remorse hit, because Carpenter came back with sushi for lunch. Tasty, yes, but by the end of the day, Mason was craving steak and potatoes. Ugh—the curse of the overfed male!

He texted *What are you doing for dinner?* to Terry.

Caught a burger. Am writing thank-you notes. Do you have addresses?

Not everyone's. Skip might.

Good idea!

Mason stared at the phone. Thought *Maybe tomorrow, Mace.* Thought it hard. Consistently. Just that one phrase. It never appeared.

Well, a night alone in his own apartment—wasn't too much to ask.

Or two nights. Or three. Or four. On Thursday night, Mason put a spare set of work clothes—casual, in deference to his and Mrs. Bradford's new resolve to dress like the sun was out to kill them—in the back of his car before he went to practice. The action was based on hope and hope alone.

Terry didn't show up until halfway through, and although he ran by Mason and patted him casually on the ass, they didn't get a chance to talk until the usual beer and bullshit session in the windless hush of sunset.

"You were late," Mason said neutrally.

"Yeah—me and Rudy were picking out posters for my bedroom and the living room. Lost track of time." He grimaced. "Low-rent move—sorry 'bout that, Skip."

"No worries," Skip said easily. "Just try to remember the game Saturday, okay?"

"Yeah! It's our last, right? Two-week break afterward."

Oh—dammit! Of all the fuckin' times!

But everyone else was nodding like this was expected, and whatever. "Do we play when it gets to be a hundred?" Mason asked, half-afraid of the answer.

"We stop at 105," Skip confirmed. "Same as the little kids."

"You know," Mason said thoughtfully, "uh, after those *really* hot games, I sort of have a pool." Danc's project that day had been cleaning and dosing the pool so it would be usable that weekend.

But right now Mason was in the middle of many admiring sets of eyes, and damn, it was great to be a hero.

"Beats the shit out of my porch," Skip confirmed. "Do you mind if Richie and I bring the monster?"

"Does he come when he's called?" Mason asked, thinking about all the places beyond the fenced-in patio the dog could get lost if he decided to disappear.

"He responds to my whistle," Richie said, and he pursed his lips and folded his tongue, and the groan of the rest of the team told Mason all he wanted to know about that.

"So," Cooper said slyly, "do we have to wait until next season? Can we maybe come by after the game Saturday?"

Terry smacked his arm. "Subtle, Cooper. Really fuckin' subtle."

"Yeah," Skip said, voice dry as the Sahara. "Subtle is our middle name around here. So, Mason, you up for it?"

"I'll have burgers and dogs," Mason confirmed. "You guys bring the beer."

"What should I bring?" Terry asked quietly while the rest of the guys whooped.

"A change of clothes?" Mason asked, so full of hope he almost hated himself.

"Bank on it."

The promise came with a kiss on the cheek, and Mason clung to it, even when Terry missed lunch on Friday.

Mrs. Bradford ran and got him an emergency sandwich from the cafeteria, and she placed it on his desk at around two, right when Terry's text pinged.

D'oh! Sorry!

No worries. I'm eating company egg salad. It's awesome.

Next time I'll text you if I'm coming—that way you don't have to plan on me.

Sure.

Sure.

THEY LOST the soccer game, but the pool party was a success. People brought food and beer and dessert—and more beer. Singh brought his wife and two kids, and Menendez and Owens brought their girlfriends. Carpenter and Dane stayed out of the pool and in the shade, talking, but most everyone else got in and out—and even used the hot tub in the corner, although it was plenty warm outside.

Skip and Richie's dog—as big as advertised, and so voracious that Skip brought him his own bag of food to inhale so he wouldn't go after burgers right off the bat—ran around the trees and down to the creek.

Every now and then, a piercing whistle would rend the air, and the whole world would look up to see Ponyboy come running to check in with his humans.

Terry stayed and frolicked, as comfortable in the water as an otter. The guys—being the guys—started an impromptu game of water polo that turned into a blood sport.

Mason was busy grilling, so he didn't participate, but Carpenter and Dane dressed a lot of wounds—and counseled a lot of bitterness about how *some* people didn't trim the eagle talons they were nurturing in the place of toenails.

Terry, being neither wounded nor wounder, put on his shirt and went running into the oak trees to throw sticks to the dog.

After Mason had gotten everyone else settled with food, he found Terry there, chucking what amounted to half a tree over and across the creek and up the rise. This was great—it ensured the dog had to run down one hill, across the water, and up the next hill, and he'd obviously been doing it for quite some time, because he was starting to slow down.

"You hungry?" Mason asked with a smile.

The expression Terry turned toward him was troubled. "Little bit, yeah."

"What's wrong?" But he knew.

"You know… Rudy—he was saying all sorts of shit, and… I know it's not true but…."

Mason grimaced. "I don't know. It might be true. Ask me."

Terry rolled his eyes. "You just using me for sex?"

"Absolutely. Next question?" Mason couldn't keep the bitterness out of his voice.

"Be serious!"

Mason took a deep breath and tried to be the grown-up. Only succeeded a little. "I am *terrified* that's the only reason you're with me. Because I put out, and I was easy, and I was there," he said soberly.

Terry looked uncomfortable. "That's how it was at first," he admitted. "I know it."

"It's more than that now."

Mason swallowed. "I was hoping. Is there anything else Rudy said?"

Shrug. "He said if you really cared about me, you would have asked me to move in with you."

Great. "I was sort of hoping you'd ask me, when you were ready."

The look he sent Mason was hurt and pissed. "Why do I have to do the asking?" The dog dropped the stick at Terry's feet, and he bent down and scratched it behind the ears.

"Because you're the one who's finally sprouting some wings, here. I don't want you to move in with me because I'm a rich old guy with a nice house. I want you to move in with me because you hate it when we don't see each other." Mason offered his hand to the damned dog, who was going to weigh more than he did when it was grown. "Hi, dog."

The dog licked his knuckles.

"I don't think of you like that!" Terry objected, chucking the stick across the creek with enough force to lose it in the trees on the other side.

The dog took off, and they were left alone.

"What *do* you think of me as?" Mason asked, wanting the answer so damned bad. *But we don't always get what we want.*

"I think of you as a friend," Terry said with dignity. "Maybe the best friend I've ever had. And the best sex I've ever had. What does that make us?"

In love. "Boyfriends." Mason went with the obvious.

"But I don't know how to have a boyfriend." Apparently Terry was going for the same.

"You… you make dates with them to do stuff," Mason said, feeling plaintive. "Even if it's stuff you think they won't like, you ask anyway. Like looking for posters. Or going to see a movie. You surprise them unexpectedly with gifts—doesn't have to be pricey. You tell them before you're going to miss a meeting, because you know they might be planning on you. You… you hug them in public and kiss them on the cheek when they've said something nice." *You hold them tight and say you love them and promise to be faithful and to never let each other go.*

"I… this is a permanent thing you're talking about," Terry said, like this had suddenly dawned on him.

"It would be if we moved in."

"Are *you* ready for me to move in?" The horror in his voice was unmistakable.

"In a hot second. Months ago. March." He couldn't have lied if he'd had a teleprompter.

"But why wouldn't you *say* anything?" Terry asked, eyes bright. "Why wouldn't you—"

"Because you weren't ready," Mason said. "You're not now. You have an apartment you want to decorate, you have friends you want to invite over. You—you get to do that, Terry. I have no right to take that away from you." The dog splashed noisily across the creek at that point, and they both watched him struggle up the side of the ravine.

"Then how do we do this? I don't... I don't have a schedule. I... I don't want to leave you hanging and...."

Mason took a couple of steps toward him, uncertain in the close heat of the woods. "Terry?" he said gently, taking his hand. "C'mere."

Terry went, hiding in his embrace like a child.

"Do you know what taking a break means?" Mason asked softly.

Terry glared at him, struggling out of his arms. "It means you're breaking up with me!"

"No." Mason pulled him back. "It means when you know how you want us to be, all you have to do is tell me. Text me and I'll be there. Knock on my door and I'll probably bang you before we make it to the stairs. Call me and I'll teleport through the phone. But... but until you tell me what you want us to be, you take your time. You go out with friends. You sit in your apartment and listen to whatever goes on in your head. You... you be *you*. And then...." His voice got wobbly. "Then you invite me along for the ride, okay?"

"Can we at least have sex tonight?" His glare was almost comic, and Mason placed a sweet kiss on his forehead.

"Only if you want to hurt me," he said honestly.

Terry blinked hard. "I never... in a thousand years, I'd never want to hurt you."

"Then let's go back and eat. The guys are going to start leaving soon."

"I should go with them," Terry said, wiping his face on his shoulder.

"Yeah."

PEOPLE LEFT in waves. Terry sat down and ate, far away from where Mason was finishing up with the grill. The first wave of people left, and he stayed to talk.

That wave of people left, and he went with them. He came to Mason and kissed his cheek hurriedly before walking with his group. Mason had heard mentions of a movie and thought wistfully of the latest action hero vehicle that had been released.

He'd had hopes.

Richie was out running the last of the go out of the dog, but Skip watched the whole thing from a conversation with Carpenter. He wandered, super-extra-casual-like, to where Mason was assembling his own hamburger, and offered him an imported beer.

Mason looked at the bottle dumbly. "I didn't bring this."

"Nope. But Richie said we should bring something fancy for you because you're smart and all."

For some reason that felt like all that was wrong with the world.

"I'm not that smart," Mason said, setting his plate down so he could use the bottle opener on the side of the grill. "But the beer is appreciated."

"You let him go," Skip said, following Mason to the now-empty, glass-topped table. Mason sat and Skipper pulled up kitty-corner, close enough to have a conversation and not be overheard but far enough away that Richie couldn't imagine something that would never be there.

"Course I did," Mason said, taking a gulp of fine import. "'Cause I'm a good guy. And he's a good guy too. And if you're a good guy and an old fart, you don't marry your newly emancipated boyfriend like a goddamned child bride."

Skipper watched impassively while Mason killed the beer and belched, then stared dumbly at his hamburger.

"I problably did that backwards," he muttered. "Probly. Probably."

"Probably," Skipper said gently, taking the beer bottle out of Mason's hand. "You eat that and I'll go get you another one."

Sure. Why lose weight when your younger lover had probably just left to go see a Marvel movie and might never see you again?

"Another beer or another burger?" Mason clarified.

"One of each. I think I'm about to watch my boss get toasted."

Mason stared at his hamburger. "Well that's embarrassing," he mumbled, taking another bite. He dedicated himself to eating for a moment, and realized he hadn't had so much as a potato chip since breakfast.

Maybe that would help.

Skipper returned with another plate and two more beers, and then Dane and Carpenter returned from seeing the last wave of people off. Richie came back with the dog—who jumped in the pool, shook himself on all of them, and collapsed at Richie's feet—and they started to talk.

Skipper talked about the last girlfriend he'd had and how bad he'd felt when he'd broken up with her.

Richie talked about the first girlfriend he'd had and how he'd tried so hard, for so long, to make her happy.

Dane talked about a boyfriend he'd had in college, the one who had triggered his big crash, and how he'd had to spend a month in a psych ward before he realized that anyone who made you choose him over your family and friends or even your principles was probably not someone you needed to appease.

Carpenter was quiet for most of the discussion, and when he spoke, he surprised everybody.

"I have an MBA," he said bluntly.

Mason almost knocked over his beer. "You what?" he said at the same time Skipper crowed, "I *knew it!*" and Dane smacked him on the back of his head.

"What in the furry hell," Richie asked, looking at everybody like they'd lost their minds. "He's got a *what*?"

"He went to school for six years to sit with me in the damned tech pool," Skipper said, and Mason recognized the anger on his face for what it was in his heart: hurt.

"Why would you do that?" Richie asked. "I mean… you could be making, I don't know, *Mason* kind of money. Couldn't you find a job?"

Carpenter pursed his lips and looked at Mason. "Mace, how many decisions you think you make a day?"

Mason tried to think past the heartbreak and beer. "I don't know." What had he done Friday after Terry hadn't shown? Oh yeah. He'd had a meeting with HR about how to retain staff. He'd said something about furthering the education of the lower-tier workers—even if they didn't use the education for Tesko, they would at least guarantee time to the company in return for the investment. He'd also mentioned stock options and a commissary for the tech crew and receptionists and even gift cards at clothing stores during the holidays, since they had a dress code requirement.

The guy in HR—Hugh Goodman—had seemed excited about the ideas and put Mason in charge of a committee making those things happen. It all seemed simple enough, and Mason's real job—mergers and acquisitions—

was often a game of hurry up and wait. He'd done all his research, made all his offers, and was in the process of waiting for people to respond to his moves. He could implement that stuff in a week, probably less.

And then he realized what Carpenter had asked him.

"I don't know?" he said, hating to think about this. "Fifty? A hundred?"

Carpenter shuddered. "I got out of school, was interviewing for a job, and it hits me. This job they want me for? The first thing they're going to ask me to do is put a hundred people out of work. And it's what the company needs in terms of instant cash availability, but it's going to fuck the company over long-term. And people are going to lose their jobs. And I can either tell them up front that this move is sucktastic, and not get hired, or I can lie, and then lie some more, and then get the job where the first thing I did was be a douche."

Mason found himself staring, openmouthed. He wasn't alone.

"So I said fuck it," Carpenter continued, knocking back a beer. "I spent the next year dodging my parents and working in a pizza joint, and finally got tired of the dirty calls from the student loan office and got the job at Tesko."

"Oh, Carpenter!" Skip said helplessly. "You can do so much more!"

Carpenter looked at him and smiled sadly. "You're the best friend I've ever had, Skipper. You think I would have met you working Mason's job?"

"I did," Mason said, jealous. Skip was the best friend *he'd* had too.

"Yeah, but that's because your mouth is still twelve," Carpenter said, smiling at him fondly. "You're an A-1 guy, Mason. You're not bad-looking—"

"He's fuckin' sexy," Richie said, surprising them all. "Seriously—would you think I'd be jealous if he was a troll?"

Mason's brown hair was getting silver. He had Dane's brown eyes, a decent jaw, and deep laugh lines around his eyes. He was pretty sure all his friends had drunk too much beer.

"So, yeah," Carpenter continued, "good-looking, nice guy, obviously smart because they keep putting your name on all the company newsletters. Yeah, I read them. 'VP Mason Hayes just acquired a property in San Francisco.' 'VP Mason Hayes just sold off a property in Burlingame, and the company netted a zillion dollars.' You're all over the place. I'm surprised they haven't hired someone to come in and wax your knob, just to make sure you stay there."

Mason shrugged, uncomfortable. "All they really have to do is not screw my boyfriend."

Carpenter spit out his beer. "And *see*! *That's* why you're here. That's why you and Skip are buddies and you're breaking your heart over an itinerant tech rat who can't track a sentence through a book. Because there's this part of your heart that still believes all men are created equal. And you live that. And until I met you and Dane, I thought the only way I could use my education was to be a douche. But don't you get it? My parents have been telling me for *years* that I didn't have to stay in the IT pool and still be able to live with myself. But they were *telling* me. Like I didn't have the sense God gave a mole. I had to *see* someone doing it, and doing it right."

Carpenter studied his beer while Dane glared at him, and Mason got the feeling there would be all sorts of shit going down he didn't want a thing to do with. Skip was looking at Carpenter like he was fading before Skip's eyes, and Richie?

Richie was staring into space like he was seeing the infinite in the falling shadows over the ravine.

"You're talking about Terry," he said after a moment, and Mason forgave him for everything, including winning Skip's heart before Mason came on the scene. "You're saying he's got to figure out for himself what Mason is like. No one can tell him."

"Yeah," Carpenter said.

"You're saying that he doesn't know his own worth, really. That he's not going to see if he's good enough for Mason unless he goes out and screws other guys."

Mason buried his face in his hands. He hadn't wanted to think about it, but yeah. The idea was there.

"Maybe not," Carpenter said, giving Mason a gentle pat on the top of the head. "Maybe he just needs to see. You know. It's not the suit or the car or the kickass house. Mason's pretty awesome just because he's Mason. And Terry's what Mason wants, so he's got to be special too."

"You're going to leave the IT pool, aren't you?" Skip asked, sadness in his voice.

Mason glanced up. "Poor Schipperke," he said, heart twisting. "Don't worry. I think Clay's point is that he's not going to leave his friends behind."

Skip shrugged like it was no big deal. "I know, I know. We'll always have soccer."

Mason made a sound. Oh God. Terry was going to be playing soccer. He was going to be trying to spot that big play and learning where he was supposed to be on the field. Skip and Mason had been working with him since February—Terry was getting to be an amazing player. Even Mason had been getting fitter and quicker. He'd managed to find the sweet spot on the side of his foot, the one that would make the ball his bitch.

Mason really loved playing soccer.

But he couldn't.

"Skip?" he said helplessly. Oh fuck. He'd enjoyed having the guys here. It had been the peer group he'd never had. For once he'd been with a group of guys who didn't censure his words, or judge him on his lack of taste in beer, or expect him to have food he didn't know the name of.

Skip glared at him. "Really?"

"I'll take his place," Dane said calmly, and everybody at the table stared at him. He took a sip of his own imported beer and shrugged. "Just a season. I'll be out of school—nothing to do but play with Holly and Jason and be on the team." He smiled with false brightness. "It'll be fun!"

"You hate soccer," Mason and Carpenter said, almost in tandem.

"Let him miss you," Dane said, his voice hard. "Let him look for you every Saturday and see me there instead. You want him to figure out what he wants? That'll do the trick."

"You know," Mason said, hoping Dane realized this, "he might not want me."

Dane shrugged, looking fierce. "Then he's not worth you, Mason. I've watched you try to build a life with loser after loser. They weren't worth your time. Unless a guy is throwing himself at your feet, trying to romance you like you were God's gift to cosmopolitan gay, don't fucking bother. If Terry comes back, I want him to come back humble. He needs to know who's been waiting for him." Dane dashed the back of his hand across his eyes. "I certainly do."

Carpenter wrapped an arm around his back, and they listened to the night—air conditioners humming, frogs screaming their hearts out from the creek, faraway traffic noises. In that moment Mason felt really small.

He thought that would be it—party over. But Skip and Richie stayed to clean up the rest of the food, and when they all went in, they stayed to watch *Guardians of the Galaxy* on cable. And then *The Man from U.N.C.L.E.*... And *The Avengers*.

They all fell asleep during that last one, and Mason woke up in the early morning on the floor of his living room, listening to four other men snoring and farting, and saw the dog pawing at the sliding glass door to the backyard.

Mason took the dog outside and let him run around and relieve himself in the rapidly heating day. He thought about cooking breakfast for his friends and maybe going shopping and planning a meal—something nice he hadn't cooked for a while—and inviting people over for something besides a hamburger cookout.

Thought about how his new project at work was something worthwhile, and maybe he should pay attention to what he was doing there when he was just doing what he was supposed to because that's what his job description said.

Thought that it was working—he was making plans for life without Terry, and that he was going to be okay—and then realized he was crying, hard, and he felt gutted like a fish.

He managed to clean up the tears and hopefully the red eyes before everybody woke up to chocolate strawberry pancakes.

That empty feeling, though—that gutted one, like his heart was aching, bleeding, torn apart, somewhere far from his body?

That stayed.

He wasn't sure it was going anywhere. Not for a long, long time.

Reports from the Front

"MRS. BRADFORD, that is a lovely frock you are wearing this morning. I highly approve."

In fact, the bright red-and-yellow tailored dress was probably the best thing about Mason's Monday morning. He was still eating lunch with Skip and Carpenter, so things could possibly improve, but he'd woken up that morning with the same big throbbing emptiness in his chest.

He sort of doubted improvement could happen.

"Why thank you, sir. I notice you, too, have decided to throw yourself into business casual."

He mostly couldn't have faced putting on a suit. The middle of May was apparently brutally hot, and his heart just hadn't been in the whole pressed suit-and-tie thing.

Not today.

"I like green," he said with a small smile. Terry had liked green on him. He had a *lot* of polo shirts and T-shirts in his closet in this exact shade of green.

Mrs. Bradford looked at him sharply. "Mr. Hayes, if you don't mind me asking—are you quite all right?"

Mason couldn't answer her. He shrugged and looked at the files on his desk. "Mr. Goodman?" he mumbled, partly to himself. "Didn't I meet with him last week?"

"Yes, sir—he said he had some other ideas for those changes you wanted to implement."

Mason tried to pull his head in the game. "Yeah—I was going to focus on those this week."

"Good idea, sir—you won't hear back on several of your bids until next Monday. This is productive use of your downtime."

"I could always use my downtime researching my next acquisition," he said mildly, but she snorted.

"You're sort of ahead of their usual acquisition schedule at this rate anyway, sir. I don't think the company has enough capital to keep up with you."

Oh.

"Well then, let's go about changing the world," he said, trying for bright.

She paused at the door and studied him like a seventh grader studied a cow eyeball. "Sir.... Mason?"

"Yes, Mrs. Bradford?" He couldn't meet her eyes.

"Did something happen with your young man?"

"He's not my young man anymore."

Mrs. Bradford's bright red-and-yellow dress approached Mason's desk, and he finally made himself look into her sympathetic face. "I'm sorry, Mason," she said gently. "He seemed like a sweet kid."

Mason grimaced. "I'm a grown-up," he said with dignity.

She nodded. "Of course you are. But are you still having lunch with Mr. Carpenter and Mr. Keith?"

This smile was unforced. "Until they leave Tesko for greener pastures," he said grandly. "Good friends are good friends, Mrs. Bradford."

"Indeed."

CARPENTER BROUGHT Noodle House for lunch. They chatted about video games and movies while Mason tried to eat pad thai without making an ass of himself. He gave up when he flipped a noodle on his shirt and couldn't get rid of the stain.

"Oh well," he muttered. "It's not like I'm trying to impress Hugh Goodman."

"Who's a good man?" Skipper asked, and Mason had to look at him twice to see that his eyes were twinkling.

"Very funny. He's the guy who might be able to give our tech pool education benefits and get us a commissary that's decent and available to everybody so you guys don't have to drive to Noodle House every Monday."

"Ooh," Skip said, eyes wide. "Could he get us a Starbucks? I mean... a *Starbucks*."

Mason shrugged. "Why not? We're trying to minimize company turnover in places like the tech pool and the administrative assistant pool. Little stuff, big stuff—it all adds up."

Skip gazed at him in admiration. "Lookit you—you really *are* an executive."

Mason rolled his eyes.

Which was good, because he had it all out of his system when Hugh Goodman knocked on his door. A slightly built man with thick blond hair, high cheekbones, full lips, and just enough laugh lines in the corners of his green eyes to show he was over thirty, Hugh Goodman had a charming smile and a way of making you feel like you'd just pleased your fourth-grade teacher.

Mason had spent his morning typing up outlines and personnel requirements and a cost/benefit analysis, and he laid things out for Goodman in a short hour. When he was done, he sat back and waited for a reaction.

It wasn't long coming.

"This looks… this looks *amazing*, Mason. I'm not sure where you got your inspiration, but most of these things are minimal-cost sort of ideas. The ones that aren't can be written off, but even if they couldn't—I'm just very impressed. Most executives aren't this in touch with their employees. Tesko was very lucky to snap you up."

Usually you keep your tender bits away from stuff that snaps.

The quip crossed his mind, but he… just didn't. Not enough energy, maybe. Maybe he just couldn't be the only one to laugh at his own joke.

"Thank you, sir," he said humbly. "I'm glad you appreciated the idea." He started to gather his files up and organize, smiling every so often in Hugh's direction. Why wasn't he moving? Mason needed him to move so he could call Mrs. Bradford in and they could plan on stage two. He needed time to study his computer and see if any of those bids had been reported early. He had at least three-dozen e-mails to answer.

Finally he couldn't stand it anymore. "Mr. Goodman?"

"Call me Hugh." He smiled then, a sort of odd, hooded smile that made Mason think of gecko lizards.

"So, uh, Hugh—is there anything else you needed?"

"Are you married, Mason?"

"No, sir."

"Seeing a woman?"

"No, sir, I'm gay."

"Good!"

Mason looked at him sharply. "Mr. Goodman?"

"Hugh!"

I'm not Hugh, you're Hugh! But again, he kept it to himself. "Uh, Hugh—can I help you with anything else?"

An odd expression crossed Hugh's face at this point—something between exasperation and longing. It was the same sort of face Terry made when he was planning a vacation he couldn't afford to take.

"Uh, no, Mason. I'll…." He brightened. "I'll see you tomorrow—same time. Let's see if we can't have a hiring schedule and a budget request drawn up by the end of the week!"

"Sure," Mason said. "That will be fine. Thank you so much for asking me to work on this."

They shook hands, and if Hugh's hand lingered in Mason's a little longer than necessary, Mason was already figuring out how they could get Skip into upper-division humanities classes so he could use his new benefits to go for his BA. He barely noticed when Hugh left.

But he did notice Mrs. Bradford's rather determined walk into his office.

"Mason?"

"Yes, ma'am?" When she used his first name, he could tell she was getting maternal.

"Was that handsome young man trying to hit on you?"

Mason thought about it. "No—why would he do that?"

She closed her eyes as though begging for patience, and Mason had a sudden urge to go fetch her a Kool-Aid and vodka. "No reason, Mason. No reason at all."

HE SAW a lot of Goodman that week. In fact, they had lunch together on Friday, since Mason wasn't expecting any sandwiches delivered at his door. Goodman brought bento boxes from home, each one made up with homemade sushi and chilled ahi and salmon. Mason appreciated the artistry, but he had to plan on getting a hamburger or something on his way home.

"That was, uh, very kind of you, Hugh," he said quietly, putting the lid on his bento box and handing it back so Hugh could put it in the little case. "I had no idea people packed their own sushi."

Hugh blushed, twin red crescents popping up on his high cheekbones. He cast an appealingly shy look in Mason's direction. "It's a hobby of mine. Do you cook?"

"Sometimes. For company, I guess."

"Do you want to come to the farmer's market with me? There's a couple—one by Sunrise Mall and the other one is out in Roseville—and—"

"I usually just go to Whole Foods. I'm not as excited with open-air markets as everyone else seems to be." This was no more than the truth, and Mason was damned if he was going to end up with another Ira, who hauled him from one thing that he absolutely loathed to another.

"Oh," Hugh said, seemingly lost. "So this weekend—"

"I'm cooking for my brother and his boyfriend and a couple of friends of ours," Mason said, because Skip and Carpenter had planned this with him on Monday. He knew they were humoring him by planning a dinner party on Saturday night, but he was so depressed about Saturday without Terry that he was letting them. "What were you planning to do?"

"Nothing," Hugh said, and this thought apparently made him a little sad, but Mason couldn't fix that. He could barely fix himself.

THE NEXT Friday Hugh brought him salmon risotto, expertly prepared. He said something about a music festival at Fair Oaks Park—something about chickens that Mason didn't get, although the damned things seemed to be everywhere. Mason and Dane were taking advantage of their last weekend before soccer to go visit their parents on their anniversary, though, and Mason had to give his regrets.

Well, they were polite regrets. He didn't see Hugh as the kind of guy who would go to a chicken festival and play all the stupid games and buy too many tchotchkes and spices he might never use. Mason was that guy. He really didn't want to put anyone else through that.

MASON AND Dane took their parents out to dinner at Baumé for French food because that was their mother's favorite. Dane had argued fiercely for Wakuriya in the car on the way down, but they needed reservations much further in advance.

The service was excellent, the food superb…

But the conversation?

Not Mason's favorite.

"So," his mother said, tracing her finger through the sauce on her plate after the first course. "Your new young man…?" She smiled coquettishly, and Mason thought for the thousandth time that she was the prettiest woman in the world. The gray in her hair and the lines around her eyes only made her more Mom.

"Is no longer mine," he filled in, looking at his brother to help. It was only fair—Mason had toned down the severity of Dane's meltdown that March. Dane owed him.

Dane apparently didn't think so.

"Terry finally moved out of the house at the tender age of twenty-five, and Mason told him they should take a break while Terry figured out what he wanted from life. This is fine for Terry, who can apparently go out and hump like a champion if he wants, but it's depressing as hell for me, because Mason's broken heart is fucking bleeding all over the kitchen."

Mason stared at him. "You are no longer my brother."

"Whatever. If you actually cared about me, you'd go date someone and at least try to pretend you were happy."

"I don't feel like dating. Remember the last time you suggested I date? I think it was in December. And that brings us to now, when I don't feel like dating."

Dane narrowed his eyes. "You're leaving out the part where you went and fell in love with someone completely unsuitable who, by the way, I'm pretty sure loved you back."

Mason glared back. "How would you like to be the first person assaulted with a fork in Baumé?"

"Now boys," Roger said, his voice tinged with impatience. "I'm really more interested in hearing about the good things in your life."

"The good things?" Mason thought about it. "I may be able to get Dane's boyfriend an entry executive job at Tesko and get his adorable best friend a job as his assistant."

"Dane has a boyfriend?" his mother said, looking at Dane in shock. Well. Dane had been phoning home for the past two weeks—apparently he'd neglected a few details.

"I hate you," Dane muttered.

"I got Carpenter and Skipper better jobs for better pay, and Skip can go to school," Mason sallied. "Hate me now."

"He may not take the job," Dane said staunchly, and Mason rolled his eyes.

"He'll do anything to look like your hero. Jesus, you two are stupid."

"Tell us about him, Dane," Roger said eagerly, and while Dane glared at Mason, that did not stop him from launching into an epic poem about the mighty hero and slayer of psychological dragons that was Clay Carpenter, muscular and scruffy god with an MBA and champion of the working class. In fact, his dissertation on Carpenter's virtues kept them rolling through the next five courses.

Of course, in mentioning Carpenter, he had to mention Skipper and Richie and their gargantuan brown dog who, Mason suspected, kept crapping in the neighbor's yard on the other side of the ravine. He also had to mention soccer.

"So you're not playing soccer this season?" his mother asked, concerned.

Mason smiled as though he didn't miss it severely when the season hadn't even started. "Dane's playing my spot this next session. I'll go back when it's over."

"Mason?"

Mason looked up at the unfamiliar voice at his shoulder. "Uh...."

"George? George Williams? I'm a friend of Ira's?"

George Williams (stupid name!) was tall—as tall as Mason—and a carbon copy of John Cena with a Jem Finch style Boy Scout cut instead of a buzz cut. He had a square face, deep laugh grooves around his lean mouth, a square jaw, and piercing gray eyes.

Dane looked at him and made a little sucking sound through his teeth.

Mason smiled through a locked jaw. "Ira and I broke up."

"I know. I'm sorry. I kept expecting to run into you after that—you know, restaurants and such, but I never did. I wanted to tell you Ira shouldn't have gotten all of the friends in the split."

Wonderful. "Well, I moved to Sacramento in August—you're only seeing me here because I'm here with family." *C'mon, George—get the hint.*

"That's excellent. Can I join you for dessert?"

"Of course you can," Janette said warmly. "Any friend of Mason's is welcome here."

George sat down, and Mason's father ordered another helping of crème brûlée and Mason steeled himself for polite small talk.

George wasn't a *bad* talker. He was on a rec league softball team, and when he found out about Mason's soccer team, he genially compared notes.

Dessert was not awful, but Mason's father yawned twice during the first cup of coffee, and Mason stood up.

"It was so nice to see you again," George said, standing up to go with them. "Give me your phone number, and I can call you the next time I'm in Sacramento."

"I actually live in a suburb a few miles out. It's not really next door." Of course, Sacramento was one big sprawl of feeder suburbs, so that was probably not news.

"Which one? My sister lives in Folsom, and I visit her all the time!"

"Fair Oaks," Dane said eagerly. "We're practically neighbors." Mason didn't even bother to glare at him. That look obviously had no power, and his eyes were getting tired. "Here," Dane continued, oblivious and irritating to the extreme. "Let me give you Mason's number—meeting up would be great! Mason and I have a pool."

"Dane!" Mason hissed, shocked. Meddling brat!

"Well, we do." Dane batted his eyelashes at Mason, and Mason fought off a headache.

"I'm sure his sister does too."

"No, actually—and she regrets it!" Dane handed George back his phone, and George's lean mouth stretched into an impossibly wide smile. "I'll be sure to call!"

Mason didn't realize he was growling until he was helping his mother into the SUV.

"Mason, what's wrong? He seemed like a nice man!"

"He's peachy," Mason said. "Whatever. I'm just not—"

"I know you're not," Dane said, shamelessly crawling into their conversation as he climbed into the passenger seat. "That's why you need to."

"That's the furthest thing from the truth. It took me a few months to recover from Ira—"

"Oh, this is worse—way the fuck worse than Ira," Dane said seriously. "Dad, are you in?"

"In the car, yes. In this conversation? Not if you paid me."

"Smart man," Mason said, smiling at his father benevolently. Roger winked at him, letting Mason know whose side he was on.

Mason got into the car and started it up, and Dane got rolling too.

"So aren't you going to ask me?"

"I can't. I'm not talking to you."

"Look, I know you're hurting," Dane said, because he was the king of not taking the hint. "But Terry's going to come back or he's not. You know how you need him to be okay being alone? You're already okay being alone. So maybe look at being okay with someone else besides Terry."

"This makes no sense. None. Not to my head, not to my heart. And you know something else? I'm tired of being with people who *don't* make me feel like Terry did. So if all I have of that feeling is the memory and the hurt, I'm going to cling to that until someone comes along who's worth leaving that behind for. So far? No contenders. Throwing people at me isn't going to help."

"I don't have to throw people at you. I understand you've become gay-nip."

"Who besides George? And there's no such thing as gay-nip."

Behind them, their mother chortled, and Mason and Dane made the exact same sound at the exact same time.

"Stop picturing John Barrowman without his shirt," Roger said mildly. "It's scaring the children."

Janette's throaty chuckle was enough to make them both groan.

"Mom!"

"Oh my God, yeah, could you not?"

"I could, but I won't," she said unapologetically. "Go on and tell us about how Mason is gay-nip, Dane. This is the best anniversary present *ever*."

"So let me tell you about Hot Hugh," Dane said, obviously relishing the gossip.

"Oh Lord," Mason muttered. "He's not that hot."

"Smoking hot. Hot Hugh. Hugh of Hotness. Blond god of human resources—Skipper and Carpenter verified. Hugh the hottie, who is even hotter for Mason."

"Jesus," Mason mumbled, negotiating off of De Anza Boulevard toward his parents' house. "This is not my life."

But it was. It was his life. And that night—after harboring a deep grudge for the treasonous Mrs. Bradford, who apparently dished to Skipper and Carpenter way more than Mason ever suspected—he had a little talk with Dane about letting it stay his life.

"You can't keep doing this," he said as they settled into the same queen-size bed they'd shared as children.

"I'm worried about you."

"Don't be. It's a broken heart. They happen every day."

Dane's sigh shook the bed. "Not to you. You usually just bounce off the thing that breaks you and blame yourself for not being good enough to be happy."

Mason grunted. "That's fair. This time's different."

"I know. This time Terry got you. He *got you*. And he thought you were perfect. And you couldn't have him. And you're… you're broken. I had to hear about Hot Hugh from Carpenter, Mason. *Carpenter*. Not one word about George Williams and how he had the most boring name in the world and muscles like forged steel so maybe he was Superman."

Mason chuckled. "See, I was thinking John Cena," he said. "Superman is inspired."

"Mason—"

"I'm hurt," Mason said. "Remember all the times you said that to me? You said 'I hurt, but I'm still functioning. Just stop worrying about the hurt and let me function.'"

"This isn't—"

"No. It's not mental illness. It's less. It's temporary. And if it isn't, I'll still live with it."

"'It's less' is bullshit, Mason. There's no fucking yardstick for this type of pain. You can't shove a ruler into a wound and say, 'Oh, Dane's is three feet deep and Mason's is only two.' They both fucking hurt, so don't weenie out, okay?"

Mason faked a snore, and Dane walloped him over the head with a pillow.

Mason stole it.

Dane smacked him on the back, snarling, "Asshole!"

"You kids quiet down in there!" Janette called. "Don't make your father spank you!" Then she giggled, and so did Roger, and Mason threw the pillow back.

"Please, Mason?" Dane said softly.

"Time, Dane. It's a thing."

"Fine."

THE NEXT week soccer started. Without him.

He was having Skip and Richie over for dinner again, and Carpenter, and Mrs. Bradford and her husband. Mrs. Bradford had been a last-minute invitation, but she'd started bringing him lunch on Tuesday, Wednesday, and Thursday. When he'd asked her why, her response had been puzzled.

"I have no idea. I've never felt the urge to cozen you before. It's very strange. If you don't mind, sir, simply shut up and enjoy it. I don't cook this much for my husband."

"Okay, then," he said, baffled. "Well, I can return the favor. Saturday I'm making something new and interesting that I plan to find on the Internet on Friday. Would you and your husband like to join us?"

"Yes, sir," Mrs. Bradford said, apparently charmed. "I'd love that. And my husband would too. Should we bring wine?"

"That would be excellent—or beer, if Mr. Bradford prefers."

Her smile was damned near girlish. "Sixish?"

"Sixish it shall be." Which meant he had to get his game on, because last time they'd eaten at nearly eight. "Alfresco—and we have a pool." He paused. "And, uh, you'll be the only girl. I mean woman. I mean double *x* chromosome. And, uh, Mr. Bradford shall be the only straight male."

"Oh Mason," she said, sounding a little teary. "We'd love to come. Anything to hear you sounding like yourself again."

He omitted mentioning the dinner party to Hugh (Hot Hugh, Hugh of Hotness) because he'd feel guilty for not inviting him.

And he left the house Saturday morning at the same time Dane and Carpenter were leaving for soccer—timed on purpose. He told himself he'd get a workout fighting the crowds at Whole Foods.

The kid with the man-bun and the blue eyes who was stocking the meat counter winked at him and gave him extra pork tenderloin for the regular price.

The kid with the brown eyes and short blond hair who was spraying off the produce aisle produced cilantro, basil, garlic, and limes from boxes that hadn't been unloaded yet, and patted him on the ass as he'd walked away.

The actual adult behind the counter (he had gray hair and kind eyes and looked surprisingly fit) blatantly asked him if he'd want one more for dinner.

By the time Mason got home with his groceries and a plan for burritos that should knock Mrs. Bradford's socks off, he was starting to see Dane's point about gay-nip.

Which actually fortified him for the postgame breakdown.

Dane and Carpenter showed up at one, and Mason put them on housecleaning duty after their shower. Richie and Skipper showed up an hour later, Ponyboy in tow, and they got patio sweep and pool cleaning. When it dawned on Skip that they were usually the company and they were being asked to help spiff up the place to impress someone, he had the gall to ask if Mason had a date.

"No!" he protested. "My secretary, Mrs. Bradford. You know her. She's bringing her husband."

Skip smiled then—the smile that showed all his teeth. "Richie, did you hear that? You'll get to meet Mrs. B—she's the one who ran me down the cold medicine and who gave us Easter eggs with chocolate in them. She's coming for dinner."

Richie popped his head inside the kitchen from the patio. "Seriously? Aw, man—Skip, can I run out and get flowers? That's what you get for women, right? I mean mother-like women? 'Cause we owe her."

Skip nodded seriously. "Yeah—you go take care of that. Something pretty. Maybe a vase too."

Richie grunted and popped back out again, moving with purpose. Mason watched him go, remembering that long-ago conversation with Skipper about a mom who hadn't mommed.

And wondered if Terry might not want to meet Mrs. Bradford socially someday.

For a whole five minutes, he hadn't thought about Terry. It had been nice.

"Jefferson likes her too," Skip said mildly.

Mason grunted and went back to adding beer and cilantro to the simmering tenderloin. "That obvious?"

"I've just gotten used to that look on your face."

Fan*tastic*. "It's comfortable. I'll keep it." *How was he today? Is he sleeping with that Rudy kid yet? Did he kiss Rudy's cheek? Did Rudy treasure it like he should have?*

"I think Terry misses you, if that's any consolation."

"And you would know this how?" Because it might be.

"Well, he came running down the field, that Rudy kid at his heels, and he couldn't stop looking for you. That look on his face when he realized Dane was in your spot—it's the same as your look a minute ago when you thought he might like to see Mrs. Bradford at dinner. So that's something."

"How'd he play?" Mason asked. He knew they'd lost heinously, but he hadn't asked for details.

"Like shit. You were real good at feeding him the ball in the midfield—Dane tries, and he's not bad, you'd be surprised, but you guys had a rhythm, there's no denying it."

Mason took a breath and braced himself to ask the hard question, but Skipper jumped on it first.

"And I don't think he's sleeping with that Rudy kid either."

Oh thank God. "What makes you say that?"

"For one thing, Rudy hogs the ball a lot, and Jefferson looks at him like he hates him and can't shake him every time he does it. I don't know—I can't imagine him looking at someone he's banging that way. But he knows *we* don't like the guy, and that's important too."

"How does he know that?" Mason tried very hard to leech the glee out of his voice. Failed. He'd lost his entire social Rolodex when Ira had moved out. God, it was good when someone had your back.

Skipper's chuckle was damned evil. "Well, for starters, your brother never kicked to him, and he played midfield. Dane would kick to Jefferson or Menendez but never that Rudy kid, who—by the way—screamed, 'Me, goddammit!' at least six times."

"Heh heh heh heh…." He couldn't help it. Well, he was a petty man. Now Skipper knew.

"And if that didn't give him the hint, Richie slide-tackled him when he didn't pass the ball."

Mason was in the middle of taking a drink of water, and he had to cover his mouth or he would have sputtered into the tenderloin.

"He *what*?"

"Yeah—I thought it was pretty funny. Rudy was screaming for a yellow card, and the ref looked at me and shrugged. Said he couldn't yellow card a guy for cleating his own player, which may or may not be horseshit, but Rudy was screaming at him the whole game anyway, so I don't blame him one bit."

Mason couldn't help it. He felt his first real smile in three weeks break over his face. "That's pretty… uh, that's a shame. Poor Rudy. Was he bleeding?"

Skipper's grin went positively demonic. "Yup. I told him to go wash it off in the bathroom. He must have sulked there for the rest of the game, because I sure didn't play him."

"Schipperke?"

"Yes, boss?"

"Thanks."

"Any time. We miss you, though. Come back when you're ready."

Mason made eye contact. "I guarantee it."

THE REST of the dinner was a success. Mrs. Bradford and her husband arrived at six, as planned, and Richie presented her with the flowers that they used as a centerpiece.

Mrs. Bradford was delighted and promised to have the boys over to her house that summer. The way the two of them melted around her made Mason feel like he'd done a good thing, when the truth was, he'd just been gathering the people who made him happy.

Where Mason had feared things might be awkward, the Bradfords shared stories from the military. Some were bawdy and some were boggling, but they were always entertaining, and Skip and Richie could often return with stories of Richie's job at the auto parts store or Skip dealing with executives at Tesko.

"Oh!" Skip said, taking a swig of beer. "That reminds me—your buddy Hot Hugh—"

Mrs. Bradford burst into laughter.

"Not my buddy," Mason corrected. "He just seems to be the thing that wouldn't leave."

"Well, that thing that wouldn't leave offered me and Carpenter a way out of the IT pool. Did you have anything to do with that?"

Carpenter's dry laugh suggested he had no doubts. "I didn't put 'MBA' on my application, Skipper. That was all Mason."

Mason shrugged and tugged at the label of his beer bottle. "See, all those things we were doing, with the education program and the lower-tier benefits and upward mobility, they needed someone to help monitor them and make them happen. Also, we needed someone to present them to new employees. So I figured that the executive part would be right up Carpenter's alley, because it wasn't douchey and he could be proud of it, and the teacher part would free Skip up to take classes for his BA and maybe his teaching degree."

"Really?" Dane said, licking the last of the cake off his fork. He and Carpenter had made the cake—double chocolate with chocolate frosting—and everyone agreed it had been worth breaking a diet for. "That's what you were doing?"

"Well, I was thinking about them when I started the program—it was only logical."

Dane shook his head. "Ladies and gentlemen, my brother."

Everybody applauded, and Mason managed two whole and unfettered smiles in the space of the same day.

SO IT was a good day—but it wasn't *better*. Not by a long shot.

Mason still got updates about Terry from Skipper after every game. One week he came to the game with his hair cut short and dyed blond. One week a friend who was *not* Rudy came to watch him.

One week he'd cut off the blond and brought no friend at all.

The next week he had to thread dental floss through the reopened holes in his ears when he took off his jewelry for the game.

The week after that, he had a new car and new soccer shorts for the first time in six years.

Mason fed greedily on every detail and even celebrated their wins with a mostly happy heart, especially when he heard that all his and Skip's coaching had come to fruition and Terry was starting to play the whole field and not just squirrel-with-a-ball.

Saturday-night dinner got to be a thing—the dog was such a fixture that Dane started talking about getting one.

Mason was still expecting the karma police to land on his doorstep about Ponyboy's habit of dumping ginormous poops in the backyards of the people who lived on the other side of the ravine.

One Saturday morning in July, Mason went out extra early to the Whole Foods. He assumed people were coming over to sit in the pool and pray for heat relief, because the day before had been 112, and this day promised to be worse. Skip had canceled the soccer game that morning, and basically a pool, shade, and air-conditioning were everybody's best friend.

When he got home with bags full of chips and soda and lunch meat, ice, and beer (because who wanted to barbecue), a man he didn't know was standing in the shade of his porch.

Tall, lean, and tan, he looked vaguely familiar, and Mason thought he might have seen him gardening in front of one of those houses he shared a yard with.

Wonderful. Hello, karma police.

"Heya, let me help you out with those!"

"Uh, okay. That's nice of you."

"Not a problem. What's the matter, you've never heard of good neighbors?"

The guy had gray eyes contrasting with that tan, and a few strands of silver in his dark hair, and when he smiled and winked, the effect was indeed appealing.

"I, uh… I'm feeling guilty. My friend's dog must have crapped in your yard sixty to eighty times. I was sure you'd be on my porch with a bag of dog shit and a restraining order."

Nice-neighbor-man blinked slowly, and Mason thought, *Oh excellent—good to know that part of my personality isn't dead. Maybe my libido will come back in another year too.*

"Well, that red-headed kid has taken care of most of the land mines—no worries."

Oh! "Richie? Good. He's the dog's owner, actually. Him and Skip." Mason fumbled and managed to unlock his front door while juggling bags. Neighbor-man had his own armloads, so Mason had no choice but to let him in.

"Yeah—they seem nice. I mentioned that you seemed to have people over on Saturday a lot, and they asked me if I wanted to come by. I'm—"

"Single and gay?" Mason hazarded.

The stranger dropped his bags abruptly on the ground. "I was going to say Stuart Conrad, but yeah. Yeah, I am both single *and* gay, now that you mention it."

Of course he was. "Well, you're very welcome to stay and chill," Mason said politely. "Skip and Richie will be here in an hour with the dog, so, you know, you'll know people. Feel free to use the pool, and I'll just set up in here and—"

"Hey!" Stuart said, laughing. "This sounds like a whole lot of nice 'no.'"

Mason managed a smile. "It is. I'm sorry. You really are welcome, but I'm sort of… well, I don't know if I'm taken still, because he might not come back. But he might. And until I'm not hoping anymore, that's just not fair."

"Well, that's disappointing," Stuart said frankly. "For one thing, I'm lazy, and you're right in my backyard."

He smiled charmingly, and Mason shrugged. "I'm not great at doing things easy."

"Fair enough—but I'm going to help you set up. I'd feel like a bum if I didn't."

Mason accepted the help graciously, but inside he was feeling a bit off-balance. He'd gotten a rhythm in these past weeks, an easiness with company, with being the grown-up at the party, and this guy was in his space. It wasn't until Stuart came in asking for a vacuum cleaner to get the living room that Mason realized how protective he was of that space. He directed Stuart to the laundry room and tried to pinpoint the moment this house had become home, and the soccer team had become family, and his space had become *his* space.

He still hadn't figured it out when people started to arrive.

Skip and Richie were at the beginning of the second wave, and Mason dragged them upstairs on the pretext of getting towels from the linen closet, mostly so he could chew them out.

"Are you kidding me?" he hissed, gesturing vaguely down the stairs. "I've got stock boys groping my ass randomly and you have to bring home Hot Neighbor? For what? So I can tell him no and he can go find a stock boy?"

"Make sure it's the stock boy from the meat department," Skip said laconically. "That would kill two gays with one bone."

Richie doubled over laughing and Mason sputtered.

And then managed a chuckle.

"You could always introduce him to Hot Hugh," Richie said helpfully.

"So what? I could have Hot Hugh and Smooth Stuart? It sounds like a radio news show."

"Don't forget Gorgeous George," Dane said, scampering up the stairs like a mutant lemur. "'Cause I invited him too."

Mason stared at him blankly. "You used my phone?"

"Duh. Anyway, he's downstairs, helping with the ice chest. And Carpenter invited Hot Hugh, so you can't blame me for him."

And then all the cars wrecked inside Mason's brain and he stood there gaping. "Why?" he said after a moment. "Why would you do this? I thought you all loved me."

Skip and Richie met eyes, and Skip spilled. "He's coming today. He's bringing a friend, but no one he's serious about. He asked Richie if that would hurt you, and Richie said—"

"I said no, not at all, why would that hurt you when you've had guys throwing themselves at you for the last two months? Because I know he's, like, permanently socially handicapped by his mother, but any idiot could see that setting him free was like ripping your heart out of your chest and he shouldn't have even asked to bring a friend. So we wanted a... a...."

"*Phalanx*," Dane said passionately. "We wanted a *legion* of hot suitors wandering your home, asking everybody if they'd seen you. I don't give a shit if these guys are viable dates or not—I just want them all to be saying your name."

"You couldn't have raided Whole Foods for the twenty-year-olds?" Mason asked, thinking of three very nice guys who were going to feel sort of used.

"These guys will be okay," Dane said. "You've told them *all* no—except Stuart, but, you know, he's new."

"No, I turned him down when he walked through the door. You know this is all going to backfire radically when they end up over at Smooth Stuart's house making the human caterpillar in his hot tub, right?"

The three conspirators shrugged. "But Jefferson doesn't need to know that," Skip said, unconcerned. "He just needs to know you're wanted, and not even *you* can wait forever."

"It's only been two months," Mason sighed. "I was planning on at least a year."

They all gaped at him, horrified. Dane especially.

"You weren't going to get laid again for a year? God help us. That much sexual energy has to go somewhere, Mason—that's not healthy."

Richie broke the shock by cackling. "Heh heh heh... yeah, if it bled off on us, we'd fuck each other raw. It'd be better if you guys made up."

"Thanks, Richie," Skip said, fair skin flushed and rosy with embarrassment. "I'm so glad they know that."

"Well, we're friends now. It's only right."

"I've got an idea," Mason said, shaking his head. "How about you guys all go downstairs and talk about the kinetics of sexual energy, and I'll hide up here?"

From three guys he didn't care about and one guy he did.

"Not on your life," Dane said, grabbing his arm and dragging him down the hallway.

"I was getting towels!"

"Skip, Richie—"

"Got it, Dane," Skip said, voice mild. "Be careful. He might bruise, and then Jefferson would kick your ass."

"Terry doesn't care about me," Mason snapped for Dane's ears only. "He's supposed to be out living independently and learning how to date."

"I think that's a great idea. How about if he lives independently and learns how to date *you*!" Dane snapped. "Because right now, I'm going to start slipping lithium into your oatmeal."

Mason glared at him, outraged, because from Dane that could be kidding or not kidding. Then he was down the stairs and thrust into his own living room.

Where Hugh had been welcomed by the guys with open arms, and George was standing talking to Galvan and Owens from the team, looking happy as a clam.

"We need to know women," Mason muttered. "This looks like Fire Island circa 1980."

"Good thing George brought his sister and her kids," Dane supplied easily. "And Carpenter got his niece and nephew, and Singh brought his family again. Voilà! Women."

Mason shook his head and walked past the gaming tournament in his living room toward the card game in his kitchen, picking up bottles and soda cans and putting them in the recycler, while making sure everyone had a fresh drink and the chip bowls were full.

As a chilling out in the house and pool party went, it wasn't bad. People moved slowly, spoke quietly, and simply enjoyed the fact that they *weren't* somewhere it felt like 112. The guest rooms were put to use for quiet television and naps, and the expensive pool pump pretty much paid for itself by not sucking too much power and continuing like a champion.

Mason worked hard at being a host and managed to avoid meaningful eye contact with George, Stuart, or Hugh, although he couldn't seem to take a step without one of them asking him if he needed help. He managed to make small talk and appear to listen attentively, but the whole time…

His eyes were on Terry.

The hair on the back of Mason's neck had risen the minute Dane let him in. Dane had been polite, shaken hands with Terry's new friend, and told them to make themselves at home.

"Where's Mason?" Terry asked, and Mason had closed his eyes in the middle of Hugh's riveting tale of being stuck in traffic over the Folsom Bridge, and tried to decide if he sounded excited about seeing Mason or not.

"He's around," Dane said airily. "You'll have to fight past his swarm of guys to get to him."

Mason had blinked, not wanting to be seen with his swarm. Not wanting to be seen at all.

"Excuse me," he said politely. "I need to check on something upstairs." He separated himself from Hugh and was heading for the stairs like a laser pointer when George interrupted his trajectory.

"Hey, Mason—where are you off to? We were just going to start a game of Qwirkle!"

Mason was fishing for an excuse—any excuse—when Terry came and touched his elbow. "Hey, Mason."

Mason turned and looked at him full on.

And drank him in.

His hair was cut a lot like Skip's now—parted to the side and brushed back from his brow. It looked sweet and grown-up, both at the same time. His earrings had apparently healed, because he had a big fake diamond in each ear, but it suited him. He was wearing a T-shirt—something new and striped and not full of holes—and cargo shorts with flip-flops that looked relatively new and not like they'd fall off his feet.

And the smile he leveled at Mason was tentative, and a little worried.

"Hi," Mason said, the emptiness in his chest filling for the first time in months. "I'm glad you could come."

"I brought a friend—not a boyfriend, okay? Just a friend. I didn't want you to think... you know."

Exactly what Dane and Skip and Richie *had* been thinking. Mason knew.

"That's kind of you," Mason said, nodding. "That would have hurt."

"You seem to have a lot of... friends." With an arched eyebrow, Terry gave George a once-over. George gaped at him and then sort of faded into the background.

"Just friends too," Mason said soberly. "I wouldn't have three men here if I was trying to date them."

"I know you wouldn't." Terry bit his lip and looked at Mason shyly. "That would be mean, and you're anything but mean."

Mason smiled at him, his heart so full of the compliment that he could barely breathe.

And something crashed and someone screamed by the poolside, and Mason turned his attention outside for just a minute—

And Terry was pulled away, his friend chatting excitedly about the gaming system and how they had up next.

Mason went outside and cleaned up the mess—Ponyboy had gotten excited at the kids in the pool and knocked over a planter. He had plenty of help, because in spite of Mason having no interest in any of them, his three suitors would not leave him alone.

And Terry's friend—and his other teammates—seemed hell-bent on keeping Terry's attention divided as well.

The rest of the day felt like a haze of people that Mason could never remember talking to, and glimpses of Terry's brown eyes peering at him from his own haze.

They were the only two souls in the whole house, but they never had a chance to touch.

Until night fell, and people left.

Terry went somewhere in the middle—after Hugh and George but before Stuart—and Mason managed to catch him before he got to his car.

"So," he said breathlessly, wilting in the heat. "I just wanted to say I'm glad you came."

Terry smiled and, unbidden, stood on his tiptoes and kissed Mason's cheek. "I'm glad I came too. Are you coming to see our game next week?"

Of course he wasn't. "I can try," he said brightly. "If nothing comes up." He refrained from raising his hand to cup his cheek.

"I'll look forward to seeing you." Terry raised his hand and rubbed Mason's lower lip with his thumb, and Mason's libido woke up with a bang. "Maybe we can go out afterward."

"I'd like that," Mason whispered.

And then Terry turned and was gone, leaving Mason in the humid dark, alone.

Or so he thought.

"Oh," Stuart said, coming out of the shadows by the doorway. "I was wondering."

"Wondering what?" Mason headed back into the house—sweat was running down his neck and back already.

"You said you weren't over someone, and I was wondering. Is this guy really mooning for someone he doesn't have a chance with, or is maybe there still a thing going?"

Mason shrugged and cupped his cheek, unable to stop the smile that pulled at the corner of his mouth. "We're still friends," he said with dignity.

Stuart's low laughter was probably sexy, but Mason wasn't feeling it.

"Well, I got the phone number of that blond guy—"

"Hugh?"

"Yeah. And I think your other prospect was flirting with one of your soccer guys—"

Mason frowned. "I had no idea so many people on Skip's team swung our way. Who was it?"

"I have no idea. He was young and hot—but that's the entire team, so, you know. Whatever. But I'm sad I never had a chance with you."

Mason shrugged. "We'll probably be better neighbors this way."

"Yeah. As long as you have the parties, my friend. You know way more interesting people than I do."

They walked inside together and, in fact, had a nice conversation over cookies and soda. Stuart was the last to leave, trailing in Skip and Richie's wake as they towed the exhausted dog into the car.

Mason was left with surprisingly little cleanup, which Dane and Carpenter helped with. He took a final dip in the pool before dousing it with chemicals to help counteract the people and the sunscreen and the heat, and then started up to bed while the cool on his skin remained.

As he fell asleep to the hum of the air-conditioning, he could still feel the tingle on his cheek.

Time and Space

MASON DID *not* make it to the next soccer game. He had to go give a damned speech in San Francisco instead.

Hugh was actually very sweet on Monday. He came in, they talked about their new project and about promoting Carpenter and Skip, and then, almost shyly, he brought up the party.

"So, uh, I sort of figured out why you weren't... you know. Inviting me places on the weekends."

Mason stared at him, unsure of what to say. "Because...."

"Because you're in love with someone else."

Mason was wearing another polo shirt and khakis, and he pulled at the collar. "Uh, well, we're on a break."

"Good," said Hugh, rolling his eyes. "I'd hate to think of what you guys are like in the same room when you're *not* on a break. The sexual tension alone would up the temperature twenty degrees. But don't worry—you've been a gentleman this whole time, and I'm not vindictive. But I *do* have to say I have no compunction about throwing you at this whole speaking engagement thing. I was going to try to save you from it if you had any interest in me at all, but buddy, I've got a date on Saturday, and you are on your own."

"Speaking engagement?"

Yes. Speaking engagement.

Apparently their new program had caught the eye of a company in the Bay Area, and the president had received an invitation for one of the two people who had spearheaded the changes.

Mason skimmed the memo Hugh handed him with dawning horror.

"No," he said seriously. "Please. No. I'll blow you to not do this— Terry would totally understand."

Hugh laughed as though genuinely delighted. "That kid I saw Saturday? He'd gnaw his toothbrush into a shiv and gut me with it if he ever found out. No—I'm afraid you're on your own."

He left and Mason sank down into his desk chair, muttering "Fuuuuuuuuuck!" as he sat.

"Sir?" Mrs. Bradford said crisply, apparently summoned from the very air by his salty language.

"I have to take a business trip on Friday. I have to give a presentation Friday afternoon, and I'm the keynote speaker at a dinner on Saturday."

"Well, sir," Mrs. Bradford said kindly, "you've spoken at meetings before. We can work on what you're going to say before you leave. It's not the end of the—"

"Given by my old boss."

"I'm sorry?" Mrs. Bradford pulled up the chair in front of the desk and sat down gracefully. She really was lost in the twenty-first century, Mason thought distractedly. She would have been wonderful as an actress in one of those movies made in WWII.

"My old boss. Who is now living with my old boyfriend. Which is only right, since they were having an affair for two years when we lived together in my old house and I worked my old job."

"Well, he sounds like a ripe old prick, if you don't mind me saying so."

"I'm sure his ex-wife thinks so too," Mason said, and tried to remember the name of his last administrative assistant. He couldn't, because Roy Carruthers had spun the secretary pool like a game of roulette, and Mason hadn't seen the same assistant for longer than a month.

"I'm far better off without that situation," he said sincerely. "But that doesn't mean I want to go back to my old turf and tell them how they're fucking up their business."

Mrs. Bradford started to laugh, and it had a surprisingly evil ring to it.

"Really, sir? Are you *sure*? Are you *sure* you don't want to go back to your old turf and tell them how they're fucking up their business? Because it seems to me that you were *invited* to go back, and *invited* to talk to them about their business, and you'd have to be pretty damned angelic to resist that sort of temptation."

Mason stared at her and thought of all the ways Roy Carruthers had made him feel like a complete asshole even *before* Mason had found out about the affair.

"I'm not an angel," he said, a perfect chord of beautiful, sweet revenge opening up in his soul.

"For which I am damned grateful. Angels are boring to work with, and they're irritating as hell as friends. Now how about you write up two lists for me, okay?"

"Sure," he said, not sure when she'd taken over this situation but not minding in the least. "What's on them?"

"Well, one list is the ways you think your old boss could have run his company better. The other list is the series of notes you need to make about your project. I'm going to see if we can't combine these lists into a thing of beauty."

"Mrs. Bradford, I adore you."

"Yes, you do, Mr. Hayes, and I have the flowers to prove it." She paused then. "Sir, if you don't mind me asking… about your young man?"

Mason sighed. "I was going to go watch him play soccer on Saturday morning. He asked me special."

She pursed her lips. "Well, sir, grown-ups know how to take setbacks."

"That," he said grimly, "is a *very* good point."

And a very good test, whether he'd thought of it that way or not.

SORRY *I can't make it to the game. I was looking forward to seeing you play.*

Mason stared at the text and debated whether or not to push Send. The car was packed, his best evening suit hung from the hook in the back, and he had a small bag of gifts from his present boss to his old boss.

He was good to go.

He just needed to decide how he was going to tell Terry he wasn't going to make it.

"What are you doing? Why aren't you moving? You're just standing in the driveway like a moo—Jesus, Mason, let's go!"

Mason looked up from his phone irritably. "You know, you could have signed up for summer courses."

"In the *loony bin*. No. I'm taking downtime, and you're avoiding the question. What. Are. You. Doing?"

"I was just going to text Terry about—"

Dane, wearing pajama bottoms and nothing else, reached out an imperious hand and grabbed the phone. His hair was down, falling from a natural part in the middle, and his scruff was almost beardlike. Mason had been calling him Hipster Jesus all morning. "Done. Texted. Now leave."

"You and Carpenter are going to have sex in the kitchen, aren't you? I knew it—no details. I want no details. That's why you're in such a hurry for me to leave."

Dane recoiled. "Ew. No. Who *does* that?" His eyes widened in horror. "Don't answer that. For the love of God. Gross. But no—we want you to leave so we can watch the Star Wars trilogy from beginning to end. Not your favorite, I know."

Star *Trek*, yes. Star Wars, not so much.

"Heathens," Mason grunted. "Now give me my phone back. And be sure to tell him that—"

"I know, I know. Someone held a gun to your head and made you go to San Francisco to give a speech. And maybe blow your old boyfriend. Because that's fun."

"Not even when we were together. Go away."

Dane rolled his eyes. "Drive safe. Call me before you get home. The kitchen, no, but the living room is fair game."

"Deal."

After a brief, hard hug, Dane went back inside and Mason took off.

ROY CARRUTHERS didn't believe in casual Fridays, employee commissaries, or getting to know your administrative assistants well so you could work as a team. Mason wasn't sure how his company had survived so long in the ultra-competitive world of the Bay Area corporate shark tank, but it sure wasn't because people wished him well.

However, in the past two months, Mason's company had managed to stave off lower-tier turnover by half and had saved some money doing so.

Mason got to tell everybody how he'd done that, and boy, did he enjoy it.

"So," Roy said when Mason's presentation was over, "I see you've found your niche."

"I've found my home, yes," Mason said levelly. "Nice of you to ask."

"Do you have a plus one to bring to the banquet tomorrow night?"

Oh, classy, Roy. Asking if Mason was going to be alone. "All my plus people are back in Sacramento," Mason replied with a smile. "Not even a trip to San Francisco was worth sitting through a corporate dinner."

Roy startled. "You don't like corporate dinners? Really? You used to try so hard to fit in!"

Ass. Hole. "Well, that should have been my first clue," Mason said. "Anyplace you have to *try* to fit in really isn't your place." He was going to say *Sort of like fitting a cock into your tight ass*, but he suddenly realized he didn't have to. What a relief.

"Sounds like Sacramento has some good points," Roy said genially. "Ira and I will have to check it out sometime."

"Let me know when you'll be there, Mr. Carruthers." *So I can have my posse slash your tires.* He was pretty sure Dane would just make bitchy comments over dinner, but Richie would definitely slash his tires, and Skip would help because it was Richie. And Carpenter would pull lookout duty.

And Terry would probably dismantle his engine, whether or not he and Mason were going out.

"So you can get out of town?" He smiled coquettishly like he *lived* to make people uncomfortable.

"So you can meet my friends," Mason said, not blinking. "I'm pretty sure you don't know how to behave around decent people."

He gathered the rest of his notes into his briefcase then and turned to Roy's second-in-command, Janice Collins. She was a vibrant woman, maybe a little younger than Mrs. Bradford, who streaked her blonde hair and liked bright red lipstick. She was lucky she could carry it off.

"Janice," he said warmly. "It's so good to see you again. Now I understand you got me accommodations nearby?"

"Sure, Mason. But did you want to come out to eat with us? Nowhere fancy—there's an El Torito around the corner from the Marriott, if that's okay."

Oh awesome. "The place with the karaoke?" he asked, because he and Dane had loved that place when Dane had been in school.

"That's the one. No champagne, no caviar, just really big margaritas. C'mon—I'll give you a ride. Everyone else can meet us there."

Everyone else turned out to be the people Mason most missed from leaving work. He'd forgotten he'd had people in San Francisco—and they had a good time.

But as they sat and waxed lyrical about how shitty it was to work with Roy Carruthers and his new leader of the graphics department, Ira, Mason had a moment of clarity.

He'd take Monday lunch with Skipper and Carpenter over these nice people any day of the week. He'd take Saturday dinners with the guys from the soccer team and his brother too. Skipper had been right—he really had found his people, and knowing who his people were made it so much easier not to feel like an asshole in front of everybody else.

THE NEXT night's corporate dinner wasn't nearly as awful as he'd anticipated, mostly because Janice had put him at the table with the same people he'd stayed up drinking with the night before. They were eating in the banquet room of the hotel Mason was staying at, and as Janice had a generous hand with the champagne, Mason could only be glad.

He finally put a hand over his glass and murmured, "I have to give the speech in twenty—we maybe don't want my inhibitions lowered."

"Aw, c'mon, Mason—I've been dying to hear you say something to put Ira and Roy in their places. They're grossing me out!"

Mason looked over to where his ex-boss and ex-lover were simpering in each other's eyes, and fought the urge to hurl.

Then he had the strongest, sharpest, most painful pang of missing Terry in two and a half months of barely being able to breathe for the same pain.

Terry would… he'd make Mason feel like they didn't matter.

Oh God. They didn't. They didn't matter.

"They're grossing everybody out," Mason whispered back. "And Ira's in charge of the graphics department, so that means *everybody*. Your new advertising looks like shit. Seriously. If Roy doesn't replace him, you're going out of business."

Janice shivered. "Tesko got any upper-management positions open?"

"No--I'll drop you a line if any open up. But don't worry about putting them in their place. Mrs. Bradford wrote my speech. It's a masterpiece of passive-aggressive backhandedness that would do a politician proud. Seriously—it's going to be one of those things that has everybody laughing but Roy and Ira. I wouldn't change it for the world."

Janice was staring at him with wide, bright eyes and a rather besotted smile. "Oh, Mason—self-control and a masterstroke. I *like* this new you!"

Mason laughed wickedly. "Oh, hon. You haven't seen anything yet."

At that point he was called to the stage.

TWO HOURS later Mason let himself into his hotel room, feeling very pleased with himself—and still a little drunk.

He shucked off his clothes, parked himself on the bed in his boxer shorts, and plugged his phone in the charger. That's when he noticed the five messages and pulled it out again.

They were all from Terry.

Dammit—you were supposed to come today. I missed you.

I'm sorry—I should have called you over the week to make sure.

Your brother put me in my place about that—I feel bad.

Call me when you get in, okay? I'd really like to talk.

But don't feel bad if you don't get in until late. You should be having a good time.

Mason smiled, touching the face of the phone, and figured what the hell.

He wanted to brag to someone after all.

"Mason?" Terry asked excitedly. "How did your speech go?"

Oh, it was good to dish. "It was *amazing*," Mason said, practically dancing where he sat. "Mrs. Bradford wrote it for me—it was great. The first thing I said was that loyalty was really important, but you can't get it if you don't give it—it's like getting caught cheating on a spouse. The next person in line is going to know they're not going to expect faithfulness, so they might not be so committed, right? And oh my God, you should have *seen* Roy and Ira squirming. And the rest of the audience—I'm going to have to read you exactly what the speech said, but everybody was laughing, because it was funny, right? But I swear to God it was like watching my boss and my ex sitting on thumbtacks when they couldn't get up. They couldn't move, they couldn't squirm, but Jesus did their asses hurt!"

Terry was laughing by this time, chortling into the phone as Mason ran out of breath, and Mason felt bad. He'd been wanting to crow about that since he'd given the speech, but he couldn't talk this freely in front of anybody—not here, and not at home.

Dane, maybe.

And Terry. Who just happened to be on the other end of the line when Mason needed him most.

"I'm sorry," Mason said after pausing to think. "I was just so excited. I didn't even ask about the game—"

"We lost," Terry said like it didn't matter. "I… it's not fun without you."

Mason sighed and melted a little into the pillow. "Well, this wouldn't have been as fun if I hadn't been able to tell you," he admitted. "I'm so glad you called."

"*You* called," Terry said, but it sounded like he was teasing. "I just whined at you via text."

"Well, I'm glad you did that." Oh wow. They were talking. Like they hadn't been for two months. Mason hadn't realized how difficult breathing had become, weighty, as though he'd been walking around with an elephant on his chest. Until now, when he was talking to Terry, and he felt like he could fly.

"So what else did Mrs. Bradford's speech say?" Terry asked, as Mason took deep breaths of happiness oxygen. "How bad did she burn those assholes?"

"So bad," Mason told him. "It was like… like… she said stuff like 'Caring more about a person's job description or education than about their character and performance is like picking out wines and caring more about label than taste. And then gulping your overpriced chardonnay and complaining about the hangover.'" Mason giggled and then realized there was only puzzled silence on the other line.

"See, Ira, he used to throw these dinner parties where everyone came and sampled wine and cheese and stuff—"

"You like doing that?" Terry asked, sounding pretty alarmed.

"Not really. I mean, *beer* I can get into, and I don't mind stuff that tastes good, but mostly—"

"Sounds like a good way to throw up," Terry agreed.

"See? That's what I always said. But the thing is, Ira and Roy like to do this thing, and I knew it, and they *knew* I knew it, so—"

"It let them know you thought they were douche bags." Terry chuckled as he caught on. "That's good. And you didn't have to *say* they were douche bags, which is even better, 'cause what are they going to do? Complain 'cause you used an example?"

"Right? And she did that all throughout the speech. And…." His voice dropped, because he was sort of ashamed about this, even though Ira had it coming. "She used examples about graphics, which was sort of mean, because Ira is the head of their graphics department now. But he sort of sucks—I mean, really sucks. He used to make our Christmas cards. Dane would laugh at them and draw mustaches and stuff on them because they were dumb. So really, that whole part was to—"

"Make him feel like shit," Terry said. "I approve."

"It wasn't… kind," Mason said, coming down a little. "I… I mean, comeuppance is nice, but…."

"You were kind and they hurt you," Terry growled. "I think you're even now."

"Yeah. But being a nice guy is something you like about me."

There was a thoughtful silence on the other end of the line. "I like so much about you," Terry said at last.

Mason's heart fell. "But…." That statement was *always* qualified.

"No buts." Terry's voice sounded warped when he spoke again. "Nothing in the way. Everything about you I like. Your smile. Your brown eyes. Your geeky clothes. Your pretty house. The way you laugh. The way you make me laugh." He choked a little, caught between laughter and emotion. "Your cock." His swallow was audible. "The way you touch my face when we're making love."

Mason closed his eyes, the last of the champagne fizzing out of his blood and the heady liquor of Terry's words taking its place.

"I love your laugh," Mason said. "The unexpected things you notice. The unusual way you think. Your eyes that hit me in the gut whenever you look at me. Your pride. The way you've grown. The things you've done with yourself without my help." And his throat grew thick. "I really loved that you texted me tonight."

"I wanted to call you all the time, these last two months," Terry confessed. "But… but it wouldn't be fair, calling you, unless I knew what I wanted. You'd been so… so damned fair. If I was just calling to tell you about my day or about a guy I'd talked to—that's not right. So I had to wait."

"For what?" Mason asked, heart in his throat.

"Until I knew what I wanted."

"What do you want?" *Oh please. Oh please oh please oh please….*

"I want you."

Thank you. Oh God, thank you.

"I want you too."

They talked longer than that—they talked for *hours*, actually. Some of it was silly: the lizard who climbed in through Terry's bedroom and then kept running across the covers at night had Mason burying his face in his pillow to stifle his laughter.

Some of it was painful: Terry's stories of trying to date other men weren't exactly welcome. One guy tried for the car blow job when Terry didn't want to put out; another called him bottom boy before they even went to the movies. The best and worst story was the last one, though.

"What was wrong with him?" Mason asked, wondering. Because Terry actually described a pretty nice, normal date—dinner, a movie, looking at comics on Terry's phone and laughing their asses off.

"He wasn't you," Terry said softly. "When I realized that's what it came down to, that's when I knew what I needed to do."

"So you came to the party," Mason realized. Oh.

"Well, yeah. My friend came with me—"

"I never did catch his name—"

"Porter. Like the steak, right? Or the liquor?"

"Port is the liquor and porterhouse is the steak, but porter is the guy who carries your luggage. Like transporter, right?"

"Whatever. His name does too damned much. But he was nice, and he was cute, and he was even my age. But at the end, he went to kiss me, and he wasn't you. So I told him about you. Spent the whole rest of the night talking, and he said I may want to go see you somewhere, I don't know. Neutral. Not a date. Someplace with people. And Thursday night we could barely breathe 'cause of the heat, right? And everyone was talking about your place with the pool, and I asked Dane, and…."

Mason understood. "Well, my brother didn't want me to look… I don't know. Alone and foolish, I guess. Which is how I ended up with all the extra men."

Terry chortled. "Which did you no goddamned good at all. You… you followed me with your eyes that day, and I'd been feeling so low. So stupid for not knowing what I wanted and maybe losing you. But the way you looked at me—it reminded me of all the things I really love about you."

Mason must have made a sound, a helpless, yearning sound.

"Yeah, love. You heard me right. Don't shit your pants—you're probably on a really fancy bed."

Mason's laugh was broken. "I… I need to say some of these things to you in person," he apologized. "I—" His phone beeped. "I'm running out of power, and I have to plug my phone in."

"It's okay if you say it over the phone," Terry said, his voice gentle. "You didn't say it that day when I left because you didn't want to tie me up. It's okay if you say it now."

"It hurts," Mason admitted, feeling small. "I'm sorry, but—"

"No. Don't be sorry. This here is my job, Mason. I'll make sure it doesn't hurt anymore."

Mason's phone beeped again, and this time they could both hear it.

"You drive home safely tomorrow. I've got to take my mom to Concord—"

"Concord?"

"She's doing some sort of rally where they take buses to DC and protest queers getting married and people using bathrooms. Whatever. It'll take a month and hopefully she'll get abducted by aliens, but I told her I'd take her to the meet. But you'll hear from me between now and Saturday. I promise."

"Saturday?" Mason almost hated to ask.

"The game. I'll see you—"

And Mason's phone died right then. He plugged it in and responded to Terry's good-night text while it was charging, and then climbed into the crisp, impersonal sheets of the hotel room bed.

He fell asleep hugging that phone conversation around his shoulders like a blanket. It kept him warm and safe as he settled down to dream.

Fall into the Future

MASON GOT home around one the next day and found Dane and Carpenter swimming—wearing trunks, thank God.

"Did you expect an orgy?" Dane asked acidly.

"No. I expected orgies all through college. They never materialized. I learned to live without."

"Right?" Carpenter asked, treading water without getting breathless. "Everyone told me I'd get girls in college. Heinous disappointment."

"I got laid," Dane told them both as though bored. "Frequently. I think you two just had no game."

"I suspect you're right," Mason said, standing up to take his stuff in the house and change into his suit. The pool was big enough to do laps in and still avoid Dane and Carpenter, and that was the best way ever to recover from a long, hot car trip.

"Hey—speaking of game. Go through the kitchen on your way upstairs. I think your game is better than you think."

Mason blinked at him, feeling stupid. He'd needed ibuprofen to get out of bed that morning, because champagne was just not as good for him as he always thought it was.

"Where in the kitchen am I looking?" he asked. "In case my head is throbbing and I'm blind with pain?"

"The counter, Mason. It's not going to test you too badly."

Oh thank God.

"If you killed a bug and left it for me, I'm disowning you."

"Promises, promises. Go drink some water and come back when you're human."

There might have been some more banter, but Mason missed it in his desire to get out of the heat and redose himself.

But when he saw the thing on the counter, the headache, the heat, the tiredness—it all went away.

Flowers.

There was a vase—new—full of flowers on his counter, with a six-pack of sparkling cider next to it.

And a card.

You sounded a little loopy last night. I figured this might help if you wanted to keep a clear head next time we talked. Call you tomorrow—promise.

The flowers were standard grocery-store daisies and carnations—he'd apparently bought a bunch of each and then mixed them up in the vase.

Mason didn't care. They were flowers, and they were beautiful, and they were for him.

He'd never drink champagne again in his life. Not if flowers and sparkling apple cider made him as high as he felt right now.

TERRY CALLED Monday night, and they talked for hours. He asked if he could bring lunch, and Mason had to tell him that he was in lunch meetings all week.

"Yeah, suddenly I'm Mr. Popular. It won't last. We can do lunch next week. If, uhm, you're still available."

"I'm planning on it," Terry said, and Mason wished they were having this conversation face-to-face so he could see how Terry meant that. "But this week is sort of crazy. A lot of our vendors got new machines, and everybody is working twelve-hour days to get stuff installed. It should all die down by Saturday, though. Uh…."

"Yeah?"

"You're going to be there this Saturday, right?"

Mason had double-checked with Mrs. Bradford. "Unless something dire happens. Like a hurricane or an inferno or a massive hippopotamus migration, yes."

"So, uh… do you want to see a movie Saturday night?"

"Pixar?" Mason prayed.

"Oh my God yes! Like, Porter, when we went out, wanted to see one of those inspirational movies? I almost cried when I realized I was gonna have to sit through that."

"So it's a date," Mason said, trying not to jump up and down on the bed.

"It's a sleepover," Terry said grimly. "And a talk some more. And I'll pay for the movie if you pay dinner. And we can flip for donuts and coffee."

Ohhh… Mason liked this.

Mason *loved* this. "That's definitely a date," he said. He hadn't been this excited since he was twelve years old and found the two bikes in the garage the day before Christmas.

Except this was better, because Dane wasn't getting the red one Mason wanted, and there was *sex* involved.

"You sound very determined," he said, feeling warmth seeping back in what used to be the hole in his chest.

"Look, Mason, I know grown-ups are supposed to be patient and all? But I had the perfect boyfriend in my life since January, even if I didn't know what that was. Now that I've got it figured out, I'm not fucking around. I want you back. I want sexy Saturdays and sleeping in Sundays and something, even if it's just a phone call or a text, all of the other days. I may have been clueless, but I ain't stupid. Now that I've caught a clue, you need to speak up now or get used to us being us again, but better."

"We're us?"

"Yeah, Mason. We're us. We're… dating. Exclusive. Boyfriends. And I swear to Christ if I see one more old guy hitting on you, I'm gonna get the tool kit out of Richie's car and slash some fucking tires. It was all fine when you were just looking at me all heartbroken, but I'm not throwing you out there like chum to catch big rich men."

"Deal," Mason said with relief. "And if you ever bring that Rudy kid to practice again, I'm cleating him myself."

Silence. "Crap. Mason, he's… he's not trying to get in my pants anymore. But I'm sort of the only friend he's got."

"You ever think that's because he's a *prick*!" Mason snapped.

"Well, yeah. But… but you helped me not be such a fucking squirrel. And I don't want to be the same thing for him, but… but someone needs to help him."

Mason pinched the bridge of his nose. "That is so not fair," he said, feeling twelve.

"No, it's not," Terry admitted. "But I'm hoping you don't need fair if you've got me."

Oooh. "Nice one."

"Thank you. I've been planning a lot of this in my head since *last* Saturday. Practice. Helps."

"Truth," Mason conceded. "I'll still cleat him if he's mean to people." Okay, be truthful. "I'll *try*. I mean, I've seen Richie do it, but I'm not that graceful—you know that."

"Yeah, but it's real sweet of you offering to protect my virtue. You don't need to do that. That's not your job."

And suddenly Mason could care less about Rudy. "What *is* my job?" he asked seriously. Because it sounded like Terry had the whole grown-up thing down.

"Take care of my heart, Mason. You're the only one who can."

Oh. "It's what I was born for," Mason said. "I just didn't know it until I met you. Now I do."

"Me too. That's my job. My real job. First four months were training. Last two months were making sure I wanted the position. I want it. I want it with everything in me. I'm going to make sure you never doubt that. I promise."

THAT WAS Monday night. Mason got texts on Tuesday during Terry's lunch hour and a card in the mail Wednesday. Thursday night was another scorcher, so practice was called. Terry was still working anyway, so Mason—with Dane's help—left a small ice chest in front of his apartment, two half gallons of ice cream sealed inside. When Terry got home two hours later, he said that it wasn't even soupy—he was very impressed.

"It was the foil and the foam we packed around the outside," Mason said, pleased. "I just wanted to do something nice for you."

"Well, I've got one more day of being a grown-up—I'm getting a promotion and a raise out of this, so you know, it's not just me working a bullshit job."

Mason blinked. "I never thought it was." Of all the things that were once wrong in Terry's life, his job had never been on Mason's complaint list. "You do what makes you happy, Terry. I never wanted you any other way."

Terry's reply was muffled in a bite of ice cream, but it sounded like he was happy with that too.

FRIDAY NIGHT there was a break in the heat, and Mason stayed out on the porch, feeling the breeze off the river and ravine revive the air and the growing things around him. Dane and Carpenter were out, but Mason found himself missing companionship. Terry had just gotten home and texted him that he was falling into bed, and that was good.

Maybe someday he'd be like Richie and Skip and would get a dog.

Maybe someday he and Terry would live here together, and they'd get a dog together.

The future beckoned joyfully, and Mason wasn't going to put money down on anything, but… he could hope.

Tomorrow would be a big day.

HE WAS rusty on the soccer field. Dane dragged him and Carpenter there early to kick the ball around. As the rest of the team got to the field, the warm-up drill sort of built around the three of them.

The rules of the game were to kick the ball to someone not trying to steal it from you. That could change with every pass—so don't get too complacent, and don't take your eyes off the ball.

Mason was so invested in the warm-up, in remembering how to hit the ball with the sweet spot on the inside of his foot, in remembering how to fight someone for the ball without using his hands, and just generally orienting himself with all those bodies swarming around, that he forgot to look for Terry.

Until he heard Terry's voice snapping, "Get out of my way, assholes, he's mine for a minute."

That was all the warning he had before Terry came hurtling down the rise to the field and leapt into Mason's arms.

Mason was a tall guy, built like a tree. Not awesome as a soccer player, but strong and sturdy and able to take Terry's weight and hold on.

And meet Terry's kiss head-on.

It was better—so much better—than he imagined.

Terry smelled of bodywash and tasted like coffee and toothpaste, and none of that mattered. It was his body in Mason's arms, his legs wrapped around Mason's waist, his breath mingling with Mason's as they kissed again and again and again.

Mason could have kissed him forever, could have made out with him for hours, standing in the middle of the soccer field, but, unnoticed by anyone on Skip's team, the other team had arrived.

"Oh God, do we have to?" one of the other guys complained.

"You got a thing against gay?" Skipper asked, voice flinty.

"*I'm* gay, Skipper—I don't give a shit. But we're here to play some fuckin' soccer!"

"Yeah, that's fair. Terry, get off him!"

Terry pulled back far enough to laugh, brown eyes bright, Kewpie-doll mouth ripe and swollen with Mason's kisses. "We'll finish that when we're done with the game," he promised.

Mason smiled besottedly into his eyes, not caring if the world could see. "I love you, you know that, right?"

Terry hopped down and kissed his cheek. "That's what I'm talkin' about," he said, and then skipped to his position on the field.

The other team gave an "Oh thank God!" moan, and the game was underway.

THEY WON.

Part of it was that—like Richie and Skipper—Mason and Terry had a rhythm. They could read each other's minds. It was as simple as that.

But Skipper told him that part of it was just that Mason and Dane were there, and they had four guys on the sidelines ready to go in, and everybody got a break. That helped too.

All Mason knew was that rush—one minute he was passing the ball to Terry, and the next minute the ref blew the whistle and they were up by two goals. Mason was engulfed in a big, sweaty hug of guys who were glad to see him—with the added benefit of Terry, right by his side, hugging those guys back too.

The celebration broke up, and Cooper and Menendez asked the logical thing. "Hey—are we gathering at Mason's house today or Skipper's?"

"Mason's!" Dane called out, and just as Mason was wincing, because… because *Terry*, Dane met his eyes and gestured with his head.

"C'mon," Terry muttered in his ear. "My place. We can shower and talk and go over later."

Well, Dane had the keys to the Lexus.

Mason and Terry slipped away together and rode back to Terry's apartment in his new vehicle, a used Ford Explorer. Mason's legs fit better, and he approved. As they pulled up to the apartment building, Mason felt something in his chest untwist.

"What?"

They slid out into the heating air, and Mason said, "It was rough, passing this place on the way to my house every day. This last week, it's been… better."

Terry grabbed his hand and tugged at him gently. "Come see," he said, sounding proud.

Throw rugs, framed posters, pillows on the couch. A toaster, magnets on the fridge, a computer desk, wall hangings in the bedroom in brown and red. An apartment that looked like a home, like someone who cared about themselves lived there.

Looked like a grown-up's apartment.

It was beautiful.

"This is your place?" Mason said, looking at the changes with bright eyes.

"Yeah." Terry came up behind him, wrapping his arms around Mason's waist and nuzzling his shoulder. "What do you think?"

"It's beautiful," Mason said sincerely. "Someone really amazing must live here."

Terry chuckled. "You think this is good, you should see the shower."

"Why?" he asked. "What's in the shower?"

Terry laughed wickedly. "Me. Naked. It'll be great. C'mon!"

He ran out of the room, stripping his clothes, and Mason followed him, feeling strangely shy. Terry already had the water on when Mason got to the bathroom—decorated sweetly in seafoam green—and he looked at Mason in surprise as he began to undress with reluctance.

"What's the matter?" he asked, stepping into Mason's space. "Don't you want to?"

Oh God—Mason had never wanted sex more.

"You… you cleaned house and… and decorated and…." Mason looked around. "What if I don't measure up?" he asked, throat swollen. "You… this is a commitment. You promised. I can't do this and walk away again."

"Sh." Terry cupped Mason's face in his hands. "C'mon, Mace. We'll get clean and it'll be like we're brand-new. I promise."

Mason nodded and allowed Terry to help him off with his socks and his uniform, rolling the Under Armour tightly down his sweaty thighs.

The water ran down his back, just warm enough not to hurt, and Terry's hands rubbing his chest, his shoulders, his waist and thighs, all of it helped to ground him, helped to ease that painful feeling of unreality.

That terror still possessed him, the fear that he'd wake up and this would be all gone—he'd be back to missing Terry, and Terry would be asking for another six months, another year, to get his shit together and figure out what his life was.

Terry caught his face then, the water beating down on both of them, and made Mason look him in the eyes.

"I promise," he said fiercely.

"Jesus, Terry," he said, feeling it in the pit of his groin. He wouldn't get over this if it went away again. "You'd better."

"I promise," Terry whispered again, pulling Mason in for a kiss. And another. And another. This time they didn't have to stop.

This time they didn't.

Terry remembered to turn off the water, but Mason grabbed the towels, wiping them both off roughly while the kiss went on. Terry walked him out the bathroom door into the bedroom, and Mason pulled the comforter down behind him as Terry pushed him into the mattress.

Their bodies, naked, cooling in the air-conditioning, became a real thing, and Terry's nibbles down Mason's chest, his pulls on Mason's nipples, shocked Mason into the here and now and the very real sex they were going to have to consummate their very real relationship.

Terry kept going, mouth headed for Mason's cock, and Mason grasped the comforter to keep from flailing. Oh! Everything was so sensitized, so open to Terry's touch. Terry pulled Mason's cock into his mouth, tongue flirting with the bell, with the slit, with the taut cord of flesh that drove Mason the most insane. Mason pulled both feet up to the bed and braced them against the mattress so he could thrust slowly as Terry squeezed his length.

"Wider," Terry murmured before torturing him with a lick. "I'm gonna fingerfuck ya, 'kay? Get you ready?"

Mason gasped at what that meant just as Terry was thrusting two lubed fingers into his backside. "Oh wow… you're gonna… why're you gonna…."

Terry sucked his cock for a moment while his two fingers penetrated, spread, stretched, and prepared him for what was to come.

"Because," Terry gasped, pulling his head up to look Mason in the eyes. "Because you'll believe me when I'm inside you. You'll believe I'm never letting you go."

Mason let his knees fall open as Terry positioned himself, hard and dripping already, in the spread of Mason's thighs.

"You ready?" he asked, pushing just enough.

"Yeah," Mason whispered, reaching up to stroke his taut stomach. "I've been ready for you since before you were born."

Terry grinned. "You horny little bastard!" And then he thrust in.

Mason groaned long and slow as Terry penetrated, spreading him, pulsing inside his body, and Terry went slow and easy. Mason closed his eyes and thought about the empty space in his heart over the past months, and when he opened his eyes, Terry was gazing at him with such purity, such tenderness, that Mason's heart healed, right in that minute.

"Love you," he gasped.

"Love you too," Terry returned, voice strained. He fell forward and pulled back, slow and gentle, before he thrust forward again.

Mason found he was smiling stupidly into those brown eyes. "Do you really?" he teased. "Do you really love me?"

Terry chuckled, low and evil. "God, yeah."

"Then fuck me, dammit. Fuck me fucking blind."

"Boo*yah*!"

Hard and fast and strong—oh dear Lord, Mason had waited his entire life to be fucked like this. Terry pounded inside of him without pause, without fear—hell, without even getting out of breath. And Mason's climax crested like a tsunami, first sucking all the air out of his body, then prickling along his arms and the back of his neck in warning, and then rolling, big, and bigger, up and up and up, until he was looking into the heavens to see the top. And then…

Whoosh!

In a giant surf crash of nerve-ending explosions, Mason orgasmed, crying out, spurting along his belly from his untouched cock.

He lost his grip on the sheets and flailed, catching Terry's shoulders and crying out again as an aftershock rocked him—and Terry's hips started a series of short, quick thrusts that hammered Mason's sweet spot with every plunge.

"Oh God," he chanted. "Oh God, oh God, c'mon, Terry, c'mon, c'mon, need to feel you in there, need to feel you inside me, need you to fuckin' *come!*"

With a roar and a final, epic thrust, he did, collapsing across Mason's chest, twitching, still in Mason's body.

Terry gulped air frantically for a minute, and finally, when his shudders stopped, he asked, "You believe me now?"

Of course Mason did. But he was happy and free, and he could say anything to this man and be forgiven.

"Maybe," he panted. "Maybe we'll have to do it one or two more times."

Four months later

THIS TIME Mason topped, fucking Terry from behind while he collapsed onto one shoulder and yanked frantically at his dick for climax. When they'd both roared to the finish together, Mason piled on top of him, squishing him into the mattress. He kissed the shell of Terry's ear and breathed softly into it, just to tease.

"You keep doing that," Terry grunted, "and we're going to go again before we meet everyone at Skip and Richie's."

Now that autumn had arrived, Skip and Richie had taken over hosting duties, which felt right, since it had been Skip's team to begin with.

"Dane and Carpenter will probably be there already." Dane and Carpenter, their own romance cruising to an agenda only they understood, were still living at Mason's house, which Mason didn't mind. One more year of vet school—Mason would do anything to see his little brother graduate, to have a chance to be happy. They'd go house shopping soon enough. Mason was just hoping the house would still be in the same neighborhood.

"Yeah. We'll get there. We have to—we made cookies." Terry grinned over his shoulder, particularly proud of those cookies.

Well, they were decorated, and he'd looked them up in a recipe book. It was a new skill, and he'd been using it a lot, and Mason was proud of him.

"Mmm…." Mason kissed some of the sweat off the back of his neck, moving his shaggy hair as he did so. Terry was going for the same sort of hipster thing that Dane had going on. Mason didn't mind the look, but he still sort of preferred the Boy Scout thing he'd had going in the summer.

But seriously—not picky.

He had Terry to himself as often as they could meet, and that was about five days a week.

Sleeping alone in his own bed was starting to feel like something fundamentally wrong had happened to his life.

"Hey, Mason," Terry murmured, rolling to his side.

Mason did the same. "What?" he asked, staring at his lover in wonder. God—he sent Mason flowers. At least once a month. It was such a silly, simple thing, but Mason didn't take it for granted. A silly, simple thing that meant the world.

"My lease is expiring."

Mason blinked. That was not where he'd expected this to go. "That's weird. I thought you'd have a year."

"Well, I should have, but I asked for six months, and they gave it to me."

Mason frowned. "Why'd you do that?"

Terry's smile was all teeth. "'Cause I know this guy with this really big, nice house who could probably build a mother-in-law cottage to fit all my stuff."

Slow blink. "You want to live on my property?"

"No, I just want to build the cottage with you. I want to live with you in your house, forever. Is that a problem?"

Mason felt this bolt of transcendence pierce him then. Joy. Happiness he'd dreamed not of.

"God, no. I can't wait. Can you move in now? Like right now? Like *today*?"

"Next month," Terry said smugly. "Just in time for Thanksgiving."

"Wow," Mason murmured. "We're going to see the years unfold. We're going to live together. It's going to be amazing."

"I reckon," Terry said. "You think I learned enough this summer to make that work?"

"I think we both did."

Terry chuckled lowly. "Did we learn enough to have one more quick one before we leave?"

Mason's chuckle was just as evil. "I think we knew that already."

"Yeah. Me too. Let's practice, just in case."

Practice was good. Mason would practice with him as often as he wanted. You learned more that way.

AMY LANE is a mother of two college students, two grade-schoolers, and two small dogs. She is also a compulsive knitter who writes because she can't silence the voices in her head. She adores fur-babies, knitting socks, and hawt menz, and she dislikes moths, cat boxes, and knuckle-headed macspazzmatrons. She is rarely found cooking, cleaning, or doing domestic chores, but she has been known to knit up an emergency hat/blanket/pair of socks for any occasion whatsoever, or sometimes for no reason at all. Her award-winning writing has three flavors: twisty-purple alternative universe, angsty-orange contemporary, and sunshine-yellow happy. By necessity, she has learned to type like the wind. She's been married for twenty-plus years to her beloved Mate and still believes in Twu Wuv, with a capital Twu and a capital Wuv, and she doesn't see any reason at all for that to change.

Website: www.greenshill.com
Blog: www.writerslane.blogspot.com
E-mail: amylane@greenshill.com
Facebook: www.facebook.com/amy.lane.167
Twitter: @amymaclane

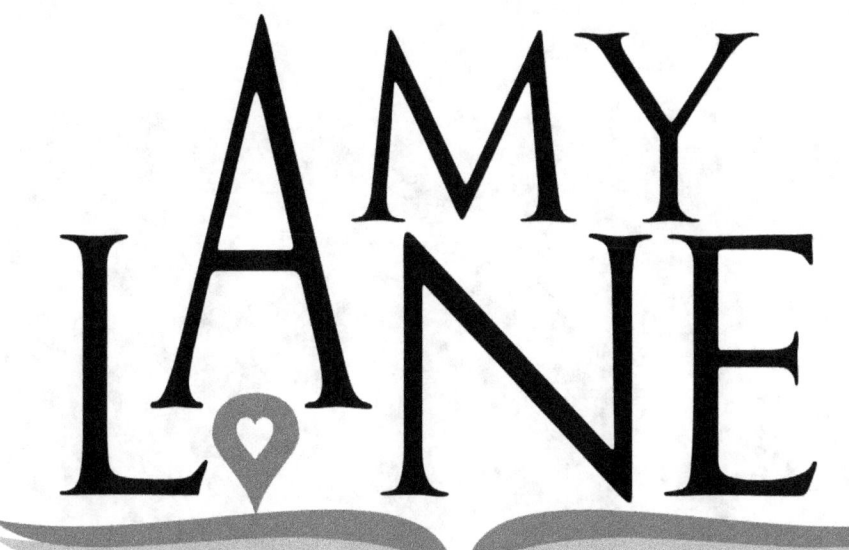

Choose your Lane to love!

Yellow

Amy Lane Lite
Contemporary Romance

Available at
www.dreamspinnerpress.com

The plays that matter
don't happen on the field...

Winter Ball

"Simple,
sweet story"
*Publishers
Weekly*

AMY LANE

Through a miserable adolescence and a lonely adulthood, Skipper Keith has dreamed of nothing but family. The closest he gets is the rec league soccer team he coaches after work—and his star player and best friend, Richie Scoggins.

One brisk night in late October, a postpractice convo in Richie's car turns into a sexual encounter neither of them expected—nor want to forget. Soon Skip and Richie are living for the weekends and their winter league soccer games—and the games they enjoy off the field. Through broken noses, holiday decorating, and the killer flu, they learn more about each other than they ever dreamed possible. Every new discovery takes them further beyond the boundaries of the soccer field and into the infinite possibilities of the best relationship of Skipper's life.

Skipper can't dream of a better family than Richie—but Richie's got real family entanglements he can't shake off. Skipper needs to convince Richie to stay with him beyond winter ball so the relationship they started on the field might become their happy future in real life!

www.dreamspinnerpress.com

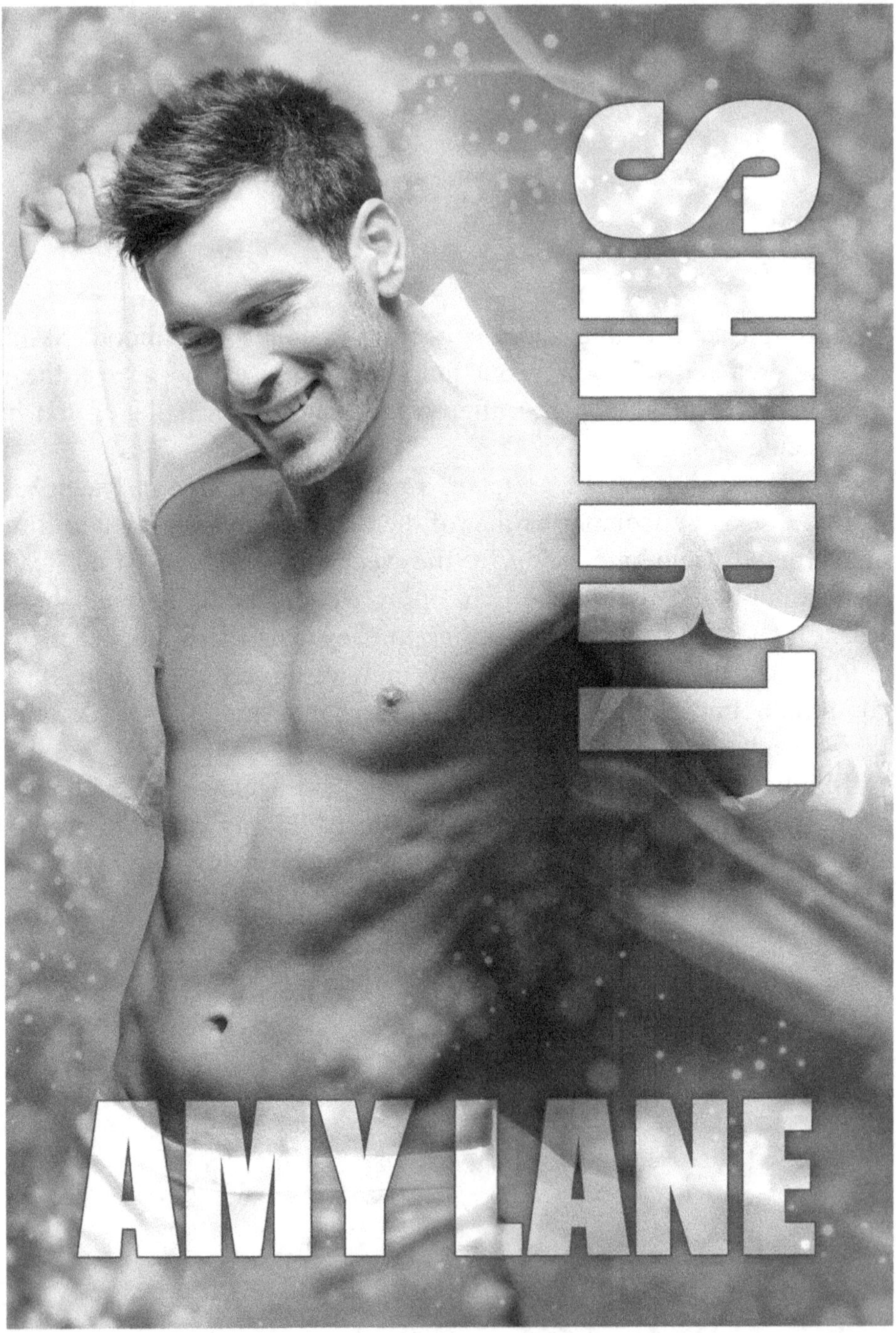
SHIRT
AMY LANE

After a meet-cute in a bathroom and a whirlwind courtship, Ryan is ready to introduce Scotty to his parents. But a misunderstanding and some stubborn cuff buttons tangle Ryan up in an oxford shirt at a *really* inopportune time. Can Scotty take this opportunity to teach Ryan one or two more lessons about falling in love?

www.dreamspinnerpress.com

PHONEBOOK

AMY LANE

Stuck away from home on business, all Ryan can do is talk with his lover, Scott, on the phone. But the conservative Ryan finds no comfort in phone sex—he's far too embarrassed. Fortunately, his playful lover has not only planned ahead, but he can think on his back as well. It turns out that the heart really is where good sex starts!

www.dreamspinnerpress.com

Amy Lane

Candy
MAN

A Candy Man Book

Adam Macias has been thrown a few curve balls in his life, but losing his VA grant because his car broke down and he missed a class was the one that struck him out. One relative away from homelessness, he's taking the bus to Sacramento, where his cousin has offered a house-sitting job and a new start. He has one goal, and that's to get his life back on track. Friends, pets, lovers? Need not apply.

Finn Stewart takes one look at Adam as he's applying to Candy Heaven and decides he's much too fascinating to leave alone. Finn is bright and shiny—and has never been hurt. Adam is wary of his attention from the very beginning—Finn is dangerous to every sort of peace Adam is forging, and Adam may just be too damaged to let him in at all.

But Finn is tenacious, and Adam's new boss, Darrin, doesn't take bullshit for an answer. Adam is going to have to ask himself which is harder—letting Finn in or living without him? With the holidays approaching it seems like an easy question, but Adam knows from experience that life is seldom simple, and the world seldom cooperates with hope, faith, or the plans of cats and men.

www.dreamspinnerpress.com

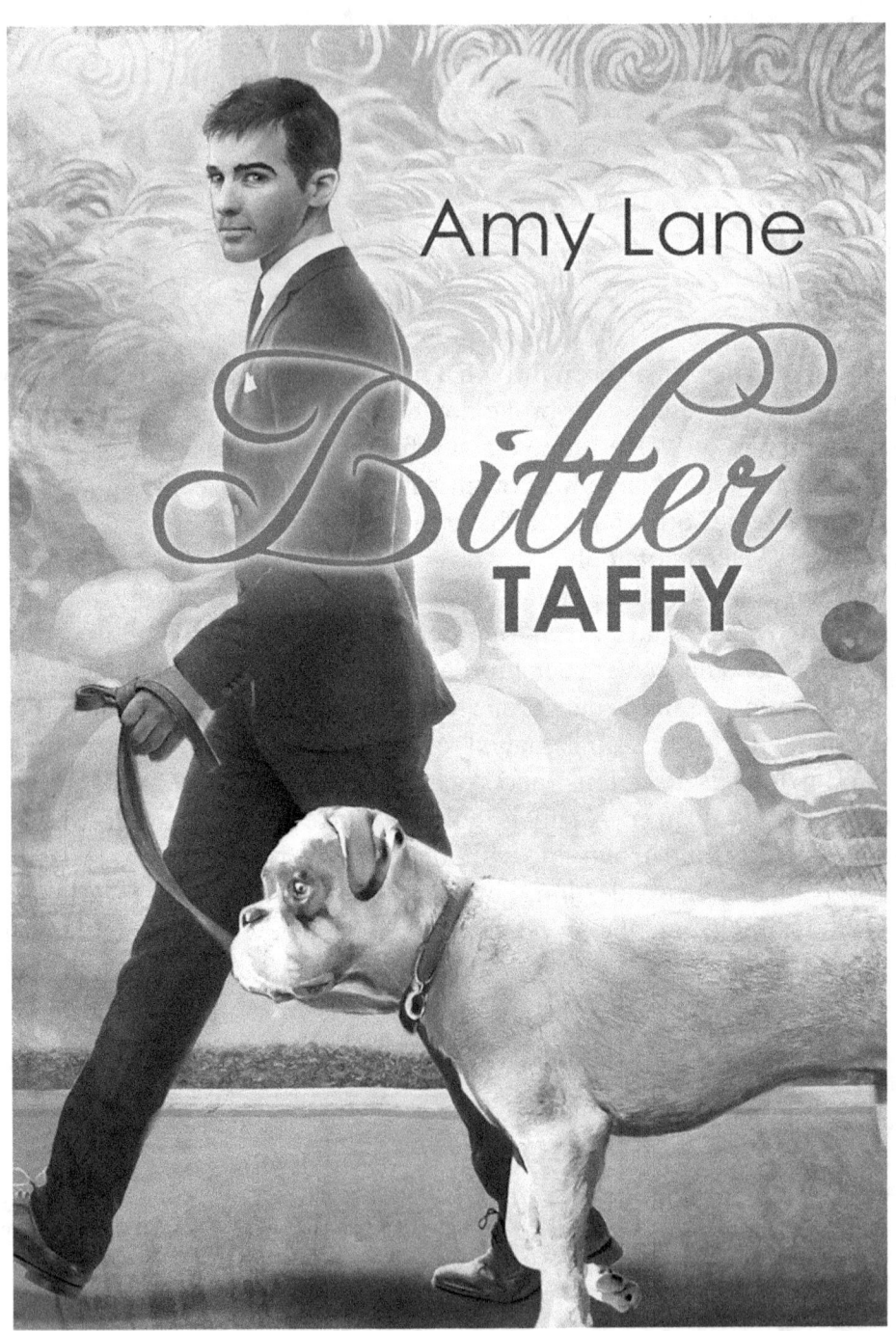

Amy Lane

Bitter
TAFFY

A Candy Man Book

Rico Gonzalves-Macias didn't expect to fall in love during his internship in New York—and he didn't expect the boss's son to out them both and get him fired either. When he returns to Sacramento stunned and heartbroken, he finds his cousin, Adam, and Adam's boyfriend, Finn, haven't just been house-sitting—they've made his once sterile apartment into a home.

When Adam gets him a job interview with the adorable, magnetic, practically perfect Derek Huston, Rico feels especially out of his depth. Derek makes it no secret that he wants Rico, but Rico is just starting to figure out that he's a beginner at the really important stuff and doesn't want to jump into anything with both feet.

Derek is a both-feet kind of guy. But he's also made mistakes of his own and doesn't want to pressure Rico into anything. Together they work to find a compromise between instant attraction and long-lasting love, and while they're working, Rico gets a primer in why family isn't always a bad idea. He needs to believe Derek can be his family before Derek's formidable patience runs out—because even a practically perfect boyfriend is capable of being hurt.

www.dreamspinnerpress.com